本书为上海市高校高峰学科建设计划资助"中国语言文学"研究成果,上海市教委创新项目(15ZS042)研究成果。

中国古典小说
西译文选读

宋丽娟 编选

By Song Lijuan

Selected Western Translations
of Chinese Classical Novels

中州古籍出版社
·郑州·

图书在版编目（CIP）数据

中国古典小说西译文选读：汉、英 / 宋丽娟编选 . — 郑州：中州古籍出版社，2021.1

ISBN 978-7-5348-9573-9

Ⅰ.①中… Ⅱ.①宋… Ⅲ.①古典小说—文学欣赏—中国—汉、英 Ⅳ.①I207.41

中国版本图书馆 CIP 数据核字（2021）第 023933 号

中国古典小说西译文选读

责任编辑	李　芳
责任校对	李晓文
装帧设计	曾晶晶

出　版　社	中州古籍出版社（地址：郑州市郑东新区祥盛街 27 号 6 层　邮编：450016　电话：0371-65723280）
发行单位	新华书店
承印单位	河南新华印刷集团有限公司
开　　本	640 mm×960 mm　1/16
印　　张	23.75
字　　数	200 千字
印　　数	1—1000 册
版　　次	2021 年 1 月第 1 版
印　　次	2021 年 1 月第 1 次印刷
定　　价	58.00 元

本书如有印装质量问题，请与出版社调换。

序 言

文化的交流是双向的。明清之际,与"西学东渐"相呼应,中国传统文化在西方也得到了较为广泛的传播,我们称之为"中学西传"。中国古代典籍的翻译就成为"中学西传"的主要方式和途径。从16世纪到20世纪初,翻译出版的中国古代典籍涵盖了经、史、子、集等各个领域,其中,中国古典小说作为中国传统文化的一部分,亦构成"中学西传"的有机组成部分。

1735年,杜赫德(Jean-Baptiste Du Halde,1674—1743)编撰的《中华帝国全志》[1]在巴黎出版,该书第3卷所收三篇中国小说的译文是迄今为止我们所知最早译成西文的中国小说,在没有新的文献资料发现之前,暂以此作为中国古典小说西译的起点。1911年,随着清王朝的灭亡,中国古典小说在明清时期"中学西传"这一特定历史语境下的翻译活动结束了,步入其现代转型期。1735年至1911年近两百年的中国古典小说西译活动,经历了18世纪末期和19世纪中叶两次转折,形成了滥觞、发展和成熟三个历史阶段。这种划分主要

---

[1] P. J. B. Du Halde, *Description Géographique, Historique, Chronologique, Politique et Physique de L'Empire de la Chine et de la Tartarie Chinoise*, Paris: P. G. Le Mercier, 1735. 1736年被译为英文: *The General History of China, Done from the French of P. J. B. DU HALDE*, trans. Richard Brookes, London: Printed by and for John Watts at the Printing Office in Wild-Court near Lincolns-Inn Fields, 1736.

以西方翻译中国古典小说的实践为据：18世纪翻译的小说数量有限，但开启了中国古典小说西译的风气，选译的小说题材集中在才子佳人小说和话本小说，译者以在华传教士、商人和欧洲教士为主体，大多采取了归化的翻译策略，是为中国古典小说西译的滥觞。19世纪初，随着欧洲汉学的兴起，一批优秀的欧洲汉学家投入到中国小说西译的事业中，推进了中国小说西译的渐次拓展，不仅选译的小说题材日益多样，且翻译策略也呈现出归化和异化并存的局面，新的翻译载体也不断问世，构成了中国古典小说西译的发展期。1840年鸦片战争以后，西方列强对华签订的一系列不平等条约，为西人在中国开辟了更为广阔和自由的活动空间，为其认知中国提供便利条件，从客观上促进了中国古典小说西译的逐渐深入和成熟，这一时期不仅翻译的小说数量大幅度增多，且外文报刊这种古典小说西译的新载体风行一时，古典小说译文选集的编纂及译本体例也不断完备，成为中国古典小说西译的成熟期。

以上划分主要以中国古典小说西译的实践为标尺，尝试描绘出中国古典小说西译的历史演进轨迹，其中18世纪末至19世纪初的世纪之交是西方由启蒙主义进入浪漫主义的转折时代，1840年亦与中国近代史起点的划分相合，这在一定程度上反映了文化思潮及政治权力关系对翻译等文化活动的影响和制约。

一、开启风气与确立范式：中国古典小说西译的滥觞
（1735—1799）

最早被翻译和介绍到西方的中国典籍是儒家经典，后逐渐扩展

至包括小说在内的中国古典文学。1735年《中华帝国全志》在巴黎出版，该书第3卷收录了耶稣会士殷弘绪（François Xavier d'Entrecolles，1662—1741）译自《今古奇观》中的三篇中国小说:《吕大郎还金完骨肉》、《庄子休鼓盆成大道》和《怀私怨狠仆告主》。这是迄今为止我们所知最早译成外文，并正式出版的中国古典小说。[①] 1761年，伦敦多利兹出版社出版了《好逑传》英译本，此书引发了欧洲日后翻译出版《好逑传》的热潮。但自1735年至1799年间，西人翻译的中国古典小说大抵只有以上四部（篇）[②]，是为中国古典小说西译的滥觞期。

（一）翻译动机

在中国古典小说西译初期，译者对中国小说的了解还处于起步阶段，且受语言限制，不可能在大量阅读和充分了解中国小说的基础上再做选择，因此选译小说具有很大的偶然性。但译文的前言和注释或多或少透露出编译者选译这些小说的动机。

首先，看重中国古典小说的道德教化作用。《今古奇观》入选的小说或谴责女子的薄幸，或阐明为恶的祸果，或宣扬行善的荫庇，大

---

① 由于《中华帝国全志》没有标明译文的中文底本，学术界最初认为殷弘绪三篇译文是从"三言二拍"中选译的。王丽娜的《中国古典小说戏曲名著在国外》（上海：学林出版社，1988年，第170页）、黄鸣奋的《英语世界中国古典文学之传播》（上海：学林出版社，1997年，第176页）均持此观点。后马祖毅、任荣珍《汉籍外译史》（武汉：湖北教育出版社，1997年，第171页）、严建强的《18世纪中国文化在西欧的传播及其反应》（杭州：中国美术学院出版社，2002年，第147页）已经注意到了其底本应是《今古奇观》而非"三言二拍"，但未作具体论证。笔者发现，《今古奇观》作为根据"三言二拍"选编而成的小说集，编撰者在选编时，对作品也进行了再加工，在行文内容方面做了一定的增删和润色。殷弘绪译文在《今古奇观》改动之处，也作出了相应的改动。所以说，译文是根据《今古奇观》选择而成的。

② 旅居巴黎的华人黄嘉略（Arcade Houange，1679—1716）曾于1714年之前将《玉娇梨》前三回译成法文，惜乎译文未正式付梓。

都具有道德教化的主旨。而《好逑传》中主人公处处恪守道德的行为也为西人所赞赏，托马斯·帕西（Thomas Percy，1729—1811）在献词中说："正当海淫海盗小说故事充斥国内市场的时候，这本来自中国的小说，作为一本讲究道德的书，还有劝善惩恶的作用。"① 可见西人翻译中国小说的一个重要原因是对其道德教化功用的认可。

其次，中国古典小说被视为西人了解中国和中国人最生动有效的媒介，并为西方传教士在华的宣教事业提供参考。殷弘绪从《今古奇观》中选译的小说，向西人生动地展示了中国人对"天"的崇拜，而传教士认为中国的"天"与西方的"上帝"具有某些共通之处。帕西在《好逑传》前言中指出："一个民族自己创造的东西最能说明该民族的风俗人情……它不是对每个细节巨细无遗的描摹，而是通过人物自己的行动来表现他的思想、感情等。"② 因此他不遗余力地为译文编写了大量的注释，对中国的社会政治、风俗人情、宗教信仰等做出详细阐述，并通过中国人性格特征、宗教思想与西方基督教传统的比较，分析基督教在华传播的可行性。

最后，中国古典小说成为西人学习中文的汉语读本。《好逑传》的译文手稿有许多段落先用铅笔写成，后又用钢笔改正重写，字里行间还有许多修改，这显示译稿原来很可能是为学习中文而作的练习。法国汉学家马若瑟（Joseph Henri Marie de Prémare，1666—1736）在18世纪早期编写的《汉语札记》（*Natitia Lingae Sinicae*）已从《水浒传》《画图缘》《醒风流》等小说作品中选取只言片语作为学习汉语的实例。

---

① Thomas Percy, ed., *Hau Kiou Choaan or The Pleasing History*, trans. James Wilkinson, London: R. and J. Dodsley, 1761, vol.I, Dedication.

② *Hau Kiou Choaan or The Pleasing History*, vol.I, Preface, p.xiii.

这说明西人从开始就把小说作为学习中文的重要媒介,从而建立了中国古典小说西译和汉语读本编撰之间的联系。

以上最早翻译成法文的《今古奇观》中的三篇小说和《好逑传》,是西人最早接触到的中国古典小说,虽然西人对中国小说的评价褒贬参半[1],但毕竟为西人认知中国古典小说提供了可资参考的直接样本。

(二)翻译范式

《中华帝国全志》所刊三篇中国小说的译文皆加有注释和批注,或介绍中国作者的时代,或解释中国作者的观点,数量虽不多,但为后来中国古典小说的编译者所继承,初步形成了西人翻译中国小说添加注释的惯例。

1761年,伦敦出版的《好逑传》英译本,由詹姆斯·威尔金森(James Wilkinson)翻译,并经托马斯·帕西编辑出版,题为《好逑传或愉快的故事》。[2]全书分为序言、正文、注释及附录四个部分。帕西在序言中交待了译本的基本情况,正文共四卷,正文后附三种附录,分别为1719年在广州上演的中国戏剧的情节介绍、《中国格言选辑》和法国汉学家尼古拉·弗莱雷(Nicolas Fréret,1688—1749)关于

---

[1] 如帕西认为,据欧洲批评标准,《好逑传》存在诸多不足:事件不够充分,布局不够精细,想象不够准确生动,叙述过于琐碎,且枯燥冗长。但帕西同时也注意到中国小说讲究真实自然的特征:"值得肯定的是,如果说中国小说缺乏其他东方国家小说中大胆的想象,却也没有其作品中随处可见的荒谬。中国人十分重视文学,所以他们比其他亚洲国家更注重小说叙事的真实自然。《好逑传》与东方其他作品相比,叙事巧妙井然,缺少奇异非凡的描述,却更加真实合理。故事情节有全局整体的规划,每一个事件都指向同一个终点,情节流畅连贯,叙事自然真实。"(*Hau Kiou Choaan or The Pleasing History*, vol.I, Preface)

[2] 《好逑传》最早的英译本为英国东印度公司职员詹姆斯·威尔金森所译,由托马斯·帕西编辑出版。因帕西对《好逑传》最早英译本的出版问世贡献颇大,学术界一般称之为帕西译本。本书从之。

中国诗歌的一篇论文节选。同时,《好逑传》英译本亦附大量的注释,内容涉及中国社会生活的方方面面,在一定程度上成为反映彼时中国的微型百科全书。

《好逑传》英译本出版后,在欧洲影响巨大,引发了翻译出版《好逑传》的热潮,并迅速地被转译为法语、德语、荷兰语等多种语言。《好逑传》的法、德、荷兰译本均直接从英译本转译而成,大抵继承了《好逑传》英译本的翻译和编排体制,进而形成了由序言、正文、注释和附录组成的中国古典小说西译的翻译范式。

(三)翻译策略

由于中西方文化的异质性,中国小说和西方小说在体制结构、语言修辞、审美旨趣等方面都存在着诸多不同,这就使译者面临一个选择,即在翻译的过程中是完全遵循中国小说的传统,还是根据西方的价值取向对中文进行改编,使之符合西方小说的体例习惯。在中国古典小说西译的初期,编译者大都选择了后者,译文和中文原文间出现了一定程度的差异,这种差异表现在体制、情节、词语等各个方面。

1. 对故事单元做出调整和组合,以符合西方小说的章节特点

中国古典小说具有特殊的小说体制,如章回小说有回目和开头诗词,话本小说在正话之前往往有入话;西方小说则为章节体,开篇即进入正文,没有回目、诗词或入话。殷弘绪在翻译《今古奇观》的三篇小说时,将译文分为四篇作品,或直接删去入话,或以入话单独构成一篇作品,并对中文的故事单元重新组合。

《好逑传》为传统的章回体小说,是根据故事情节发展来划分小说章回的,共有四卷,前两卷每卷五回,后两卷每卷四回,共十八回。《好逑传》英译本为了适应英国小说的编排体例,将中文原本的章回

重新排比划分为四十章。特别是第十六、十七、十八回，译文明显打乱了原文的回次安排，有些章节包涵四五个故事情节，有些仅有一个故事情节，这种安排在一定程度上破坏了原有故事情节发展的连贯性。①

2. 添加解说性文字，为西方读者提供中国文化的背景知识

这主要指对作品中具有中国特色的事物或文化，在正文中添加背景知识的介绍，便于西方读者理解。如《庄子休鼓盆成大道》：

原文：原来是老苍头吃醉了，直挺挺的卧于灵座桌上。婆娘又不敢嗔责他，又不敢声唤他，只得回房。捱更捱点，又过了一夜。②

译文：when she found the old domestick laid upon the table placed before the coffin, on which perfumes were to be burnt, and offerings set at certain hours; he lay there to sleep himself sober, the lady having given him too much wine; any other woman would have shown a resentment for such irreverence to the dead, but she burst not complain, nor even disturb the sleeping sot; she went therefore to lie down, but it was not possible for her to take any repose.（她发现老苍头躺在棺材前边的桌子上，这个桌子是用来焚香并在规定的时间摆放祭品的。他因为女子给了太多的酒而沉沉地睡着。任何其他的女子都会憎恨这样对死者的打扰。但她既不敢嗔责他，又不敢声唤他，只得回房躺下，却又不能入睡。）③

译文解释了灵座桌子的功用，从而点明老苍头在灵座桌上沉睡

---

① 参见宋丽娟、孙逊：《中国古典小说的早期翻译和传播——以〈好逑传〉英译本为中心》，《文学评论》2008 年第 4 期。
② 抱瓮老人：《今古奇观》，北京：人民文学出版社，1957 年，第 368 页。
③ *The General History of China, Done from the French of P. J. B. DU HALDE*, vol.III, pp.147–148.

的行为是对死者的大不敬。女子对老苍头的容忍则反映出女子对逝去丈夫感情的漠然,使读者更易于理解中文所表达的对人物心理活动的描摹。

3.增加细节和心理描写,使人物形象的塑造更贴近西人的写作技巧

根据西人小说创作的惯用技巧为作品增加细节描写和心理描写,使人物的刻画益发形象真切,这是译者常用的手法。如《怀私怨狠仆告主》:

原文:刘氏含泪道……刘氏又劝慰了一番,哭别回家,坐在房中纳闷。①

译文:The Lady Lieou withholding her tears, that she might not add to her husband's grief…he was going on when they obliged the Lady to withdraw, because night approached. It was then she gave vent to her grief which she had smother'd in her bosom; she went to her own house all in tears, and retried to her apartment, where she was wholly taken up with the distress and melancholy situation of her husband.(为了不增加丈夫的悲伤,刘氏止住哭泣……天色已晚,刘氏不得不辞别丈夫。这时她再也忍不住内心压抑的痛苦,含泣到家。她回到房内,内心充满着对丈夫不幸遭遇和悲惨境况的担忧。)②

译文通过刘氏在丈夫面前和独处时的不同表现,丰富了刘氏复杂的心理活动,更好地刻画了刘氏坚强贤惠的品质。

4.因价值观念差异对情节内容进行删节和改写

因价值观念差异而对原著的情节做出删改。如《吕大郎还金完骨肉》:

---

① 抱瓮老人:《今古奇观》,第544页。
② *The General History of China, Done from the French of P. J. B. DU HALDE*, vol.Ⅲ, pp.180–181.

原文：吕玉少年久旷，也不免行户中走了一两遍，走出一身风流疮。服药调治，无面回家。捱到三年，疮才痊好。①

译　文：and a tedious distemper wherewith Liu was seiz'd, kept him three years in that province.（吕玉得了一场重病，稽留他乡三年。）②

"行户"即妓院。这里译者删去吕玉逛妓院一节，很可能是因为这样的行为不仅有损于吕玉的德行，而且与译者的信仰相左，所以译者有意识地将之删除。

以上我们从翻译动机、翻译范式和翻译策略三个方面，对中国古典小说西译滥觞期的大致情况作了简略分析。这一时期虽然翻译的作品数量不多，尚属起步阶段，但它对西方文学已经产生了一定的影响，为西方文学增添了富有东方色彩的故事因子。如法国大文豪伏尔泰撰写的小说《查第格》，其中第2章的内容吸收模仿了《庄子休鼓盆成大道》的情节，成为中西文学交流在文学创作上首次有益的尝试，为西方文学加入了东方的素材。③而1762年出版的英国作家奥利弗·哥尔德斯密斯（Oliver Goldsmith，1728—1774）创作的书简体作品《世界公民》，在第18封信中亦搬用庄子夫妻的故事④，并借此讽刺当时英国人对待婚姻的不严肃态度。更有甚者，有西方学者以《庄子休鼓

---

① 抱瓮老人：《今古奇观》，北京：人民文学出版社，1957年，第568页。
② *The General History of China, Done from the French of P. J. B. DU HALDE*, vol.Ⅲ, p.115.
③ 伏尔泰：《查第格》第2章仅将人物改名换姓，并将"扇坟"改成"引溪水别流"，"心痛"改为"脾脏作痛"，"劈脑"改为"割鼻"，故事情节明显模拟《庄子休鼓盆成大道》。
④ Oliver Goldsmith, *The Citizen of the World, or Letters from a Chinese Philosopher, Residing in London to His Friend in the East*, London: Vernor, 1792. 第18封信的故事以"庄子是最温柔的丈夫，田氏是最可爱的妻子"开始，讲述了庄子、田氏与执扇女子、庄子弟子间的感情纠葛，故事情节大抵沿袭自《庄子休鼓盆成大道》，但亦对其做出部分改编，如添加庄子与执扇女子完婚的情节等。

盆成大道》的故事为对象进行专题研究，如德国学者爱德华·格里泽巴赫（Eduard Grisebach，1845—1906）的著作《不忠贞的寡妇及其在世界文学中的演化》，以《庄子休鼓盆成大道》的故事为中心，不仅详细介绍了故事的来龙去脉，还叙述了其在世界文学中的传播过程[①]，体现出中西文化的互动和交融。

在中国古典小说西译的滥觞期，虽然翻译的小说数量不多，但它改变了西方人重视中国儒家经典、轻视中国文学的态度，开启了中国古典小说西译的风气，在翻译标准上形成了一定的范式，成为后人翻译和传播中国古典小说的效仿对象，并为西方文学创作增添了东方文学的元素。

二、题材的多样与中国古典小说西译的拓展
（1800—1840）

随着西人对中国了解的逐渐深入，中国古典小说的西译亦得以渐次拓展。这主要表现在：翻译小说的数量大量增加，选译小说的题材有所拓宽，翻译策略逐渐多元，且出现了一些新的小说西译的载体。

（一）题材的多样化

进入19世纪，中国古典小说引起了更多西人的关注，一些传教士和欧洲汉学家亦加入到中国古典小说西译的活动中，从1800年至1840年，西方翻译中国古典小说的数量由滥觞期的四种增加到三十余种，且选译的中国古典小说在题材上也有所拓宽，涵盖了志怪小说、

---

① Eduard Grisebach, *Die Treulose Witwe. Eine chinesisch Novelle, und ihre Wanderung durch die Weltliteratur*, Wien: L. Rosner, 1872.

神魔小说、历史演义、才子佳人小说及公案小说等各种题材，文体则包含了文言小说和白话小说，其中尤以话本小说数量最多。

这一时期翻译的神魔小说、志怪小说从明刊《三教源流搜神大全》、清代文言小说《子不语》中选译，并翻译了清代白话小说《白蛇精记》。其中从《三教源流圣帝佛帅搜神大全》中选译《释氏源流》和《道教源流》两篇；从《子不语》中选译了《良猪》《铁匣壁虎》《黑柱》和《十三猫同日殉节》四篇。《白蛇精记》最早的西译本为法文本 *Pé-Ché-Tsing-Ki, Blanche et Bleue ou les deuzx couleuvres fées*，由法国著名汉学家儒莲（Stanislas Julien，1797—1873）翻译，1834年在巴黎查尔斯哥塞林（Charles Gosselin）出版社出版。同年，《皇家亚洲学会学报》（*Journal of the Royal Asiatic Society*）刊载了《白蛇精记》的英译文。

这一阶段翻译的历史演义小说有《三国演义》和《五虎平南狄青后传》两种。前者主要翻译了和"董卓之死"相关的章节，后者围绕小说的主人公之一段红玉，节译了与她相关的情节。翻译的才子佳人小说有《玉娇梨》《平山冷燕》和《好逑传》三种，其中《好逑传》在1829年由德庇时（John Francis Davis，1795—1890）再次译成英文 *The Fortunate Union, A Romance, Translated from the Chinese Original*，是《好逑传》第二个英文全译本，并迅速被转译成法、德等各种文字。公案小说则从《龙图公案》中选译《石狮子》一篇，收入帕维（Théodore Pavie，1811—1896）的《故事小说选》（*Choix de Contes et Nouvelles*），1839年由巴黎迪普拉（B. Duprat）出版社出版。

话本小说在这一阶段继续受到重视，除再译了《今古奇观》中的《庄子休鼓盆成大道》和《怀私怨狠仆告主》外，亦从《今古奇观》中选译了《宋金郎团圆破毡笠》《蔡小姐忍辱报仇》《三孝廉让产立高名》《念亲恩孝女藏儿》《滕大尹鬼断家私》《王娇鸾百年长恨》《灌园叟晚逢仙女》《李谪仙醉草吓蛮书》和《俞伯牙摔琴谢知音》九篇。并翻译了《警世通言》中的《范鳅儿双镜重圆》，《拍案惊奇》中的《李公佐巧解梦中言 谢小娥智擒船上盗》及《醒世恒言》中的《大树坡义虎送亲》和《刘小官雌雄兄弟》两篇。另外，还从李渔《十二楼》中选译了《三与楼》《合影楼》和《夺锦楼》三篇。另外，有些篇章不止一次被翻译，且出现了先被译为一种西文，再被转译成其他西方语言的现象。

（二）翻译策略的多元化

中国古典小说翻译题材的多样化之外，西人翻译中国小说的策略也呈多元化趋势。除采取以读者所在国文化为标准，对中文做出改编使之符合西人的价值观念之外，亦出现尊重原著，在翻译中尽可能保留原著面目的做法。如《好逑传》第二个英文全译本德庇时译本，与帕西译本相比，在故事单元的编排整合、回目诗词的解释翻译、文字语言的选择修饰和情节内容的安排设计等各个方面都更接近中文原本。

例如关于故事单元的编排整合。帕西译本对中文原著的故事单元重新编排和整合，将中文《好逑传》十八回划分为四十章，打乱了原著故事发展的脉络，在一定程度上破坏了故事情节的紧凑感和章回小说的传统结构。德庇时在重新翻译《好逑传》时认为："这部小说原有的章回，经过不合理的排比，在帕西的《愉快的故事》中，变得混乱了，不清楚了。"① 因此，德庇时翻译的《好逑传》避免了帕西译本对小说原有章回不合理的编排整合，遵循了中文原著的章回安排，译文分为十八章。

再有关于回目和诗词的翻译。回目用概括的语言提炼出每回的主要内容，置于回首，起到"题眼"作用，是中国古典章回小说的惯例。帕西译本省略了对章回目录的翻译，德庇时译本则将其一一翻译出来，使译文更为完整。另外，中国古典小说在故事情节的叙述中往往使用诗词歌赋来描摹人物形象，烘托环境氛围，概括故事主题，提引情节线索，对情节的发展起转承启接的作用，是小说的有机组成部分。帕西译本删去了《好逑传》中诗词歌赋的翻译，在一定程度上损害了小说的完整性。德庇时译本在翻译时则补足这种缺失，对诗词歌赋重新进行翻译。

还有文字词语的选择修饰。帕西译本和德庇时译本对相同情节内容的翻译，选择了不同的文字词语。如：

原文：韦佩立在道旁相送，心下又惊又疑，又喜又感，象做了个春梦一般，不敢认真，又不敢猜假，恍恍忽忽，只立到望不见铁公子的马，方才回去。②

帕西译本：Wey-phey stood amazed and motionless, with his eyes fixed on Tieh-chung-u 'till he was out of sight, not knowing whether what had happened was real or a dream.（韦佩惊奇地、一动不动地站着，注

---

① John Francis Davis, *The Fortunate Union, A Romance, Translated from the Chinese Original*, London: Printed from the Oriental Translation Fund, and Sold by J. Murray, 1829, vol.I, Preface, p.viii.
② 《好逑传》，大文堂藏版，第一回第六叶。

视着铁公子,直到望不见他,不知道刚刚发生的一切是真或是梦。)①

德庇时译本:The young man, overwhelmed with conflicting emotions, stood by the way-side and followed him with his eyes. The whole appeared liked a dream, which he hardly dared to think was true, and yet would not willingly believe to be false. In this state he lingered until Teih-chung-yu and his horse vanished from his sight: and then, turning round, walked pensively towards his home.(韦佩立在道旁目送,心内五味杂陈。所发生的一切像梦一般,不敢认作是真的,又不愿认作是假的。在这种状态下一直耽延到看不见铁中玉和他的马,才转过身,愁眉苦脸地向家走去。)②

两个译本都描摹出了韦佩复杂的心理状况,但文字词语选择修饰的不同,使得其表现的效果亦不等。相较而言,德庇时译本和原文比较接近,用细致的语言刻画出韦佩内心相互矛盾的感情,帕西译文的描写则相对比较笼统,表现力稍弱。

最后关于情节内容的安排设计。帕西译本根据编译者自身的主张对《好逑传》的情节内容做出一定的改写和删节;德庇时译本则往往根据原著纠正帕西译本的改写,如帕西认为《好逑传》第四回中关于冰心小姐"南庄拜扫"的描写提前说明了冰心小姐怎样设计躲过其祖的圈套,破坏了故事发展的悬念,因此删除了该段情节。德庇时译本则根据原著补足这一段描写,复原了原著故事情节的铺陈安排。

德庇时译文对原著的遵循为中国古典小说西译提供了"西化原著"之外的另一种翻译途径,丰富了中国古典小说西译的翻译方法。

---

① Hau Kiou Choaan or the Pleasing History, vol.I, p.21.
② The Fortunate Union, A Romance, Translated from the Chinese Original, vol.I, p.14.

同时，这一阶段仍有相当一部分译者根据西方习惯对中文小说进行改写，如德庇时翻译的《三与楼》在 1822 年被编入《中国小说》(Chinese Novels)时，对 1816 年的译文进行了较大程度的改编，不仅删去了回目、诗歌的翻译，而且文中某些词语的翻译也更贴近西人的表达方式。如原文"不肯破费分文"，1816 年的译文为：would not spend as much as a candareen or a cash①，按照原文的表达方式，只是以欧洲的货币名称代替中文的"分""文"；1822 年则改译为：was determined to take care of his money②，即"决定好好照管自己的钱财"，显然更接近西人的表达方式。

（三）新载体的出现

最初，中国古典小说译本的载体不外乎两种，或收入综合类书籍发行，或以单行本出版。此时出现了三种新的载体：外文报刊杂志、中国古典小说译文选集以及作为汉语读本的中国古典小说译本。

19 世纪，报刊杂志作为一种新的传播媒介在西方迅速发展。1800 年至 1840 年间，已有几份以中国或亚洲为主题的外文报纸创刊，如 1816 年在伦敦创办的英文杂志《亚洲杂志》(Asiatic Journal)，1822 年在巴黎创办的法文杂志《亚洲学刊》(Journal Asiatques)等，这些外文报刊都曾刊载过一些中国古典小说的译文。但是，此阶段报刊上登载的中国古典小说译文还十分有限，外文报刊作为一种新兴的中国古典小说译文的载体，要到 19 世纪中后期才得到迅猛发展。

本时期亦出版了几种中国古典小说译文选集，或把先后从同一

---

① *Asiatic Journal*, vol.I, 1816, p.40.
② John Francis Davis, *Chinese Novels, Translated from the Originals*, London: J. Murray, 1822, p.156.

个小说选集中选译的单个故事编辑成集，或从同一系列的中国古典小说集中选译几篇结集出版。前者如德庇时翻译的《三与楼》，最早于1815年在广东刊行，1816年又刊载于《亚洲杂志》，1822年德庇时从《十二楼》中又选译了《合影楼》和《夺锦楼》两篇，并与《三与楼》结集出版，取名为 Chinese Novels, Translated from the Originals，由伦敦默里（J. Murray）出版社出版。后者如1827年出版的雷慕沙（A. Rémusat）编辑的法文《中国小说选》，内容为从《十二楼》《今古奇观》和《警世通言》中选译的十篇小说。

中国古典小说在西译之初已经被视为学习汉语的材料，在本时期更出现了正式的汉语读本，如1814年与1815年在伦敦出版了韦斯顿（Stephen Weston，1747—1830）和斯当东（George Thomas Staunton，1781—1859）翻译的《范希周》(Fan Hy Cheu，即《范鳅儿双镜重圆》译文)，体例为英汉对照，且附有注释和中文语法讲解，专门为外国人学习汉语而用。在版式上，汉语遵循中国体式，采用从右往左的竖排版，英文则沿用西方从左往右的横排版。

1800年至1840年的四十年间，西译的中国古典小说在题材的拓展、翻译策略的使用、翻译载体的多元化等方面取得了进展，且这一时期翻译者的汉语水平明显提高，出现了一批汉学家；出版地虽仍然集中在欧洲，但是在中国内地，主要是广州，亦开始刊印中国古典小说的译文，如德庇时的《三与楼》、罗伯聃（Robert Thom，1807—1846）的《王娇鸾百年长恨》及英文报刊《中国丛报》均在广州出版。

三、名著翻译、体式完备与中国古典小说西译的成熟（1841—1911）

1841年至1911年期间，被翻译成西文的中国古典小说篇目大幅度增多，名著进入译者的视野；近代外文报刊成为中国古典小说西译的重要载体，中国古典小说译文选集的体式也不断完善。另外，这个阶段出版的中国小说译本往往附有插图，这都说明中国古典小说西译的体式日臻完备。

在异质文化交流初期，由于文化间的隔膜及偶然性等因素，所选译的作品不一定是源文化中最为优秀的作品。在中国古典小说西译的滥觞和发展期，除节译了《三国演义》的一些章节外，其他翻译的小说多属二三流作品。而进入小说西译的成熟期，随着文化交流的深入、知识的积累等，译者对所选译的作品具有了较强的把握和鉴赏能力，更多地选译了源文化中的经典名著。《红楼梦》《水浒传》《西游记》和《金瓶梅》等皆在这个阶段被译成西文。其译文（本）大都为小说某些章节的选译，或登于外文报刊，或收入综合性书籍，或以单行本的形式发行。如英国在华外交官乔利（H. Bencraft Joly）翻译的《红楼梦》前五十六回的译文，由别发洋行（Kelly & Walsh）于1892年和1893年在香港、上海、横滨、新加坡四地同时以单行本的形式发行，这是《红楼梦》第一个较为系统的外文译本。《水浒传》最早较为系统的译文为法译文，收入巴赞（Antoine Pierre Louis Bazin，1799—1863）编著的《元代》（*Le Siècle des Youên*），并以 *Extraits du Chouï-Hou-Tschouen* 之名转刊于1850年和1851年的《亚洲学刊》，是原书中鲁智深和武松等相关故事情节的翻译①。《西游记》的译文亦见《亚洲学刊》，刊于 1857 年，题为 *Etude sur le Sy-Yéou-Tchin-Tsuen, Roman Bouddhique Chinois*，是以《西游真诠》为底本翻译而成的。《金瓶梅》最早的西译文收入巴赞编译的《现代中国》(*Chine Moderne*)，题作 *Histoire de Wou-song et de Kin-lièn*，标注为《金瓶梅》第一回的法译。② 1845 年和 1851 年巴黎迪普拉书局出版了《三国演义》法译本 *San-Koué-Tchy. Ilan Kouroun-I Pithé: Histoire des Trios Royaumes*，乃小说第一回至第四十四回的全译，这不仅是首次以单行本发行的《三国演义》译本，也是《三国演义》最早的较为系统的译本。③ 以上几部作品其他片断的译文也多次见于近代外文报刊或以单行本印行。

本阶段不仅中国小说中的经典名著被陆续翻译成西文，在西方广为传播，而且小说西译的体式也日益完备，主要表现在以下几个方面。

（一）近代外文报刊成为中国古典小说西译的重要载体

随着西方报刊传媒的发展成熟，在 1841 年至 1911 年之间，不仅前一时期以中国或亚洲为主题的外文杂志继续刊印发行，更有十余种相同主题的外文杂志相继创刊，外文报刊主要以在华传教士、商人、外交官、汉学家为撰稿人和读者；内容涵盖了关于中国和亚洲地区的

---

① M. Bazin aîné, *Le Siècle des Youên ou Tableau Historique de la Littérature Chinoise Depuis L'avénement des Empereurs Mongols Jusqu'À la Restauration des Ming*, Paris: Imprimerie Nationale, 1850. 关于巴赞《元代》可参见宋丽娟《巴赞〈元代〉及其文学史学史价值》，《文学评论》2020 年第 3 期。

② M. Bazin, *Chine Moderne*, Paris: Firmin Didot Frères, 1853. 又笔者查阅了法国国家图书馆东方馆中国书目，内中记载《金瓶梅》有另一种节选法译文：Maurice Jametel, *L'argot Pékinois et le Kin-ping-mei*, Paris: Maisonneuve, 1888.

③ 对译文版本的介绍参考王丽娜：《中国古典小说戏曲名著在国外》，上海：学林出版社，1988 年；王尔敏编：《中国文献西译书目》，台北：台湾商务印书馆，1975 年。

政治制度、文化风俗、文学风貌等各个方面，成为西人认知中国的重要凭借。其中，对中国文学的译介构成这些外文报刊的重要主题，而对中国小说的翻译则占据了相当大的比重。

这一时期继续发行和相继创办的外文报刊，以中国或亚洲为主题，以法文或英文为主要语种。法文报刊主要有《亚洲学刊》《东方杂志》《法国东方教育公报》等，英文报刊主要有《中国丛报》《亚洲杂志》《凤凰杂志》《远东杂志》《中国评论》《亚东杂志》等。这些报刊刊登了大量中国小说的译文，其中相当一部分作品是首次被翻译为西文。这些译文不仅丰富了中国古典小说西译的篇目，而且使外文报刊成为中国古典小说西译的即时资料源。具体情况见下表：

外文报刊所刊部分中国古典小说一览表

报刊	办刊时间	语种	出版地	刊载的中国古典小说
《亚洲学刊》Journal Asiatique	1822年至今	法文	巴黎	《红楼梦》《画图缘》《大树坡义虎送亲》《水浒传》《三教源流》《西游真诠》《种梨》等
《东方杂志》Revue de L'Orient	1848—1865	法文	巴黎	《白蛇精记》
《法国东方教育公报》Bulletin de L'Ecole française d'Ex trême-Orient	1901—1938	法文	巴黎	《阳羡书生》
《中国丛报》Chinese Repository	1832—1851	英文	广州	《三教源流》《智囊补》《聊斋志异》《笑得好》《今古奇观》等
《凤凰杂志》The Phoenix	1870—1873	英文	香港	《蒋兴哥重会珍珠衫》《杜十娘怒沉百宝箱》《庄子休鼓盆成大道》《疗妒缘》等

《远东杂志》 The Far East	1870—1878	英文	东京 上海	《好逑传》《薛刚反唐》 《粉妆楼》《二度梅》 《俞伯牙摔琴谢知音》 《金玉奴棒打薄情郎》等
《中国评论》 China Review	1872—1901	英文	香港	《水浒传》《荡寇志》 《东周列国传》《三国演义》 《麟儿报》《穆天子传》 《南柯梦太守传》《镜花缘》 《四游记》《笑林广记》 《智囊补》《今古奇观》 《好逑传》等
《亚东杂志》 The East of Asia Magazine	1902—1906	英文	上海	《双凤奇缘》《三国演义》 《西游记》《聊斋志异》 《今古奇观》等

这些译文往往以连载的形式刊登，但有些译文的划分没有遵循中文小说的章回编排，而是打乱中文的情节单元重新整合，如《中国评论》刊载的译文 The Young Prodigy，即清代小说《麟儿报》，译文分为五个部分，于《中国评论》1873 年第 2 卷第 1 期至第 5 期上连载。外文报刊以连载的方式刊登中国古典小说译文的做法，在某种程度上开启了中文报刊的小说连载。中文报刊最早的小说连载始于 1892 年韩子云创办的《海上奇书》，分期刊登了长篇小说《海上花列传》，它晚于外文报刊连载小说译文近 70 年。

（二）中国古典小说译本选集编撰体制的完备

这一时期中国古典小说译本选集的编撰日渐增多，其中比较重要的法文本有：儒莲编撰的《中国小说选》[①]，德理文（d'Hervey-

---

[①] Stanislas Julien, *Nouvelles Chinoises*, Paris: L. Hachette et C, Benjamin Duprat, 1860. 书中收有《董卓之死》《滕大尹鬼断家私》和《刘小官雌雄兄弟》3 篇译文。

Saint-Denys,1823—1892)编译的两种《三种中国小说》[1]和《六种中国小说》[2],以及由中国驻巴黎公使馆的陈季同将军编译的《中国故事集》[3];英文本主要有:道格斯(Robert K. Douglas,1839—1913)编译的《中国故事集》[4],师多马(Thomas G. Selby,1846—1910)选译的《中国小说中的中国人》[5];毛继义(J. A. Maung Gyi,1871—1955)和陈途宏(Cheah Toon Hoon)合译的《天镜》[6];德文本有爱德华·格里泽巴赫编译的两种《中国小说》[7]等。这些译文选集或把先后从同一个小说选集中选译的单个故事编辑成集,或从同一系列的中国古典小说集中选译数篇结集;也出现了把同一主题、不同题材和属系的中国古典小说编译成集的形式,如师多马的《中国小说中的中国人》,其中选译了7篇中国作品,侧重于家庭内部纠纷:或兄弟失悌,或婆媳不

---

[1] d'Hervey-Saint-Denys, *Trois Nouvelles Chinoise*, Paris: Ernest Leroux, Editeur, 1885. 书中所收3篇译文是:《夸妙术丹客提金》《看财奴刁买冤家主》和《钱秀才错占凤凰俦》。d'Hervey-Saint-Denys, *Trois Nouvelles Chinoise*, Paris: Editeur, 1889. 书中所收3篇译文是:《蒋兴哥重会珍珠衫》《徐老仆义愤成家》和《唐解元玩世出奇》。

[2] d'Hervey-Saint-Denys, *Six Nouvelles Choinoise*, Paris: J. Maisonneuve, 1892. 书中收有《赵县君乔送黄柑子》《金玉奴棒打薄情郎》《裴晋公义还原配》《吴保安弃家赎友》《崔俊臣巧会芙蓉屏》和《陈御史巧勘金钗钿》6篇译文。

[3] Tcheng-Ki-Tong, *Contes Chinoise*, Paris: Calmann Levy, 1889. 此书从《聊斋志异》中选译了《王桂庵》《白秋练》《青梅》等26篇故事。

[4] Robert K. Douglas, ed. and trans., *Chinese Stories*, Edinburgh and London: William Blackwood and Son, 1893. 书中收有《好逑传》《怀私怨狠仆告主》《夺锦楼》《金玉奴棒打薄情郎》《女秀才移花接木》《夸妙术丹客提金》《续玄怪录·薛伟》等译文。

[5] Thomas G. Selby, *The Chinaman in His Own Stories*, London: Charles. H. Kenny, 1895. 书中收《好秀才》《瓜棚遇鬼》《横柴纹》《生魂游地狱》等译文。

[6] J. A. Maung Gyi and Cheah Toon Hoon, *The Celestial Mirror*, Rangoon: D'vauz Press, 1894. 书中收有《闵损御车》《骗马》《鹿随獐》《叶生》等译文。

[7] Eduard Grisebach, *Chinesische Novellen*, Leipzig: Fr. Thiel, 1884. 书中收有《女秀才移花接木》和《杜十娘怒沉百宝箱》两篇译文。Eduard Grisebach, *Chinesische Novellen*, Berlin: Lehman, 1886. 书中收有《卖油郎独占花魁》的译文。

和，或妻妾相迫，或亲家相斗。作品围绕人们的家庭生活可能出现的各种纠纷，在纠纷产生和解决的过程中宣扬谦让恭敬的品性，劝人为善，在日常生活中致力于德行的培养。而《天镜》以中国孝义和判案故事为主题，由《聊斋志异》《搜神记》和《龙图公案》中选译的24篇作品编辑而成。该书列为闽南图书系列（Hokkien Library Series I），1894年由仰光德瓦兹（D'Vauz）出版社出版。

另外，这一时期中国古典小说译文单行本继续发行，如首次以单行本形式出现的《大明正德皇游江南传》《红楼梦》的英译本；《龙图公案》《二度梅》的法译本等。其中，《大明正德皇游江南传》早在1843年已经被译成英文，题为 The Rambles of the Emperor Ching Tih in Keang Nan, A Chinese Tale。译者为英华学院的中国学生何进善（Tkin Shen），译稿经英国著名汉学家理雅各（James Legge, 1815—1897）修订，由伦敦朗文（Longman）出版社出版，是这部小说最早的西文全译本，也是首次由中国人完成的西译小说。

（三）插图的添加和插图艺术性的提高

明清时期的中国古典小说大都配有插图，与文本相互补充，相得益彰。早在中国小说西译之初，译本已开始有附加插图的做法，如《好逑传》的英、法、德译本皆有4幅插图，分别置于每卷之首，描画小说中4个故事情节。进入明清时期，附加插图的做法日益普遍，且插图风格多样，艺术性增强。从总体上讲，中国古典小说译本的插图大抵可以分为四类：

第一，直接套用中国古典小说中的插图。如甘淋（George T. Candlin, 1853—1924）译著的《中国小说》，从《三国演义》《西游记》中选译了部分章节，书中相应地附有从《三国演义》绣像本中搬用的关

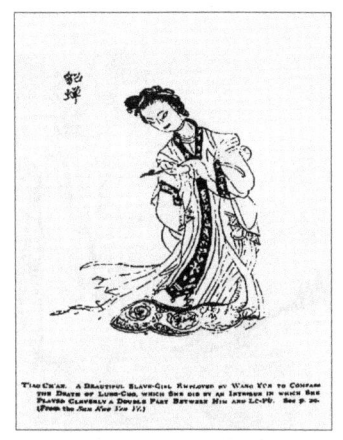 

图 1

羽、貂蝉等 8 幅人物的绣像，以及《西游记》中"四圣试禅心""孙行者三调芭蕉扇"等 3 幅回目画。（见图 1）

第二，以其他中文书籍的插图临摹而成的插图。如《亚东杂志》第 5 卷所刊载《双凤奇缘》的英译文 *Chao Chuin, A Novel, Translated from the Original Chinese*，配有 20 余幅插图，生动再现了小说的一些重要情节，英译文的插图与中文原本插图完全不同。《双凤奇缘》现存的版本主要有嘉庆十四年忠恕堂刊残本、嘉庆二十四年玉茗堂本及道光二十三年卧云阁本等，附有插图 16 幅，为文中主要人物绣像。译本则省去单个人物绣像，而是根据主要情节为小说配画。译文图画刻画比较细致，亦注意景色氛围的烘托，生动地描绘出小说中的故事情节及人物形象。但人物形象在服饰装扮等方面与原书插图存在诸多差异，译本的插图明显没有以原本插图为依据，而大抵是依其他中文书籍临摹而成。（见图 2）

第三，西人根据中国古典小说的情节内容而创作的插图。其中最典型的代表是 1884 年由巴黎拉于尔出版社出版的勒格朗（E. L. J.

图 2

Legrand, 1841—1903）翻译的《宋国的夫人》（*La Matrone du Pays de Soung* 亦即《庄子休鼓盆成大道》的法译名），书中附有 20 余幅彩色精美的插图，图中有画者的签名和日期。这些画作于 1883 年，是西人根据特定内容而作，且具有浓厚的日本浮世绘风格，这应与 19 世纪中后期日本浮世绘在西方绘画界的流行相呼应。（见图 3）

图 3

第四，请中国本土画家为译本所作的配图。1905年由别发洋行分别在上海、香港、新加坡出版了豪威尔（E. B. Howell）编译的《今古奇观：不坚定的庄夫人及其它故事》（*The Inconstancy of Madam Chuang and Other Stories from the Chinese*），书中有插图12幅，并在扉页注明插图为中国本土画家所作。（见图4）

图4

中国古典小说译本中的插图除了起到对文本引导、阐释和形象化传播的作用，亦具有一定的史料价值。这种史料价值主要表现为，插图在一定程度上反映了西人对中国人的认识及其历史发展过程。在西人最初编撰的有关中国的书籍中亦时或附有插图，其中所描画的中国人的形象大都是西人凭借想象创作

图5

的。如 1736 年出版的《中华帝国全志》第 1 卷卷首附有孔子画像，其人物特征和服饰打扮俨然是西人的模式。（见图 5）

进入 19 世纪，随着西方人对中国了解的积累，对中国人的形象认识也逐渐增多，译本插图所描摹的人物已不再有典型的西方人特征。但是，他们对中国人的认识似乎仍是一个笼统的概念，往往对整个东方的认识相混淆。如上述为《宋国的夫人》所创作的插图采用了日本浮世绘的画法，庄子亦为日本人形象，对中国与其他东方国家人物形象的区别并没有清晰地区分。同时，这些小说插图成为了解那个特定历史阶段的重要史料，如道格斯的《中国故事集》所附插图中女子小脚、执扇和男子蓄长辫是当时西方人认识的中国人的典型形象，这种典型的中国人形象与译者所处的特定历史时代相呼应。

综上所述，1841 年至 1911 年间，更多数量的中国小说被介绍到西方。这一阶段西译的中国小说承接并发展了此前所确立的翻译范式和灵活多元的翻译策略，在此基础上，外文报刊成为重要载体，译文选集体式日趋完备，译文单行本继续发行，添加插图的做法逐渐普遍，且插图的艺术性有所提高。另外，译文发表地除集中在欧洲的巴黎、伦敦和莱比锡外，在亚洲的香港、上海和广州形成了另外的中心。这都体现了中国古典小说西译的成熟。

四、中国古典小说早期翻译的文化解读

以上我们按历史时期大致勾勒了中国古典小说西译的发展轨迹。文学作品的翻译当然首先是两种语言文字符号的转换，但语言文字只有在其作用的文化背景中才有意义。因此翻译不仅仅是两种语言的简

单转换，更是深深植根于两种语言所处的不同文化之间的对接，是一种文化的再造。不仅如此，西方对所翻译的中国古典小说的选择，以及在翻译过程中所进行的文化改写和阐释，都无不经过了西方"滤色镜"的过滤，从而从一个侧面折射出"中国形象"在西方人眼中的历史演变。

（一）从文字的转换到文化的再造

如上所述，文学作品的翻译不只是两种语言文字符号的转换，而且还承担了更深层次的文化转换的功用，是一种文化的再造。这种文化的再造具体通过文化认同、文化阐释、文化承载与文化改写来实现。

文化认同指接受文化对源文化的认识和首肯，从而构成文化交流的动机和基础。如中国古典小说所具有的道德教化功用从其被译成外文之始就备受西人的赞赏和肯定，不仅成为译者翻译中国小说的主要动机之一，也在西方读者中引起较大的反响。除《歌德谈话录》中常被人引及的那段引文，《中华帝国全志》也有一篇文章论及中国小说："中国小说与我们时下流行的小说不同。我们的小说大都是一些爱情故事，给读者带来消遣和娱乐，但是往往过于鼓吹激情，使之变得十分危险，尤其是对一些年轻读者。然而，中国小说则充满教训，具有教化作用，引导人们改进行为礼节，提倡高尚的德行操守。"[①] 对中国小说讲究道德的认同显然引发并推进了西人对中国小说的关注和翻译。

文化阐释指对源文化中特定的事物、概念、礼仪、习俗等做出解释，为接受者提供背景知识的介绍，从而为不同文化间的理解和沟

---

① "Of the Taste of the Chinese for Poetry, History and Plays," *The General History of China*, Done from the French of P. J. B. DU HALDE, vol.III, p.113.

通消弭距离与障碍。而文化承载是指在将汉语转换为外语的过程中，外语作为汉语文化的载体，通过添加与中国人生活相关的内容，起到文化承递的作用。如《怀私怨狠仆告主》对主人公狱中情况仅寥寥数句概括而过，而译者则在此拟出一个颇具光彩的人物龙（Lung），并通过曾与龙在相同境遇中一个神形枯槁，一个处之泰然的截然相反的表现，引出一段很有意思的儒道之辩，展开了儒道之间关于未知、死亡及来生的论辩，从而对中国最为重要的两大主导思想做出大致的介绍，且嵌儒道之辩于故事之中，情节的衔接合乎情理而不显突兀。

文化改写指译者在翻译过程中，对原作进行一定的调整和改动，使其符合译入语文化的价值标准。如《夸妙术丹客提金》原文止于潘氏悔悟、终身不再相信炉火之事，旨在警示世人炉火丹术的虚无缥缈，对以丹术骗人的丹客的下场则只字不提。译文则添加了官府通缉丹客的情节，符合西人讲求对恶者进行法律制裁，使作恶者得到应有惩罚的价值标准。译者对中文内不符合西方文化价值的事件或情节作出调整，使之更易为西方读者接受和理解，完成了对原作的文化改写。

通过文化认同、文化阐释、文化承载和文化改写，中文所代表的部分源文化流失；同时，译文又为中文添加了其所不具有的文化因子，在文化缺失和文化增值的双重功能下实现了文化的再创造，完成了文本在异域的"再现"。

（二）西方人眼中"中国形象"的历史演变

中国古典小说的早期翻译也从一个侧面折射了西方人眼中"中国形象"的历史演变，这里所谓"中国形象"是指西方对中国的一种认识和想象，是在中西交流的过程中，伴随着中西文化自身发展的步伐，在特定的历史时段和文化语境下，由不同类型的文本构筑而成的具有历史延续性和社会集体性的话语谱系。①

西人对中国及其文化的关注可以追溯到纪元前后,在早期的描述中,中国以"丝人国"的形象出现在西人对中国最初的想象之中,但由于记录的零散,并不能构成真正意义上的"中国形象"。直至13世纪中后期,随着《柏朗嘉宾蒙古行纪》《鲁布鲁克东行纪》和《马可·波罗游记》等游记的流行,才将遥远神秘、富庶强大的中国构想引入西方的文化视野,成为西方"中国形象"的起点。此后,随着西方和中国交流的密切,西人关于中国的著述日益增多,从而构筑起西人眼中纷繁多样的"中国形象"。简言之,构筑西人"中国形象"的文本在形态上主要有旅行家的游记、传教士的书信、外交使节的报告、西人关于中国的专门著述、西人创作的"中国主题"的文学作品、西人翻译的中国儒家经典、西人创办的以中国和远东地区为主题的外文报刊和西人翻译的中国古典小说等。

自1735年法国杜赫德编撰的《中华帝国全志》上刊登了三篇中国小说的译文肇始,中国古典小说的译文亦成为西人构筑"中国形象"的重要文本支持。在这方面,中国古典小说译本具有天然的有利条件。首先,中国古典小说是由中国人自己创作的,作者凭借小说这种叙事文学体裁,通过复杂巧妙的结构、持续发展的情节、绵延拓展的时空、丰富详致的细节,赋予小说表现社会的内涵和功用,从而使小说成为中国及中国人真实生活和风俗世态的"自我投影"。因此,中国古典小说往往被西人视为了解中国和中国人最有效生动的媒介,最直接的

---

① 有关西方的"中国形象"可参见梅克热斯(Colin Mackerras)的《西方的中国形象》、贝尔格(Willy Richard Berger)的《启蒙时代欧洲的中国形象与中国模式》、周宁的《天朝遥远——西方的中国形象研究》等。本文论述仅就中国古典小说翻译的实践做出论断,与其他论著关于西方"中国形象"的论述不尽相同。

窗口。其次，中国古典小说早期的译者大都是西方人，受译者自身思维范式、知识结构、学术素养与文化积淀的影响，在翻译的过程中难免带有偏见，以"他者审视"的态度有选择地翻译中国小说，自觉不自觉地以西人的标准添加或改写其中的某些情节，并注重中西文化之间的比较和差异。正是在"自我投影"与"他者审视"的双重作用下，中国古典小说的翻译成为构筑西方人眼中"中国形象"的重要文本依据。

中国古典小说翻译构筑西人"中国形象"具体有四种方式：（1）西人对中国古典小说的选择。西人翻译中国古典小说的选择标准和价值取向在一定程度上折射出西人对"中国形象"的构想。（2）西人在翻译过程中对中国小说的改写。通过对中文小说的增益或删节，展示和凸现西方眼中的"中国形象"的某个侧面。（3）译本中前言和注释的添加。译者为译本添加的前言或注释往往包含大量的信息，或为译者对所译小说的介绍，或是对小说中出现的典章制度的解释，或将中西文化进行比较，或对小说本身的内容、人物做出批评，成为西人构筑"中国形象"的重要凭借。（4）中国小说译本在西方的刊印和流传。中国古典小说通过在西方的传播，将关于中国社会生活、思想文化等各个方面的知识带入西方世界，成为西方读者理解和认识中国的依据，从而在更广的范围内构筑起西方人眼中的"中国形象"。

与中国古典小说西译的进程相一致，西方通过小说翻译构筑的"中国形象"，先后出现了三种类型："道德理性之乡""中国情调"与"多面的中国"。这三种"中国形象"的话语谱系大抵与西方启蒙主义运动、浪漫主义思潮与现代性的历史进程相一致。首先，"中国形象"在启蒙主义思潮的背景下进入西方的文化视野，中华帝国作为"道德理性之乡"被西人定格和放大,在一定程度上反映了西人在启蒙主义影响下对理性的推崇。进入19世纪初期,随着浪漫主义的蔓延,西方发出了一种对人的感情自由抒发的呼唤,形成了对人为理性的反弹,在这样的文化语境下,中国"道德理性之乡"的形象逐渐隐退,取而代之的是一种作为异国风尚而出现的"中国情调"。进入19世纪中叶,随着中西交流的频繁和一些重大历史事件的发生,特别是伴随着中西力量对比的悄然变化和西方现代主义的推进,西方中心主义思想开始形成,因而其对中国的评价也逐渐带有负面的成分,形成了西人眼中"多面的中国"。

18世纪的欧洲充斥着一股"中国热潮",法国的舞台上演着《中国孤儿》《丑角、宝塔和医生》等表现中国人的戏剧;时髦的贵族夫人们品尝着传说能治愈偏头疼的中国茶叶;中国瓷器、屏风、漆器等成为欧洲宫廷和贵族家庭装饰的风尚;中国的绘画、文学和哲学也成为西人竞相谈论的话题和模仿的对象,此时的欧洲对遥远的中国普遍怀有一种仰慕之情。18世纪选译的4部(篇)中国小说或通过中国式因果循环宣扬道德教化的主旨,或因主人公以理性控制情感的高尚品质而备受西人的称赞。这4部(篇)小说都展示了"中国形象"美好的一面,即对"高尚的道德理性"提倡的一面,并将其和西方流行的"鼓吹激情""诲淫诲盗"的小说进行比照,凸现了"道德理性之乡"的"中国形象"的完美。

18世纪末期至19世纪,西方文化在法国大革命的冲击下,由启蒙主义进入浪漫主义时代。后者在对人为理性的质疑中退回到对内在自由精神的探索,追求人类情感的自由倾泄,在西方社会文化中形成了一股非理性主义的审美思潮。这一时期,西人翻译的中国古典小说在数量上从18世纪的4种增加到30余种,其中大量才子佳人之间那种以诗酒自娱、放纵才情的生活及其诗歌传情、共效于飞的爱情方式构筑起西人眼中瑰奇的"中国风情";一夫多妻的婚姻制度和女子间因共同的爱情对象不仅不起纷争,反而互生倾慕之情的感情模式更增添了一种不可思议的异国情调;无怪乎戈蒂耶会将中国想象成"多愁善感的爱情国度"。① 美酒、月夜、少女轻盈的脚步、布满亭台楼阁的花园等"中国情调"更是在西方表现中国的文本中屡屡出现。可以说,正是从中国爱情小说的翻译中,西人获取了文学创作的灵感,将瑰丽多情、色彩斑斓的"中国风情"置入西方的文化中,渲染出西人眼中"中国情调"的多彩多姿。

  19世纪40年代,中英鸦片战争的爆发及战后签订的不平等条约,为西人开辟了在中国更为广阔和自由的活动空间,一个真实落后的中国裸露在西人的视野之中。同时,伴随着中西力量对比的悄然变化和西方现代主义的推进,西方中心主义逐渐形成,西人对中国的态度从仰慕变为俯视。这一时期,中国古典小说译本通过改写、释读、品评和配图等环节,营造出西人眼中"多面的中国"形象:一方面,中国小说中道德感知力的余风尚存,中国风格仍令人愉悦;另一方面,中国社会的一些阴暗面被西方译者植入中国古典小说的译文中,并在某种程度上加以放大,如中国人吸食鸦片的恶习、中国监狱的悲惨场景、中国社会的自杀现象等。道格斯便在其选译编辑的《中国故事集》中为从官员、士人到仆卒等人物添加了抽吸鸦片的嗜好,强化了中国人对鸦片的依赖。如根据《金玉奴棒打薄情郎》翻译的《再婚的夫妻》,

---

① 米丽娜·德特利:《19世纪西方文学中的中国形象》,孟华主编:《比较文学形象学》,北京:北京大学出版社,2001年,第241—262页。

添加了原作中所没有的男主人公（原作叫莫稽，译文改姓王）对于鸦片的依赖：

Wang was so completely unnerved that he was scarcely able to stand. "Shall I bring your Excellency some opium?" suggested the man, seeing his condition. "Yes, quickly." The materials for a pipe of the drug were always at hand in Wang's household, and before many minutes had elapsed he was stretched on the divan greedily inhaling the "foreign dirt". Gradually under the soothing influence of his pipe his eyes lost their wild excited look, his features relaxed, and his hand recovered some of its steadiness. （王完全地身心疲惫，简直不能站起。看到这种情况，他的仆人问："老爷，要不要我给你拿些鸦片？""要，快点。"抽鸦片所需的物件是王家里常备的。不一会儿，王已经躺在长椅上贪婪地抽着鸦片。渐渐地，在鸦片的缓和作用下，他的眼睛失去了先前狂野过激的神色，身体也松弛下来，手也恢复了正常。）①

译文通过王对鸦片的依赖，塑造和强化了中国人喜食鸦片的嗜好。道格斯还在《处于危境》中将《怀私怨狠仆告主》简单交待的监狱生活铺陈为一段详细描述，大肆渲染了面黄肌瘦的囚犯、污浊肮脏的空气、四处蔓延的皮肤病、狭窄犹如野兽笼子般的空间等中国监狱的简陋肮脏，非人性化的制度及囚犯的悲惨生活。而师多马编译的《中国小说中的中国人·泼妇》则讲述了漂亮妻子为了报复丈夫的父母、兄弟对自己的不满而自杀，从而引起一连串为报复而自杀的行为，展示的也是中国负面的形象。其他诸如中国女子小脚、男子蓄辫的体貌

---

① Robert K. Douglas, ed. and trans., *Chinese Stories*, p.155.

特征以及中国人呆滞的目光和狡诈的内心都被定格为中国人的典型形象而反复渲染。

从"道德理性之乡"到"中国情调"再到"多面的中国",中国古典小说早期翻译在其历史进程中,因具有"自我投影"和"他者审视"的特性,成为西方对中国进行想象的重要文本依据,构成了三种具有一定象征性并被集体认同的"中国形象"。这一由中国古典小说西译所构筑起的"中国形象",遂成为西人眼中整体"中国形象"不可或缺的一部分。

以上我们简要论述了在"中学西传"背景下,中国古典小说西译所走过的漫长发展历程,并就中国古典小说西译的诸多特征和文化蕴涵作了初步的阐释。历史的经验告诉我们,不同文学和文化间的双向交流是人类文明进步的必由之路。和"西学东渐"给中国带来了欧风美雨一样,包括中国古典小说西译在内的"中学西传"也为西方带去了回味隽永的中国风尚。作为中国他者的"西方形象"和作为西方他者的"中国形象",都对彼此的文明和进步产生了积极的影响。今天,我们比以往任何时候都更需要这样的互动和交往。

(本篇序言原载于《中国社会科学》2009年第6期,原标题为《"中学西传"与中国古典小说的早期翻译(1935—1911)——以英语世界为中心》。收入此书稍有修改)

目 录

殷弘绪《庄子休鼓盆成大道》（1736）……………………………… 1

帕西《好逑传》（第一回）（1761）…………………………………… 29

马礼逊《三教源流·释氏源流》（1812）……………………………… 41

汤姆斯《著名丞相董卓之死》（1820—1821）………………………… 49

德庇时《三与楼》（1822）……………………………………………… 97

乔治·加德纳·亚历山大《貂蝉》（第三幕）（1869）……………… 136

奥古斯塔·韦伯斯特《俞伯牙摔琴谢知音》（1874）………………… 170

乔利《红楼梦》（第一回）（1892—1893）…………………………… 233

道格斯《续玄怪录·薛伟》（1893）…………………………………… 269

师多马《俗话倾谈·横纹柴》（1895）………………………………… 284

后　记 …………………………………………………………………… 343

殷弘绪《庄子休鼓盆成大道》
（1736）

导　读

　　《庄子休鼓盆成大道》最早见于冯梦龙编撰的《警世通言》，后被辑入抱瓮老人选编的《今古奇观》。《庄子休鼓盆成大道》讲述了庄子与妻子田氏的婚姻波折，并从中参破世情的哲理故事。其中"女子扇坟""庄子鼓盆而歌"等为其经典情节。目前所知，最早将《庄子休鼓盆成大道》翻译成西文的是法国传教士殷弘绪[①]（François Xavier d'Entrecolles, 1662—1741）。

　　殷弘绪将《庄子休鼓盆成大道》《怀私怨狠仆告主》和《吕大郎还金完骨肉》三篇拟话本小说译成法文，译文收入法国籍耶稣会士杜赫德（Jean-Baptiste Du Halde, 1674—1743）编著的《中华帝国全志》(*Description Géographique, Historique, Chronologique, Politique, et Physique de L'Empire de la Chine et de la Tartarie Chinioise*)，1735 年由巴黎勒梅尔西埃（P. G. Le Mercier）出版社出版。这是迄今为止，我们所知的最早翻译成西文并正式出版的中国古典小说。殷弘绪的法

---

①　殷弘绪为其所取中文名。

译文载于《中华帝国全志》第三卷，译文分为四个部分：

Histoire où l'on voit qu'en pratiquant la vertu on illustre sa famille 积善之家，必有余庆。（《吕大郎还金完骨肉》，但省去了"金员外毒杀亲儿"的入话部分）

Trait d'Histoire où le crime étant d'abord absous, le Ciel au moment qu'il triomphe, le confond le punit avec éclat 恶人逃罪，沾沾自喜；天公明判，惩治恶人。（《怀私怨狠仆告主》的入话部分）

Trait d'Historie où l'innocence accablée prête à succomber, vient tout à coup à être reconnuë, vengée par une protection particuliere du Ciel 无辜蒙冤，服罪认命；天公明断，为之昭雪。（《怀私怨狠仆告主》）

Autre Histoire: Tchoang tse après les bizarres obseques de sa femme, s'adonne entierement à sa chere philosophie, devient célèbre dans la Secte de Tao 另一部小说：庄子在妻子葬礼之后，投身于所钟爱的哲学，成为道教名哲。（《庄子休鼓盆成大道》）

《中国帝国全志》出版后，被转译成英、德、俄等多种语言。其中英译本有两种，一为由约翰·瓦茨（John Watts）主持翻译的四卷本《中华帝国全志》（*The General History of China*），1736 年在伦敦出版。该书第三卷包括《吕大郎还金完骨肉》（*A Novel, wherein is shewn that Practice of Virtue renders a Family illustrious*）、《庄子休鼓盆成大道》（*Another Novel: Tchouang tse, after the Funeral Obsequies of his Wife, wholly addicts himself to his beloved Philosophy, and becomes famous among the Sect of Tao*）和《怀私怨狠仆告主》（*Two Pieces of History: or rather two kinds of judgment; the one where the Guilty being acquitted, Heaven, in the midst of his Triumph, confounds and punishes him in a remarkable manner; the other where Innocence being oppressed, and ready to sink under the Misfortune, is suddenly discovered and revenged by the particular Interposition of Heaven*）三篇作品。一为爱德华·凯夫（Edward Cave）主持的两卷大开本《中华帝国全志》（*A Description of the Empire of China and of Chinese Tartary from the French of P. J. B. Du Halde*），1738 至 1742 年在伦敦出版，亦包括《吕大郎还金完骨肉》（*A Novel, call'd Hi eul or Virtue rewarded*）、《怀私怨狠仆告主》（*Two Stories. The Guilty punish'd by Heaven, and oppressed Innocence justified*）和《庄子休鼓盆成大道》（*Another Story, called Tyen, or the Chinese Matron*）三篇小说。

此篇译文选自 1736 年在伦敦出版，由约翰·瓦茨主持翻译的《中华帝国全志》。

译　文

ANOTHER NOVEL

Tchouang tse, after the Funeral Obsequies of his Wife, wholly addicts himself to his beloved Philosophy, and becomes famous among the Sect of Tao.

The Chinese Author's PREFACE

THE Riches and Advantages of this World are like an agreeable Dream of a few Moments; Honour and Reputation are like a bright Cloud that is soon dissipated; even the Affection of those who are untied by the Ties of Blood is often nothing but a vain Shadow; the most ender Friendship often changes to a deadly Hatred; let us not be pleased with a Yoke because it is Gold, and with chains because they consist of Jewels; let our Desires be reasonable, but especially let them be moderate; let us free our selves from too great an Attachment to the Creatures, for it is like taking up a handful of Sand; let us look upon it as the principal Point to preserve our selves in a State of Liberty and Joy, which is independent.

The Sects of Tao and Fo, tho' greatly different from the Sect of the Learned, agree with them in the Principal Duties, without attempting to oppose or weaken them; however it is true that the Love of Fathers to Children ought not to make them over and above anxious when they are about to be settled in the World; on which account it is commonly said, *The Fortune of Children ought to be procur'd by themselves.*

As for what relates to Man and Wife they are united together by Sacred Ties, and a Divorce or Death often dissolve this Union: This we are taught by the Proverb which says, *Husband and Wife are like Birds of the Field, in the Evening they meet in the same Bush, and separate in Morning*: Yet it must be own'd there is much less to be fear'd from the Excess of Paternal Affection than Conjugal Love; the latter is nourish'd and grows secretly by mutual Endearments and reciprocal Confidence, insomuch that it is no uncommon thing for a young Wife to become Master of her Husband, from whence proceeds the Coldness of the Son to the Father: These are gross Faults, from which Men of Sense know how to preserve themselves.

Upon this Subject I shall give a Sketch of the Life of the famous *Tchouang tse*, but I solemnly declare that it is with no Intention to weaken the Union between Man and Wife, my only Design is to shew that we ought to be careful in distinguishing between true and false Merit, in order to regulate our Affections; and as it is very dangerous to be a Slave to a blind Passion, it is likewise of great consequence to our Repose to keep within the Bounds of Moderation; generally speaking those who constantly strive to subdue their Passions will at length become Masters; then Wisdom will be their Portion, and a calm and serene Life will be the Fruit of their Labour: But let us come to the History.

TOWARDS the end of the Dynasty of *Tcheou* there was a famous Philosopher appear'd in China, called *Tchouang tse*, he was born at Mong, a City of the Kingdom of *Song*; he had a small Mandrinate, and became a Disciple of a famous Sage of those Times, and Author of the *Sect of Tao*; his Name was Ly, and his Surname Eul; but as he came into the World with white Hair he was called the Infant Old Man.

Every time *Tchouang tse* slept his Sleep was interrupted by Dreams; he imagined himself to be a large Butterfly fluttering about either in some Meadow of Orchard: The Impression of this Dream was so strong, that even when he awaked he could not help fancying he had Wings fasten'd to his Shoulders, and that he was ready to fly away, not being able to guess at the meaning of a Dream so extraordinary and frequent.

One Day making use of a proper Opportunity, after a Discourse of his

Master *Lao tse* on one of the Canonical Books, he told him his Dream that had been repeated so often, and desir'd the Interpretation.

This reply'd the wonderful Man, who was well acquainted with the Secrets of Nature, The Cause of this Dream ought to be sought in the Times preceding those in which you live; you must know that at the Time that the Chaos began to be unravell'd, and the World to be formed, you was then a fine white Butterfly: The Waters were the first Production of Heaven, the second was the Trees and Plants, wherewith the Earth was adorned, for every thing flourished and looked gay in an Infant: This fine white Butterfly wander'd at pleasure, and went and enjoyed the Scent of the most excellent Flowers; he knew how even to derive from the Sun and Moon an infinite Delight, insomuch that at length he procured himself the Gift of Immortality; his Wings were large and almost round, and his Flight was swift.

One Day as he was taking his Diversion he alighted upon the Flowers of the Pleasure-Garden of a Great Queen, wherein he found the Secret to insinuate himself, and spoil several Buds scarcely blown; the mysterious Bird, to whom was committed the Care of the Garden, struck the Butterfly with his Beak and killed him.

The Butterfly's Body was then left without Life, but his Soul being immortal could not be destroyed; it has passed into other Bodies, and at present possesses that of *Tchouang tse*: This gives you the happy Disposition to become a great Philosopher capable of raising yourself, and acquiring the Art which I teach, and also of purifying your self by an en-tire Detachment from the World, and establishing your self in the perfect Knowledge of the Mind and Heart.

From that time *Lao tse* discovered to his Disciple the deepest Mysteries of his Doctrine, and the Disciple perceived himself all of a sudden become another Man, and following thenceforward his original Form he had in reality the Disposition of a Butterfly, which is continually fluttering without fixing upon any Object how charming soever; that is, *Tchouang tse* began to discover more fully the Emptiness of every thing that amuses and enchants Mankind; the most illustrious Condition was not capable of laying a Temptation in his way; his Heart became insensible to the greatest Advantages, for he found them as light as a thin Cloud that is the sport of every Wind, and as unstable as the Water of a Brook whose Stream is extremely rapid; in short his Soul no longer adhered to any thing.

Lao tse seeing his Disciple entirely weaned from earthly Amusements, and having a Taste of Truth, initiated him into the Mysteries of Tao te king, for the 5000 Words of which this Book is composed are all mysterious; he kept nothing secret form such a worthy Disciple.

Tchouang tse for his part gave himself up entirely to study; he read without ceasing, he meditated, he put in practice the Doctrine of his Master, and in proportion as he examined his interior Part to purify it, and if the Expression may be allowed to refine it; he perfectly comprehended the difference between what is visible and invisible, between the Body which is corruptible, and the Spirit which leaving its Abode acquires new Life by a kind of wonderful Transformation.

Tchouang tse, struck with these Lights, renounced the Office he was possessed of; he even took leave of *Lao tse* with a Design to travel, hoping to acquire agreeable Knowledge, and to make fresh Discoveries.

However tho' his Ardor was great to be entirely disengaged, and to enjoy uninterrupted Repose, he had not renounced Conjugal Pleasures, he married successively three times; his first Wife was taken away suddenly by a Distemper, a second he divorced for Unfaithfulness that he had surprised her in, the third shall be the Subject of this History.

Her name was *Tien*, and was descended from the Kings of *Tsi*: *Tchouang tse* was greatly esteemed throughout the Kingdom, and one of the Principal of this Family, called *Tien*, engaged by his Merit gave him his Daughter in Marriage.

This new Bride far outdid both her Predecessors; she was well shaped, had a fine Skin, and a Disposition that had a due mixture of Mildness and Vivacity; so that tho' the Philosopher was not naturally passionate he tenderly loved this last Wife.

However the King of *Tsou*, being informed of the great Reputation of *Tchouang tse*, designed if possible to get him into his own Dominions; he deputed Officers of his Court, with rich Presents of Gold and Silks, to invite him to enter into his Council in Quality of Prime Minister.

Tchouang tse, far from being blinded with these Offers, made his Apology after his manner: A Heifer appointed for Sacrifice, and delicately fed for a long time, walked in Pomp loaded with all the Ornaments usual to Victims; in the midst of this kind of Triumph she perceived in the Road

Oxen yoked, which were sweating at the Plough; this Sight redoubled her Pride, but after she was introduced into the Temple, and saw the Knife lifted up ready to stay her, she wished to be in the Place of those whose mean Lot she had before despised; these Wishes were fruitless for it cost her her Life: In this manner *Tchouang tse* courteously refused the Presents and Offers of the King.

Soon after he retired with his Wife into the Kingdom of *Song*, his native Country, and chose for his Abode the agreeable Mountain *Nan hoa*, in the District of *Tsao tcheou*, there to spend his Life in a Philosophical manner, and to enjoy, far from the noise and Tumults of the World, the innocent Pleasures of the Country.

One Day, as he was walking and enjoying his Meditations at the foot of a Mountain, he found himself insensibly near the Sepulchres of the neighbouring Place; he was struck with the Multitude of the Tombs: Alas! *cried he, sighing*, behold all are equal, here there is neither Rank nor Distinction; the most ignorant and stupid of Mankind are confounded with the prudent and wife; a Sepulchre is the eternal Abode of every Man; when once he has taken his Place in this Habitation of the Dead he must never expect to return to Life.

After he had busied himself for some time with these melancholy Reflexions, he advanced to the Side of the Burying-Place, when he found himself without design near a Sepulchre newly built; the little Eminence made of tempered Earth was not yet entirely dry; very near it sat a young Woman, whom at first he was not aware of; she was in deep Mourning, that is she was clad in a long white Gown of coarse hempen Cloth without ever a Seam; she was placed a little on one side the Tomb, holding in her Hand a white Fan, wherewith she incessantly fann'd the upper part of the Sepulchre.

Tchouang tse surprised with this Adventure, Dare I, *said he to her*, demand of you to whom this Tomb belongs, and why you take so much Pains in fanning it? Doubtless there is some Mystery in it which I am ignorant of: The woman without rising, as Civility seemed to require, and continuing still to move the Fan muttered a few Words between her Teeth, and shed Tears; this made it plain that Shame, rather than the natural Timidity of her Sex, hindered her from explaining herself.

At length she made his Reply: You see a Widow at the foot of her Husband's Tomb; Death has unfortunately snatch'd him from me, and he whose Bones rest in this Tomb has been dear to me during Life; he loved me with an equal Tenderness, and even when he expired left me with Reluctance; these are his last Words: *My dear Wife, said he, if afterwards you think of marrying again, I conjure you to wait near my Sepulchre till the moistened Earth of which it is composed shall be intirely dry, and then I will allow you to marry again*; wherefore thinking that the Surface of this Earth, newly heaped up, will not readily dry, you see me fan it continually to disperse the Moisture.

At so simple an Acknowledgment the Philosopher had much ado to forbear laughing; however he kept his Countenance, and said within himself, This Woman is in great haste, how can she dare to boast of loving her Husband, and of being belov'd by him What would she have done if they had hated each other? Then addressing himself to her, You desire, said he, that the top of the Tomb may be quickly dry, but your Constitution being tender you must needs be weary very soon, and since you will want Strength permit me to help you; at these Words the young Lady rose up; and making a profound Reverence accepted the Offer, and presented him a Fan like her own.

Then *Tchouang tse*, who had the Art of raising Spirits, called them to his Assistance, and giving a few blows with the Fan upon the Tomb, immediately all the Moisture vanish'd; the young Lady, after she had thanked her Benefactor with a gay and smiling Countenance, drew a silver Bodkin from her Hair, and made him a Present of it, with the Fan that she used herself, beseeching him to accept of them as a Token of her Gratitude; *Tchouang tse* resufed the Bodkin, but took the Fan; after which the Lady withdrew well satisfy'd, Joy appearing in her Countenance and her Gait.

As for *Tchouang tse* he remained quite astonished, and abandoning himself to Reflexions, which arose from such an odd Adventure, he returned to his Habitation; when sitting in the Hall, where he thought himself alone, he viewed for some time the Fan that had been given him; and then fetching a deep Sigh repeated the following Verses.

Do not they say that two Persons join themselves together only on account of an inveterate Hatred they bore each other in a precedent Life[①],

---

① This relates to the opinion of the Transmigration of Souls. 本书英语译文的所有注释，如无特别说明，均为译者注。

and seek each other in Marriage?

His Wife *Tien* was behind her Husband without being perceived; after hearing what was said, she advanced a little, and shewing herself, May one know, says she, what makes you sigh, and whence comes this Fan that you hold in your Hand? *Tchouang tse* related the Story of the young Widow, and all that had passed at her Husband's Tomb.

The Story was hardly ended but the Lady *Tien* discovered sighs of Indignation and Anger in her Looks, and, as if she had sought the young Widow with her Eyes, loaded her with a thousand Curses, called her the Scandal of Mankind, the Shame of her Sex; then looking upon *Tchouang tse*, I have said it, and it is true, she is a Monster of Insensibility.

Tchouang tse was not over and above attentive, but following the Emotions of his own Mind repeated these Verses: *While a Husband is living how does his wife flatter and praise him! When he is dead, she is ready to take the Fan, and dry his Sepulchre as fast as possible: A Picture represents well enough the ouTside of an Animal, but it cannot shew what is within; one sees the Countenance of a Person, but not the Heart.*

At these Words *Tien* fell into a great Passion, Mankind said she, are all alike as to their Nature; it is Virtue or Vice that makes a Distinction between them: How have you the Boldness to speak after this manner before me to condemn all Women, and to confound unjustly those who are virtuous with Wretches that do not deserve to live? Are not you ashamed to pass such an unjust Sentence? And are not you afraid to be punished for it?

To what purpose are all these Exclamations, replied the Philosopher?

I would have you candidly own, that if I was to die this instant, and you such as you are now, in the flower of your Age, beautiful and sprightly, could you persuade yourself to spend three or even five Years, as ancient Custom requires, without thinking of a new Husband? Is it not said, reply'd the Lady, That a Grandee who is faithful to his Prince renounces all Offices after the Death of his lawful Master? A virtuous Widow never thinks of a second Husband: Was it ever known that Ladies of my Quality, who after they were married have passed from one Family into another, and quitted their Nuptial-Bed after they have lost their Husbands? If I should be so unhappy as to become a Widow, I should be incapable of an Action that would dishonour my Sex, and should never be tempted by a second Marriage; I do not say after the Term of three or five Years, but as long as I live; nay such a Thought as this could never come into my Head even in a Dream; this is my Resolution, and nothing can shake it.

Such Promises are these, replied *Tchouang tse*, are easily made, but not so easily kept: These Words put the Lady into an ill Humour, and she could not forbear disrespectful Reproaches; Know, said she, that a Woman has often a more noble Soul, and is more constant in conjugal Affection than a Man of your Character: Can it be said that you are a perfect Pattern of Fidelity? Your first Wife died, soon after you take a second; her you divorc'd, and I am now the third; you judge of others by yourself, and hence you judge wrong; as for us that are married to Philosophers, who make profession of a severe Virtue, it is least of all allowed for us to marry again; if we did so we should become Objects of Derision: But to what purpose is this Language to me, and why do you take pleasure in making me uneasy? You are well in health, why then do you endeavour to disconcert me by making the disagreeable Supposition that you are dead, and that—

Then, without saying any thing more, she fell upon the Fan that her Husband had in his Hand, snatch'd it from him, and tore it in pieces. Pray be easy, said *Tchouang tse*, your Resentment gives me Pleasure, and I am glad you take fire upon such an occasion; Upon this the Lady grew calm, and they began to talk of some other Subject.

Some Days afterwards *Tchouang tse* fell dangerously ill, and lay at the last extremity; the Lady his Wife never left his Bedside, shedding Tears, and fetching continual Sighs: As far as I can see, said *Tchouang tse*, I shall not get over this Distemper, this Night or tomorrow we must take an eternal Adieu: What pity is it that you tore in pieces the Fan that I brought! It would have served you to have dried the Composition which my Sepulchre shall be made of.

For Heaven's sake, Sir, cry'd the Lady, in the condition that you are in let on Suspicions enter into your Head so uneasy to you, and so injurious to me; I have studied our Books, I understand the Customs, my Heart has once been united to yours, and I swear it never shall be to any other; If you doubt of my Sincerity I consent and demand to die before you, that you may be fully persuaded of my faithful Attachment.

It is sufficient, reply'd *Tchouang tse*, I am satisfied of your Constancy with respect to me: Alas! I perceive that I expire, and my Eyes are going to be closed for ever; after these Words he remained without Respiration, or the least sign of Life.

Then the Lady was almost out of her Senses, and with the most piteous Cries embraced the Corps of her Husband, and held him a long time in her Arms; after which she dressed him, and placed him in a proper manner in his Coffin, and then went into deep Mouring; Night and Day she made the Neighbourhood echo with her Complaints and Groans, and gave all possible Demonstrations of the most lively Concern; nay she carry'd it so far that she might have been thought to be half distracted, refusing both Sleep and Nourishment.

The Inhabitants that lived near the Mountain came to pay their last Duty to the deceased, whom they knew to be a Sage of the first Rank; when the Croud began to withdraw there appeared a young Batchelor, well-shaped, and of a florid Complexion; nothing could be more gallant than his Dress; his Cloaths were of a violet-colour'd Silk, with a handsome Cap, such as are wore by the Learned; his Girdle was embroider'd, and his Shoes neatly made; he was follow'd by an old Domestick; this Gentleman made it known that he was descended from *Tsou*: It is some Years since, said he, that I acquainted *Tchouang tse* with my Design of becoming his Disciple; I am come for this purpose, but I learn'd at my Arrival that he is dead: What a Disappointment! What a Loss!

He immediately threw off his coloured Habit, and went into Mourning; he then went near the Coffin, beat his Forehead four times against the Ground, and cried with a Voice mixed with Sighs, "Sage and learned *Tch-*

ouang! How unfortunate is your Disciple in not attending upon you during your Life, and profiting by your Lessons; I am desirous however of testifying my Regard and Acknowledgment in staying here to mourn a hundred Days." After these Words he prostrated himself again four times, bedewing the Earth with his Tears.

After this he desired to see the Lady, in order to pay his Compliments to her; but she excused herself from appearing tow or three times; *Ouang sun*, which was the Name of the young Lord, represented that, according to ancient Custom, Women might shew themselves when the intimate Friends of their Husband pay them a Visit: I have still more reason, added he, to enjoy this Privilege, since I was to have lived with the learned *Tchouang tse* in quality of his Disciple.

These instances prevailed upon the Lady, who came from her Apartment, and in a slow manner advanced into the Hall to receive the Compliments of Condolence, which were over after a few Words spoken in general Terms.

When the Lady saw the genteel Behaviour, Wit, and Attractions of this young Lord, she was charmed with them at once, and felt in her Soul the Motions of a growing Passion, which at first she did not rightly understand, but only wished he was not to retire so soon.

Ouang sun prevented her by saying, Since I have had the Misfortune to lose my Master, whose Memory will be always dear to me, I am desirous of procuring a Lodging where I may remain the hundred Days of the Mourning, when I will assist at the Funeral; I shall likewise be very glad to read, during that time, the Works of this illustrious Philosopher, which will supply the place of the Lessons I am deprived of by his Death.

This will be an Honour for our House, reply'd the Lady, and I feel no Inconveniency at all in it; upon which she prepared a small Repast, and served it in; while this lasted she laid, upon a handsome Desk, the Compositions of *Tchouang tse*; to which she added the Book of *Tao te*, a Present of the famous *Lao tse*, and came and offered it herself to *Ouang sun*, who received it with his natural Politeness.

On one side of the Hall, where the Coffin stood, there was on one of its Wings two Rooms that looked into the Hall, which were designed for the Lodging of this young Lord; the young Widow came frequently into the Hall to weep over her Husband's Coffin, and when she withdrew she said some engaging thing or other to *Ouang sun*, who came to salute her: In these frequent Interviews many a kind Glance passed between them, which betrayed each others Hearts.

Ouang sun was already half smitten, and the young Widow was downright in love; that which pleased her greatly was that they were in a solitary place, and at a House little frequented, where any Failure in the Mouring-Ceremonies would not be taken notice of: But as a Woman is always backward to make the first Advances, she bethought herself of an Expedient; she sent secretly for the old Servant of the young Lord, and entertained him plentifully with Wine, she flattered and cajoled him , and then went so far as to ask him if his Master was a married Man: Not yet, replied he. Well, continued she, what Qualities does he desire in the Person he designs to marry?

The Servant, who was got merry with drinking, instantly answered, If he could meet with one that resembled you it would be the height of his Wishes. She reply'd immediately, Tell me the truth, are you certain that he spoke in this manner? An old Man as I am, reply'd he, is uncapable of Lying, much less would he impose upon a Person of your Merit. Well, continued she, you are a fit Person to bring about a Marriage with your Master, you shall not lose your labour; speak of me to him, and if you find that he likes me assure him that I shall look upon it as the greatest Happiness to be his.

There is no need of sounding his Inclinations, said the Servant, because he has owned me freely that such a Marriage would be intirely agreeable to his Taste; but, added he, this is not possible because I am a Disciple of the Deceased, and what would the World say of it?

This Obstacle is a Trifle, reply'd the passionate Widow, your Master is not truly a Disciple of *Tchouang tse*, he only promised to be so; besides being in the Country, and quite out of the way, who can ever talk of our Marriage? Go, and if any other hindrance lies in the way, you have Ingenuity enough to remove it, and I will make a liberal Acknowledgment for your Services; At the same time she filled him several Glasses of excellent Wine to put him in a good Humour for the Undertaking.

He promised to take care of it; but as he was going she called him back, Harkye, said she, if the Gentleman accepts my Offers come as soon as possible, and bring me the News, let it be at what Hour of the Day or

Night it will, for I shall expect it with Impatience.

As soon as he was gone she was greatly uneasy, and made several Pretences to go into the Hall, but in reality it was to be near the young Gentleman's Room; it being extreamly dark she went to listen at the Window belonging to his Room, flattering herself she should hear something of the Affair she had so much at heart.

Then passing near the Coffin she heard a sort of a Noise, and trembled for fear: Alas! said she, in great Emotion, can it be the deceased that gives signs of Life? She enter'd her Room immediately, and taking the lamp went to see what was the occasion of the Noise, when she found the old Domestick laid upon the Table placed before the Coffin, on which Perfumes were to be burnt, and Offerings set at certain Hours; he lay there to sleep himself sober, the Lady having given him too much Wine; any other Woman would have shewn a Resentment for such Irreverence to the Dead, but she durst not complain, nor even disturb the sleeping Sot; she went therefore to lie down, but it was not possible for her to take any Repose.

The next Day she met the servant walking about carelessly, without thinking of returning an Answer to his Message; this Coldness and Silence gave her the greatest Disturbance, and calling him and taking him into her Chamber, Well, said she, how goes the Affair that you undertook to manage? There is nothing to be done, reply'd he dryly. Alas! Why so? said she, doubtless you forgot what I desired you to say on my part, or have misrepresented it: I forgot nothing, return'd the Domestick, my Maters knows not how to act; he acknowledges the Offer is advantageous, and is satisfied with what you said concerning the Obstacle in his being esteemed a Disciple of *Tchouang tse*, therefore this is no farther hindrance; but he told me there are three Obstacles that cannot possibly be got over, and which I am not very willing to mention.

Let us see a little, reply'd the Lady, what these three Obstacles are? These are they, reply'd the old Domestick, exactly as they were mentioned by my Master. 1. The Coffin of the Deceased yet standing in the Hall is a very mournful Scene, how then can one rejoice there, or celebrate the Nuptials? 2. The illustrious *Tchouang* having loved his Wife tenderly, and she having testified the like Affection, founded upon his Virtue and great Capacity, I have reason to fear that her Heart will always be united to her first Husband, especially when she finds so little Merit in me. 3. In short I have no Equipage here, nor have I Furniture, or Mony, how then shall I defray the Charge of the Ceremony, and make the usual Feasts? In the Place where we are there is no Person to borrow of: These, Madam, are the things that hinder him.

These three Obstacles, reply'd the passionate Lady, may be removed in an instant, and without a great deal of Thought: As to the first Article of the mournful Coffin, what does it contain? An inanimate Corps, an infectious Carcass, from which there is nothing to hope, and nothing to fear; I have in the corner of my Yard an old ruined House, and some of the neighboring Peasants, whom I shall send for, will soon carry the Coffin thither, so that the sight of it will be troublesome no longer; thus here is one Obstacle removed.

As to the second Article, Alas! was it true that my late Husband was what he appeared to be, a Man of uncommon Virtue and of great Capacity! Before he had espoused me he had divorced his second Wife; 'twas a sly Trick, as you may easily guess: The Fame of his Reputation caused the last King of *Tou* to send him rich Presents, and he would have made him his Prime Minister: He, who was conscious of his own Incapacity, and knew that it would appear if he accepted the Office, fled away, and came and hid himself in this solitary Place; about a Month since, as he was walking alone at the Foot of the Mountain, he met a young Widow employed in fanning the top of her Husband's Sepulchre in order to dry up the Moisture, because she had promised not to marry again till it was dry; *Tchouang* accosted her, cajoled her, took the Fan out of her Hands, and began to play with it with a design to please her in drying the Tomb faster than ordinary; afterwards he kept the Fan as a Pledge of her Kindness, and brought it hither, but I snatch'd it from him, and tore it in pieces: Being at the point of death, he brought this History upon the *Tapis*, which increas'd the difference between us: What Kindness have I received from him, and what Proofs has he given me of his Affection? Your Master is young, loves Study, and will certainly be famous in the learned World; he is already illustrious on account of his Birth, for, like me, he is descended from Royal Progenitors, so that there is between us a Conformity of Circumstances, and Heaven itself has conducted him hither to unites us; such is our Destiny.

There remains only the third Hindrance to be removed; as for the

Ornaments and Nuptial Feasts, I will take care to provide them: Can you believe that I have been so simple as not to lay up something against a Day of Necessity? Here, take twenty Taels, and give them your Master to buy new Cloaths; make what haste you can, and let him know that I have said; if he gives his Content I will go and prepare every thing for the Marriage this very Evening.

The Servant took the twenty Taëls, and went and inform'd his Master of the whole Discourse, who at length gave his much wish'd-for Consent. When the Lady was told the agreeable News she discovered her Satisfaction a hundred different ways; she immediately threw off her Mourning-habit, dress'd, adorn'd, and painted herself, while in pursuance of her Orders the Coffin was transported into the old ruin'd House; the Hall was immediately cleans'd and adorn'd for the Ceremony of the Interview and Nuptials; at the same time a Feast was getting ready that no time might be lost, nor any thing wanting for the Rejoicings.

In the Evening they Prepared the Nuptial-Bed with exquisite Perfumes, the Hall was illuminated with a great number of fine Lanthorns, and at the bottom of the Table was placed a great Wax-candle, being the Marriage Taper: When every thing was ready *Ouang sun* appeared in a Habit and Ornament for the Head that greatly set off his Shape and Features; the Lady came soon after to join him, dress'd in a long Silk Gown richly embroider'd, when they placed themselves near each other overagainst the Nuptial Flambeau; the Sight was surprisingly charming, for being thus seated by one another they added to each others Lustre, as precious Stones and Pearls set off the Beauty of Cloth of Gold, and appear more splendid themselves.

After making the usual Compliments that the Ceremony required, and being wished all kinds of Prosperity in their Marriage, they went hand in hand into the inward Apartment, where they practiced the grand Ceremony of drinking after each other in the Cup of Alliance, and then sat down at the Table.

The Feast ended, and when they were just going to Bed, the young Bridegroom fell into horrible Convulsions, his Visage was disfigured, and his Mouth dreadfully distorted; he could not walk a step further, for endeavouring to get upon the Bed he fell on the Floor, where he lay extended, rubbing his Breast with both his Hands, crying out as loud as he could, That he had a Sickness at his Heart that would be his immediate Death.

The lady, who was inamour'd to the last degree with her new Spouse, without thinking where she was, or the Condition she was in, cried out for help, and threw herself on the Body of *Ouang sun*; she embraced him, rubbed his Breast where his Complaint lay, and asked him what was the nature of his Distemper? *Ouang sun* was in too great an Agony to make any Answer, for he seemed just ready to expire.

His old Domestick ran in at the Noise, took him in his Arms and shook him: Has my dear *Ouang sun*, cry'd the Lady, been subject to such-like Accidents? This Distemper has seized him several times, reply'd the Servant, there seldom passes a Year but it attacks him; there is only one Remedy that can possibly cure him: Tell me quickly, reply'd the Bride, what the Remedy is? The Physician to the Royal Family, continued the Servant, has found a Secret which is infallible; he must take the Brain of a Man newly killed, and drinking it in warm Wine, his Convulsions will immediately cease, and he will be as well as before; the first time that this Distemper attacked him the King, his Father, executed a Prisoner who deserved Death, and took his Brain, which cured him in an instant; but alas! where shall we find such a thing at present?

But, reply'd the Lady, will not the Brain of a Man that died a natural Death have the like Effect? Our Physician, reply'd the old Domestick, let us know that, in case of absolute Necessity, he might use the Brain of a dead Person, provided he had not expired too long, because the Brain not being quite day preserves the Virtue.

If it be so, cry'd the Lady, you need only open my Husband's Coffin, and take from thence the salutary Remedy. I thought of it myself, reply'd the Servant, but durst not propose it lest it should fill you with Horror: A mighty matter, reply'd she, is not *Ouang sun* my Husband at present? If he wanted my own Blood to heal him, should I think it too much? How then can I hesitate to meddle with a vile Carcass?

At these Words she left *Ouang sun* in his Servant's Arms, and took an Ax which was used to cut Firewood in one hand, and a Lamp in the other, and running with precipitation towards the old House, where the Coffin was, turn'd up her long Sleeves, and taking the Axe in both Hands, lifted it up, and with all her Strength struck a great blow on the Lid of the Coffin, and clove it in two.

A woman's Strength would not be sufficient for an ordinary Coffin, but *Tchouang tse*, by an unusual Precaution and Love of Life, had ordered that the Boards of the Coffin should be very thin, because he had heard that many had returned to Life after they had been supposed to be quite dead.

Thus at the first blow the Board was split, and a few more knock'd off the Lid; as this extraordinary Motion had put her out of Breath she stopt a moment to recover herself; at the same instant she heard a very deep Sign, and, casting her Eyes towards the Coffin, she perceived her first Husband move and rise up.

One may judge what a Surprize the Lady was in; the Consternation made her give a great Shriek, her Legs fail'd her, and she was so confus'd she let the Ax fall out of her Hands without her Knowledge.

My dear Spouse, said *Tchouang* to her, assist me a little that I may stand up: When he was got out of the Coffin he took the Lamp and went towards her Apartment, the Lady followed, but with trembling Steps, and sweating large Drops, because she had left *Ouang sun* and his Servant there.

When he entered into the Room every thing appeared gay and splendid, but *Ouang sun* and his Servant had fortunately left it; this recovered her a little, and she began to think of means of glossing over this troublesome Affair; therefore casting a kind Look upon *Tchouang tse*, Your humble Slave, said she to him, since the moment that you died had been intirely taken up with your dear Memory; at length having heard a Noise proceed from the Coffin, and calling to mind the Stories that have been related of certain dead Persons returning to Life, it gave me hopes that you might be of this number, for which reason I ran as fast as I could and opened the Coffin, and, thanks to Heaven, my Hopes were not deceiv'd! What a Happiness is it for me to regain my Dear, whose Loss I continually bewailed!

I am obliged to you, reply'd *Tchouang tse*, for your great Regard for me, but let me ask you one short Question, Why are you not in Mourning? How do you come to be dress'd in a rich Brocade?

The Answer was ready: I went, said she, to open the Coffin with a secret foreboding of my Happiness; the Joy that I expected did not required a melancholy Dress, nor was it agreeable to receive you when recovered in a Mourning-Habit, for which reason I put on my Wedding-Cloaths.

Very well, said *Tchouang tse*, let us pass over this Article: But why was my Coffin plac'd in the old House, and not in the Hall where it ought to have been? This Question embarrass'd the Lady, and she could not tell what to answer.

Tchouang tse casting his Eyes upon the Dishes, Plates, and the other Signs of Rejoicing, considered them very attentively; and then, without explaining himself, required hot Wine to drink, and swallow'd several Cups without speaking one Word, while the Lady remained in the utmost Confusion.

After this *Tchouang tse* said to her, Behold these two Men that are behind thee, pointing to them with his Finger; she turned about and perceived *Ouang sun* and his old Servant ready to enter the House; this was a new Subject of Terror to her, and turning her Head a second time she found they were gone.

In short the unhappy Woman, finding her Intrigues all discovered, and not being able to survive the Shame, withdrew into a private Place, and taking off her silken Girdle fastened it to a Beam, and hanged herself; a deplorable End occasioned by a shameful Passion!

Tchouang tse finding her in that condition cut her down, and without farther trouble mended his old Coffin, and laid her in it, from whence she had not the good Luck, like her Husband, to return.

After this *Tchouang tse* took a Resolution to travel, determining never to marry again; in his Travels he met with his Master *Lao tse*, to whom he was attach'd the rest of his Life, which he spent agreeably in his Company.

思　考

1. 仔细阅读译文，辨析此篇《庄子休鼓盆成大道》译文是译自《警世通言》还是《今古奇观》？请阐明理由。

2. 比较伏尔泰《查第格》与《庄子休鼓盆成大道》，并谈谈你的看法。

参考文献

- *Description Géographique, Historique, Chronlogiquee, Politique, et Physique de L'Empire de la Chine et de la Tartarie Chinoise*, Paris: P. G. Le Mercier, 1735.
- *The General History of China, Done from the French of P. J. B. Du Halde*, trans. Richard Brookes, London: Printed by and for John Watts at the Printing Office in Wild-Court near Lincolns-Inn Fields, 1736.

扩展阅读

- *The Citizen of the World: or, Letters form a Chinese Philosopher, Residing in London to His Friends in the East*, by Oliver Goldsmith, London: Venor, 1792.
- *The Matrons, Six Short Histories*, by Thomas Percy, London: R. and J. Dodsley, 1762.

帕西《好逑传》(第一回)

(1761)

导　读

《好逑传》又名《侠义风月传》,编次者署名"名教中人"。全书共十八回,主要描写铁中玉和水冰心的婚姻爱情故事。故事情节跌宕,矛盾冲突紧凑,人物形象比较鲜明,文辞亦流畅优美,是我国明清之际出现的一部较为优秀的小说。《好逑传》在十八世纪已被译成西文,并在欧洲广泛流传,是十八世纪欧洲声名最著的中国小说。

《好逑传》最早问世的是英译本,译者为曾在广州居住的英国东印度公司职员詹姆斯·威尔金森(James Wilkinson),译稿完成于1719年。译文经托马斯·帕西(Thomas Percy,1729—1811)编辑,1761年由伦敦多利兹(R. and J. Dodsley)出版社出版,题为《好逑传或愉快的故事》(*Hau Kiou Choaan or The Pleasing History*)。

全书分为四个部分:序言、正文、附录及注释。帕西在序言中交待了译本的基本情况,并发表对中国小说的基本看法。译稿为四卷中国纸对开本,前三卷为英文,第四卷为葡萄牙文,且笔迹与前不同,编者在出版时将葡萄牙文转译成英文。帕西在序言后亦附一份参考书目,其中多数为耶稣会士的报告文集。正文分为四卷,由中文翻译而成。附录有三：一为1719年在广州上演的中国戏剧的情节介绍；二为《中国格言选辑》，帕西认为格言最能直接地体现和反映一个民族的性格和智慧；三为法国汉学家尼古拉·弗莱雷（Nicolas Fréret, 1688—1749）关于中国诗歌的一篇论文的节选。附录后还附有一个索引，列出注释中出现的条目，便于读者查找。另外，《好逑传》英译本的一个重要特征是附有大量的注释，注释内容庞杂而详尽，从婚俗到科举、从政治体制到宗教思想，涉及中国社会生活的方方面面，在一定程度上成为反映中国及其文化生活的百科全书。

《好逑传》帕西译本问世后，又作为底本被翻译成法语、德语和荷兰语，从而引发了欧洲翻译出版《好逑传》的第一次热潮。此处所选译文为帕西《好逑传》第一回之英译文。

译 文

HAU KIOU CHOAAN

OR

THE PLEASING HISTORY

A TRANSLATION FROM THE CHINESE LANGUAGE

BOOK I

CHAP. I

IN the city of *Tah-ming*①, formerly lived a student named *Tieh-chung-u*, of great endowments of body and mind: for the beauty of his person, which equaled that of the finest woman, he was called *the handsome Tieh*: yet was his temper no less rough and impetuous than his form was elegant and pleasing: bold and resolute in resenting affronts, without any regard or awe of his superiors; yet strictly just, humane, generous, and noble, never so happy as when employed in assisting and relieving the distressed.

His father, whose name was *Tieh-ying*, was a Mandarine of justice: his mother's name was *Sheh-sheh*: his father belonged to one of the tri-

---

① *Tah-ming-foo* or *Tai-ming-fou*, as it is written by *Du Halde*, is a city of the first order, and is south of *Pe-king*, being in the same province with it. See Pere Du Halde's Description of China, in 2 vols. folio, printed for Cave 1738, which is the translation always referred to in the following notes.

N. B. *Foo* or *fou* signifies a city.

bunals in the palace, but becase of the violent temper of his son, confined him at his house in another city①, lest he should involve him in any trouble at court. There he lived and kept house, pursuing his studies, and at proper intervals unbending his mind with company. When he had attained his sixteenth year, his father and mother began to think of marrying their son. They acquainted him with it; but he was no way disposed to concur with their intentions: on the contrary, he urged that marriage was not like an acquaintance of friendship, which could not be quitted on any dislike or disagreement: that whenever he should incline to marry, he would take more than common care in his choice: but should hardly think of it, 'till he could meet with a lady possessed of every perfection of mind and person. These arguments weighed so deeply with his parents, that they left him to himself.

When he had arrived at his twentieth year, one day as he was amusing himself with reading an ancient history, and drinking between whiles②, he met with the story of an Emperor, who sent to one of his Mandarines, named *Pé-kan*, for his heart to make a medical potion for his queen, who was sick. *Pé-kan* immediately suffered himself to be opened, and his heart to be taken out in obedience to the Emperor's order. Here the young *Tieh-chung-u* saw how much the great were exposed to the fatal caprice of Princes, and how far more desirable was a life of obscurity. But more particularly struck with the great resignation of *Pé-kan*, he was led to re-

---

① 'Tis the custom in China for Mandarines to have their houses in a different place from that where they hold their office. Translator.

② The Chinese drink often between meals.

flect on that duty and obedience he had been wanting in to his parents. So deeply was he stung with remorse, that he passed the night without sleep. At length he resolved to go and throw himself at their feet; and to implore their pardon for that stubbornness of temper, which had kept him so long apart from them.

Full of these resolutions he arose in the morning, and taking with him only one servant named *Siow-tan*, left his house and set out for the court. He had been now two days on the road, and so impatient to see his father, as to neglect almost all repose and refreshment, when he found himself on the approach of night far from any house of reception for travellers①. At length he came where at some distance was a large village, but near were only a few scattered cottages of very poor people: at one of these he alighted, and calling, an old woman came to him: who seeing him drest in his student's habit, said to him, "*Siang-coon*, or young gentleman, I suppose you are come from court hither to visit *Wey-siang-coon*, or our young student of this village." He said he knew no such person. She enquired what then could bring him thither. He told her he had lost his road, and intreated her to give him room in some part of her house to pass the night. She said he was welcome, and that she was only sorry she could not entertain him as he deserved. His servant *Siow-tan* brought in his bed and other travelling furniture: and the old woman shewed him a place for his horse,

---

① The inns in China are commonly mean, being generally four walls made of earth, without plaister or floor, except in the greastest roads of all, where they are large and handsome: but it is necessary for travellers to carry their beds with them (commonly a quilt or two) or they must lie on a mat. See P. Du Halde, &c.

furnished out a room for him with clean straw, and brought him tea.

Tieh-chung-u having refreshed himself a little, asked why she was so inquisitive at his arrival, and who the young student was whom she had mentioned. "You don't know perhaps, said she, that this village was not formerly called as, as it was at present, *Wey-tswün*①, but received that name from a family that lives here, who were once great people at court, but are now reduced to the meanest condition. But thank heaven, there is one of the family, who altho'poor, understands letters: he went to court to undergo his examination②: there he met with a friend, a learned man, named *Han-yuen*, who conceived a great fondness for him; and having one only daughter would give her to him in marriage: for which purpose he

---

① *Tswün* in the Chinese language signifies a village. Trans.

② Called by the Chinese *Kow-shé*. As all civil offices in China are bestowed according to personal merit, no wonder that the study of letters is in the highest esteem, and that the examinations of students are conducted with the greatest decorum, solemnity, and exactness. There are several lesser examinatoins before the students are admitted to be examined for the degree of *Sieou-tsai* (answering to Batchelor of Arts in our universities): the examination for which is made once in three years in each of the largest districts of the province before the Mandarines, who seldom confer it on more than four or five out of hundred. —The examinations for the second degree, or Kiu-gin (answering to *Master of Arts* or *Licentiate* in Europe) are also once in three years at the capital of the whole province, at which all the Sieou-tsai are obliged to attend: out of ten thousand of whom perhaps only sixty are admitted. This degree intitles them to lower offices: but the highest employments are sure to be conferred on those who can obtain the degree of Tsin-seé (or Doctor) which they are examined for the year after they have obtained the former degree (but this they are not obliged to attend) at Peking before the Emperor himself: who seldom confers this degree on more than one hundred and fifty out of five or six thousand candidates. Each of these degrees is conferred according to their proficiency in history, politics, morality, but a particular regard is had to their skill in composing in their own language, and the knowledge of their laws. Similar examinations and degrees are also appointed for their militray people. P. Du Halde, vol.I, p.376.

caused him to take a pledge. 'Tis is now four years since he was betrothed, without ever fetching home his wife, not having wherewithal to maintain her. Some time since she happened to be seen by a great Mandarine, who fell in love with her, and would have her for a second wife, or concubine, which the father and mother would by no means consent to. This enraged the nobleman, who contrived many ways to get her, and at last carried her off by force. *Wey-siang-coon* was advised of his loss, and repaired to the court to make his complaint: but not knowing how to apply for relief, and unable to learn news of his wife or her relations, all whom the Mandarine had secured, he returned home in despair. Since that time, his mother, fearing he might make himself away, hath desired the assistance of her neighbours to prevent such a misfortune."

While she was yet talking, they heard a great noise and disturbance in the street: they looked out and saw a crowd of people, and in the midst of them a young man clad in blue[①], who wept and lamented. In the crowd the old woman saw her husband, whom she called to her, and informed of their guest: he blamed her for having delayed to provide a supper for the stranger, and commanded her to hasten it. Of this man *Tieh-chung-u*

---

① The habit of those who have taken the lowest degree, or *Sieou-tsai*, is a blue gown, with a black border round it, and a pewter or silver bird on the top of their cap.—MThose who have taken the second degree, or *Kiu-gin*, are distinguished by a gown of a dark colour with a blue border: the bird in their cap is gold, or copper gilt.—The first degree, or that of *Tsin-seé*, is also distinguished by a habit different from the former, but more particularly by a girdle which they always wear at their governments, but is more rich and precious according to the offices they are advanced to.

P. Du Halde ubi supra. Semedo's hist. p.46. &c.

enquired whether the student's wife was carried off by night or by day? He told him, in the day time. He then asked if there were none that saw it. He was answered there were several, but none that durst open their lips: for who would be forward to appear against so great and powerful a Mandarine? Here the old woman interrupted, begging them to talk no more of it, for that now there was no remedy. *Tieh-chung-u* smiled and said, "You people of the villages are so saint-hearted and doubtful! but perhaps you know not the truth of the story, and all you have been telling me is a fiction." "By no means, she replied, nettled at his affected incredulity; I know it to be true: a cousin of mine who sells straw at the court, by great chance was present, and saw both the young woman and also her father and mother carried into the Mandarinc's house, which is a palace of retirement given him by the Emperor, who hath made it sacred to every body but himself and to whom he please." "Why did not you advise the young man of this?" said Tieh-cheng-u. "To what purpose? said the other: it is in vain for him to contend." He then enquired where this palace stood: she told, him without the city: but though he should find it, no one durst look into it. Supper being ready they ended talking: after which he called his servant *Siow-tan* to lay his bed, being fatigued and sleepy.

In the morning when he had breakfasted, he ordered his servant to weigh out five *mace*① to pay the old woman: he then took leave of her with many thanks for her kind treatment: she in return asked him pardon for

---

① About 3^s. 4^d. English money. Trans.

any thing that was amiss; but particularly intreated him not to open his lips about what she had told him, as well for his own safety as hers.— "What is that affair to me? he replied, your kind entertainment of me is all I have to remember: fear nothing." The old woman waited on him to the great road, and there took her leave of him.

Tieh-chung-u mounted his horse, and was got two or three *lee*① on his way, when he perceived at some distance before him *Wey-siang-coon* stamping and raving by himself, calling out to heaven and complaining of his fate. *Tieh-chung-u* no sooner discovered who he was, but he made all haste to come up to him: when dismounting② from his horse, he ran to him and clapped him on the shoulder: "Brother, said he, yield not up to despair: your cause of grief may be removed: I'll use my endeavours, and doubt not but to get your fair mistress restored to you." Surprised at being accosted in this manner, the student lifted up his eyes and looked stedfastly at him; when seeing him to be a person of good and genteel aspect, but utterly unknown to him, he was the more astonished: nevertheless he said, "Sir, you seem to be a man of rank and consideration: I am a poor and mean person. Till this moment I never had the honour to see you. I am plunged in the deepest sorrow and affliction: but I cannot account for your knowledge of it. The words you spoke just now have so rejoiced me, that I think they could only come from Heaven. But, alas! 'tis is all in vain!

---

① A *lee is* as far as a voice can be heard: ten of them make a league. Trans.
    N.B. The French missionaries write it *ly*, or *li*.
② 'Tis the custom in China to dismount, when they salute equals or betters. Trans.

My misfortune is so great that it is not possible for you, tho' you were an angle①, to afford me relief." *Tieh-chung-u* laughed, and said, "This is no more than the sting of a bee: if I can't untye this knot, let the world laugh at me. In former times there were heroes who could perform great achievements: and why not now?" *Wey-siang-coon* thought there was something in this more than ordinary: "Sir, said he, I perceive you are a person of uncommon merit: I ask your pardon: pray, how am I to call you?" "That, replied *Tieh-chung-u*, it is not necessary for you to know at present: but I must beg to be informed of *your* own original name②, and where you would betake yourself, for I have something to say to you farther." "My name, said he, is *Wey-phey*, and I should go find out some way to end my life, but for my mother, who is a widow, and depends on me alone for her support. For her sake I endure my misfortunes, and have sought all means of relief: none offers now but to write a petition and carry it to court, there to present myself with it to some Mandarine: if he refuses to accept it I will go to another; and so on 'till I find one that will: if none will do me justice, I can then but dye: I shall dye in the face of the world, and not meanly in secret." And taking out his petition, he gave it to *Tieh-chung-u*; who read it, and found the wife's father to be a Doctor of law③, of the

---

① The Chinese believe there are a kind of tutelar spirits, or *good Genii*: in the cities there are temples to them, in which the Mandarines offer sacrifice: as also to the spirits of the rivers, mountains, four parts of the world, &c. P. Semedo's hist. part.I. chap.18. p.86.

② The other was his complimental name, bestowed on account of his prosession. Trans.

③ The second degree, called *Kiu-gin*, perhaps answers better to the degree of Master of Arts or *Licentiate* in the European universities: however, as it is rather a civil distinction, *Doctor of law* seems to convey a more adequate idea. See note above. See P. Du Halde, vol.I. p.377.

second degree. The Mandarine also, who had committed the violence, was not unknown to him. "Very well, said he, this petition is right, and must be presented to the Emperor; he has power: to apply to any other audience beside will be to no purpose: nor would it avail to carry it to the Emperor yourself. Intrust it to my care, perhaps I may have an opportunity to serve you." *Wey-phey* bowed down and embraced his feet. "Sir, said he, the joy your compassion excites in my heart is like the springing forth of tender leaves from the withered branches of a tree. If you do me this favour in procuring my petition to be seen, 'tis is not sitting I stay here: let me rather follow your horse's feet and wait on you to court." "Should you go with me, answered *Tieh-chung-u*, it might alarm the world: it is much better for you to return to your village: within ten days expect to hear from me." "Sir and brother, said *Wey-phey*, this favour you do me is as great as the heaven and the earth." He then shed some tears, and made him a profound reverence. *Tieh-chung-u* exhorting him to be comforted, took the petition and put it in his sleeve; then bidding him adieu, mounted his horse and put forward. *Wey-phey* stood amazed and motionless, with his eyes fixed on *Tieh-chung-u* 'till he was out of sight, not knowing whether what had happened was real or a dream.

思　考

1.《好逑传》作者署名为名教中人，如何理解"名教"及其在小

说中的作用？并思考帕西《好逑传》对"名教"的翻译及其效果。

2. 比较《好逑传》的帕西译本与德庇时译本有何异同？

参考文献

- *Hau Kiou Choaan or The Pleasing History, A Translation from the Chinese Language. To which are added,* Ⅰ. *The Argument or Story of a Chinese Play,* Ⅱ. *A Collection of Chinese Proverbs, and* Ⅲ. *Fragment of Chinese Poetry*, London: R. and J. Dodsley, 1761.
- *Thomas Percy,* by Bertram H. Davis, Twayne Publishers, 1981.

扩展阅读

- "Thomas Percy and His Chinese Studies" by Chen Shouyi, *Chinese Social and Politics Science Review*, 20.2 (July, 1936), pp.202–230.
- *The Fortunate Union, A Romance Translated from the Chinese and a Chinese Tragedy,* by John Francis Davis, London: Printed from the Oriental Translation Fund, and Sold by J. Murray, 1829.

马礼逊《三教源流·释氏源流》

(1812)

导 读

《三教源流圣帝佛帅搜神大全》,作者不详,书中收录了儒、释、道三教一百八十一位中国人所信奉的神道仙圣,较为详致地记叙了这些神道仙圣的姓名、爵里、生平神迹等,在一定程度上反映了中国人的宗教信仰。正是因为其与中国人宗教思想的紧密联系,这本书很早就受到西方人的关注。十九世纪初,马礼逊(Robert Morrison,1782—1834)已从《三教源流圣帝佛帅搜神大全》选译了《释氏源流》与《道教源流》两篇,收入其编译的《中国春神》(*Horae Sinicae: Translations from the Popular Literature of the Chinese*),1812年在伦敦由布莱克及帕里(Black and Pary)出版社出版。

马礼逊作为十九世纪第一位来华的新教传教士,为中西文学文化交流作出了突出贡献。此处所选译文为马礼逊《中国春神》之《释氏源流》。

译文

ACCOUNT OF FOE

Foe was the founder of a sect, which in Japan and China now prevails to a great extent. This account of him is translated from a Chinese work, entitled, *San-kiao-yuen-lieu*, "*The rise and progress of the three sects,*" viz. those of *Kung-fu-tsi*, *Foe*, and *Tao-szi*.

The work begins with the life of *Confucius*, and after the accounts of *Foe*, and *Tao*, gives the lives of a great number of subordinate deities.

Foe

The surname of *She-kia-meu-ni-foe*, [the lord of religion in the middle ages,] was *Chai-li*. His father was the king of *Tsing-fan*. His mother's name was *Tsing-tsing-miao-wei*. When at *Pu*, she bore *Foe*, then called *Teu-sio-tien-kung*: he was also called *Shing-shen-tien-jin*, ["the virtuous, heavenly man:"] and *Hu-ming-ta-szi* ["the great and illustrious learned man."] He was the restorer of the multitude, and the supplier of that which was wanting. He exhibited his person, every where, as an example.

It is written in the book *Pu-yeu*, that *Foe* was born of the royal family *Chai-li*. He exhibited great wisdom and splendour; and was manifest in every place. Wherever he sat cross-legged, the earth produced the golden *lien* flower. He walked seven steps to the east, west, north and south; with the finger of his right hand he pointed to heaven; with that of his left he pointed to the earth, and speaking with the voice of a lion, said, " Above, below, and all around there is none more honourable than I." He was born on the 8th day, of the fourth moon, of the 24th year, of the reign of the king *Chao*; during the dynasty *Cheu*. On the 8th day, of the second moon, of the 42nd year, of the same reign, when 19 years of age, he begged of his parents that he might be permitted to leave the family, and deliberated with himself, whither he should go. He went and looked out at the four doors, and saw the old, the sick, the unburied and the distressed. In the midst of joy, his heart was filled with compassion. He thought—were but age, sickness and death avoided, it would be well. That night, at midnight, a heavenly person, whose name was *Tsing-kia*, appeared in the middle of the southern window, and stretching out his hand said, "O prince, the time which you have mentioned to leave your family is now come; you may go." When the prince heard this, he was exceedingly glad, and immediately, having passed over the walls of the city, went to the midst of the hill *Tan-te* to cultivate reason. He at first remained three years at *O-lan* and *Kia-lan*, where he found that they were unprofitable places. He was fully convinced that they were bad, and therefore he left them, and went to *Yu-teu-lan-foe* and remained three years. That place, also, he found extremely unfavourable to study; and being persuaded that it was bad, he left it, and went to *Siang-teu* hill, where he lived with other religionists who were not of his sect; with them he daily ate hempseed and wheat. Here he passed sixteen years. Hence the Classic says, "without having such intention;

without pointing out [that it should be so] he completely subjected all the other religionists to himself. He first repeatedly tried their depraved arts, and then declared to them the square and expedient [the rule of doing that to others which we ourselves like.] He exhibited [to them] uncommon appearances, and commanded them to advance to goodness.

The book *Pu-tsie* says, " On the 8th day, of the second moon, when the bright stars appear, *Pu-sa* [the universal deliverer] in the time of ———① was 30 years of age. It was the third year of king *Mo*, and the year of the cycle *Kuei-wei*. There, in the midst of the garden *So-ye*, to ———② five persons he communicated the four truths, and the law of returning in a circle [the metempsychosis;] and he discoursed on reason and certain retribution." He remained in the world and spoke of his laws forty years. Afterwards he taught his pupil the honoured *Mo-ho-kia-ye*, saying, —

"The law of purity; the duty of trusting in the wonderful heart of *Nie-puon*, [he who sits cross-legged, the posture in which Foe is always represented,] the doctrine of real appearance and no appearance; the true and supremely excellent law, I now take and deliver to you. It is your's to preserve it. Do not say that it is distressing or difficult. You will be able to assist me in promulgating my doctrines and renovating the world; do not cause them to be discontinued." He then uttered this *Ki*, [enigma.]

"Law, the foundation of law, no law.

No law, law, also law,

---

① Chasms unsupplied in the original.

② Chasms unsupplied in the original.

Now is delivered in the time of no law.

Law, law, where is law?[①] "

At the same time that *Foe*, the honoured of the age, delivered this *Ki* to *Mo-ho-kia-ye*, he further added, "I now take my robe, composed of golden threads, and deliver it to you, that you may place it in the sanctuary of deity, and preserve it from injury till the age of mercy shall arrive, when *Foe* shall appear."

When *Mo-ho-kia-ye* heard the *Ki*, he stooped with his head and face towards his feet and said, "Most excellent! Most excellent! it is mine to obey with the most profound submission the doctrines of *Foe*."

Foe, the honoured of the age, then went to the city *Kiu-shi-no*, and addressed a vast multitude saying, "I am greatly distressed because of the people of the age. I wish to enter and sit down in the posture of meditation." He immediately went to the side of the river *Hi-lien*, and under two So-so trees, on the right side, folding his legs, he instantly expired.

He again rose from his coffin in consequence of a law which he had not delivered. He then uttered a *Ki* respecting death:

"All actions are improper:

Hence is produced the law of destruction.

In life destruction is instant; men destroy themselves.

After death all is repose."

His disciples all immediately hastened, and took fragrant wood to

---

① Though apparently there be no fixed law or rule of conduct, yet there must really be such a law. *Exposition of the Translator's Chinese Tutor.*

burn① him. After he was burned the coffin② yet remained as before.

The multitude immediately arranged before *Foe*, praised him by the following *Ki*.

"In all common persons is depraved fire;

How can they burn thus excellently?

We beg that honoured *Foe* will display his three splendid fires,

And surround his golden-coloured body."

His golden-coloured coffin then ascended high in the air, by the So-so tree; and was carried backwards and forwards, and then converted into three splendid fires. The ashes were instantaneously changed into valuable globules that filled eight *hu* and four *teu*.③

This took place on the 15th of the 2nd moon, of the year of the cycle *Jin-shin*, in the 52nd year of king *Mo*.

A hundred and seventeen years after the burning of *Foe*, the honoured of he age, his religion arrived in China, the middle empire. It was in the time of the latter dynasty *Han*. The emperor *Ming* dreamed one night that he saw a golden man, of a tall stature, large neck, and splendid as the sun and moon. When he enquired of all his ministers respecting it, one said, "In the West there is a deity whose name is *Foe*: is it he of whom your majesty has dreamed?"

Messengers were then sent to the kingdom *Tien-lo*, to enquire re-

---

① It is yet the practice for the priests of *Foe* to be burned after death.
② The tradition is, that the fire was put within, yet the coffin was not consumed.
③ About a gallon.

specting their religion; to obtain their books, and bring some of their *Sha-muen*, [priests.]

The *Sha-muen* said that *Foe* was fifteen cubits tall, of a yellow golden colour, his neck large, and that he shone like the sun and moon. He is capable of endless transformations. There is no place to which he cannot go; he can understand all things, and he greatly commiserates, and delivers, the multitude of living men.

The above account is accompanied by an engraving, representing *Foe*, sitting cross-legged on a pedestal, and two of his pupils by his side. Around the head of each are diverging rays of light.

The speak of three appearances of *Foe*: the first, *Nan-mo-o-mi-to-foe*, who presided over the state of things that preceded the present heavens and earth. The second, *Nan-mo-she-kia-meu-ni-wen-foe*, the lord of religion during the middle heaven, that is, the present state of things. The third, *Nan-mo-mi-le-tsun-foe*, who shall appear on the state of things which shall succeed the present. 120,000 years are allowed to each *Sun-hwue*, complete revolution or state of things.

In the temples of *Foe*, these are represented by the symbols of three persons seated by the side of each other. In the middle is he who presides over the present state of things. The names made use of, and which have been just now recited, are in a foreign dialect and unintelligible to the Chinese.

思 考

1. 马礼逊的《释教源流》如何翻译诸如"释迦牟尼""涅槃""沙门"等专有术语？请思考这样的翻译是否合理正确？

2. 请判断此处译文是译自《搜神记》还是《三教源流》，并阐明理由。

参考文献

- *Horae Sinicae: Translations from the Popular Literature of the Chinese*, By Rev. Robert Morrison, London, Black and Pary, 1812.
- *Memoirs of the Life and Labours of Robert Morrison*, by Eliza A. Robert Morrison, London: Nabu Press, 2010.

扩展阅读

- *Vie de Bouddha*, par J. Klaproth, *Journal Asiatique*, 1830.
- 汤森著、王振华译《马礼逊：在华传教士的先驱》，郑州：大象出版社，2000年。

汤姆斯《著名丞相董卓之死》
（1820—1821）

导　读

　　《三国演义》，亦称《三国志通俗演义》，描写了自东汉末年至西晋初年近百年间魏、蜀、吴三国的政治军事斗争，是中国第一部长篇章回体历史演义。目前所知，最早将《三国演义》选译成西文的是英国人汤姆斯（Peter Perring Thoms，1790—1855）。

　　汤姆斯于十九世纪初叶来华，是马礼逊的得力助手。汤姆斯在协助马礼逊负责印刷事宜的同时，亦致力于中国语言与文学的学习，曾先后将《三国演义》《宋金郎团圆破毡笠》《花笺记》及《博古图考》等翻译成英文。其中，《三国演义》的译文载于《亚洲杂志》（the Asiatic Journal and monthly）1820 年卷 10 和 1821 年卷 11，题为 The Death of the Celebrated Minister Tung-cho，即《著名丞相董卓之死》，为《三国演义》第八回和第九回相关情节的选译。这是迄今为止，可以考知的《三国演义》最早的西译文。

　　汤姆斯以故事情节为标的，从《三国演义》中选出与"董卓之死"情节相关联的内容进行翻译，并以《著名丞相董卓之死》为标题，代替中文的回目。译文省去了中文第八回开头"孙坚尸换黄祖"的情节,而直接从董卓以为孙坚已死,心腹已除,因此愈加娇纵僭越述起。译文止于"二贼手起,众贼杀了王允,一面又差人将王允宗族老幼,尽行杀害。士民无不下泪"。至此,"董卓之死"的主要谋划者王允的结局已交代清楚。因此汤姆斯删除了第九回结尾点引下文的关于"李傕、郭汜立意叛乱,杀入长安"的描述。这样的编排使得整个译文紧紧围绕"董卓之死"的情节,故事相对独立和完整。

此处译文选自《亚洲杂志》所载汤姆斯翻译之《著名丞相董卓之死》。此外,值得注意的是,汤姆斯以注释的形式译介了《三国演义》的部分序言,并经由序言的翻译将"才子书"的观念介绍给西方读者。

译　文

THE DEATH OF THE CELEBRATED MINISTER TUNG-CHO[①]
TRANSLATED FROM THE CHINESE BY MR. P.P. THOMS
(Originally communicated to the Editor of the Asiatic Journal)

At the death of Tsze-këen, Tung-cho was residing at Chang-gan.

---

① The narrative in the text is extracted and translated into English from the San-kwo-che, a Chinese history of the most celebrated of their civil wars. This history is much esteemed by the Chinese, not only for its literary merit, but because it contains (as they imagine) a copious and accurate narrative of the wars and calamities of the period to which it relates. The following extracts from the preface to the work are laid before the reader in order that he may judge of the estimation in which the work itself is held by the Chinese literati. This preface is from the pen, or rather pencil, of Kin-jin-suy, who flourished in the reign of Shun-che, about one hundred and fifty years ago.

EXTRACTS FROM THE PREFACE TO THE SAN-KWO-CHE.

When I published my comments on the six literary works which bear the respective titles of Chwang, Saou, Ma-che-she-ke, Too-che-leuh, shwuy-fo and Se-leang, the learned of the empire applauded my labours, and were pleased to assure me that I had shewn myself not badly versed in the authors whom I had presumed to expound. Encouraged by their approbation, I now venture to submit to them the observations which I have made in perusing the History of the San-kwo. The first of these observations is, that it is not, like some pretended histories, a mere work of imagination, but accurately accords with what is elsewhere related of antiquity, and may be as safely relied on as the Standard History of China itself. But if we consider the History of the San-kwo in the light of an authentic narrative of facts, we shall find that all other histories, however admirable, fall far beneath it both in interest and in literary merit. But since all history, from Tsin and Chow upward and from Han and Tang downward, is bottomed in the Standard History of China, why, it may be asked, is the History of the San-kwo entitled to peculiar admiration? To this I answer, that the wars of the San-kwo, when compared with all other wars, whether ancient or modern, are wars of the most interesting nature; and that the historian of those wars, when compared with all other historians, whether ancient or modern, is an author of unrivalled merit. What is there in the affairs, whether civil or military, of any other age that can compare in interest with those of the San-kwo? And as to all other historical productions, are they not, when contrasted with the History of the San-kwo, the productions of ordinary pens?

As often as I reflect upon the power and resources which were possessed by each of the three parties engaged in these mighty struggles, so dark and incomprehensible do I find the ways of heaven that I almost lose my confidence in its wisdom and its justice. When on the death of Hëen-te (who was the last Emperor of the Eastern Han Dynasty, died about A.D. 226. On his death the civil wars began), of the dynasty Han, the government of the empire was usurped by the minister Tung-cho, a host of veteran soldiers started up in arms and the nation was thrown into confusion. If Heaven had earlier blest Lew-pe with the sage counsels of Kung-ming, he would in the first instance have made himself sure of the country of King-Leang; and then proceeding to Ho-pih, would have thence dispatched advices to Wae-nan, Keang-tung, Tsin and Yung; the affairs of the distracted empire would have been peaceably adjusted, and in power and reputation he would have rivalled Kwang-woo, the illustrious restorer of the family of Han. Had Heaven given this turn to the affairs of the empire, I should not have ventured to question either the wisdom or the justice of its decrees. But in the events which actually happened we see nothig but a scene of confusion: we behold Tung-cho seduced by his ambition to usurp the throne, but losing his life in the attempt, and Tsaou-tsaou dictating to the nobles unders the guise of imperial authority. For though in the first month of each year, and on the first day of each month, that ambitious minister ostensibly held council on the affairs of the nation in the name of the Emperor, the substantial powers of Government were exercised by himself. Unable to restore tranquillity to the state, what was Lew-pe to do? The northern and southern portions of the empire were seized upon by usurpers, who formed out of those districts the kingdoms of Woo and Wae. The only portion of the empire which still obeyed Lew-pe was the country of Se-nan, where he established his government. If, indeed, he had not been aided by the wisdom and valour of Kung-ming in the wars which he waged on the eastern and western sides of this remnant of his dominions, Leang-yeh with many other places would have been subdued by Tsaou-tsaou; the kingdom of Woo, unable to subsist as an independent power, would also have fallen under his yoke; Tsaou-Tsaou, like another Wang-mang, would have held the whole patrimony of Han in subjection to his usurped authority; and in the absolute triumph of that atrocious tyrant posterity might well have questioned the wisdom and the justice of the Heavens. Adverting as I pass to the arrival of Tsaou-tsaou at Tung-ying, when in consequence of his repeated defeats the three independent states which had arisen out of these contests were firmly and equally established, I now proceed to draw a hasty sketch of the history of his life: of the life of the tyrant, whose whole exixtence was a tissue of enormous crimes, and who was no less abhorred by the gods than he was dreaded and detested by men. And here I can only relate, in the most general terms, that there was a period in his eventful career in which libels were put forth against him in every town of the empire; in which he was insulted and reviled to his face; and in which his life was openly sought with the javelin, and covertly aimed at with poison and the dagger. But though assailed by these and a thousand dangers beside; though compelled to cut off his beard that he might escape his enemies in disguise; though so close upon the brink of destruction as on one occasion to have his teeth knocked out, and on another to be thrown from his horse and dragged along the ground; though pursued by that relentless hatred which was justly due to his atrocious crimes; still did he escape the untimely end to which his destiny seemed to lead him, still did the multitude of his enemies hardly outnumber the host of his adherents. Whether the escape of the tyrant from an ignominious end accorded or not with the will of heaven, it is not for me to determine. This is certain: had his life been other than it was, the three hostile dynasties which arose out of the civil wars would have never existed. Here I shall dismiss Tsaou-tsaou, the formidable foe of the dynasty of Han, and who, like

When he heard of the late Emperor's decease, he said within himself, "Now will I turn a deaf ear to my conscience, and listen only to my ambition." The youth and inexperience of Tsze-këen's son and successor, who was

---

some corroding insect, gnawed his way to the very heart of their empire.

But not content with one successful rebel, the Heavens raised up another in the person of Chou-yu—the founder of the kingdom of Woo, and in wisdom, valour and fortune the worthy and equal rival of the loyal Kung-ming. In addition to Tsaou-tsaou and Chôw-yu, the Heavens gave birth to Szĕ-ma-e—the successor of Tsaou-tsaou in the kingdom of Wae, and his successor also in crime and in infamy. In its fears that some one of the three states which it had just established might be oppressed by one or both of the other two, Heaven placed on the thrones of all of them sovereigns of equal ability.

From the most remote antiquity downward, usurpers have from time to time arisen, and of these usurpers many have succeeded in establishing themselves as kings. Thus, during one period, there were subsisting at one and the same time twelve independent states; during another period, seven independent states; during another period, sixteen independent states. Thus, the northern and the southern dynasties reigned through the same period. Thus, the eastern and western Wae dynasties existed together. Thus, the former Leang dynasty was superseded by the later Leang dynasty. But it is remarkable that in these instances the contentions for power were speedily determined. What distinguishes the wars of the San-kwo is this, that they were contiued through sixty years; and that as the three independent states which were parties to the contest were established at one and the same period, so were they at once annihilated.

Of the literary merits of this admirable work, I may observe, that they are equally felt by all classes of readers. The scholar is delighted with it; the mere man of business is interested by it; the soldier warms with pleasure at the perusal of it; the very vulgar are moved by it.

Having one day called on a friend, I saw upon his table the rough draft of a commentary which Maou-tsze had composed on the History of the San-kwo. On the very first inspection of it, I found that the sentiments of Maou-tsze accorded with my own. This emboldens me to declare, both to my contemporaries and to posterity, that the Te-yeh-tsae-tsze (the work which evinces the highest literary talent) is "The History of the Civil Wars of China." These few words, by way of preface, I therefore send to Maou-tsze, in order that he may prefix them to the next edition of the History of the San-kwo, and that posterity may thence be informed of the conformity of our opinions with regard to its literary merits.

only in his seventeenth year, emboldened the minister in his wickedness; for he concluded that his designs would meet with no serious obstacle in any opposition that the young prince could offer to them. Accordingly, he assumed the title of Shang-foo (guardian or protector of the prince) .Whenever he went abroad, or returned to his palace, he surrounded himself with imperial state. His brother, Tung-yan, he raised to the rank of duke and to the station of lieutenant-general in the imperial army. His nephew, Tung-hwang, he appointed to the offices of attendant at the imperial palace and commander of the Emperor's body-guard. Every member of his family, young as well as old, assumed the title of duke.

At the distance of two hundred and fifty le from Chang-gan he founded a new city, to which he gave the name of Me-too. In the building of this celebrated city he employed two hundred and fifty thousand workmen. He enclosed it with a wall, which, in height and breadth, rivalled the solid and lofty wall of the imperial city Chang-gan. Within the city he erected a palace, a treasury, and also store-houses large enough to hold twenty years' provisions for a numerous army. He chose from among the women of the empire eight hundred comely damsels, and sent them to his new city to aid in the peopling of it. To this city he removed the whole of his family, and also deposited there his treasure; which last consisted of an immense quantity of gold, diamonds, pearls and rich silks.

In the course of his administration, Tung-cho was often obliged to visit, and sometimes to reside for a month or fortnight at a time at the imperial city Chang-gan. On his return from any of these visits, the ministers of state would accompany him to the outside of the eastern gate of the imperial city, there to take their leave of him; but before they took their leave, would drink wine in company with Tung-cho, in a tent which he ordered to be pitched for that purpose just without the city gate.

On one of these occasions, and whilst he and his guests were in the midst of their carouse, some hundreds of deserters, relying upon a proclamation in which he had promised a general pardon, came in from the northern provinces and yielded themselves up to the clemency of Tung-cho. Instantly he commanded them into his presence. Regardless of his word, he sentenced them upon the spot, some to have their hands and feet lopped off, others to have their eyes torn out, and others, still more miserable, to be cast alive into boiling cauldrons; and whilst the cries and groans of the wretched sufferers rent the very heavens, and the ministers, aghast with horror, dropped the chopsticks① from their nerveless hands, Tung-cho reclined himself at his ease, drinking, jesting and laughing, as though nothing in the world had happened to mar the festivity of the assembly.

On another occasion, whilst he was feasting at a great entertainment in the city, with the ministers of state about him, and had drunk plentifully of wine, Leu-poo entered the banqueting room, and walking up to Tung-cho, whispered a few words in his ear. The ministers turned pale with terror, when Tung-cho answered with a smile: "It is thus, is it? Seize Tsze-kung (the Chang-wan) and drag him from the apartment." The order was

---

① With these the Chinese lift their food to their mouths.

obeyed; and in a few minutes an inferior officer of the guards entered the room, and presented Tung-cho with the head of the Chang-wan lying in a blood-coloured trencher. At this woeful spectacle, the very souls of the ministers fainted within them; but Tung-cho, with a smiling aspect, exhorted them to take courage, informing them "that the Chang-wan had conspired with Wae-shǔh to destroy him; that a letter addressed by the Chang-wan to his fellow-conspirator, and containing intimations of their treason, had been delivered by mistake into the hands of Tung-cho's adopted son, Fung-sëen①; and that on this discovery of the Chang-wan's guilt, Tung-cho had ordered his head to be struck off; that they, the ministers, were not implicated in his guilt, and ought not therefore to take alarm at his punishment." To this exhortation, the ministers only answered, "True, true;" and then took their leave of Tung-cho with all possible expedition.

Wang-yun, the Tsze-too, who had been one of the guests, returned to his home sorrowfully pondering on what had happened at the banquet. Unable to rest, he took his staff, walked out by moonlight into the garden behind the house, and leaning against a rail which supported some rose-bushes, gazed at the passing clouds and wept. Whilst thus engaged, he was surprised at hearing the sighs and lamentations of some unknown person, who was concealed in an adjoining arbour. Gently drawing nigh, that he might find out who it was, he was astonished at discovering Teasou-shin, a girl whom in her early childhood he had adopted into his family, and

---

① A name borne by Leu-poo.

carefully instructed in the arts of dancing and singing, whom he had ever treated with the tenderness of a father, and who having grown up to the age of sixteen under his fostering care, was now a beautiful and attractive young woman. Hearing her sighs, he asked her, in a tone of rebuke, why she grieved, and of what offence she had been guilty? "Offence!" answered the girl, falling at the same time on her knees, "how can I, who am supported by your bounty, and who am ever thinking on your kindness, how can I have ventured to offend?"— "If you have not offended," replied her master, "why are you here at this late hour of the night sighing and grieving?"—"Do you wish me, " said Teaou-shin, "to open my whole heart to you?"—"Do so," answered Wang-yun, "and remember that you cannot hide the truth from me." — "Let me begin, then," replied Teaou-shin, "by thanking you from the bottom of my heart for your goodness in bringing me up, and more especially for the instructions which you have given me in the arts of dancing and singing. Such, and so unvarying has been your kindness to me, that though I died in your service, though, to serve you, I gave up my flesh to be stripped bit by bit from my bones, and my bones to be ground to powder, never, never could I require you one ten-thousandth part of the manifold benefits which I have received at your hands. I have marked of late that the brows of my honoured master have been knit together by some inward grief; I have not presumed to pry into the cause of your unhappiness, but I cannot but feel convinced that it is some public care which thus presses upon your spirits. When I beheld you this evening restless and uneasy, I was grieved at your unhappiness; and, little suspecting that you would follow me into the garden, I stole to this sequestered spot that I might indulge my grief in secret. If I can assuage your sorrows, if aught that I can do will avail my generous benefactor, command me: you shall find that I will not shrink from ten thousand deaths."

"Who could have thought it!" exclaimed Wang-yun, striking the ground with his staff, "who could have thought that the tottering dynasty of Han was destined to find support from this orphan damsel! Follow me to the painted chamber."

As soon as they had reached the painted chamber, he commanded the female attendants, who were then in waiting, to leave the apartment; and when they had withdrawn, he touched the ground with his forehead, prostrating himself before Teaou-shin. Alarmed at these unwonted marks of respect, she fell upon her kness and exclaimed, "Why is it that my honoured master thus abases himself before his servant?"— "Will you not," answered Wang-yun, "will you not take compassion upon the fallen state of the family of Han? will you not do your best to snatch your legitimate sovereign from destruction, and to rescue the people from oppression?" And when he had thus spoken, the tears gushed from his eyes faster than the water bubbles from the spring.

"If you can believe the professions which I have just made to you," said the damsel, "you need say no more; only command me, and that command will I do my best to execute in the teeth of ten thousand deaths." Wang-yun, still kneeling before her, thus resumed: "The lives of the Emperor and of his faithful servants, the ministers, are as a pile of eggs, liable to be crushed at every instant; and as for the people, their misery is not less excruciating than if they were hanged up by the heels writhing under the bamboo of the executioner. It lies with you to save and deliver us: should you refuse your aid, or should you fail in your attempt to save us, the usurping minister Tung-cho will thrust himself into the throne of his sovereign; for though the faithful ministers have long perceived his traitorous intent, their wisdom can supply them with no device which looks as if it were likely to prevent it. Now hear me. Tung-cho has an adopted son, who by reason of his extraordinary strength has acquired the name of Leu as a prefix to his original name of Poo. I have discovered that Tung-cho and this his adopted son Lea-poo are much given to go astray with women. Upon this weakness of theirs I have raised a scheme, in which, I trust, I shall entrap them both. My intention is, first, to promise you in marriage to Leu-poo, and then to make an offer of your person to Tung-cho. It will be for you to set the father and son at variance by every artifice that you can think of; and by working upon the jealousy of Leu-poo, to incite him to the destruction of the tyrant. If you should succeed to the full extent of my wishes, you will put an end to the tyranny under which we are now groaning; you will establish the throne in safety; and Keang-shan, the ancient and venerable capital of the empire, will again become the seat of government. All this it lies in your power to accomplish; say, will you do it or not?"

"I have already assured you," said Teaou-shin, "that to serve your Excellency I am ready to brave ten thousand deaths. Proceed with your scheme, and rest assured that I will go through my part in it with fidelity and zeal." "If," said he, "you betray a single tittle of this matter, I and my whole family shall be utterly rooted out from the earth." "Banish such idle fears," said Teaou-shin: "if I do not do my best to requite you for your unexampled goodness to me, may I be cut into the minutest particles." Wang-yun, again prostrating himself before her, thanked her and retired.

The next day Wang-yun ordered an artizan to make a golden helmet. This helmet, which was surmounted by a ball of the same metal, and set with the richest and most brilliant of his family diamonds, he privately sent to Leu-poo. When Leu-poo beheld it, he was greatly elated at receiving so splendid a present, and immediately went to Wang-yun's palace for the purpose of offering him his thanks. Wang-yun, who expected this visit, and who had prepared an elegant repast for his reception, went forth to do the honours of his house to Leu-poo as soon as he saw him approaching; conducted him into the innermost chamber; and then pointing to the highest place at the table, requested his guest to take it.

Leu-poo, surprised though gratified by this extraordinary politeness, addressed himself to Wang-yun and said, "How is this? How can I, who am but a subordinate officer to a minister of state, how can I be entitled to such marks of distinction from one who is himself a minister?" "These attentions," answered Wang-yun, "may not perhaps be due to the rank of Leu-poo, but I think that these and even greater attentions are justly due to his unrivalled talents and courage." With this compliment Leu-poo was greatly elated.

Through the whole of the repast, Wang-yun pressed his guest to drink, and talked without intermission of the abilities of Tung-cho and Leu-poo. Leu-poo drank freely, laughing the while with pleasure at the compliments which were paid him. As soon as dinner was over, Wang-yun ordered his men servants to withdraw, and commanded his maid servants to serve them with wine. When they had drunk plentifully of wine, Wang-yun commanded that his daughter should come forth into the banqueting room; and in a few minutes Teaou-shin, elegantly attired, and attended by two female servants, made her appearance in the apartment. Leu-poo was struck with her grace and beauty and asked Wang-yun who she was? "It is my daughter Teaou-shin," said Wang-yun, "and as I look upon Leu-poo in the light of a relation, I have commanded her to come into the room and shew herself to him." He then commanded her to present Leu-poo with a cup of wine. This she did; and whilst she was in the act of presenting it to Leu-poo, their eyes met and were withdrawn together.

Wang-yun, feigning intoxication, said to Teaou-shin, "My daughter, present our honoured guest with another cup of wine. It is to him that we are indebted for the protection which we enjoy; let us not fail in the attentions which are his due." Leu-poo requested Teaou-shin to be seated; and on her making a motion as if she were about to withdraw, Wang-yun said to her, "My daughter, Leu-poo is amongst the most intimate of my friends: what should deter you from taking a seat?" She immediately seated herself by the side of Wang-yun; and Leu-poo feasted his eyes upon her, drinking the while large draughts of wine.

Wang-yun pointed with his hand at Teaon-shin, and said to Leu-poo, "There is nothing I should like so well as to have Leu-poo for my son in law. I would offer you my daughter there in marriage, but I am afraid that the proposal would not meet your wishes." Leu-poo, starting from the table and thanking Wang-yun for his offer, said, "If you will indeed make me the husband of your daughter, neither the horse nor the dog shall surpass me in fidelity." "Then be it so," said Wang-yun: "on the very first lucky day that falls I will send her to your house." Leu-poo, drunk with joy no less than with wine, resumed his couch, and gazed upon Teaou-shin; and as Teaou-shin responded to his amorous glances, his bosom hove like the autumnal wave.

Shortly afterward the table was removed; and Wang-yun, apologizing to Leu-poo, told him, "that he wished he could pass the night there, but was afraid that Tung-cho might hear of it and be displeased." Leu-poo, bowing thrice and thanking him as often, politely took his leave and withdrew.

A few days afterward Wang-yun went to the imperial court, where he saw Tung-cho. As Leu-poo was not at the time in attendance, Wang-yun accosted the minister (first making his obeisance) and said, "Wang-yun humbly desires of your greatness that your greatness will condescend to eat of a dinner at his house, and earnestly hopes that nothing will happen to prevent you from complying with his request." With this invitation Tung-cho complied. Wang-yun took his leave, and hastened homeward to prepare for the minister's reception. The couch of the expected guest was spread out in the great hall, which was covered with a rich carpet and hung round with sumptuous curtains.

The next day, about noon, Tung-cho was seen approaching. Wang-yun went forth to receive him, and after making him the appropriate obeisance, requested him to enter the house. Tung-cho alighted from his carriage, and entered the house through a passage formed by his guards, who extended themselves in two lines as far as the door-way which led into the great hall. As soon as he had entered the hall Wang-yun again bowed himself to the ground, but Tung-cho ordered one of his attendants to raise him up, and then graciously commanded him to take his seat by his side.

During the repast Wang-yun plied the minister with compliments, assuring him "that the fame of his administration had spread itself over the whole earth, and that the ancient sages and statesmen Yen and Chow could not for a moment be compared with him." Tung-cho, elate and joyous with the compliments which he received, drank freely; and as Wang-yun was a pleasing companion, the wine retained its flavor to a late hour in the day.

After they had passed some time at table, Wang-yun requested Tung-cho to retire with him into an inner apartment. With his invitation Tung-cho complied, having first commanded his guards not to follow them. Wang-yun then presented Tung-cho with a cup of wine, and addressed him as follows: "I have studied astrology from my youth upward, and can clearly discern in the present aspect of stars that the dynasty of Han is fast approaching to its close. Your great abilities are known and acknowledged by the whole empire. Nay, start not. If, in the olden time, Yaou was supplanted by Shun, and Shun in his turn succumbed to Yu, we may conclude that both gods and men were consenting to these changes." —"How," said Tung-cho, "how can I venture to look so high?"—"There is an ancient saying," answered Wang-yun, "that fools must give way to the wise, and the wicked yield to the virtuous. Why should this ordinary course of human affairs be interrupted in the instance before us?"—"If heaven," replied Tung-cho, "raise me to the throne, Wang-yun, the Tsze-too, may look to be promoted to the office of Yun-kewen." Wang-yun, thanking Tung-cho, commanded his female servants to light the ornamented lamps and to place wine upon the table. He also ordered music, telling Tung-cho that it was unworthy of his ear, but that he had commanded it to attend because there was an actress in waiting, who, if it pleased him, would accompany it with her voice. On Tung-cho's expressing his assent, a curtain was lowered across the room, the musicians playing in front of it, and Taou-shin singing behind it.

When Teaou-shin had concluded her performance, Tung-cho requested that she might be introduced into his presence; and she accordingly came from behind the curtain and made him three low curtesies. Struck with her beauty, he asked who she was? "It is one Teaou-shin an actress," answered Wang-yun, requesting her at the same time to take the musical boards and sing them a soft air. As she sung Tung-cho was loud in her praise.

At the command of Wang-yun she presented a cup of wine to Tung-cho, who as he received it from her hands said to her, "blooming beauty! what may be your age?" "Twice eight," answered the damsel with a bewitching smile. "You are an angel among men," was the reply of the enamoured minister.

"I would fain present this woman to your greatness," said Wang-yun, "but I am not certain that the gift would be acceptable to you." "For such generosity," said Tung-cho, "how could I sufficiently requite you?" — "In waiting upon your greatness," said Wang-yun, "this damsel will be the happiest of mortals." Tung-cho thanked him thrice.

By Wang-yun's order, a carriage was got ready, and Teaou-chin was conveyed to Tung-cho's palace. Shortly after, Tung-cho followed her. Wang-yun accompanied him home, and then took his leave of him.

When Wang-yun had taken his leave, he mounted his horse and rode homeward. He had hardly got half way home before he saw two rows of lanterns moving towards him. In the front of them was Leu-poo with a javelin in his hand. As soon as he saw Wang-yun, he stopped his horse, and seizing the rider by the collar of his vest, said to him, in a rude tone, "Tszetoo, since you promised me Teaou-shin in marriage, you have presented her to his grace: are you trifling with me?" Wang-yun, hastily stopping him, said, "This is not the place to speak of that subject! I beg that you will accompany me to my house." Leu-poo accompanied him home, and went with him into the inner hall. When they had gone through the usual ceremonies, Wang-yun said, "Why were you so rude with me?" Leu-poo answered, "I am informed that you have taken coach and driven Teaou-shin to his grace's palace: why have you done so?" "It would appear," replied Wang-yun, "that you are unacquainted with the circumstances of the case.

When I was at court yesterday, his grace said to me, 'I have a favor to ask of you, and you may expect me at your house tomorrow.' On receiving this intimation, I made ready for his grace's entertainment, and waited his coming.

"While we were taking wine," continued Wang-yun, "his grace said to me, 'I hear that you have a daughter named Teaou-shin, and that you have promised her in marriage to my son Fung-sëen; I am afraid that you do not mean what you have said, and am therefore come to request that it may be so; let me see her.' I could not presume to object to this command, and therefore ordered Teaou-shin to come forth to pay her respects to the father-in-law. His grace said to me, 'as this is considered a lucky day, I will take your daughter home with me, and give her in marriage to Fung-sëen.' Consider, I pray you, that his grace paid me a visit, and that I was compelled to receive him with courtesy." Lee-poo replied, "Tsze-too, pardon me; Leu-poo sees his error, and tomorrow will bring a bundle of brambles and do penance for his fault." Wang-yun said, "my daughter has a small dowry, which is to be sent to you as soon as she goes to your house." Leu-poo thanked him, and withdrew.

The next day Leu-poo went to Tung-cho's palace for the purpose of inquiring into what had taken place. Entering the hall, he began with inquiries of the servants, who informed him that their master had brought his bride home with him the night before, and was still in bed with her. Enraged at hearing this, Leu-poo stole into Tung-cho's bedchamber, posted himself behind a screen by which the space allotted to the bed was separated from the body of the apartment; and looking over this screen, observed the motions of Teaou-shin, who having partly dressed herself, was finishing her toilet at the window. Teaou-shin, who discerned the figure of Leu-poo reflected from a fish-pond under the window, was no sooner aware of his presence than she put on the semblance of the deepest grief; knitting her eyebrows, and from time to time applying her handkerchief to her eyes, as if to wipe away her tears. Leu-poo observed her for some minutes, and then retired from the chamber with the same fancied secrecy with which he had entered it. Shortly afterward he re-entered the room and accosted Tung-cho, who had dressed himself in the interim, and was then sitting in the middle of the apartment waiting for his morning repast. Tung-cho, asking him whether he had no business to attend to elsewhere, and being answered that he had none, permitted him to remain.

Whilst Tung-cho was occupied with his breakfast, Leu-poo every now and then cast an eye at the screen, and observing Teaou-shin passing and repassing behind it, was so affected that he could not altogether conceal his emotion from Tung-cho. Tung-cho conceiving some jealousy at the emotion which he betrayed, ordered him to leave the apartment; an order with which he reluctantly complied.

Tung-cho was so besotted with the love of his new concubine, that nearly a month elapsed before he could attend, as usual, to the business of his ministry; and his love was still further inflamed by the sedulous attentions which he received from her during the course of a long illness with which he was shortly afterwards attacked.

During his convalescence, Leu-poo waited upon him in his bedchamber for the purpose of making inquiries after his health. When he entered the chamber he found Tung-cho asleep, and Teaou-shin attending at the side of his bed. As soon as she was aware of Leu-poo's presence, she began to weep, laying one hand on her bosom and pointing with the other to Tung-cho. Before Leu-poo could recover from the emotion with which these demonstrations of sorrow affected him, Tung-cho awoke, rubbed his eyes, turned himself to the several quarters of the room, and observing that Teaou-shin was standing beside his bed, and Leu-poo gazing at her from behind the screen, he was so moved with jealousy and anger that he exclaimed, "Do you mean to seduce my best beloved concubine from me? Here, servants, drive this intruder from the chamber, and see that he never enter it again." Leu-poo, enraged at the harsh treatment which he had received, went homeward, and meeting Le-joo on his way, could not refrain from telling him of the indignity which he had suffered. Le-joo hastened him thus: "How can your Lordship, with your designs upon the imperial throne, have so far forgotten your own interest as to offer an indignity to Leu-poo? He is the ablest and most powerful of your partizans; and if he fall off from you, the high enter-prize which you have in hand will never be accomplished."—"What is to be done?" said the other. "Send for him tomorrow," replied the adviser; "appease his anger with flattering words, and with costly presents of silks and gold."

In conformity with this advice, Tung-cho sent for Leu-poo on the morrow, and in a conciliatory tone addressed him thus: "The day before yesterday my mind was disturbed, and my spirits ruffled by a return of my sickness. I pray you to forget the angry words which then escaped me, and which had no deliberate meaning. As a token that my kind intentions toward you have undergone no change, I request that you will accept of these twenty pieces of rich silk and of these ten pounds of find gold." Leu-poo received this peace-offering, thanked the giver, and with the accustomed ceremonial of respect, took his leave and withdrew.

In spite of all that had passed, Leu-poo's thoughts were still fixed upon Teaou-shin.

As soon as Tung-cho had got the better of his illness, he went, as usual, to the imperial court. Leu-poo, who attended him with his javelin in his hand, no sooner observed him in close consultation with the Emperor, than he left the imperial presence (still holding his javelin in his hand), mounted his horse, and rode with all expedition to Tung-cho's palace. On his arrival, he dismounted, fastened his horse to the gate of the palace, and made his way to the inner hall (still holding his javelin in his hand) in quest of Teaou-shin. As soon as she saw him, she said, "Go to the Fung-e's summer-house, and there await my coming." Leu-poo, with his javelin, went into the garden, and leaning against the railing of the summer-house, awaited her promised arrival. At length she made her appearance, waving in her gait, like the young and delicate branches of a tree gently moved by wind, and looking indeed not so much like an earthly creature, as like some fair genius from the palace of the moon. Weeping, she addressed herself to Leu-poo, and said, "Although I am not Wang-yun, the Tsze-too's daughter, he always treated me as such. From the first time I saw you, Colonel, and was promised in marriage to you, the desires of my life seemed realized. Who would have thought that his Excellency cherished an impure mind, or would violate and defile my person! I detest him even unto death. Having determined on seeing you, I have endured this disgrace, and am now happy in meeting you. As my person in defiled, and I am thereby unworthy to serve the valiant of the age, my desire is to die in the presence of my lord, that he may witness my integrity." When she had thus spoken, and attempted to throw herself into the lily-pond. Leu-poo hastily caught hold of her, and preventing her purpose, said, with tears in his eyes, "I have known your mind for a long time, and have been grieved that we could not converse together." Teaou-shin, taking hold of Leu-poo by the hand, said, "Though I cannot now be your wife, I hope to be so in a future state of existence." Leu-poo replied, "If I do not make you my wife in this life, I am no man of valour." Teaou-shin said, "Each revolving day seems a year, I beg that you, my lord, will have pity on me and rescue me." Leu-poo said, "As I have now come by stealth, I am apprehensive that the old traitor will be suspicious; I must therefore make haste and go." Teaou-shin, seizing him by the arm, said, "If you, my husband, are thus afraid of that old traitor, I cannot live to see the light of another day." Leu-poo, stopping, said, "Wait till I have devised some practicable plan for accomplishing our purpose." When he had thus spoken, he took his javelin as if about to leave her. Teaou-shin said, "When I was in the inner apartments and heard your name, it sounded in my ears like thunder, for there is not your equal in the whole world: who do you imagine would object to receive such a man's addresses?" When she had thus spoken, the tears fell from her eyes like drops of rain. Leu-poo, laying down his javelin, blushed, and was confounded. He turned himself around, and embracing Teaou-shin, spoke to her in an affectionate manner. In a moment they were so fast locked in each other's embrace, that they found it impossible to separate.

It is further related, that shortly after Leu-poo had left the imperial presence, Tung-cho, turning himself round, and not seeing Leu-poo, immediately conceived a suspicion of what he was about; took an hasty leave of the Emperor, mounted his chariot, and rode homeward. When he arrived at his palace he beheld Leu-poo's horse fastened to the gate; and finding from his inquiries of the porter that the duke had gone into the garden, he chid the servants for their negligence, and went into the inner hall in quest of him. Unable to find him there, he then sought for Teaou-shin. She also was not to be found. He hastily interrogated the female servants; the servants replied, that Teaou-shin was in the garden looking at the flowers. Tung-cho hastily entered the garden, where he saw Leu-poo and Teaou-shin by the side of the Fung-e summer-house, conversing together, and Leu-poo's javelin placed against the wall. Tung-cho uttered an exclamation of rage. Leu-poo, seeing Tung-cho approach, and being greatly alarmed, turned himself round and endeavoured to escape. Tung-cho seized the javelin, and pursed Leu-poo; but Leu-poo running with great agility, Tung-cho was unable from his corpulency to overtake him; he therefore threw the javelin after him. Leu-poo struck the javelin to the ground. Tung-cho seized the javelin, and again pursued him. Leu-poo had got without its reach, and Tung-cho was pursuing him beyond the garden gate, when a third person hastily entered, and suddenly encountering Tung-cho laid him prostrate on the ground. This person is Le-joo. Le-joo raised Tung-cho from the ground, led him into the library, and placed him on a bench. Tung-cho said, "Why did you enter in such haste?" Le-joo replied, "When I came to your residence, I heard that you had gone out into the back garden in anger, in search of Leu-poo; therefore I hastened. When I really met Leu-poo flying, and exclaiming, 'His lordship means to murder me!' I hastened the more in order that I might appease your rage. I did not think of encountering your lordship as I have done, and I hope that you will pardon me my involuntary offence." Tung-cho said, "I cannot endure the thought of losing my beloved concubine; I swear that I will slay the seducer." — "With submission to your excellency," returned Le-joo, "I must tell you that you act unwisely. When Chwang, the monarch of Tsoo, prudently granted an amnesty to his enemies, he never thought of calling Tseay-ling to account for the seduction of his favourite concubine: and well was he rewarded for his forbearance; for when he was afterwards surrounded by his own rebellious troops, his life was preserved by a desperate effort of this same Tseay-ling. Imitate his prudence. One woman is as good as another; but the friendship of the veteran Leu-poo is beyond all price. Contend not for such an object. Let him have this Teaou-shin. He will feel your generosity, and will be ever ready to requite you by dying in your service. I implore your lordship to weigh well the faithful counsel which I give you." Tung-cho considered for a moment, and then replied, "What you say seems to be just; I will think of it." Le-joo thanked him, and withdrew.

Tung-cho went into the inner hall, and inquiring of Teaou-shin, said, "What were you doing just now with Leu-poo?" Teaou-shin, weeping, replied, "I was in the garden looking at the flowers, when Leu-poo suddenly rushed in upon me. Alarmed at his abrupt entrance, I attempted to make my escape. Leu-poo said to me, 'I am his Excellency's son, why should you leave me?' and seizing his javelin, drove me into the Fung-e summer-house. Perceiving his intentions, and fearing that he might use violence, I determined to die in the lily-pond rather than submit to dishonor; but the faithless wretch, embracing me, prevented my purpose. I was really between life and death when your excellency came to my assistance."

Tung-cho said, "What objection have you to my giving you to Leu-poo?" Teaou-shin, astonished, weeping, replied, "Hitherto I have attended on persons of rank, are you all at once determined on giving me to a slave! I had better die than disgrace myself." So saying, she snatched a sword from the wall, and attempted to plunge it into her bosom; but Tung-cho hastily caught hold of the sword, laid it aside, and embracing her, said, "I was only trifling with you." Teaou-shin fell on Tung-cho's neck, and concealing her face, wept aloud, saying, "This must be a device of Le-joo. Le-joo is the intimate friend of Leu-poo, and therefore has devised this plot; but they are wanting in respect to your excellency's person, and to my happiness. I could tear their flesh from their bones." Tung-cho said, "How could I endure to be separated from you?" Teaou-shin said, "Although I am thankful to your excellency for your kindness, love, and compassion towards me, I am apprehensive that we cannot remain here long, for Leu-poo will certainly seek our destruction." Tung-cho said, "You shall accompany me to-morrow to Metoo, where you shall be a partaker of my happiness, and where we shall have nothing to annoy us." Teaou-shin ceased weeping, and making a courtesy, thanked him.

On the following day Le-joo came to pay his respects, and said, "This is esteemed a propitious day; now, then, is the time to give Teaou-shin to Leu-poo." Tung-cho replied, "I have been thinking that Leu-poo and I are as father and son, and that it would not be right in me to give her to him. Inform him that I cannot comply with his wishes; but make the communication in a conciliatory manner." Le-joo said, "Your excellency should not be deceived by a woman." Tung-cho changed countenance, and said, "Would you give you own wife to Leu-poo? Speak no more of Teaou-shin! Another word and I cut you down." Le-joo withdrew, and lifting his eyes to heaven, said, with a sigh, "We shall all die by the hands of a woman!"

That very day Tung-cho issued orders for his return to Metoo. All the officers of state attended to take their leave of him. Teaou-shin rode in an open carriage, and saw Leu-poo at a distance, among a concourse of people, looking towards the carriage. Teaou-shin drew aside the blinds, and appeared as if she were weeping violently. When the carriage had gone to some distance, Leu-poo ascended a mound of earth, and continued gazing after the carriage till it was lost in a cloud of dust. Suddenly he was roused from his reverie by the voice of a person behind him, who said, "How is it that Leu-poo stands here lost in thought, instead of accompanying his lordship to Me-too." Turing round, he perceived Wang-yun, the Tsze-too, at his elbow. When they had interchanged the compliments of the day, Wang-yun said to him, "I have been confined to my house for several days past by sickness. To-day I have ventured abroad, though still far from well, for the purpose of taking my leave of his lordship; and I am heartily glad that this has given me the present opportunity of paying my respects to my esteemed friend Leu-poo. But how is it, I ask again, that you stand here lost in sadness, instead of attending his lordship to Metoo?" "In truth, Sir," said Leu-poo, "it is your adopted daughter that I was thinking of. I fear that she is lost to me for ever."—"How can that be," said Wang-yun, with an assumed air of astonishment; "was she not affianced to you in marriage?"—"She was," replied the other, "but the hoary traitor, Tung-cho, has nevertheless taken her from me."—"Impossible!" Leu-poo informed him, point by point, of all that had occurred. Wang-yun, lifting his eyes to the heaven and stamping on the ground, uttered nothing but incoherent cries of astonishment for many minutes. At length he said, "I really could not have believed that his lordship would have thus descended to the level of the brute animals; would have so far lost sight of all discrimination in his desires, as to take the affianced bride of his adopted son to his own bed. Come home with me, and we will consult on this matter."

Leu-poo followed him. On their arrival at Wang-yun's house, Wang-yun invited Leu-poo to partake of a repast which had been prepare in a private apartment. When they had finished their repast, Leu-poo recounted the particulars of the incident which had happened near the Fung-e summer-house. "His grace", said Wang-yun, as soon as he had heard the narrative, "has cheated me of my daughter and robbed you of your wife. The whole empire will laugh at our expense. As for me, I am old and infirm, and must put up with his dishonour as well as I may. But shall Leu-poo, shall the hero of our age be thus sported with, and shall he not revenge?" Leu-poo, inflamed by these suggestions, struck the table with his clenched fist and raved loud. Wang-yun, interrupting him, said, "I ought not to have disclosed what was passing in my mind: really, you must not give way to these transports of anger." "Anger!" retorted the other, "I swear by all the gods that I will wash away my dishonour in the blood of the miscreant." "Stay," said Wang-yun, stopping his mouth with his hand, "Utter not, I implore you, another word of the kind, lest you implicate me in the consequences of your rashness." "What," continued Leu-poo, "shall any man dare to dishonour me and hope to live? By heaven I will slay the tyrant. What to me are the ties that bind father and son together, wronged and humiliated as I am? And yet, if I slew him, they might call me *parricide*! My memory might be handed down to posterity loaded with execrations." "Parricide!" said Wang-yun, with an incredulous smile, "remember that you are at most but his adopted son: and where, I pray, were these tender ties when he aimed at your life with your own javelin?" "By heaven," said Leu-poo, "what you say is true: farewell remorse!"

Wang-yun, seeing him bent upon the death of the usurper, threw off all further disguise, and addressed him thus: "If you lend your powerful support to the tottering house of Han, your fidelity to your lawful sovereign will win you the respect of your contemporaries; the faithful historian will record your virtue; and your fame will descend through a hundred age:—adhere to the cause of the usurper, and your memory will stink in the nostrils of posterity for ten thousand thousand years!" "Say no more", said Leu-poo, rising from the table and bowing to Wang-yun: "I am firmly resolved on the destruction of the tyrant, and you need not fear that I shall faulter in my purpose." "I fear it not," replied the other; "my only fear is that you may fail in the attempt, and that that abortive attempt may involve us all in one common ruin."

Leu-poo unsheathed his dagger, and piercing his arm, pledged himself to what had uttered by a solemn vow. Wang-yun, in a transport of joy, knelt before him and addressed him thus: "Now, indeed, will the family of Han be rescued from destruction, and to Leu-poo will redound the glory of their salvation. But drop not a word of this: I will now retire and digest the plan of our conspiracy. As soon as I see my way clearly you shall hear from me." "Be it so," said Leu-poo, and taking his leave, returned home.

As soon as Leu-poo had retired, Wang-yun sent to Shun-suy, the Poo-shay-tsze, and to Whang-wan, the Sze-le-kaou-nae, requesting their attendance at this house.

These persons obeyed the call, and on their arrival fell into close consultation with Wang-yun. In the course of their deliberations, it was suggested by Shun-suy that the Emperor had lately been unwell, and during his illness had intermitted his attention to state affairs; that a message from the Emperor might therefore be sent to Tung-cho, requiring his attendance at the imperial city on business; and that on his arrival he might be put to death by soldiers, whom Leu-poo might post in ambush for that purpose in one of the antichambers of the palace. Wang-yun approved of the scheme, but asked who would undertake the proposed message? Shun-suy answered that Le-shuh, the Ke-too-nae, had been refused promotion by Tung-cho, and was on that account his secret enemy. Wang-yun exclaimed, "Excellent!" and immediately sent to Leu-poo, requesting his presence at the consultation.

A similar message was also sent to Le-shuh. On the arrival of the latter, Leu-poo, who had previously made his appearance, addressed him thus: "You know that that traitor Tung-cho aims at the destruction of the Emperor; and that from his unrelenting cruelty to the people, and his other enormous crimes, mankind and the gods abhor him. We have determined on the death of the tyrant, and expect that you will assist us in carrying our intention into effect. What we want of you is this; you must proceed immediately to Me-too, assuming the character of bearer of an imperial message, and announce to Tung-cho that his presence is required at the Emperor's palace. I in the mean time will secrete soldiers in one of the antichambers, and as soon as he makes his appearance, will give the word to them to fall on him and put him to death. Say, are you ready to bear your share in this endeavour for the salvation of the Emperor?" Le-shuh replied, "I have long desired to be rid of the tyrant. I swear immortal hatred, not only to him, but to all who hate him not as I do. Now that Leu-poo has conceived the same sentiment, I doubt not that we shall accomplish his overthrow: it is the will of heaven!" Having thus expressed himself, he took an arrow, broke it in twain, and bound himself to persist in the enterprize by a solemn vow.

"Gentlemen," said Wang-yun, "I trust that you will not be losers by your loyalty: should we succeed in our attempt to save him, be assured that the Emperor will not forget his deliverers."

The next day Le-shuh, with several companies of horsemen, proceeded to Me-too; and on entering the city, announced that he was the bearer of a letter from the Emperor. Tung-cho ordered him into his presence. Le-shuh accordingly presented himself and made his obeisance. Tung-cho asked him, "what letter have you from the Emperor?" Le-shuh replied, "the Emperor has recovered from his illness, but finds himself to enfeebled by it that he has determined to abdicate the throne. He thinks that a worthier successor than Tung-cho could hardly be found amongst his subjects; and has called a meeting of the chief civil and military officers of state, in order that he may make, in their presence, a formal transfer of the empire to your excellency. This is the purport of the letter which I now present to your excellency." "Indeed!" said the minister; "But how stands Wang-yun disposed?" "Wang-yun, the Tsze-too," replied the other, "is amongst the most zealous of your excellency's well-wishers: he has issued orders for convening the intended meeting, and nothing delays it but your excellency's absence. " "My dream, then, is out," exclaimed the exulting minister; "I dreamt, last night, that I was arrayed in the imperial robes; and since gods and men conspire to call me to the throne, oh! time, that will never return, I must not lose thee!" Then addressing himself to Le-shuh, he said, "As soon as I am seated on the throne you may look to be my Chih-kin-woo." Le-shuh bowed and thanked him.

He immediately ordered his favourite generals, Ko-fan, Chuy-tsee and Fan-teaou, to take command of three thousand invincible flying troops, and keep guard in Me-too during his stay at the imperial city.

He then went into the inner apartments, to take leave of his mother. His mother, who was upwards of ninety years of age, said to him, "my son, whither are you going?" Tung-cho replied, "Going! I am going to ascend the throne of the house of Han: think of that mother; only imagine that a few days hence, you, my honoured mother, will bear the title of Tae-how!"

His mother replied, "I have of late been affected with an involuntary trembling, and my mind has been much disturbed; I fear that these symptoms are ominous of some impending disaster." "Why expect misfortune?" replied her son; "are you not to be the mother of the empire? and what more natural than that the approach of such an event should manifest itself in the symptoms which you talk of?" He then took leave of his mother, and went to bid adieu to Teaou-shin. He told her what had passed, and assured her that when he was crowned emperor she should be the honored concubine. Teaou-shin, who had already received an intimation of what was intended, made him a low courtesy, and affected the most lively joy.

Having bid adieu to his family, Tung-cho mounted his chariot and went on his way to Chang-gan; a large concourse of people preceding and following him through the whole of his journey. He had hardly gone ten miles when the axle of this chariot broke with a fearful crash. He alighted from his chariot, and mounted a led horse; but hardly had he gone three miles further, when his horse turned restive, neighed vehemently, and with a sudden jerk snapped the bit of his bridle. Tung-cho, disconcerted by these incidents, addressed himself to Le-shuh, and said, "the breaking of the axle and the snapping of the bit, what do they portend?" "As your excellency," answered Le-shuh, "is on the eve of ascending the throne, these incidents clearly indicate nothing more than that your old equipage has served its turn, and will immediately be replaced by a new; that for the chariot in which you have been riding, and for the bit which hangs at your horse's mouth, you will shortly substitute a bit made of fine gold, and a chariot studded with gems." Tung-cho, pleased with this interpretation of the omens, implicitly believed the assurances of this wily companion. The next day, as they were pursuing their journey, they were encountered by a violent gale of wind, bearing along with it clouds of dust; and on the evening of the very same day, they were suddenly enveloped in a thick and impenetrable mist. Tung-cho, abating in his confidence, again turned to Le-shuh, and said, "the wind which bore with it clouds of dust, and the mist around us which obstructs our sight, what do *they* portend?" "Ere many hours shall pass over our heads," was the answer of Le-shuh, "your lordship will ascend the dragon's seat: the very elements are aware of the approaching change, and shew their sense of it by these unusual manifestations of their power." Tung-cho was again satisfied with the interpretation, and resumed his former cheerfulness.

On his arrival at Chang-gan he was received in form by all the officers of state, except Le-joo, who was confined to his bed by an opportune sickness. Amongst the foremost of those who paid their respects to the minister, was Leu-poo. Tung-cho promised him that, on his accession to the throne, he should be invested with the command of all the troops in the empire. Leu-poo thanked him, but persisted notwithstanding in the resolution which he had previously formed.

That same evening, as Tung-cho was in bed, he heard the voices of children singing in the street. The wind bore the sound to the ears of the sleepless minister. This was the burthen of their song:—

"*The verdant grass of a thousand le*

Fades ere it attains the age of ten days."①

The strain was melancholy; and Tung-cho was so moved by it, that he said to Le-shuh, "The song which the children are singing, does it promise me good, or is it ominous of evil?" "The song," answered Le-shuh, "has no other meaning than its obvious one; or if it foretokens anything, it foretokens the fall of the dynasty of Han and the rise of the dynasty of Tung."

The next day, Tung-cho proceeded in great state to the imperial palace. On his way he was encountered by one of the followers of Taou, clad in a black vest and a white turban, and holding a flag of white cloth in his

---

① These lines are made up of the component parts of the characters which form Tung-cho's name. Tung, the first, is compounded of *grass*, *thousand*, and *miles*; Cho the second, is compounded of *above day*, and *ten*. This is a specimen of the wit which the Chinese delight in.

hand. On two corners of the flag was inscribed the character which signifies "a mouth."① Tung-cho turned round to Le-shuh, and asked, "what does this priest do here?" Le-shuh, replied, "he is mad;" and ordered one of the guards to remove him. Tung-cho was borne in his chair of state into the imperial palace, where all the ministers were in waiting, dressed in their court dresses. Le-shuh drew his sword, and held by the chair as it entered. When they came to the eastern gate, Tung-cho's guards were ordered to remain without; and only the chairbearers, with about twenty persons more, were permitted to proceed further. Tung-cho, perceiving that Wang-yun and many others of the ministers were posted at the avenue leading to the throne, each of them holding a naked sword, was somewhat disconcerted at this unusual appearance, and asked Le-shuh what it meant. Le-shuh made no answer, but urged the chair-bearers onward. At the moment, Wang-yun exclaimed, "the usurper is come: soldiers, do your duty!" Instantly, a hundred armed men rushed from the sides of the palace, and attacked Tung-cho with their spears; but as he wore a suit of mail under his vest, they were unable to pierce his body. He fell, however, with the shock; and as he was falling, cried aloud, "where is my son Fung-sëen?" Leu-poo, who was behind the chair, exclaimed in a voice of thunder, "miscreant, I have an imperial order for beheading you;" and therewith pierced his throat with a javelin. The moment after, Le-shuh severed his head from

---

① Of the two characters which form Leu-poo's name, the first is compounded of "*mouth*," repeated, with a line uniting them; the second of "*cloth*," which was implied in the flag; so that the flag was intended to apprize his Lordship to beware of Leu-poo.

his body, and held it up in his hand; whilst Leu-poo, grasping his javelin in his left hand, and with his right drawing the imperial mandate from his bosom, called aloud to the surrounding assembly, "here is the imperial order for putting to death the usurper Tung-cho. Let no one be alarmed; he is the only person to whom it extends." The guards responded to this brief address with a loud shout, "may his majesty live for ever!"

As soon as the tyrant was dispatched, Leu-poo exclaimed, "the man who abetted Tung-cho in all his infamous projects, was Le-joo. Who will seize him?" As Le-shuh was about to obey the call, a noise was suddenly heard from without the gates. This was found, on inquiry, to proceed from Le-joo's servants, who had bound him fast, and were dragging him to the imperial palace. At the command of Wang-yun, he was taken to the market-place, and there beheaded. The head and trunk of Tung-cho were also, at the same command, taken into the street, that the people might be convinced of his death, and might behold the punishment which awaits disloyalty. Fire was placed on his navel by the guards; and as it burnt, the fat from his carcase streamed along the ground. The people vied with the soldiery in heaping indignities upon his remains; beating his head and spurning his trunk as they were dragged through the streets of the city.

The punishment due to his crimes stayed not here. Wang-foo-sung and Leu-poo were commanded by Wang-yun to march at the head of sixty thousand men to Me-too, and to root out the whole family of the traitor.

When Le-chuy, Ko-fan, Chang-tsee, and Fan-chow, heard of Tung-cho's fall, and of Leu-poo's approach at the head of an invincible army, they fled in the night to Lang-chow. On the arrival of the imperial army at Me-too, the first care of Leu-poo was to make himself master of Teaou-shin's person. Having secured his not unwilling captive, he proceeded to issue, in concert with Wang-foo-sung, the following orders: the inhabitants of Me-too were commanded to liberate all the women who had been forcibly brought to that city by the tyrannical orders of Tung-cho: they were further commanded to aid in the apprehension of Tung-cho's family; who, as soon as they were secured, were put to death, without regard to age or sex. Even the mother of Tung-cho escaped not the common fate: and, as an additional punishment, justly due to their pre-eminent treasons, the heads of Tung-yan, the usurper's brother, and of Tung-whang, his nephew, were stuck on the tops of poles, and exposed, for several days, to the view of the people. Orders were also issued for seizing the treasure which the usurper had collected in Me-too. This treasure, consisting of many hundred thousand pieces of gold, of many million pieces of silver, and of an immense quantity of silks, diamonds, precious stones, and plate, was accordingly seized and sent to Wang-yun, who divided it amongst the soldiery.

These measures having been carried into effect, a splendid banquet was prepared by Wang-yun in the hall of audience. To this banquet all the ministers of state were invited. Whilst they were feasting, news was brought to them that a certain man was lying on the ground in the marketplace, weeping over the mangled remains of Tung-cho. Wang-yun, enraged at the audacity of the man, exclaimed in a loud and angry tone, "Who would have thought that any subject of the emperor, whatever his station in society, would regret the destruction of the usurper? Who is this insolent traitor that dares to lament his fall? Guards! Seize him, and drag him into the hall!" In less than a minute, the guards dragged the man into the presence of Wang-yun. To the astonishment of the assembly, he proved to be no other than Fze-ying, the Se-ze-chung. Wang-yun indignantly said to him, "The carcase of the usurper is lying in the public street, and the nation is rejoicing at his hall: how is it, that you, a minister of Han, instead of sharing in the general joy, are weeping over his remains?" "Though not gifted with superior talents," was the submissive reply of Fze-ying, "I am not altogether ignorant of the leading principles of morality. Do you suppose me so unprincipled as to regret the death of an usurper? I once received an important service from this unhappy Tung-cho; and the tears which I shed over his mangled remains were not tears of regret at the fall of a tyrant, but tears wrung from me by a grateful remembrance of the service which he had rendered me. I know that even this is criminal; and shall, therefore, cheerfully submit to any punishment which you may please to impose upon me. Cut off my feet, brand my forehead; in fine, afflict me in any way short of death. I earnestly wish to live, that I may complete the annals of the house of Han, and thereby atone for the offence into which my criminal gratitude has betrayed me."

Most of the officers of state, recalling to mind the signal talents of the man, were moved to pity and sorrow; and used every effort in their power to rescue him from death. Ma-jih-shen, the great historian, said aside to Wang-yun, "Fze-ying is a man of unrivalled talents; if he be permitted to finish the annals of the Han dynasty, they will be ably and faithfully written. Besides, he is universally known and respected as the most dutiful of sons; and should he be put to death at our bidding, I fear that we shall lose the confidence of the people." "Heaou-woo," answered Wang-yun, "spared the life of Sze-ma-tsëen, and afterwards appointed him imperial historian. The consequence was, that, Sze-ma-tsëen, more mindful of his previous enmity than of the clemency which had been extended to him, belied his age; and the characters of his contemporaries have descended to our times, not as they really were, but as distorted by his malignity. The evil passions of men have been put in motion by our recent convulsions. Shall we, at such a period, commit the pencil of the historian to a man whose loyalty may be suspected? Shall we hire an enemy to vilify ourselves?"

Ma-jih-shen uttered not a word in reply; but addressing himself aside to one of the ministers, he said, "the name of Wang-yun will never descend to posterity!" Wang-yun, regardless of what Ma-jih-shen had said, ordered Fze-ying to be strangled in prison. When the officers heard these orders given, they all wept. The more recent historians and moralists are universally of opinion that it was wrong in Fze-ying to weep over Tung-cho; but that it was equally wrong in Wang-yun to put him to death for it.

It is further related, that as soon as Le-chuy, Ko-fan, Chang-tsee and Fan-chow arrived at Shin-se, they dispatched a message to Chang-gan, imploring a pardon. "Tung-cho," said Wang-yun, on the receipt of this message, "was abetted in his crimes by these four men; and though we will extend our pardon to all the other subjects of the empire, we must not extend it to them." The messenger returned, and informed Le-chuy of Wang-yun's resolution. "Well," said Le-chuy, "as we have asked for a pardon and cannot obtain it, we must each of us do his best to escape, and save his life if he can." Hea-yun, the general's secretary, thereupon said, "General, if you disband your troops, you will infallibly be betrayed by some of them to your implacable enemy. Rouse yourselves: incite the people of Shin-se to embrace your cause, and embody as many of them as will join you with the regular army; then boldly fight your way to Chang-gan, openly proclaiming yourselves the partisans and avengers of Tung-cho. Should you be victorious, you will rule the empire; should you fail, you can run for it then as well as you can now." Le-chuy approved of his advice; convened the people of Le-lang-chow, and told them that Wang-yun had determined to extirpate them to a man. "Since nothing," he continued, "can be gained by submission, enter the ranks of my army, and join us in our resistance to him." The inhabitants, struck with a panic, embodied themselves with his army to the number of a hundred thousand men. The army, thus reinforced, was divided into four divisions, and moved forward to Chang-gan. On their route they fell in with New-poo, the son-in-law of Tung-cho, at the head of a corps of five thousand men. Le-chuy united this corps to his army and ordered New-poo to take the command of the van; the four generals following in the rear.

When Wang-yun was informed of their advance, he hastened, in a panic, to ask the advice of Leu-poo. "Be not alarmed," said Leu-poo, "depend upon it, this horde of rats will be stopped short in their course for want of provender."

He then ordered Le-shuh to advance with an imperial army, and attack them. Le-shuh immediately advanced and attacked New-poo. After a long and bloody conflict, New-poo was obliged to retreat. On the following night, however, and during the second watch, New-poo surprised Le-shuh's camp. Le-shuh's troops were thrown into confusion by this unexpected assault, and fled to the distance of ten miles, with the loss of half their number. Le-shuh hastened to Leu-poo, and apprized him of his defeat. Leu-poo exclaimed, "Why have you stripped me of my reputation? Guards, off with his head, and fix it on a pole by the entrance to the camp."

The next day, New-poo was attacked by Leu-poo in person. After an obstinate contest, New-poo yielded to the skill and valour of Leu-poo, and fled to the main body of the rebel army.

The night after the battle New-poo opened himself to Ho-chih-urh, his confidential adviser, as follows: "This Leu-poo is resistless. There are ten thousand chances to one against our success. How much better will it be for us, unknown to Le-chuy and the other three generals, to seize the treasure which is concealed in the camp, and in company with three or four attendants, desert the army." Ho-chih-urh consenting, they that night seized the treasure, and deserted the camp in company with three or four others. Whilst they were crossing a river in their fight, Ho-chih-urh, who had already turned over in his mind the means of getting the whole treasure to himself, murdered New-poo, and taking the head of his victim, made his way to the imperial camp, and presented it to Leu-poo. Leu-poo, inquiring into the particulars of the incident, and learning from the attendants that Ho-chih-urh had murdered New-poo, indignantly ordered Ho-chih-urh to instant execution.

Having repulsed New-poo, Leu-poo advanced upon the main body of the rebel army. In his advance he was encountered by Le-chuy, at the head of his foot and horse. Leu-poo, instead of awaiting the attack, instantly grasped his javelin, dug the spurs into his horse, and commanded his troops to follow him to the charge of the enemy. Le-chuy's troops, unable to withstand this impetuous attack, retreated to the distance of sixteen or seventeen miles from the field of battle, and entrenched themselves between two mountains. Here Le-chuy held counsel with Ko-fan, Chang-tsee and Fan-chow. He addressed them thus: "Leu-poo, though brave, is wanting in skill. Let us not be dismayed. I will daily lead out our troops to the entrance of the pass, and provoke this impetuous madman to give me the battle. You, Ko-fan, as soon as he advances to attack me, will fall upon his rear; imitating the movements which were made by Poo-yul, in the battles which he fought during the war against Tsoo. You will sound the gong as you advance the attack, and will beat the drum when you intend a retreat. In the meantime, you, Chang-tsee, and Fan-chow, will proceed by different routes to the imperial city Chang-gan. Hemmed in, in front and rear, Leu-poo will be unable to advance to the relief of Chang-gan, and it will inevitably fall into our hands." This plan was highly approved of by his colleagues.

The scheme succeeded, Leu-poo, intending an attack, led his troops to the foot of the mountain. Le-chuy advanced, as if to meet him, but no sooner did Leu-poo command his army to charge the enemy, than Le-chuy retreated and ascended the hill; from whence his troops showered down such vollies of arrows and stones, that Poo's soldiers found it impossible to proceed. At this critical moment Ko-fan's troops attacked him in the rear. Leu-poo faced to the right about, and rushed upon this fresh opponent; but as soon as he had put his troops in motion, the loud sound of the drum proclaimed that his enemy was on the retreat. Leu-poo halted. But without a moment's pause, the gong bellowed through the plain, and Le-chuy again descended from the mountain. Again Leu-poo moved forward to attack him; and again he retreated from the charge. Again, Ko-fan attacked Leu-poo in the rear, and again was the signal for retreat beat upon the drum, as soon as Leu-poo moved forward to meet the assault.

Leu-poo, whose bosom burned with rage, was thus harassed for several days. He could neither give battle to his enemy, nor repose to his own troops. Whilst thus perplexed, a messenger brought him word that Chang-tsee and Fan-chow had marched by two different routes upon Chang-gan, with large bodies of foot and horse, and that the imperial city was in imminent danger of falling into their hands. Leu-poo immediately moved towards the capital, pursued by Le-chuy and Ko-fan. Leu-poo, not venturing to give them battle, pushed onward to the relief of Chang-gan, losing a great number both of men and horses in the course of his march. On his arrival in the neighbourhood of Chang-gan, he descried the host of the enemy, numerous as the drops which fall in shower of rain. They had surrounded the entrenchments of the city; and Leu-poo's troops, instead of moving to attack them, were so disheartened by the desperate aspect of the imperial cause, that to the grief and indignation of their leader, they deserted in great numbers and went over to the rebel army.

A few days after Le-mung and Wang-fan, two of Tung-cho's partisans, who had carried on a secret correspondence with the rebel army, threw open the city gates to them. Instantly they rused in from every quarter. Leu-poo, at the head of a few hundred men, fled through the eastern gate; however, before his departure, he hastened to Wang-yun, and said to him, "embrace this opportunity of escape; mount this horse, and accompany me to another province: there we may devise some plan for retrieving our fortunes." Wang-yun answered, "If I could thereby uphold the commonwealth and restore tranquillity to the empire, I would do as you desire; as that cannot be, Wang-yun resigns himself to death. Could I avoid it I would not. I pray you, however, to take my last commands to the governors of the eastern provinces. Tell them to exert themselves strenuously in restoring the affairs of the nation." Leu-poo again and again exhorted him to embrace the opportunity of escape; but Wang-yun obstinately withstood his intreaties. By the time this dialogue had ended, every gate of the city was on fire. Leu-poo, in despair, threw up the game, and, in company with a few hundred men, made his way to the state Kwan, where he placed himself under the protection of Wae-shuh.

Le-chuy and Ko-fan permitted their troops to plunder the city. Chung-fuh, the Tae-chang-ying; Las-kwo, the Tae-po; Chow-ying, the Tae-kung-loo; Chuy-keih, the Ching-mun-Kaow-wae; and Wang-king, the Yue-ke-Kaou-wae, all of them perished amidst the disasters of the day.

When the enemy surrounded the palace, the throne was in imminent danger. The ministers in waiting requested his Majesty to appear in the balcony. When Le-chuy and his adherents beheld the imperial robes, they ordered the troops to stop, and shouted aloud, "may his Majesty live forever." His imperial Majesty, leaning over the balustres, said, "Ministers, what do you ask? What is it you intend by entering Chang-gan?" Le-chuy and Ko-fan, looking up to his Majesty, answered, "Tung-cho, the Tae-tsze, was your Majesty's prime minister of state. Why did you order Wang-yun to put him to death? Our business is to revenge him. We rebel not against your Majesty; only give us up Wang-yun, and we will withdraw our troops." Wang-yun, who was standing by the side of the Emperor, addressed his Majesty thus:—"What I originally planned was for the welfare of the commonwealth, but as affairs have taken this adverse turn, your Majesty must not think off saving me at the expense of you own ruin. I request that I may be permitted to descend to the rebels." Whilst his Majesty hesitated, Wang-yun, of his own motion leapt from the balcony, and calling aloud to the rebels, said, "Wang-yun is here." Le-chuy and Ko-fan drew their swords, and cursing him, said, "Tung-cho, the Tae-tsze, why was he put to death?" Wang-yun answered, "The ineffable crimes of that monster covered the face of the earth, and stank to the very heavens; on the day that he fell, all the inhabitants of Chang-gan rejoiced, though you, ye traitors, lamented him." "But what were our crimes that we were not to be forgiven?" Wang-yun impatiently exclaimed, "why so many words? I am Wang-yun; if I must die to-day, so be it." The two rebels raised their hands aloft, and cut down Wang-yun below the balcony.

When the rebels had put to death Wang-yun himself, they immediately sent persons to seize his whole family, and put them to death also, without respect to youth or age. Amongst the officers of state and people at large, there were none who lamented them not.

**This work mentions not the year in which Tung-cho fell. But by referring to the Standard History of China, I find, that Ling-te (of the former Han dynasty), the father of Hëen-tee, died after reigning twenty-two years, and was succeeded by his son, Tsze-p-ëen, who was then only fourteen years of age. He appointed his brother Hëe (who was only nine years of age) king of Ching-lew. Druing the seventh month, Ho-tsin, a nephew to the emperor, called in the assistance of Tung-cho to subdue a rebellion. During the eighth month, Tung-cho returned to the capital. During the ninth month, he dethroned the emperor, and appointed him king of Fan-nung, and raised his brother Hëe to the throne, when that emperor took the name of Hëen-te. Tung-cho appointed himself generalissimo of the troops. During the eleventh month, he became minister of state, when he appointed the whole family of Tung to the rank of duke, and gave to each a military command.

On the first month of the following year, the princes of Kwang-tung and other provinces declared war against Tung-cho. During the second month of the second year of the reign of Hëen-tee, Tung-cho appointed himself prime minister of the state. During the third year, and fourth month of the same reign, Wang-yun, in union with Leu-poo, put Tung-cho to death. During the ninth month, Leu-poo fled to the eastern province of Nan-yang, when Wang-yun died. On his death, Le-chuy, Ko-fan, Chang-tsee, and Fan-chow, were appointed generals of the imperial troops.

思 考

1. 仔细阅读译文，并判断汤姆斯《三国演义》选译自《三国演义》的哪个版本？

2. 请思考汤姆斯《三国演义》译文中对"才子书"这一概念的介绍及其影响。

参考文献

- *The Death of the Celebrated Minister Tung-cho,* By Peter Perring Thoms, *Asiatic Journal*, Vol.X, Vol.XI., 1820–1821.
- "Universal Brotherhood Revisited: Peter Perring Thoms (1790–1855), Artisan practices, and the Gensis of a Chinacentric Sinology", by Patricia Sieber, *Representations*, 2015, 130(1): 28–59.

扩展阅读

- *Teaou-Shin. A drama from the Chinese in Five Acts*, by George Gardiner Alexander, London: Ranken & Co., 1869.
- Luo Guanzhong, C. H. Brewitt-Taylor trans., *San Kuo: or Romance of the Three Kingdoms*, Shanghai: Kelly & Walsh. 1929.

德庇时《三与楼》

（1822）

导　读

《十二楼》又名《觉世名言》，是清代著名小说家李渔撰写的短篇拟话本小说集。全书共收入十二篇以"楼"命名的小说，即：《合影楼》《夺锦楼》《三与楼》《夏宜楼》《归正楼》《萃雅楼》《拂云楼》《十卺楼》《鹤归楼》《奉先楼》《生我楼》《闻过楼》。小说情节新奇，语言生动，早在十九世纪二十年代已经引起西人的注意，并被翻译和介绍到西方。

《十二楼》中最早被译成西文的是《三与楼》，由德庇时（John Francis Davis，1795—1890）翻译成英文，并于 1815 年由广州东印度公司出版社发行。该译文又转载于《亚洲杂志》（*Asiatic Journal*）1816 年第 1 期、第 2 期，译文中对个别词语的翻译稍做调整，但与 1815 年译本属于同一种译文。1822 年德庇时又重译了《三与楼》，收入其《中国小说》（*Chinese Novels*），1822 年由伦敦默里（J. Murray）出版社出版。书中收录《合影楼》《夺锦楼》与《三与楼》三篇小说的英译文，其中《三与楼》译文与 1815 年译文差别较大。此处所选译文为德庇时《中国小说》中《三与楼》之译文。

译文

THE THREE DEDICATED CHAMBERS:
A TALE
TRANSLATED FROM THE CHINESE

Let observation, with extensive view,

Survey mankind from CHINA to Peru;

Remark each anxious toil, each eager strife—

Vanity of Human Wishes

Note. The following Tale (for it can hardly be called a novel) has been already printed, but never yet given to the public in a regular shape. For the reasons which produced this revised Translation, see Observations, &c. The story is here taken at its actual commencement, and a tedious introduction omitted. The unnecessary recurrence of Chinese names has also been avoided.

SECTION I

During the reign of the twelfth Emperor of the Ming dynasty, in a district of the province of Sze-chuen, there lived a rich man, who was likely in time to be still richer. This person, whose name was Tang-yo-chuen, had an immense quantity of land. Whenever he got any money, it was his delight to add to his landed possessions; but he would neither build houses, nor would he supply himself with any of the comforts or necessaries of life, beyond what was absolutely indispensable. His disposition was to enrich himself by every means in his power, and his property increased daily, like the moon towards the full. Houses and furniture (he thought) were not only unprofitable, but there was always a fear lest the god of fire should destroy them, and they might in one moment become annihilated. If one had fine garments, there immediately came unpleasant fellows to borrow clothes. If there was plenty to eat, one soon had people claiming acquaintance, and taking their seats in quest of food. In short, there was nothing like being contended with coarse articles, for people in that case would not be seeking them.

He laid fast hold of this notion, and was determined to take care of his money. But not contented with being niggardly, he wished to assume credit to himself for it, and said that he was descended from one of the most ancient emperors, and that his ancestors were celebrated for their economy.

The father being thus parsimonious, his son was bound to obey his precepts. When people saw the avarice of the former, they observed, that there was an ancient proverb, which said, that "if a man was a great miser, he would certainly have a prodigal son." He must inevitably have a successor who would turn things upside down; so that Tang-yo-chuen's disposition to save was not likely to descend. To their surprise, however, the son imitated his father. From his earliest years he devoted himself to letters, seeking preferment by every means in his power, and soon became a scholar of the third degree. In his eating and drinking he did not seek for luxury; in his clothes he wished not for a super-abundance; and in his pleasures he was very sparing. It was only on the subject of houses that he differed; for there he was not contented with economy.

Being ashamed of the dwelling which they now inhabited, he wished to build a better one, but was afraid to begin, lest the means should not be forthcoming. Having heard people say, "that to buy an old house was better than to build a new one," he observed, in a consultation on the subject with his father, that if they could purchase a handsome dwelling, fit for them to live in, they might then think of a garden, and build a library in it, to suit their own taste. As the father had an object① in humouring his son, he deviated on this occasion from his usual maxims. He replied, "There is no necessity to be in a hurry; we shall have a handsome house and garden in this very street. The house is not yet completed, but the day of its being finished must infallibly be the day of its sale; so let us wait a while."

The son observed in answer to this, that "when people wanted to sell houses, they did not often build; when they built houses, they did not often intend to sell them. Where, then, was the probability of this house being sold as soon as it was completed." The father replied, "Pray where did you

---

① When a man in China attains to high literary rank, certain honours are conferred on his *father*. A Hong merchant at Canton, whose son was a member of the Imperial College, had the privilege of erecting certain poles or masts in his grounds, indicative of the favour of the emperor.

get that crochet? If a man possesses ten thousand pieces of money, he may build a house which costs him only one thousand: but if his possessions in houses equal one half of his whole fortune, he may be compared to a large tree without a root, which must inevitably be blown down when the wind comes. Then how much more may this fellow, who without possessing an hundred acres in land, builds all at once a house with a thousand rooms, be called a tree without a root! He will not wait for the wind's blowing, but will tumble down of himself. There cannot be a doubt about it."

When the son had heard this reasoning, he agreed with his father. He went about seeking for land, and said nothing more concerning houses. He was impatient, however, that the abovementioned house should be built, in order that, the present owner being gone, the finishing stroke might be given by himself. The rich man's plan proved successful: the result justified his prediction. There are two lines of the *Book of Odes* which are applicable to the case.

> "*The nest one bird constructs with anxious toil,*
> *Ere long another seizes as her spoil.*"

He who was building the mansion was named Yu-soo-chin. He delighted in amusing himself with books of poetry, and fancy, but did not seek eminence as a scholar. From the indolence of his disposition, he had a great aversion from any office, and was not born to be a mandarin. He therefore detached his thoughts from a great name, and give himself entirely up to odes and wine; by which means he could not but be reduced to beggary.

During his whole life he had scarcely any other delight than in arranging and building gardens and summer-houses. From the beginning of the year to the end, not a day passed without his doing something in this way. He was desirous that the place about which he was now engaged, should be quite perfect, and superior to the common order of things. He said, "Let other men have their numerous acres: ostentation and riches were the concerns of others: on him they had no influence." There were only three things in which he really felt interested, and which he was determined to have of the best. These were, the house which he inhabited in the day, the bed in which he slept at night, and the coffin which was to contain him when dead. Having these ideas in the breast①, he went on with his work, and laboured at it in an indefatigable manner.

Tang-yo-chuen's son, having waited several years without seeing him come to a conclusion, began to feel somewhat vexed and irritated, and said to his father, "Why have we delayed in vain for such a length of time? That man's house is not yet finished, nor is his money yet expended. It would seem from this, that he is a fellow of ways and means; and the point of his selling it hereafter appears to be somewhat doubtful." To this Tang-yo-chuen replied, "Every day later makes it a day more certain, and each succeeding day will make it more advantageous for us. There is no occasion for you to fret about it. The reason why his house is not finished, is simply this. When any part is completed, it does not suit his ideas of per-

---

① The Chinese suppose that the abdomen is the seat of ideas.

fection, and he must take it to pieces to build over again. If it is excellent, he seeks for still higher excellence; so that of every day, during which it is delayed, the alterations and improvements are wholly for our own advantage. The reason why his resources are not yet expended, is the willingness of the usurers and the workmen to give him credit, as long as he goes on building. The labourers do not sue him for their claims, because they fancy that by every additional day of work, they may get a day's wages; while, if they were to press him hard, he would certainly stop the building for a while, and they would get no employment. It is thus that his money is not yet expended; but this may be called 'taking flesh to feed an ulcer.' Do not be afraid that he is possessed of ways and means. Having arrived at the period when he can draw together no more, those who have him in their books will certainly press him in a body, and begin to curse him. He will then seek, in the first place, to sell what he has in land: but as that will not suffice to pay them, he must inevitably have recourse to his house. If he begins to collect now, at an early period, and before his debts are very large, he may stay for a good price before he sells it. Our right plan will be to wait until a later day, when his debts are a little increased, and anxious to sell, he will be willing to come down with his terms. This is all exactly as we should wish it; why, then, go and obstinately torment yourself?"

The son, when he had heard this, applauded and acquiesced in his father's sentiments. Indeed, after a few years, Yu-soo-chin's debts gradually accumulated, and his creditors came daily to his doors to claim them; and there were some who would not go away again. The house which he had so long been building, could not be completed; and he at last wanted to seek a man who would buy it.

All those who are selling houses, are differently circumstanced from the venders of lands. They must naturally desire to find out a purchaser in some neighbouring or contiguous situation; for should a person from a distance wish to buy, he will make enquiries of those in the neighbourhood. If the neighbours utter a word of disadvantage, he who before was desirous to purchase, will be unwilling to do it. Not like lands, or any other property, concerning which people are less particular. Therefore in selling a house, it is certainly desirable to sell it to a neighbor.

Tang-yo-chuen was a wealthy man, and since it was as well not to trifle with him, the owner of the house of course went to offer it to him first. Both father and son, though at their hearts they greedily coveted it, merely returned for answer, "that they did not want it." They waited until he intreated them earnestly, and then went over—just to give a look. Pretending not to admire it, they observed, "that he had built it but indifferently. The apartments were not suited to a private gentleman, and the winding avenues would only impede business. The fine carved doors, when they were required to keep out thieves, would have no strength. Rooms, which should be different, were all alike. The ground and the air were very damp. It certainly could not sell for much. The flowers and bamboo shrubberies were like plantations of mulberry and hemp. Those who came to saunter here must be served with wine and eatables. Such a place as this was fit only to be turned into a nunnery①, or a residence for the priests of Fo. If one wished to make family apartments for one's children, it would never answer."

Yu-soo-chin might be said to have spent his heart's blood upon it, and when he perceived that it met with nothing but disapprobation and contempt, was not altogether pleased. However, since this man was the only person who was likely to buy the house, it was as well not the quarrel with him.

The people present advised Tang-yo-chuen not to say too much against it. The price was not altogether high; and even though he took it to pieces, and built it over again, it would pay for the workmen and their maintenance. The father and son of course praised and dispraised it, still they brought it down to an exceeding low price: not above one fifth of its real value.

Yu-soo-chin had no alternative, and must endure the pain of selling it. Every thing was delivered over in the bonds, with the exception of one set of apartments, which had occupied his whole life, and which he had brought exactly to suit his own taste. These he would not insert in the deeds, but wished to build a partition wall, and make a separate entrance, that he might inhabit them until his death.

The son was for decidedly compelling him to sell the whole together,

---

① There are receptacles in China for the religious of both sexes, who devote themselves to celibacy. The strange and unaccountable resemblance, which many of the leading tenets of the religion of Fo bear to those of the Roman Catholic church, led the Jesuits to assert, that the devil had invented them in spite.

in order that it might be complete. His father seemed to agree with the rest of the people. Screwing up his mouth, he exclaimed, "Let him sell it or not, as he pleases: it is a pity to force him. He merely wishes to keep this small shred①, that it may be the means of his recovering the property hereafter, when he has improved his circumstances. It will then revert to its original master, which will be a very good thing." When the people present heard this, they all said it was the speech of a benevolent man. They little knew that it was far otherwise; that it was altogether the language of contempt! He concluded that it could never be recovered, and therefore left him this shred. Indeed it was quite useless, and the whole must inevitably become one house, sooner or later. They listened to his requisition, and entirely acquiescing with him in words, they divided the property, of which the new owner obtained nine parts, and the old possessor one.

The apartments, which Yu-soo-chin retained, were in the style of a Pagoda, consisting altogether of three stories. In each chamber was a tablet, written upon by some person of rank and eminence, with whom he was acquainted. In the lowest room were carved lattices, crooked railings, bamboo seats, and flower stands. It was the place where he received his guests. On the tablet were inscribed large characters to this effect,

DEDICATED TO MEN

The chamber in the middle story was adorned with bright tables

---

① There is some law existing in China, that if a man in selling his property, retain but a small portion of it, he is entitled to receive back the whole, if hereafter his improved circumstance will allow of his redeeming it. This observation may serve to explain his motive in wishing to retain this shred.

and clear windows, together with pictures and other furniture. This was his study, where he was accustomed to read and write. On the tablet was largely inscribed,

DEDICATED TO THE ANCIENTS

The highest chamber was empty and light. There was nothing in it, besides a chafing dish for incense, and a sacred book. It was here that he retreated from the crowd, retired from noise, and shut himself up in complete solitude. On the front of the tablet in this chamber was written, in large characters,

DEDICATED TO HEAVEN

Having divided the building into compartments for these three different uses, he likewise took them unitedly, and formed a tablet, calling them,

THE THREE DEDICATED CHAMBERS

Before he had parted with the rest of his property, those three appellations, though well chosen, had still been vainly applied, since he had not made use of the apartments. The lowest chamber only could be excepted, for as he was exceedingly fond of entertaining guests, and if a person came from a distance to visit him, immediately placed a bed in it, the appellation of "Dedicated to Men" was certainly applicable. As to the two upper chambers, he had hardly been in them. But now, since his summer houses were gone, besides the chamber "Dedicated to the Ancients," he had no place in which he could read or write; and except that "Dedicated to Heaven," none to which he could retire from noise, or retreat from the crowd. All the day long he sat in them, and the names which he had dictated became truly applicable. He now fully understood that a great deal might be effected in a small and confined residence, and that it was better to despise the name, and adhere to the reality. These four popular lines are not inapplicable.

> "*Lord of ten thousand acres, flowering fair,*
> *A few small morsels quell thy appetite;*
> *A thousand spreading roofs demand thy care,*
> *And lo! six feet suffice thee every night!*"

The strength which he possessed had hitherto been dissipated in vain. He now applied his inventive genius collectively at a single point, and caused his dwelling to be decorated to an extraordinary degree. Residing in it, Yu-soo-chin not only forgot the misery of parting with his garden, being in fact very much relieved by the absence of that burthen, but also remained secure from a violent neighbor at his side. How he could live unmolested in this habitation will be shewn in the next section.

SECTION II

When Tang-yo-chuen and his son had purchased their new residence, the rich man's taste unfortunately proved quite different from that of the former owner, and he wanted to alter it once again. But there was no necessity to take it to pieces, or to change the main parts of the structure. It was like some beautiful landscape, where the only thing requisite was to add a blade of grass, or take away a tree. The appearance of it did not suit his idea of a picture. When he had worked at it for a time, he found that he had departed from his original pursuit of turning iron into gold, and contrary to his expectation, was turning gold into iron.

The persons who came to view it, agreed in saying that "the pleasure-ground was large and unsuitable, and that, after all, it was not to be compared with the Three Chamber;—though if they were both united, it would be well enough. It was no wonder (they added) that the other retained the small part, and despised the large one; or that he held it tenaciously and refused to sell it. The partition turned out to be one inch of gold and the cubits of iron."

Both the father and son, when they heard these observations, became very sorry, and repentant of the bargain: and they then learned that a man may be rich, without being altogether satisfied. They applied to the brokers, and going over to annoy their neighbour, required that he should insert the Three Chambers in the deeds, and give the whole over to them. Yu-soo-chin, since selling the pleasure-ground, had employed no workmen, and had not been at all extravagant. As his debts were all paid, and he was short neither of money nor food, what should make him wish to sell his property? He therefore said to them in answer, "Tell me where I should repose myself, when this habitation was gone?—but I will still hold out, though you try to starve me into compliance with your demands." As his circumstances improved, he became more and more determined in his resolution.

The brokers came over, and talked on the subject with the son. The latter could not help taking his father to task, and telling him, that "Though he had been all his life studying mankind, he seemed, on this occasion, for once to have been quite mistaken." The father replied, "That fellow may be as determined as he pleases during his life-time, but he will be very quiet when he is dead. He is now an old man, and without heirs. When the breath is out of his body, his whole household must inevitably revert to strangers, and doubtless the Three Chambers among the rest. All his property will become our own; there is no fear of its flying away up to heaven." The son, when he had heard thus far, replied, that "Though all this might be very true, yet the man's duration seemed to be without a limit; it was impossible to wait for his demise; and the sooner they obtained possession of his house, the better." From this time, they made Yu-soo-chin the chief subject of their thoughts; and though they imprecated his death heartily, they rather hoped that his ruin would anticipate that event: for they still thought that it would be impossible for him to hold out, when his food and raiment had failed him.

Who could have conceived, that when men had such virtuous wishes, heaven would not comply with them! He continued to live on prosperously, in spite of all their hopes and imprecations. Indeed he seemed to grow stronger, as he became older. Neither was he troubled with a want of clothes, nor did his subsistence fail him; and he had no necessity to sell his Three Chambers.

Tang-yo-chuen and his son were vexed and enraged beyond measure, and after having deliberated on the next plan to be pursued, they applied to the brokers, insisting that Yu-soo-chin should redeem back what they had purchased. "Two families," said they, "cannot live in the same premises. Exalted on high in his Three Chambers, he looks down upon our dwelling; and is able to see into our private rooms, while his own are secure from our view. This is an unequal bargain, and will never answer."

Yu-soo-chin was informed of what they said; but he knew very well that their wish to be off the bargain was all feigned, and that the real truth was, they greedily desired to get possession of the whole. He therefore repeated what he had said before, and returned a very sharp and decisive answer.

Both father and son were of course exceedingly angry, and it now only remained for them to oppress him with the Mandarin's power. They made out a document, announcing in open court their wish to undo the bargain; hoping, that by a little bribery, they might be able to buy over and manage that officer, and through his assistance obtain the whole property.

They were little aware that the person, with whom they had to deal, was incorruptible; that he had formerly been a poor and obscure scholar, and was oppressed and insulted by a wealthy man. He said to them "This is a very poor person: how then is it possible for him to redeem it? Your's is evidently a plot to ruin and devour him. You are people of property, and wish to be rich, rather than virtuous: it is my business, as a magistrate, to be virtuous, rather than rich." Then in open court, he rebuked them for a while, and tearing up the deed, turned them both out.

Yu-soo-chin had an old and very worthy friend. He was a person from a distant part of the country, and one who possessed great wealth. It was his delight to expend his riches in performing acts of kindness. Happening one day to come and converse with Yu-soo-chin, he observed that he had sold his garden and pavilion; and heaved a deep sigh. When he found, also, that people had been plotting against him, and that he could not live unmolested even in this little nest, but might hereafter be compelled to yield it up entirely, he offered immediately to produce the money, and redeem the whole back for his friend.

The latter was a man of a most independent spirit. He would not merely avoid being indebted to another for some hundreds or thousands; but if one had offered him the smallest sum, without at the same time proving that he had a claim to it, he would have declined the acceptance. Having heard what his friend had to say, he observed, that "his warm-heartedness was all in vain, and that he was mistaken in his view of the subject. The possessions of this world were altogether transitory, and never remained for many generations in the same family. A man might take good care of them during his life time; but there was no securing them after death. Though now (said he) you interest yourself in my cause, and would advance large sums of money to redeem a portion of my property, yet I cannot live beyond a few years, and some day hence, when I die without heirs, every brick and tile must revert to strangers. Though now, from a generous motive, you are willing to make light of your money, I am afraid you cannot assist me hereafter. Though now, alas! you may redeem for me my former possessions, wait till a little while hence, and you cannot be of any service to my ghost!" The friend, perceiving this to be his mode of thinking, was unwilling to press him farther.

He lodged with Yu-soo-chin for several nights in the Three Chambers, and when he took leave on his return home, addressed him thus, previous to commencing his journey. "While I was reposing at night in the lowest chamber, I observed a white rat, which ran about for a while, and then quickly darted into the floor. This circumstance is, no doubt, indicative of some wealth being concealed there. Do not on any account part with this house, for you may chance hereafter to dig up some treasure; at least such is my idea." Yu-soo-chin laughed at this as a mere joke, and having thanked his friend, they separated.

The old saying, that "No unlooked for wealth ever fell to him, who was destined to be poor," is a very true one. The purchasers of houses are the only people who dig up hidden treasures; no seller of his property ever yet found a single brass coin in his own ground. Yu-soo-chin knew this, and was too wise to entertain any such visions. He therefore replied to his friend's observation with a cold laugh, and did not begin to rout up the bricks and dig the earth.

Tang-yo-chuen and his son, since they had experienced the Mandarin's wrath, were as much abashed, as they had before been vexed and angry. However, they were more busy than ever with their plots, and lived in hope that their neighbour would soon die; that he would soon become a childless ghost; for they might then enter his house with a good face.

Who could have conceived, that when a rich man had been right in all his conjectures, there should still be the two circumstances of life and death, which would not acknowledge his control! Their neighbour not only continued to live on, but when he had arrived at upwards of sixty years, seemed to grow young again, and was fortunate enough to have a son born to him.

The Three Chambers were immediately crowded with congratulatory guests, who all exclaimed, that "now the whole property must be redeemed!" Tang-yo-chuen and his son, when they heard of the unlucky event, were very much disturbed. They were before only afraid of not obtaining the remaining portion, but their apprehension now was, that they should lose the whole:—and they were anxious beyond measure on the subject.

After the lapse of a month, several brokers came to them unexpectedly, saying, that "their neighbour, after the birth of his son, had been reduced to poverty by his guests, who had completely eaten him up. He had now no other means of subsistence left, than to sell the house in which he was living. The cards of sale were already issued, and the bills pasted on the doors. They ought to seize this opportunity, and pounce upon it as quickly as possible."

On hearing this, both father and son were transported with joy; which was only allayed by the fear, that he would remember and hate them for past circumstances; chusing to sell it to some other person, in preference to having any dealings with them.

They were not aware, that his way of thinking was quite different from their own. "The descendants of our two families (said he) are peculiarly circumstanced with respect to one another. His remote ancestor conferred the Empire on mine, who had nothing to give in return. Now, since the obligation has descended to the posterity, it would be nothing more than what was right, were I to give him this small property as a present; I may surely, then, let him have it for a price. I will not, for the little resentments of these days, obliterate the memory of former favours. Let him not be anxious on the subject, but trust to me to fix a moderate price for it, and deliver it over into his possession."

Tang-yo-chuen, when he heard of this, was happy beyond measure; as was also his son. The former said, "I always delighted in dwelling on my ancestors, and have ever experienced their favourable influence. Had it not been for their ancient generosity, I should never have obtained this elegant residence. It is thus that men may rejoice in having had virtuous forefathers." He then went over with the brokers, and settled the bargain. Though his disposition had always been to seek for an advantage on such occasions, yet since old things had been brought forward, he was willing for once to practise a little liberality. His neighbour, on the other hand, did not higgle about it, but imitated the generosity of Tang-yo-chuen's ancestor, who had given up his throne and his kingdom, and sought some thatched cottage, where he might live in retirement.

There were a few honest friends, who could not bring themselves to justify Yu-soo-chin. They said to him, "When you had your house, why did you not sell it to any body rather than to him who envied and plotted against you? He has now succeeded, and both the father and son will go about to every one, chattering and exulting. As long as you were without an heir, you would not abate in your resentment. Since you were so fortunate as to obtain one, he might have proved the means of recovering back the whole property; and even though you had not recovered it, that which remained to you was sufficient. Why then did you deliver over the last remnant of your possessions to that man?"

Yu-soo-chin, having heard what they had to say, smiled, and replied, "Your intentions, gentlemen, are very good; but you regard merely what is before your eyes, without considering the hereafter: I judge that his plots will eventually benefit me. In order to redeem back the whole property, I must have waited until my son was grown up, when it might have been possible to recover it. But I am an old man, and conceive that I cannot live so long; and who can tell, whether, after my death, my son would not have sold the Three Chambers to Tang-yo-chuen? Having at length succeeded in getting it from the son, he would have laughed at, and abused the memory of the father. It is better that the father should sell the property, and then people will compassionate and assist the son."

"The above, however, might not have been the worst evil. It is ten thousand to one, that I should very soon have died, while my son was yet an infant. My wife, being content to strive with hunger, would not have parted with the property to our enemy. He, seeing that the new would not come into his hands, and fearing, also, that the old might be redeemed, would certainly have laid plots to cut off my heir. Thus I am fearful, that not only the property would have been lost, but my son sacrificed besides.

This indeed might be called a loss! By selling it cheap to him now, I have merely made a kind of deposit, and caused him to incur a debt, which will be paid into the hands of my son. If he does not pay it, I think it possible that others will. The old proverb says, 'To endure injuries is the sure policy.'"

When they had heard this, his friends, though they were somewhat startled by his reasons, still maintained their former opinion. The old man died suddenly, a very few years after he had sold his whole property, and left his son, a child, under the protection of his widow, who possessed scarcely any thing. Their sole reliance was on the price which had been obtained for the house, and which produced a little interest, just enough to subsist upon. Tang-yo-chuen's possessions became every day greater. He knew how to make money, and his son knew how to take care of it. Every thing came in; nothing went out; and the property which he had bought seemed so secure, that it might last for a thousand years.

Every one arraigned the wisdom of Heaven, saying, that "the descendants of those persons, who had been liberal and just, possessed little or nothing; while the progeny of those, who had enriched themselves by unworthy means, were so well off." The saying of the ancients, however, is very true, that "when virtue and vice have arrived at their full, they must finally be recompensed; the only difference being, whether sooner or later." Those words are constantly in men's mouths, but leave very little impression on their hearts. Though the recompense come late, it is the same thing as if it came early; and indeed his lot, who waits for his punishment, is the worst.

The subject of late or early recompenses very much resembles laying out money, and receiving back the interest. If you receive it one day sooner, you receive one day's less interest: if you leave it for a year longer, you get a year's additional interest. Should you look for the reward of your good deeds with an anxious heart, Heaven may not immediately send it, and it may seem as if no reward awaited you. But when you have lost all expectation, and given up the hope, the recompense will suddenly arrive; like a bad debt of many years' standing, which, when the lender has forgotten it, comes unexpectedly to his door, with an exceeding large accumulation of interest. This is far better than an early payment.

When Yu-soo-chin's son, who was called Ke-woo, had reached the age of seventeen or eighteen, he soon acquired a literary title. He was created governor of a district, and being called to court, was afterwards raised to a still higher office. As he was a person who dared to speak in the cause of rectitude, he became a great favourite with the reigning Emperor.

At length, when his mother became old, he requested leave to retire and take care of her. Making the best of his way home, and being as yet some miles from it, he perceived a woman, not much more than twenty, with a paper in her hand, kneeling by the way side, and exclaiming to him aloud, "I intreat, sir, that you all receive and examine this." Ke-woo told her to come into the boat①, and taking the document from her, looked at it. It turned out to be a deed, or bond, in the name of her husband, who desired, with his family and effects, to come under his protection, and become his slaves②. Ke-woo said to her, "If I may judge by your appearance, you are of a respectable family, why do you wish to throw yourselves under my protection? How happens it, too, that your husband does not shew himself, instead of permitting you, a woman, to come to the road side, and cry out aloud?"

The woman replied, "We are the descendants of an ancient family; but my father-in-law, while he lived, being very fond of buying lands, unceasingly endeavoured to add to his stock evey acre of ground, and every house, which adjoined to his own. Those persons, who sold to him their property, did not part with it willingly, but each of them hated him in his heart. Before my father-in-law died, they happened, in the first place, to be favourable times, which prevented him from breaking in upon his wealth; secondly, he was a person of some rank and influence, and if a magistrate had any charge against him, it became necessary only to spend a little money, in order to live unmolested. At length, the favourable times no longer existed, and before the expiration of half a year, my father-in-

---

① Almost all journeys are performed in China by water. The British Embassy of 1816, of which the translator was a member, travelled a distance of about 1200 miles, along canals and navigable rivers.

② "It is to be observed, that the slavery, which is recognized and tolerated by the laws of China, is a mild species of servitude, and perhaps not very degrading in a country, in which no condition of life appears to admit of any considerable degree of personal liberty and independence."—*Staunton's Penal Code, p.293, note.*

law died. My husband was young, and moreover possessed no rank. The persecutors of the orphan and widow rushed upon him in a body, and all went before the magistrate with accusations against him: so that, within a year, he experienced a great many different charges, and the larger half of his property was expended. But a still worse evil has since befallen him. He is in prison; and money alone will not release him. The only hope of his liberation rests on the zealous interference of some person of influence, and yourself are the only one to whom we can look on this occasion. Besides, sir, the business, in which my husband is involved, has considerable relation to you; and though he seems the only person concerned, it may yet be considered as your own cause. He therefore wrote this document, and desired me to come and throw ourselves under your protection, offering to you both our property and our personal services, and only intreating, that you will not consider them as worthless, but accept of them without delay."

Ke-woo was at a loss to express his surprise on hearing the above, and asked her, "Pray what may the business be, in which you are involved, and which has so much concern with myself? Doubtless during my absence from home, my household have been getting into mischief, and in conjunction with you and your husband produced this evil. Do you wish me to identify myself with a parcel of strangers, and, by affording them my countenance and protection, incur criminality through an unjust stretch of power?"

The woman replied, "This is by no means the case. In the midst of our property is a tall building, called 'the Three Dedicated Chambers', which originally belonged, sir, to your family, but was afterwards sold to us. We lived there for several years without molestation; until some unknown enemy lately presented an anonymous petition, stating, 'that my husband was one of a nest of robbers, and that the three generations, from grandfather to grandson, were all rogues: that twenty pieces of treasure were now deposited under the Three Chambers, and that when the hoard was taken up, the particulars would be understood.' When the magistrate had seen this document, he quietly sent some thief-takers forward to raise up the hoard; and contrary to all expectation, they certainly produced from under the flooring, twenty pieces of treasure. My husband was immediately apprehended, and taken to the magistrate's court. He was pointed out as a harbourer of thieves, and severely tortured and beat, with a view that he might discover his associates, together with the rest of the spoil which they might have taken."

"My husband endeavoured, as well as he could, to solve this extraordinary affair; but was unable to get at the truth. Far from having any claim to the treasure which had been discovered, he knew not whence it had flown thither. Being ignorant of every circumstance connected with it, we were unable to unravel the mystery; but might still rejoice that no one appeared to have lost it. The magistrate committed my husband to prison on suspicion, but has not yet decided on his crime. My husband considered the subject minutely, and thought it probable, that as our house and grounds formerly belonged to your family, your grandfather might have deposited the treasure in the floor, and your father, ignorant of the circumstance, never removed it. Hence, that which should have been a profitable thing, turned out to be a source of misfortune."

"We do not wish to enquire into the truth of this point, but only intreat, sir, that you will claim the money as your own. When the money is thus disposed of, my husband will be restored from death to life, and as your interference will be the cause of this, our whole property should be presented to you in recompense. The house and grounds, which were constructed by your father with such pains and labour, have a particular claim to be restored to you, and we therefore intreat, sir, that you will not reject them."

Ke-woo, hearing this, could not help suspecting that something was wrong. He said to her in answer, "My family have made it a maxim of old, to refuse all such offers. There is no occasion to speak now about your throwing yourselves under my protection. It is true that the house and grounds were formerly possessed by my family; but they were regularly sold, with all the forms of brokers and deeds, and were not conjured away by your relations. If I want them again, therefore, I must pay the original price for them, and there is no reason why you should give them back to me for nothing. As to the treasure, I have no concern with it whatever, and cannot with any propriety lay claim to it. Go now, and wait until I have had an interview with the magistrate. I will request him to investigate the subject with care, as it is highly necessary to have a clear decision. Should the charges be proved to be untrue, your husband will of course be released from prison, and certainly will not be put to death unjustly."

When the woman had heard this, she rejoiced exceedingly, and returning him ten thousand thanks, took her departure. The source, whence these misfortunes arose, and the manner in which they were afterwards got the better of, are explained in the third and last section.

SECTION III

Ke-woo, after his interview with the woman, made the best of his way home. He then fancied himself to be the examining magistrate, and considered the subject in different lights, saying to himself, "Not to mention that this treasure cannot be the patrimony of my ancestors, yet allowing that it were so, how came I, their descendant, to know nothing about it, nor my kindred to contend for its possession? On the contrary, it was a person out of the family who knew of it, and who presented a petition on the subject. As this petition was without a name, it is plain that he must be an enemy;—I have no doubt about it. At the same time, supposing that he had some cause of enmity, it was not well to charge the other with such a vile act, and to point him out as a harbourer of thieves. Then, again, at the time of taking up the treasure, the petitioner's words were verified, and it answered exactly to the amount specified in the document, without being either more or less. It is difficult to conceive that he, who presented the petition, for the sake of gratifying a secret enmity, should be willing to risk such a vast sum, and having placed it in another's ground, proceed to carry on so extraordinary a business."

He considered it for several days, but could make nothing of the matter. It was the constant subject of his thoughts, and during his sleep, and in his dreams, he cried out and muttered broken sentences. His mother, hearing him, enquired the reason of this; and he then recounted to her minutely what the woman had said to him. On first hearing it, his mother, too, was very much perplexed, but having considered it awhile, discovered the truth, and exclaimed "It must be so, indeed! This treasure does certainly belong to our family; and the man was right enough in his conjectures. When your father was alive, he had a friend who came from a distance to see him. This friend remained for several nights in the lowest of the Three Dedicated Chambers, and perceived (he said) a white rat, which ran about for a while, and then darted into the floor. At the time of his departure, he spoke to your father, desiring him by no means to sell the apartments, since he might hereafter find some unlooked for treasure. By all appearances, this treasure has now come to light. Your father, by not searching for it, made it a cause of misfortune to others: do you, therefore, go and claim it, and thereby save the man's life."

Her son replied, "There is something more to be said on the subject. An idle story like this is not fit for the mouth of a respectable person, and when I talk about a white rat to the magistrate, he will probably suspect that I covet that large sum of money, and unwilling to claim it openly, have trumped up this story, in order to impose upon simple people. Besides, neither was this white rat seen by my father, nor was this foolish story related by him. The more I consider it, the more ridiculous does it appear. It may indeed be called the dream of a fool. If the treasure were the property of our family, my father should have seen those indications; or how happened it that, instead of appearing to me, they were perceived by a stranger? The whole story is false; it is impossible to believe it. Still, however, we ought to consult with the magistrate, with a view to clearing up this mysterious business, and saving a guiltless wretch. This will be acting a correct and virtuous part."

As he had done speaking, a servant suddenly announced that the magistrate had arrived, to pay his respects. Ke-woo said, "I was just now wishing to see him: request him to walk in immediately." When the magistrate had made his bow, and talked a little on general subjects, he did not wait until Ke-woo began the subject of the mystery, but took it up himself, and requested to hear all that he knew about it, saying, that, "the person in whose house the hoard had been found, although repeatedly and strictly examined, had discovered nothing. He yesterday" (said he) "made a deposition, stating, that the place where the treasure had been taken up belonged formerly to your family, and that therefore it must have been left by your ancestors. I accordingly came here, in the first place, to pay my respects, and secondly, to request your information on the subject, being quite ignorant of the truth."

Ke-woo replied, "My family has for several successive generations been very poor, nor did my immediate predecessors accumulate any thing in money. It would therefore be rash in me to lay claim to this treasure, by which means I should acquire a bad name. There must be something in this affair which we do not understand; nor is it necessary to assert that it is a hoard accumulated by a nest of thieves. I therefore entreat, sir, that you will continue a strict investigation, and effect a decision of this doubtful business. Should you be able to bring the crime home to the prisoner, then well and good."

The magistrate said, "When your father departed this life[①], though you, sir, were still a child, and therefore, perhaps, not very well acquainted with former circumstance; yet may we not ask your mother if, before the property was disposed of, she either saw or heard of any thing particular?"

He replied, "I have already interrogated my mother, but she talks somewhat at random, and my father never mentioned a word on the subject. As I am now conversing with you on business, it would be improper to repeat any thing unadvisedly. I will therefore keep it to myself." The magistrate insisted on his telling it out: but Ke-woo was determined to say nothing.

His mother was fortunately standing behind the screen, and wishing sincerely to do a good action, desired her steward to go and recount the story in question for his master. When the magistrate had heard it, he considered silently for a time, and then said to the steward, "I will trouble you to go in again, and ask, where is the residence of him who saw the white rat; whether he is at present alive or dead; whether his family is rich or poor; on what terms of intimacy your master lived with him; and if they

---

① The Chinese have a superstitious dread of mentioning death in direct term. The expression in the original is "to pass over to immortality, or become immortal."

were in the habit of rendering each other mutual assistance. I have to request that your lady will speak with precision, as the present day's enquiry may serve in the place of a formal trial, and this obscure case be happily cleared up."

The steward went in for a while, and coming back, answered, "My mistress says that the person who saw the white rat came from a considerable distance, and lived in such and such a district. He is yet alive, and his fortune is very large. He is a person of great worth, who sets a small value on riches, and lived on terms of strictest friendship with my former master. Seeing that he had sold his pleasure ground, and that he would be compelled to part with his Three Chambers, he wished to produce the money, and redeem the whole for him. As my master would not consent, his friend pressed him no farther. The words in question are those which he uttered at the period of his departure." The magistrate, having considered a little, directed the steward to go in and ask, "if, after the death of his lady's husband, the friend had come to pay honours to the deceased; and if his lady could mention any expression which she might have heard him utter."

The steward went in and returned, saying, "When my master had been dead for more than ten years, his friend came to pay honours to his memory. Seeing that the Three Chambers were sold, he was much surprised, and asked my mistress, 'Did you, after my departure, obtain that unlooked for treasure which I predicted?' She answered, that indeed they did not. He then sighed, and observed that 'it was a fine piece of good fortune for those who had bought the property. Deceitful in their hearts, and contriving plots to get possession of the place, they had acquired wealth which they did not deserve. In a short time, however, they would experience an unlooked for calamity.' A very few days after his departure, some person brought an accusation against their prisoner, and gave rise to this business. My mistress constantly praised and admired her friend, declaring that he was one who could see into futurity."

The magistrate, having heard thus far, laughed heartily, and going towards the screen, made a low bow, saying, "Many thanks to you, madam, for you information, which has enabled me, a dull person, to make out this extraordinary affair. There is no occasion for farther enquiry. I will trouble your messenger to bring a receipt, and will immediately send the twenty pieces of treasure to your house."

Ke-woo exclaimed, "What is your reason for this?—I beg, sir, that you will inform me." The magistrate replied, "These twenty pieces of treasure were neither left by your ancestors, nor were they plundered by the prisoner. The fact was just this. That worthy person wished to redeem the property for your father, but as he possessed a very independent disposition, and was tenacious in his refusal, your friend deposited the money in the floor, as the means of redeeming the property hereafter. Not wishing to declare this plainly, he pretended the agency of some spirit, with the idea, that, when he was gone, your father would take up the treasure. When he came afterwards to pay honours to the deceased, observing that the pleasure ground had not been recovered, but that the Three Chambers were also sold, your friend knew that the treasure was in the hands of the enemy, and of course was vexed beyond measure. At his departure, therefore, he presented an anonymous petition, with the intention of waiting until the family of the prisoner was broken up, and the property dismembered. As the truth is now plain, your original possessions ought to be restored to you. What have you to say against this?"

Ke-woo, though in his heart he admired him for his decision, had still an objection to claiming the treasure, from the suspicion which might be attached to himself. He did not wish to take it in too great a hurry, but making the magistrate a bow, observed, that "he had formed an excellent conclusion, and must be possessed of admirable wisdom. That though Lung-too① himself were to re-appear, he could not equal this. At the same time (said he), though you conclude this treasure must have been left by our generous friend, still there are no persons to bear witness to it, and it would not be well for me to put in a claim rashly. I therefore entreat, sir, that you will keep it in your treasury, to relieve the wants of the people during famine."

While he was yet declining it, a servant came in, with a red ticket in his hand, and announced a visitor to his master in a whisper, saying, "The person of whom you have just now been talking② is arrived at the door. He says that he has come from a great distance to pay his respects to my mistress. The magistrate being present, I ought not to have announced him;

---

① A famous magistrate of ancient times, who is now deified, and has temples to his memory.
② This servant must have waited at the conferences. It is customary, among the Chinese, to have a great number of attendants present on all occasions of ceremony, with a view to avoid the suspicion of conspiracy.

but since he is acquainted with the business in question and seems to have come at a lucky moment, I therefore acquaint you, sir, with his arrival, in case you may wish to interrogate him." Ke-woo was greatly rejoiced, and informed the magistrate. The latter was ready to dance with joy, and desired that he might be requested to enter immediately.

He was a very respectable looking old man, with a round face, and white locks. He paid his respects to this friend, but only slightly regarded the magistrate, who was a stranger to him, and making a bow, passed onward, saying, "The object of my visit was to see the wife of my deceased friend. I came not to court the rich or powerful, nor do your affairs concern me, a person from a distant part of the country. I cannot presume to intrude on you; so shew me the way into the house, that I may visit the lady."

Ke-woo answered, "As my venerable friend has come from a great distance, it is not right to treat him as a casual visitor; but since the magistrate is engaged in an affair of difficulty, and wishes to ask you some questions, and since it is a fortunate occurrence to find you here, we entreat that you will sit down for a moment."

On this he made his obeisance, and sat down. The magistrate took some tea with him, and then bowing, said, "I believe, sir, that you are the person, who, about twenty years ago, performed an act of great virtue, of which no one was then conscious, but which it has now fallen to my lot to bring to light. Were you not the author of that hidden treasure, which was left for your friend, without any other notice than by some reference to the agency of spirits?"

The old man was taken somewhat by surprise, and for a moment did not speak. Having recovered from his embarrassment, he replied, "How should such a rustic as I perform any act of great virtue?—What can you mean, sir, by your question?"

Ke-woo answered, "Some words, respecting a white rat, were heard to proceed from your mouth. In consequence of certain suspicious appearances, they were going to impute the crime of harbouring thieves to an innocent person. As I could not bear to see this, I entreated the magistrate to set him at liberty. While we were conversing together on the subject, we by degrees got a clue to it; but being still uncertain whether the story of the white rat be true or false, we have to request a word, sir, from you to settle it."

The old man was determined in his refusal, and would not speak, until a message came from the lady of the house, begging him to give up the whole truth, in order that an innocent person might be exculpated. He then smiled, and made a complete disclosure of the circumstances, which had been profoundly secreted in his breast for more than twenty years. They agreed to a tittle with what the magistrate had said. Having directed the people to bring the treasure, in order that they might examine the letters and marks upon its surface, all these particulars corresponded exactly.

The magistrate and Ke-woo admired the old gentleman's great virtues; Ke-woo expatiated with the old gentleman on the penetrating intellect of the magistrate; while the magistrate again, and the old gentleman, dealt out their praises on the conduct of Ke-woo, who had conferred benefits, instead of cherishing resentment. "Such action as these," they observed, "would be hereafter talked of far and wide: this might be predicted without the aid of divination."

They went on with their praises of each other without ceasing, and the attendants who were present, put their hands to their mouths, in order to conceal their laughter, observing, that "the magistrate had issued orders to apprehend him who had presented the anonymous petition. Having found him out, he was sitting down and conversing with him, instead of giving him a beating. This was certainly a novel proceeding!"

When the magistrate returned to his office, he sent a messenger to deliver the twenty pieces of treasure, and to procure a receipt for the same. Ke-woo, however, would not accept it. He wrote back a letter to that officer, requesting that he would give the money over to the family of the prisoner, and redeem the property with it. That, in the first place, this would be fulfilling the intentions of his father; secondly, it would accord with the wishes of his generous friend; and lastly, it would enable the prisoner's family to purchase some other residence. Thus, neither the givers nor the receivers would be injured in the least.

All parties praised such unexampled generosity. The magistrate, in compliance with the words of the letter, released the prisoner from his confinement, and delivering to him the original price, received from him the two deeds, by which the property had been sold. A messenger being sent off with these, the pleasure ground, and the dwelling, were delivered into the possession of their original master.

On the same day, in the highest of the "Three Dedicated Chambers", he offered up wine, in token of gratitude to heaven, saying, "Thus amply has my father's virtue been rewarded; thus bitter has been the recompense of Tang-yo-chuen's crimes! Oh, how is it, that men are afraid of virtue; or how is it, that they can delight in being vicious!"

Tang-yo-chuen's son and his wife made out a deed, as before, delivering up their persons, and together with the price of the property, which they had received from the magistrate, offered themselves to Ke-woo, entreating that he would accept of their services for the remainder of their lives. He resolutely declined their offer, but at the same time soothed them with kind words. Then the husband and wife, having engraved a votive tablet, wishing him long life, took it home and made offerings to it. Though they could not prevail on him to receive them into his service, they still recognized him as their master. They not only endeavoured to recompense his favours, but likewise wished people to understand that they were a part of his family, for then nobody, they thought, would venture to molest them.

With a view to the remembrance of these events, every one had by heart a stanza of verses, which admonished persons of opulence to refrain from contriving schemes for the acquisition of their neighbours' property. The line were to this effect,

"By want compell'd, he sold his house and land,

Both house and land the purchasers return;

Thus profit ends the course by virtue plann'd,

While envious plotters their misfortunes mourn."

CHINESE MORAL

The clear judgment of the magistrate, the disinterested generosity of the old friend, and moderation of Ke-woo, in living retired without cherishing resentment, are all three deserving of everlasting remembrance. Those who are magistrates, ought to make the first their example. Persons of influence, who reside in the country, ought to take a lesson of the last. Those, however, who possess great wealth, should not altogether copy the old friend, because his conduct, in presenting the anonymous petition, cannot be held up as an example. It may be observed of the actions of such generous friends in general, that very few are fit to be imitated, and that those, whose conduct can be recommended, have always been men of justice. The difference between those who are just, and those who are only generous, consists in the conduct of the one being worthy of imitation, and that of the others, not.

思 考

1. 比较德庇时《三与楼》1815年、1816年及1822年译文,试分析形成译文不同的原因。

2. 分析德庇时对中西文学文化交流有何贡献?

参考文献

- *Chinese Novels, translated from the originals*, by John Francis Davis, London, J. Murray, 1822.
- *San-Yu-Low: or The Three Dedicated Rooms, A Tale, translated from the Chinese*, by John Francis Davis, Canton: E. I., 1815.

扩展阅读

- "*San-Yu-Low; or The Three Dedicated Rooms, A Tale, translated from the Chinese*", by John Francis Davis, *Asiatic Journal*, Vol.1, 1816.
- *The invention of Li Yu*, by Patrick Hanan, Harvard University Press, 1988.

乔治·加德纳·亚历山大《貂蝉》（第三幕）
（1869）

导 读

乔治·加德纳·亚历山大（George Gardiner Alexander，1821—1879）是英国维多利亚时代的戏剧家、小说家和汉学家。其著作主要有《貂蝉，一部中国五幕剧》（Teaou-shin, A Drama from the Chinese, in Five Act，1869）、《冒名顶替的沙皇》（Dimetri: A Dramatic Sketch from Russian History，1876）、《维多利亚医生》（Doctor Victoria: A Picture of the Period，1881）、《孔子，伟大的师者》（Confucius: the Great Teacher，1890）与《老子，伟大的思想家》（Lâo-Tsze, the Great Thinker，1895）等。

乔治·加德纳·亚历山大曾于1861年将《三国演义》中与董卓相关的情节译成英文 A Chapter of Chinese History: The Minister's Stratagem，即《中国历史中的一回：大臣之计策》，载于《周报》（Once a Week）1861年5月卷。不久之后，他又将其改编成一部五幕二十二场的英国戏剧《貂蝉》，即：Teaou-shin, A Drama from the Chinese, in Five Acts，1869年由伦敦朗肯（Ranken & Co.）出版社首次出版。该剧对应的内容主要为《三国演义》第八回"王司徒巧使连环计 董太师大闹凤仪亭"和第九回中"除凶暴吕布助司徒"的情节,但在时间、空间、人物、主题等诸多方面对中文小说进行了改写,不仅将故事发生地由长安转移到南京,而且把整个事件的时间跨度压缩在六天之内。另外,在主要人物貂蝉、董卓、王允、吕布、李肃外,又增加了何景、穆华和阿莲三人,这三人在剧中主要起到陪衬和牵引情节发展的作用。

更为重要的是,亚历山大的英剧《貂蝉》不仅在体裁上将中国小说改编成西人钟爱的戏剧形式,而且将"貂蝉故事"的主题从体现忠义思想的政治斗争改编为对真诚爱情的颂歌,并通过心理活动的细腻描写,多侧面地刻画了剧中人物,使人物形象更加真实丰满。同时,增加了剧中人物对奴隶身份的自觉及其对自由平等的追求,赋予其新的反映十九世纪西方自由精神的时代特征和文化内涵,是中国"貂蝉故事"在英语世界一次意味深长的"投胎转世"。此处所选译文为亚历山大英剧《貂蝉》之第三幕。

译　文

TEAOU-SHIN
A DRAMA FROM THE CHINESE
IN FIVE ACTS

STORY OF THE PLAY

WANG-WAN, an Imperial Councillor and Minister of State, is filled with a patriotic desire to rescue the Empire and its young Emperor from the hands of a brutal and unscrupulous adventurer, Tung-chow, who, after a long period of civil war, has usurped supreme authority, placed himself at the head of the Government as Regent, and is now secretly aiming at the destruction of the child-Emperor and his own recognition in his place. Wang-wan is also actuated by fears for his own safety; and these feelings are intensified by the tyrant causing one of the members of the Council to be cruelly executed.

Puzzled how to act, he at last finds the means of effecting his purpose through the proffered aid of a beautiful girl—Teaou-shin—who had been rescued from death by him as a babe, and brought up amongst his wife's attendants. Teaou-shin is romantic and enthusiastic; he sees that she is beautiful, and determines upon making her beauty the instrument of the tyrant's destruction. Having made her swear to carry out his wishes, he unfolds his plan to her. It is this:—

Tung-chow has an adopted son, Lew-poo, the commander-in-chief of the army and its idol, who forms the main-prop of his power. Both Tung-chow and Lew-poo are slaves to beauty. Wang-wan is to offer Teaou-shin, whom he calls his daughter, in marriage to Lew-poo, and before the arrangements for the wedding can be completed, to give her—no longer his daughter—as a slave to Tung-chow; whilst she, accepting both parts, is so to manage matters as to create and foster the most bitter and deadly animosity between them.

The trap is duly baited and set. Lew-poo becomes madly in love with

Teaou-shin, and she returns his love with romantic ardour. She is his affianced bride when Tung-chow casts his amorous glances upon her; she is given to him by Wang-wan, and, in ignorance of what has previously occurred, he takes her to his palace and places her amongst his singing-girls. Lew-poo hears of this, and the insult is too deadly to be borne even by a son.

Wang-wan, who manages to keep Lew-poo in the belief that Teaou-shin is his daughter, foments the deadly feud which has sprung up between him and his father, and induces him to join in a conspiracy against him. The result is the death of Tung-chow, but Teaou-shin falls a victim of Wang-wan's treachery, for she stabs herself at the very moment that the arrival of her lover would have rescued her from the tyrant's power. She dies in his arms, and he drives Wang-wan from him in horror on discovering how cruelly he has been deceived.

The several events of the play are supposed to take place in or near Nanking, and the time occupied by them to extend over six consecutive days.

ACT III

DRAMATIS PERSONÆ

TUNG-CHOW, *the Regent, who has usurped the supreme power, and aims at the Imperial throne.*

WANG-WAN, *a member of the Imperial Council.*

LEW-POO, *Commander-in-Chief of the Imperial Army, and Tung-chow's ad-*

opted Son.

LEE-SOO, *a General of Cavalry.*

HO-CHING, *servant to Wang-wan.*

Captain of Guard, Soldiers, Sailors, Servants, a Bouze, a Cripple, a Citizen, &c.

MUN-WHA, *a wife to Wang-wan.*

TEAOU-SHIN, *a foundling, adopted in Wang-wan's household.*

A-LINE, *servant to Mun-wha.*

Dancing Girls, Attendants, &c.

SCENE 1.—*An open space before* WANG-WAN'S *palace. Entrance to the palace on the right. Temples and other buildings in background. Entrance from a public street on the left.* Vendors *of wares move across the stage—a* Barber *piles his trade*—Punch, *and then a troupe of* Saltimbanques, *collect a crowd. A* Bouze—*a* Cripple. *Gongs sound in the distance, and the crowd hasten to the entrance of the street, but are beaten back with whips by the* Soldiers *who issue from it. These are followed by a* Guard, *variously armed,* Attendants, Officers of States, *&c. Then the* Regent, TUNG-CHOW, *in an open chair, with a yellow umbrella held over him, followed by* Officers, Attendants, *&c. The crowd shout and fall down on their knees as he passes, all but the* Cripple, *who alone remains standing. He is perceived by* TUNG-CHOW, *who motions his bearers to stop, and orders the trembling culprit to be brought before him.*

Tung.

> How now, slave? When all 'neath heaven bow down
>
> Before the emblems of the Emperor's power
>
> And our authority, thou needs must stand.

Cripple.

> Oh, my great lord! pardon thy crippled slave.
>
> Alas! he cannot kneel. The gods from birth
>
> So willed it.

Tung.

> Then thank the gods that heaven
>
> Has sent me now to cure those rebel limbs.
>
> (*To his guards*) Take him from hence and rack those stubborn joints
>
> Till death release him—away with him. Move on!
>
> (*The Cripple is carried off, shrieking for mercy. The procession moves on, and forms so as to let* TUNG-CHOW *pass through it into* WANG-WAN'S *palace. The crowd rises and disperses in silence, with the exception of the* Saltimbanques, *who crawl off on all—fours in comic dismay. The* Bouze *and a* Citizen *alone remain.*)

Citizen.

> How can the gods look on and let this be?

Bouze.

> Think ye the gods look down on deeds like this?
>
> Pollute their purity with human crime.
>
> 'Tis not the gods, but demons, such men serve,

Devils alike in all but in degree.

Cit.

But the poor cripple, he had done no crime.

Bouze.

How can we tell? Would ye arraign the gods,

Who see and know what was, what is, what will?

To whom all time and space stand forth revealed

In floods of living light, whilst our weak eyes

Can scarcely guide our steps through one short life.

Cit.

But justice, surely, still remains the same.

Bouze.

Eternal justice neither flags nor fails;

Sooner or later, in befitting time,

It will o'ertake us. Let us then beware;

The sport of demons, those the gods forsake. [*Exeunt.*

SCENE 2.—*Interior of* WANG-WAN'S *palace. An ante-chamber in* MUN-WHA'S *apartments.*

MUN-WHA—A-LINE—HO-CHING.

Mun.

How goes it with the feast, Ho-ching?

Ho.

(*affectedly*) The feast!

As feasts should ever go—most daintily,

His Grace the Regent as each dish goes round

Deigning to honour it, in right good style,

With application of his princely jaws,

Nor in his condescendence does he fail

To pledge all round in wine, with every cup

Some merry word, and when the guests all laugh,

You hear his jocund shouts above their mirth,

Like distant thunder. Oh, 'tis glorious!

But now, I'm sent to say, that in brief space

His Grace will quit the feast and rest him here,

And—but I'll give it in the very words

My master used when he besought his Grace,

"And pour, in evidence of friendly love,

A few libations to the household gods,

Within the sacred precincts." So it was,

And I was told to ask if all were ready,

And Teaou-shin prepared.

Mun.

Go tell thy master

All is arranged. He has now but to come.

[*Exit* HO-CHING.

(*To A-Lien*) How thinkest thou will Teaou-shin play her part?

A-Line.

    Indeed, my lady, I can scarcely say,

    She puzzles me, and grows from bad to worse;

    She's like a willow—weeps, and weeps, and weeps.

    I never, no, I never, saw such tears.

    If it goes on, she really must dissolve.

    Why, she has shed more tears since yesterday

    Than I have done in all my living life,

    And that's some thirty years; and goodness knows

    My heart is soft enough, if only touched

    On the right spot. I think, too, she's gone mad,

    For but last night it was I heard her say—

    (She thought I was asleep, and did not know

    I do not always shut both eyes and ears)—

    "I must, and will," says she, "'twill break my heart,

    But better break my heart than break my vow."

Mun.

    But will she sing?

A-Line.

    If she said Yes, she will.

    I'm sure of that, for I did never know

    A girl so stick to every little word.

    She's not like me; for when I say No! no!

    'Tis ten to one but what I mean Yes! yes! (*A gong sounds.*)

Mun.

> Oh, here they come; A-line, we must not stay.

> > [*Exeunt.*

SCENE 3.—*Enter* WANG-WAN *and* TUNG-CHOW, *preceded by* HO-CHING, *with* Attendants *bearing lanterns. Folding-doors are thrown back, and discover a large room, opening on a court, in which a fountain plays—the whole brilliantly illuminated.* Servants *range themselves in two rows for* WANG-WAN *and* TUNG-CHOW *to pass through them, and then retire.*

Wang.

> True, true, my lord, and now we are alone,
> I would give utterance to secret thoughts
> Which have lain long imprisoned in my breast.
> In times like these, so vexed and out of joint,
> No stripling's arm can wield the sword of state;
> It needs a soldier's hand, a hand like thine.
> Thou must be all thou art, and something more;
> The people's voice would hail thee Emperor.

Tung.

> My dear, dear lord, there's treason in these words,
> I must not hear them. To the gods of fate,
> And their decrees, I will submit myself
> In all obedience. Speak no more of this,

But rest assured, whate'er may come to pass,

Tung-chow will not forget a faithful friend. (*Seats himself.*)

Servants *enter with wine, followed by a number of* Dancing Girls. *Who precede and then group round* TEAOU-SHIN. *Whilst the wine is being served the* Dancers *form a variety of graceful figures.*

Tung.

(*drinking and pointing to the dancers*) Ah! there's no relish to your wine like these.

(*Observing Teaou-shin*) But who's yon fairy?

Wang.

A Little songstress,

Who, if your Grace permit, will do her best

To warble some few notes.

Tung.

A songstress, eh?

Aye, let her sing, each song a cup of wine;

I like all music, but I like it best

When I can love the singer—eh, my lord?

  Two gifts divine

  Are song and wine.

  But when love joins to give them zest,

  Oh then, indeed, man's trebly blest.

Ha! is't not so?

Wang.

(*affecting to laugh*) Ha! ha! it is, indeed.

I wish I had your Grace's memory.

(*To Teaou-shin*) His Grace would hear thee; do not be afraid.

TEAOU-SHIN *comes forward and sings. During the song* TUNG-CHOW *keeps his eyes fixed on her, and beats time with his fan. Dancers group.*

TEAOU-SHIN'S SONG.

A soft voice murmurs in the grove,

A soft voice whispering words of love,

Ah me! ah me! I dare not stay,

Danger lurks near—away, away!

For I've been told that maidens fair

Should of love's luring voice beware;

Yet my weak heart would bid me stay,

Oh! foolish heart, away, away!

Ah me! I hear that voice again,

In mingled tones of joy and pain.

So soft, so sweet. Ah! I must stay,

I cannot, will not, go away.

The bamboo loves the summer gale,

The dry earth the warm shower;

The twilight loves the moonbeam pale,

The dew the opening flower;

Then why should I be coy and shy

When all around, beneath the sky,

Are heard the sounds of love—whilst I

From sounds so sweet, alone must fly?

No, no, no, no, come what it may,

When love is whispering I will stay.

(*At the end of the song, the* Dancers *close and move round* TEAOU-SHIN *in a giddy whirl. They stop suddenly and remain motionless, ready to obey* TEAOU-SHIN'S *next signal.*)

Tung.

Ha! 'tis a phoenix. With what grace she moves;

And what a voice! That's what I call a voice;

'Tis neither cracked by age, nor spoilt by art.

Yes, she can sing. But hush! she sings again.

(TEAOU-SHIN *makes a sign to the* Dancers, *and they move in cadence to her voice as she sings.*)

SONG.

Come hither, my maidens.

Join hands in a ring,

And move in light cadence,

To each note I sing;

For dance is twin sister,

To music and song,

And love is the master

To whom they belong.

Oh gently, so gently, ye gay dancers move,

Whilst I sigh forth my heart in a song to my love.

A hero's my love,

Who's as brave as can be,

And I a poor maid

Oh most humble degree.

I love him, he loves me,

What can maid want more?

Oh I would I were rich,

And my love he was poor.

Oh faster, yet faster, ye gay dancers move,

For my heart it is breaking, and breaking for love.

Oh, I love my love,

And my love he loves me,

My love, for my love,

Is as deep as can be,

I love him, he loves me,

Can true love want more?

Oh love's like the sea,

None its depths can explore.

Oh faster, yet faster, ye gay dancers move.

For my heart it is breaking, and breaking for love.

But oh! if my love

Should no longer love me,

And burst from the bonds

Of my love and get free.

If storms, lurid storms

Love's calm sea should sweep o'er,

And cast me away,

Lone and lost on its shore.

Oh, slowly, more slowly, ye sad dancers move,

For my heart it is broken, and broken through love.

(*Bursts into tears.*)

Tung.

Ha! By the gods, 'twere excellently done.

I like sad songs. Your giggling fal-lal-las

Soon weary me; but that was good indeed.

(*To Teaou-shin*) *My little broken heart, come here* (*takes off his chain*), *take this.* (*places it round her neck*).

No remedy for broken hearts like gems.

How many green springs have passed over thee?

Teaou.

Most mighty lord, thy slave is just sixteen.

Tung.

Ha! a sweet age, sixteen; all bud and bloom.

My little rosebud, thou hast won my heart;

I only wish I had thee safely caged

Amongst my songsters. (*To Wang-wan*) What dost say, my lord?

Canst part with her? Thou'st but to name the price.

Wang.

Acceptance is the price that I would have—

Rapacity itself could ask no more.

Tung.

My lord; no, no; indeed it must not be;

You are too generous—I am confused.

But if you will insist, well, I give way,

And take most thankfully your charming gift.

(*To Teaou-shin*) My little lotus-leaf must come with me,

And bloom and blossom in another soil,

Where she shall have all tenderness and care.

But why this sullen look, these misty eyes?

Come, come, my pretty one, we must have smiles.

Hence and get ready; yet one moment, stay,

I'd hear you sing again before you go.

(*The* Dancers *move up and retire, dancing, a few paces with* TEAOU-SHIN. *She takes up her lute, strikes a few wild, plaintive chords, and sings.*)

SONG.

Yes, I'm a slave,

And who is free?

Tell me, ye winds,

For ye alone

Have liberty.

The chains of Fate

Are forged for all,

In every cup

Some drops of gall.

In vain, in vain

My chains they gild—

In vain my cup

With wine is filled.

For I'm a slave,

And would be free!

Tell me, ye winds!

Where shall I find

True liberty.

Hush! the winds answer:

Mortal! alas, there's slavery

In every breath.

There is but one true liberty—

'Tis found in death!

            (*Rushes out.*)

Tung.

 That song's a twang to me, I do not like,

 The last words gave a roughness to the wine.

 Come, my good lord, let us rejoin your guests;

 A short carouse, and then—for it is late—

 We must repeat again our many thanks,

 And take our leave. Indeed, the time has flown. (*Rises.*)

(TUNG-CHOW *and* WANG-WAN *retire, the latter walking backwards and bowing ceremoniously before him, as on entrance.* Attendants *come in and form as before, whilst* Dancers *group and form a passage for them to pass through, and then, whirling round rapidly in a variety of graceful figures, exeunt, dancing.*)

SECNE 4.—*The same as Scene* 2.

WANG-WAN enters, in deep thought.

Wang.

The monster gone; poor Teaou-shin in his hands!

Events move quickly towards our purposed end.

What next? what next? what next? I grow confused.

(*Rousing himself and striking his forehead*) But this will never do—rouse up, Wang-wan;

Thy rest and peace will come when all is done.

(*Goes to door and calls*) Ho-ching, Ho-ching, come here!

Enter HO-CHING, *running in an ungainly manner.*

Ho.

(*as if breathless*) My lord, my lord,

What are my lord's commands?

Wang.

I have work for thee.

It will advantage thee to do it well.

'Tis this, Ho-ching—now mark well every word—

Thou must take horse, and spare nor whip nor spur,

Until thou reach the camp. When thou art there

Ask for the general, the Lord Lew-poo,

And tell him this, "The Minister Wang-wan,

O'er whelmed with grief, entreats his presence."

Tell him no more from me. If he would gain,

By questioning thee, a more extended sense

Of what my words may mean, say only this:—

(Now heed me well, for I would have thee know

Thy life shall pay for idly added words)—

Thou know'st but this—his Grace the Regent

Was feasted by your lord, and when he left,

The Lord Wang's little daughter, Lady Teaou

(Mind thee, the Lord Wang's daughter) went with him.

Now, then, to horse! Dost hear and understand?

Ho.

I do, my lords; one word for old Ho-ching

Is quite enough; to hear is to obey.

(*Significantly*) Oh, yes! He understands! he understands!
(*Runs off by door opposite side, where he stands whilst* WANG-WAN *retires by nearest door.*)

HO-CHING *re-entering.*

Ho.

But I don't understand, and I must think over this before I get on horseback and have all my ideas jolted out of me. (*Considers*). Ah, yes! now is the time. This is the opportunity. Now the "old dolt" will be revenged. When topsy-turvy's moving round, a chance once lost may never be regained. Yes, I will, I will betray him; but who shall I betray him to?—to his Grace the Regent or to my Lord Lew-poo? 'Tis puzzling. (*Reflecting*) *Come, let me see, what't was the old lord said?* (*repeating* WANG-WAN'S *words and mimicking his tone*) " The Lady Teaou, the Lord Wang's little daughter," and "remember, your life shall pay for idly spoken words"—a very dreadful speech for anyone to hear, and said in such a tone! "Thy life shall pay." How very disagreeable! Let me think again, let me consider. Is this the time? Is this the opportunity? Come, come, Ho-ching, my good fellow, do nothing rashly. Be prudent; you have a wise head upon your shoulders, and 'twere wise to keep it there. "Thy life." What an abominable tone for one fellow-creature to assume towards another! I declare it makes me blush for humanity. No, no; I see it clearly. The time has not yet come. You must watch, my good Ho-ching, you must watch! Keep your eyes open and look ahead, but, whatever you do, don't be such a fool as to take a leap in the dark. Now then I must be off and to horse; oh, how I hate the word, for I know it means aching joints, and a pretended preference for a standing posture for at least a week. Depend upon it, this has never been a comfortable world since people have wished to go faster than their own legs can carry them. But never mind, I have philosophy to salve my sores, and I will be as patient as an over-loaded camel—till the time comes.

(*Is hurrying out, when he rushes against* A-LINE, *who is entering from opposite side.*)

A-line.

(*seizing him*) Oh, Ho-ching! can it be you? To see you running like this—you, of all people in the world, to be running about like a common coolie. I thought you knew your position better. But come, don't go; tell me where you are hurrying to.

Ho.

(*struggling to get free*) Don't stop me—I have not a moment—I'm on the road to fortune—I'm off to the camp, and about to take command of a—of a—of a body of horse. (*Aside*)That's not so bad; I only hope the horse won't take command of me.

(*Tears himself from* A-LINE, *and rushed out*—A-LINE *follows, with uplifted hands.*)

SCENE 5.—*Night. A country-place, near Nanking. The camp in the distance, with the moon rising over it.*

HO-CHING *enters, covered with mud, a whip in one hand and a broken bridle in the other.*

Ho.

How I hate obstinacy! 'Tis is bad enough in man, woman, or child, but 'tis brutish in a beast. And I to be rolled in the mud by an ill-conditioned quadruped because I posses the virtue of obedience. By the shade of Confucius this is not just. If virtue receive such wages I will none of it. My master bid me spare nor whip nor spur, and because I follow his injunctions—as, in the humble office which I fill, I am bound to do—I am carried, in a manner indescribably painful to my feelings, a mile beyond the camp, and then find myself, through some demoniacal agency—for nothing else could have borne me from my seat—upon my own back, instead of the horse's, with this broken bridle in my hand. But who comes here?

Enter Drunken Soldier.

Soldier.

Holloa! How now—against orders. No rolling about the camp in the small hours of the night permitted. I say, this won't do—you're a spy (*drawing his sword*). Come, you drunken dog, this will make short work of you. What's the word. Come, out with it quick.

Ho.

The word! What word? I thought you soldiers were for deeds, not words. No, no; I'm not going to bandy words with you.

Sol.

Come, come, none of this. I want the word—the pass-word, or—(*brandishing his sword*).

Ho.

Take care, or my Lord-General will make mincemeat of you, for I bear him a message on affairs of State from my Lord Wang.

Sol.

A puff of tobacco smoke for you and your Lord Wang. My orders are, no one's to pass; and you don't know the word.

Ho.

That is easily settled. Tell me what it is, and then I shall be as wise as you are.

Sol.

I'll see thee turned into a tortoise first, you rascal. We soldiers are men of honour. Would you insult me? But I'll be merciful. Come, exchange is no robbery; give me your purse, and you shall have the word. Out with it! (*Seizes him by the throat.*)

Ho.

Oh! most valiant soldier, have pity on a poor benighted man.

Sol.

Come, don't bandy words with me. We soldiers, as someone said, are for deeds not words. Out with it (*snatches the purse*), and now the word, for I am a man of honour. 'Tis "Mum," and to enforce it take this.
(*Makes a wild stab at* HO-CHING, *who falls, as if lifeless, and exit, flourishing the purse in triumph.*)

Ho.

(*rising slowly to a sitting posture and looking round*)This is topsy-turvy with a vengeance. I thank thee, good spirits, that thou didst turn the brute's inebriate hand. (*Rising.*) Come, come, Ho-ching, take heart, and to thy task. The camp is nearly gained—a few steps more, and then—ah! let me see. "My daughter" and "thy life."Aye, aye, "thy life." But seems to me, if things go on like this, thy life, my good Ho-ching, would scarce be worth the risk of purchase, however low the price. But never mind, when things are at the worst they are sure to mend. Ah! what a thing it is to have philosophy. With that a man can see beyond his nose, and find the whole world wrong except himself. (*A sound of footsteps.*) But who comes here? One of our jolly guards—on duty, perhaps. If so, then I'll be off. But no—I see—ye gods! the very man.

Enter LEW-POO.

Lew.

(*not observing Ho-ching*) Oh, ye night, how grateful is thy silence!

How loathsome all the noise of revelry!

Once more I am alone, yet not alone,

For she is with me. Yes, she is everywhere.

I look aloft, and in those silvery beams

I catch the radiance of her loving eyes;

The very air breathes from her fragrant lips;

The rustling breeze is but a sigh of love;

Night's sable hue, locks of her raven hair.

How changed in two short days is Lew-poo's heart;

What cares he now for Fortune's smiles or frowns?

Teaou-shin is his; he revels in her love—

A love 'fore which all earthly splendours pale.

Move on, ye sluggard Time; fly, fly, ye hours,

And bring her to these arms. Ah! now, maybe,

She sleeps, she sleeps, and dreams perchance—of love. (*Sings*)

SONG.

Sweet spirits of air,

I pray ye to take

A kiss to my love,

If she's sleeping,

>   *A soft gentle kiss,*
>   *But if she's awake,*
>   *Then watch by her side*
>   *Till she's sleeping.*
>   *Oh breathe in her ear,*
>   *So gently from me,*
>   *Soft whispers of love*
>   *Whilst she's sleeping,*
>   *Till sighs break her rest,*
>   *And all her dreams be*
>   *Of lips prest to hers*
>   *Whilst she's sleeping.*
>   *Then oh! fly ye back*
>   *With each tell-tale sigh*
>   *That's sighed by my love*
>   *Whilst she's sleeping,*
>   *Oh hasten you back,*
>   *As swift dragons fly!*
>   *But, first, kiss my love*
>   *Whilst she's sleeping.*

(*Observes* HO-CHING, *who has stood by, beating time, with gestures of approbation, during the song, and now endeavours to attract his attention.*)

But who art thou?

Ho.

    A poor, half-murdered wretch,

    Most gracious lord, robbed of his little all,

    When bringing thee a message in hot haste,

    From the Lord Wang, his master.

Lew.

    A message?

    From the Lord Wang? Speak, lose not an instant!

Ho.

    He bid me say (*becomes confused*)

    "Thy life"—no, 'twas not that,

    He bid me say "My daughter".

Lew.

    (*interrupting*) His daughter,

    Speak, slave; what of his daughter?

Ho.

    Gracious lord,

    Some hour ago, my master said to me,

    Take horse at once, and spare nor whip nor spur

    Until thou reach the camp. Your slave obeyed,

    And had been here long since, but some foul sprite,

    Urged by an evil fate, beset his path,

    Who first did hurl him from his horse's back

    And then, assuming monstrous shape and form,

Disguised in soldier's garb, did plunder him,

And sought to slay him.

Lew.

(*who has been showing signs of great impatience, stamping with fury*)
Cease this fool's babble.

Thy master's message, not another word.

Ho.

 (*reflecting*) The message. 'Twas this:—

Tell the Lord General,

The minister Wang-wan, o'erwhelmed with grief,

Entreats his presence.

Lew.

Hound! of his daughter?

Base slave, quick, speak! what said he of his daughter?

Ho.

(*slowly*) Daughter? Your slave knows nothing of his daughter, but this—

And 'pon his life, great lord, he can't say more—

His Grace, the Regent, feasted with my lord,

And when he left, his Highness took with him

The Lord Wang's lovely daughter.

Lew.

(*striking him*) Oh, villain!

Why this delay? Thou diest if 'tis too late.　　　　[*Rushes out.*

Ho.

Buffets and blows come thick as hail; thy money gone, and thy life threatened on all sides. Have a care, Ho-ching, have a care. There's no standing still in this world. 'Tis a great ladder; and people are not going down who are going up. But I'll be revenged. [*Exit.*

SCENE 6.—*Night. Interior of* WANG-WAN'S *palace.* WANG-WAN *seated at a small table, apparently absorbed in grief. Room dimly lighted by a single lamp.*

LEW-POO *rushes in, his whole appearance indicating agitation and excitement.*

Lew.

(*going straight up to* Wang-wan, *whose face is buried in his hands, and seizing him roughly by the shoulder*)

My lord, what's this? Tell me, ere I go mad.

Wang.

Ask me not. Would it were not thy father,

Whose brutal lust has robbed me of my child.

Lew.

And wherefore saidst thou not that she was mine?

His son's. Would not the sacred name of son

Have touched his heart, and turned him from the deed?

Think'st thou 'tis water, and not blood,

Which flows in crimson tide through Lew-poo's veins,

That he will suffer such a wrong as this,

E'en from a father? Ten thousand demons!

Tell me, my lord, why didst thou let it be?

Wang.

Why did I suffer this? Well mayst thou ask.

'Tis that the weak must bend before the strong;

And I am old and weak. Had I thy years

I would have sooner died than thus submit

To cruel wrong like this. Alas! alas!

And he, the doer of this monstrous wrong,

Who tramples under foot our bleeding hearts,

Is still, remember this, is still, thy father!

Lew.

Oh, hateful thought!

Wang.

There is a difference

Of blood 'tis true. Thou dost not even bear

The Regent's name; but then thou art his heir;

Forget not this. Thou must not mar thy fortunes.

Lew.

And have I fallen so low that I must lose

My life, my all—for Teaou-shin's each to me—

That I may gain a miserable—what?

No father's love, but a harsh tyrant's favour,

For which I barter freedom, hope, and love!

I will not be this slave; duty has bounds.

I cast the monster off! Lew-poo is free!

Wang.

Thou speakest now as I would have thee speak;

With all the freedom of a generous heart.

But time may change thee, and bring calmer thoughts.

Lew.

Yes; time brings change to all, but whilst its stream

Bears all things onward, so, from Lew-poo's heart

As deep a current ceaselessly shall flow

Of endless love—of never-dying hate!

Wang.

But thou needst not despair. If thou wouldst so,

Tung-chow is in our hands; speak but the word,

And I will promise, feeble as I am,

A day or so, and Teaou-shin shall be thine.

But this can never be; think well of this,

There is no other course—whilst Tung-chow (*lower his voice*) lives.

Lew.

And darest thou speak to me, of this!

I who have borne the name of Tung-chow's son?

And I can listen; yes, so deep my hate,

Can gladly listen. Would that he were dead!

Yes, let him die, but not by Lew-poo's hand.

Oh, Love! thou'st cast a softness o'er my soul

That makes my heart recoil from deeds like these.

How could I bear to have my loved one's name

Linked with a parricide's! For thus the world

Would deem the actor whilst it blessed the act.

If it be justice, let the tyrant die;

For me to take his life would be a crime.

Wang.

So let it be; but thou upholdst his power;

Thou art his prime support. Without thy aid,

Thy countenance in this, there's none dare act.

'Tis for thy sake I spoke, and for my child's.

I had no wish in this to anger thee.

Alas! alas! I would that I were young.

Lew.

Thou hast not angered me; each angry thought

Is centred on the tyrant. But time flies.

Teaou-shin is in his power. She must be saved!

Wang.

But how, whilst Tung-chow lives?

Lew.

I will see him;

Aye, and I will see her. I will see him—

I will throw myself at his feet, and beg

For mercy. I will make one last appeal

To him, as my father. If he spurn me,

Then, aye then, will I cease to be his son.

Then will I throw my scruples to the winds,

And join the ranks of his most deadly foes.

To-morrow thou shalt know how I have sped:

Till then, farewell! [*Exit.*

Wang.

Indeed, I like not this!

He may succeed. There's ruin in the thought.

But lose not heart, Wang-wan, thou'st thrown the net,

And can do nought but sit upon the shore—

The victory's oft to him who best can wait. [*Exit.*

END OF ACT III.

思 考

1. 阅读乔治·亚历山大《貂蝉》的英译文，谈谈你对此译文的看法。

2. 比较乔治·亚历山大英剧《貂蝉》与《三国演义》中"貂蝉故事"的差异，并分析形成这种差别的缘由。

参考文献

- *Teaou-Shin*, *A Drama from the Chinese in Five Acts*, by George Gardiner Alexander, London, 1869.
- "A Chapter of Chinese History: The Minister's Stratagem by George Gardiner Alexander", *Once a Week*, 1861.

扩展阅读

- *The Death of the Celebrated Minister Tung-cho*, By Peter Perring Thoms, *Asiatic Journal*, Vol.X,Vol.XI., 1820–1821.
- *Tchao-Chi-Kou-Eul, Ou L'Orphelin de la Chine, Drame en Prost et en Vers, Accompagné des Pièces Historiques Qui en Ont Fourni Le Sujet, de Nouvelles et de Poésies Chinoise*, Par Stanislas Julien, Paris: Moutardier, 1834.

奥古斯塔·韦伯斯特《俞伯牙摔琴谢知音》
（1874）

导　读

《俞伯牙摔琴谢知音》谱写了俞伯牙与钟子期以琴相识相知的故事，最早见于冯梦龙编撰的《警世通言》，后被抱瓮老人辑入《今古奇观》。自十九世纪三十年代起，《俞伯牙摔琴谢知音》已被翻译成法、英、德等多种语言。其中极具特色的乃奥古斯塔·韦伯斯特《俞伯牙摔琴谢知音》之英译文。

奥古斯塔·韦伯斯特（Augusta Webster，1837—1894）是英国维多利亚时代著名的女诗人和戏剧家。她创作的诗集有《布兰奇·莱尔》（Blanche Lisle，1860）、《莉莉安·格雷》（Lilian Gray，1864）、《戏剧研究》（Dramatic Studies，1866）、《被拐卖的女子》（A Woman Sold，1867）、《画像》（Portraits，1870）与《母女》（Mother and Daughter，1895）等；戏剧有《幸运的一天》（The Auspicious Day，1872）、《伪装》（Disguise，1879）、《一天》（In a Day，1882）、《判决》（The Sentence，1887）；小说有《莱斯利的守护者》（Lesley's Guardians，1864）等。此外，奥古斯塔·韦伯斯特还精通希腊语、法语和意大利语，她曾将《被

缚的普罗米修斯》(*The Prometheus Bound of Aeschylus*，1866)、《美狄亚》(*The Medea of Euripides*，1868)和《俞伯牙摔琴谢知音》(*Yu-Pe-Ya's Lute*，1874)翻译成英文。

奥古斯塔·韦伯斯特编译的《俞伯牙摔琴谢知音》于1874年由伦敦麦克米兰（Macmillan）出版社出版，题为：*YU-PE-YA'S LUTE, A Chinese Tale, in English Verse*。此本亦收入奥古斯塔·韦伯斯特于晚年编选的《奥古斯塔·韦伯斯特诗歌选》。奥古斯塔·韦伯斯特《俞伯牙摔琴谢知音》并非译自中文，而是根据1839年巴黎迪普拉（B. Duprat）出版社所出版的帕维（Théodore Pavie）的《故事小说选》(*Choix de Contes et Nouvelles*)法文本转译而成。

奥古斯塔·韦伯斯特认为法译文设法融合散文和诗歌两种文体，常常以严肃的语调谈论现实生活中的琐细之事，显得滑稽可笑；而有时又以敏捷的笔调或幼稚的口吻捕捉无意识的惆怅和悲伤，文体参差不齐，意蕴也不尽和谐。因此奥古斯塔·韦伯斯特并没有遵循《俞伯牙摔琴谢知音》法译文 *Le Luth brisé* 严格而拘谨的文体形式，而是将小说改译成了通篇一体的韵文，以韵文诗歌的形式叙述了俞伯牙和钟子期因琴而成就的一段千古高谊，从而将中国古典小说的体裁转化成了叙事诗篇，以诗意来见证恒久友情。此处译文选自1874年伦敦麦克米兰出版社之《俞伯牙摔琴谢知音》。

译文

YU-PE-YA'S LUTE

Friends are many, but who hath a friend?
Stars are many, but who hath a star?
Friends and stars smile fair from afar,
Friends and stars have their course to wend.

Once a star came down from its sky,
Loving a man too well to stay lone;
Sometimes friend hath met friend and known
Heart was with heart to live or to die.

Hear the tale of Yu-Pe-Ya's lute-
Friend for friend in an ancient day.
Thousands of years have faded away
But the perished chords shall never be mute.

YU-PE-YA, born where Yng-Tou's halls and fanes
Look from their slopes upon a sea of plains,
Smooth wave on wave of greenness dimpling forth
To reach the cloudy mountains of the north,

Born in the shadow of her white-boled pines

Beneath the stillness of whose bosky lines

The yellow roofs① flash singly, each a sun,

And two young rivers answer as they run

With scattered brightness as of stars thick strown,

Yu-Pe-Ya, who for his first lore had known

The story of his house's vanished power,

Nursed by long years and broken in an hour

Like some centennial aloe snapped by wind,

Went forth in youth from Yng-Tou, left behind

The meads and vineplots and the waterglens

And skyward hills of Tsou and journeyed thence

To wealth and greatness. And when years were gone

He came to his youth's land, but not as one

Who, early tired, or master of his aims,

Flies to his home and the remembered names

And oft-trod paths and all the child loved best.

He came a stranger and half royal guest,

Evony from Tsin's great monarch. So he dwelt

Under the white-boled pines again, and knelt

Beside his fathers' graves. And all his heart

Clave to the land wherein he had no part.

---

① The effect of the roofs of glazed yellow tiles on the temples and palaces of some of the Chinese towns is described as singularly glittering and dazzling.

And while he yet relearned familiar ways,

Lo, it was time: four months had shed their days

Like blossoms that fall softly and leave fruit:

His king recalled him. Then he made his suit

To Yng-Tou's lord and prayed him, "Not again,

O king, may I behold bright Yng-Tou's plain

And taste the sweetness of my natural air,

I know no home in this dear land and fair

That was my fathers', and, its limits past,

My backward yearning looks must be my last

That ever linger on it; not when laid

In the still sleep can my returning shade

Behold it ghostly, I shall have my grave

In the far southern land. And this I crave,

Send me not thitherward by the beaten road

That in too short a time has passed abroad

Out of thy realm, but let me journey down

On the great river that from town to town,

Through meadow miles, 'twixt gorges of the hills,

Sweeps through the land's whole length, and ever fills

Its widening channel deeper till it gains

The double lake beyond these snow-topped chains

And through their sleepy waters breaks its way

To where Tsou's outer wall of mountains, grey

With dusky hollows, parts to make it room

Amid the silence of their verdurous gloom.

Let me, so floating onward from her reach,

Be with my motherland, hear her still speech

And answer with farewells and, greedy-eyed,

Learn all her face like one who sits beside

Dead beauty which before the coming night,

No longer his, shall be done down from sight

Into the earthy home without a door,

And cons each line and shaping o'er and o'er

To have the likeness of his lost more true:

Let changeless shores my far-off boyhood knew

Bring me my boyhood's thoughts, its hope, its dreams,

Fed with new memories, like summer streams,

Grown faint with miles of journeying from their hills

Where they were born, to which young freshet rills

Leap down the heights they left by longer ways

And brim them full. Give me forgotten days:

Give me my birthland mine to hear with me

And see it when my eyes may no more see.

So the great river bore him smoothly down

Through the whole length of Tsou, from town to town,

Through meadow-miles, betwixt the chasmy sides

Of gorges in the hills. And oftentides

The stars waned out ere well he knew 'twas night,

And oftentides the sudden scarlet light

Of sunset seemed to follow on the noon,

While he sat rapt and watchful.

                          Then, too soon,

Came the last day that aught he gazed upon

Should wear his birthland's name. Behind him shone

Tsou's sunny-coloured peaks of snow; the grove

That leftward slanted from dun heights above

To fringe the river with its streaky blaze

From flushing maples mid the serried maze

Of oaks and glittering larches and grey domes

Of silvery willows—the small peering homes

Amid their bowers where the right bank lay low,

An emerald crescent—the drowned field ablow

With flaky roods of lilies[①], stars afloat

Amid their sombre leaves—all he could note

Of rock and brake and flower and tangled wreath

Of leafy bines, the waters underneath,

---

①   Waterlilies, which are valuable both as ornamental flowers and as edible roots, are grown along the rivers in flooded fields enclosed by embankments. See Fortune's *Wanderings in China*.

The skies above, were Tsou's. But on ahead

In their blue smoothness the twin lakes were spread.

   And then he took his lute, that second heart

Which seemed to share his pulses and be part

Of the pent heart within him and expound

In living rhythms and sweet articulate sound

Its mute dim longings and to himself reveal

Some secret of himself he could not feel

Until the music spoke it; the delight

Of exquisite solitudes when, taking flight

Some brief sweet while from life's loud talk and press,

He stole the restful joy of loneliness;

The nearest love he had, nearer and more

Than wife or babes, for ever to him it bore

The sweet and subtle echoes of his thought

And sudden answers to the things he sought,

Like soul to equal soul when each one shares

The other's fullness as it ill were theirs,

The tender darlings of the guarded bowers,

Women and children playing with their flowers,

To share men's sorrowful wisdoms learned without

On the rough ways in toils and pain and doubt:

He took his priceless lute, the lute whose name

From age to age had won an added fame

While Time still bettered what the maker's skill

Had left so best that none hath heard, nor will,

In any land its fellow, and its tone

Was like some spirit's singing at Heaven's throne;

He took his priceless lute and, listening, sang

A tender song that like a farewell rang.

And yet, because a sorrow or a bliss

Will scarcely speak itself the thing it is,

But shapes its truth into a half disguise

And, like some painter who will make the eyes,

The smile, he lives by, in an altered face,

Or like the lapwing flitting past the place

She has no thought to leave, will part conceal

The thing it tells part what it hides reveal,

No farewell trembled on his tongue at all,

He sang but of the summer and its fall.

"Too soon so fair, fair lilies;

To bloom is then to wane;

The folded bud has still

Tomorrows at its will,

Blown flowers can never blow again.

Too soon so bright, bright noontide;

The sun that now is high

Will henceforth only sink

Towards the western brink;

Day that's at prime begins to die.

Too soon so rich, ripe summer,

For autumn tracks thee fast;

Lo death-marks on the leaf!

Sweet summer, and my grief;

For summer come is summer past.

Too soon, too soon, lost summer;

Some hours and thou art o'er.

Ah! death is part of birth;

Summer leaves not the earth,

But last year's summer lives no more."

And from the resonant hill came back again
Confused and multiple his last long strain,
Voice dimly echoing voice along the shore,
As he passed on, *No more, no more, no more.*
And ere they ceased the barge had floated by
And reached the widening bay, and all the sky

Lay low before his keel in the clear deeps

That stretched far forth to Tsin's blue shadowy steeps.

    Night came amid wan stars. At either side

Embattled blackness gloomed on the black tide

New pent between. Then grew from ridge to ridge,

Spanning the stream, a dappled argent bridge

Of beamy clouds, and the round moon arose

Over a barren scarp, and floating snows

Glimmered through all the heaven, and then grew black

Suddenly, for the lurid tempest wrack

Of the swift summer storm lowered over all

And a new darkness came, and the slow fall

Of drop by drop, and then the stifling rain

Rushing like fire, and, roaring through the chain

Of stony peaks, the dense tumultuous boom

Of meeting thunders, and, from out the gloom,

The swift and snaky barbs and the blue glare

Of ravenous lightnings bursting through the air,

And the sharp shriek of winds and hiss of waves.

The captain said, "My lord, the tempest raves,

Then will have passed; but meanwhile death lurks here

Among the foams and rocks, and if we steer

To left or right what matter? a leaf blown

Upon the waters, hither and thither thrown,

Is our stout ship to-night. Must we tempt fate,

Or anchor in this sheltered creek and wait?"

"Anchor," he said. And when the moored barge lay

In the embosomed nook, tired of the fray

Of earth and skies and of the watch he kept

And of his thoughts, he laid him down and slept.

    Light and deep quite waked him. Not a sound

Save where small ripples plashed and, from the ground,

The chirp of ceaseless crickets, and a breeze

That came and went among the cypresses,

Sighing a moment with them but too weak

To stir their trailing branches①. The still creek

Beamed silver underneath a silver sky

Where, larger after storm and risen high,

The clear and solitary moon moved slow

Whitening the silent air.

                Long to and fro

In the unrest of summer nights he tossed,

Then rose and burned the scented balms, whose cost

---

① The weeping cypress, a frequent and favourite tree in China. I have seen it stated that this cypress and not the willow is the weeping tree of the famous willow pattern.

Gold trebly weighed against them scarcely told,

In the bejewelled bowl—so they of old

Bade reverence the lute, before the hand

Shall touch its hallowed chords, with odours bland

Of some sweet incense. "I will rest in thee:"

He said, "one strain of thine and I shall be

Lapped in a happier calm than dreams can know;"

And thrilled the strings to music soft and slow

Like fountain ripples. But the unfinished strain

Broke suddenly; a shiver as of pain

Crept through the unwilling lute, and then, while still

Unconsciously his fingers sought their will

Of answering sound, the few forced notes were sighs,

And a chord snapped. As when on a sudden dies

A spent-out lamp, and the strange presence there

Of instant night appals us unaware,

The silence fell.

  But then the sign he knew,

And, bending o'er the wounded lute, "Oh true,

Oh ever loving! Does there then lurk hidden

Some master of the lute to judge unbidden,

Stealing my music into greedy ears?"

He said: then pondered, "Nay, for whoso hears

Among these desolate wilds can ill have fed
A learner's soul on music and have read
Its costly lore and gained its difficult skill.
What then? Is some dense thicket of the hill
Covert for crouching robbers while they wait,
Like the motionless eager pard, their time to sate
Their blood-greed at a bound?" and in this mind
Bade search be made along the banks to find
What evil-doers cowered in their dark lair
Beneath the clustered junipers, or where
The matted copse left space or the tall throng
Of river-reeds a shelter.

     But ere long
A voice gave answer, "Make not search, my lord,
For ambushed foes. Here is no robber horde:
But the poor woodman carrying home his load,
Whom the quick tempest stayed upon his road,
Heard the air sweet with sound, and in surprise
Lingered to judge thy lute's rich harmonies."

 "Brave folly!" quoth Yu-Pe-Ya. "Do ye mark?
This boor, that hews his wood from dawn to dark,
Will judge the subtle lute!" and carelessly

Bade harm him not but let him homeward hie.

    But the man heard, and answered, grave and clear,
"I'll said, my lord; unworthy words I hear
For such as thou to speak. And art thou then
A master minstrel, yet wilt measure men
By only rich and low? But I, who, born
A peasant of these mountains, think no scorn
To toil from dawn to dark and hew my wood,
Bid thee remember wisdom's brotherhood:"
Then rose from out the shadow of a rock
And took the jagged path the wild goats' flock
Had broken round the hill, and turned not back,
Nor lingered with his load. Up the steep track
Yu-Pe-Ya watched him lessening till, when now
A step or two should carry him round the brow,
Lost out of sight, "After him, men," he cried,
"Yu-Pe-Ya prays him turn and here abide
Some while in converse—say it, and that indeed
I know him for no common rustic. Speed!
Quick! ere ye lose his trace." then turned and went
Silently to his cabin, as discontent
At his own will.

With breathless speed they ran,

And climbed the difficult track, and reached the man

Just ere too late. "So be it, if my lord will;"

He said, "for I would hear that perfect skill

Upon that perfect wondrous lute once more."

But they looked scornfully on the garb he wore,

The peasant's leafy thatch of palm-bracts twined①

For cloak and hood against the rains and wind,

The plaited straw-shoes, and the belt untanned

Whence hung the axe, and in his tawny hand

A pointed staff to prop his load and stay

His heavy steps. And all along the way

They schooled him how to bear him: "So, and so,

Look and reply; and first, when thou shalt go

Before his presence, bow thee till thy face

Has touched the floor, nor lift thee from the place

Until he bid." And, listening, he forbore

To answer them till, on the deck, once more

Roughly they warned him, then bade enter where

Their lord awaited him. "Nay, have a care,

---

① The peasants of the north of China make of the bracts of a species of palm hats and a cloak called Soe. In some southern parts of China similar garments are made from bamboos and broadleaved grasses. "Le Luth Brisé," M. Pavie's translation, says that Tse-Ky "portait sur sa tête un bonnet d'écorce de bambou et sur toute sa personne des vêtements d'herbe tressée;" but I have assumed that Yu-Pe-Ya's journey was through northern scenery.

Good friends," he said, "lest ye should too much lack

The courtesy ye teach. And now stand back

While seemly I prepare," and leisurely

Doffed his smirched outer gear and laid it by,

And wiped the earth-clods from his shoes, then, dressed

In the blue homespun cap① and scanty vest

Of the poor mountain peasant, went sedate

Before Yu-Pe-Ya seated in his state.

And deep obeisance made he, but as one

Who honouring looks for honour, nor fell prone

And did the servant's homage rightly owed

By lowly men to princes, but abode,

His reverent greeting done, erect and still,

Waiting reply.

    Yu-Pe-Ya liked it ill;

But yet, since he had made the man his guest,

He could not drive him forth, but mused how best

Pass by his boldness till its cause he knew,

And would not claim nor yet forgive his due.

"Good friend," he said, and waved his hand in the air,

---

① Chinese civility would forbid him to uncover his head.

"Thou art excused thine homages. Sit there,

And answer freely;" then, perplexed, delayed,

Scanning his garb and mien before he said,

"But art thou he who spoke? And didst thou lance

A boast by hazard or by ignorance,

Or dost thou claim in sober truth for thine

The secrets of the lute, the art divine

Of princes and of sages?"

                    "It was I

Who spake erewhile," the woodman made reply,

"And so much lute-craft have I as to love

The ancient song that reached me in the grove."

"What song?" Yu-Pe-Ya asked.

           He simled, "the lay

Of Yen-Oey perished in his summer day,

The lay Ni-Chan①, the holiest, made, and wept

---

① M.Pavie makes Tse-Ky quote the dirge said to be composed by Ni-Chan(Confucius)upon the premature death of Yen-Oey in these words:
    "Quelle douleur!Yen-Oey est mort à la fleur de l'âge.
    A cette pensée les hommes sentent leurs cheveux blanchir,
    Et Comme il se contentait de sa vie misérable au fond des rues pauvres et obscures,
    Il a pu conserver la renommée d'un sage accompli pendant des siècles infinis."

For the young brother sage that earlier slept;

The song thy lips forbore, but sweet and low

thy clear lute uttered. Are the words not so?

'So soon asleep! Now must the coming years

  Weep ignorantly their loss they cannot know

And life miss ever what hath never been:

We weep to-day, let theirs be sadder tears

Who have not seen thee near, as we have seen,

  Who shall but learn a hope died long ago.

Alas for flowers untimely winds have broken,

  That should have scattered seed of following flowers!

  Alas for ruin of unbuilded towers!

Alas for ripening words that die unspoken!

  But let them weep with sadder tears than ours

  Who shall but learn a hope died long ago,

    A world's hope long ago.'

But the strain stayed not to be the final close:

When the sweet refrain's cadenced minor rose

With 'let them weep,' the shivering lute refused;

Then fifth chord shrieked and snapped."

                    "Yet one long used

By a customary chance to every note

And married word might come to know by rote

An intricate air, and be but so possessed

Of its true worth as the numb page, impressed

With some choice sentence, of that wealth it owns"

Yu-Pe-Ya thought; then, in the careful tones

Of one who knows not whom he speaks with yet,

He said, "Too rare the times when I have met

And talked in equal hours with one of those

Whom we call master minstrels; one who knows

The answering rhythms, the complex harmonies,

The difficult skill, knows the deep mysteries

And far traditions of the lute; who hears

As lovers see, to whom each look appears

Familiar long and yet a fresh surprise

Teaching new beauty to accustomed eyes.

And if thou be of these 'tis well. Yet how

May I discern thee, save thou answer now

Some question put to try thee?"

                    "At thy will,"

The woodman said, and smiled.

                    Then with the skill

Of but a master did Yu-Pe-Ya try

The woodman's lore, he with like skill reply,

And the immortal history told aright

Of him who, praying in the silent night,

Beheld the five white flames droop slowly down,

The souls of the five planet stars, and crown

An Ouchang tree with light, and understood

Heaven's gift to Earth in that one tree of the wood

The phoenix lights on coming from the gods,

The one tree of the world in whose green rods

The body of the lute grows on and on

Through air and rains and ripening of the sun

Until the perfect moment when, maybe,

One comes who knows the signs, hews down the tree,

Measures and parts, refusing less or more,

So in a middle third finds the true core

Whence (as man's soul came not from more or less

But out of equalness) from equalness

The lute's soul, sound, is born and is a part

Of the body grown in the tree which must by art

Be shaped and carven, yet which surely grew:

A lute before the gods, though no man knew,

While the green leaves were on it and the moss.

And then the chords he named of joy, love, loss,

Of hope, and wonder, that shrill chord of grief

That, thinking on his son, the maker chief

In the stillness of his dungeon gloom first strung,

And the strong chord of triumph which first rung

When Wou-Wang bade a thousand minstrels vie

To shout his victory to earth, seas, and sky.

And the lute's times he told; the ill hours when

Its voice must be forborne by reverent men;

The fair hours for its wooing; when alone,

And when among the listeners, or as one

Who tells close secrets to the friends that know,

The player's hand should set the lute aglow

With living music and the pulse of sound.

And still he answered. "Yet might one be found,"

Yu-Pe-Ya mused, "who, feeding full on books,

As a hungry pool sucks in its nursing brooks

And sends no freshening streamlets forth again,

Has gathered many words of many men,

Adding their wisdoms to his witlessness."

He said, "Methinks I cannot call thee less

Than trebly learned. Yet, (the tale is old

And thou wilt know it) once when Ni-Chan told

A secret to his lute the notes were heard

By Yen-Oey and he knew each hidden word:

But is there one like Yen-Oey to-day,

And has indeed Yu-Pe-Ya found him?"

"Play;"

The woodman spake, "and if, like beaded pearls

Strung on a hidden thread, whose coils and curls

Tend one way variously and do but show

To take of their free selves the way they go,

The wantoning notes intangibly obey

Some one informing thought, I dare essay

An easy riddle with its answer told."

Yu-Pe-Ya took the lute, and clear and bold

The loud notes pealed, while overhead the crew

Were still and waited for the words. "What clue,

Woodman, hast thou now touched, on which have run

The beaded pearls?" he said, the strain being done.

The woodman answered him, "I knew a thought

That rose up from the valley clefts and sought

The naked hill-tops near the stars: I heard

From far below the waves of sighs that stirred

The upmost belts of pines where, after night,

A weary wind went dying. And the light

Of sanguine dawn was there; else, solitude."

    Yu-Pe-Ya spoke not back, but marvelling viewed

The rough-clad guest, and touched the lute once more.

    The woodman answered him, "The distant roar

Of leaping waters left behind, the sweep

Of a resistless river, strong and deep,

Onward and onward with an even might

Along its silent levels; and in sight,

Far off, before it a dim infinite sea:

And lo, Yu-Pe-Ya, know we what shall be?

Or can we tarry on the way we wend

With its so certain yet uncertain end?"

    And mutely earnest, gazing in his eyes,

Yu-Pe-Ya paused awhile like one who tries

A question in himself and scarce can tell

If faith or doubt be more impossible.

Then "Yet," he said, "O master, hear again:

Canst thou know this?" And 'twas the fitful strain

He made at noonday where the lilies shone.

    The woodman said, "I knew one passing on
Mid beauty that makes sad, and too fair joys,
Since he must lose them. And I heard the voice
Of summer birds, leaves merry on their trees,
Bright waters rippling; and yet under these
Dim whispers of farewell. And the sweet pain
Of present ecstasy, knowing it must wane,
Thrilled in my heart; and then the long regret
Of one who going ere nightfall gazes yet
On home or mother or the friend he had.
Delight was all, and all delight was sad."

    At that Yu-Pe-Ya rose. "Oh joy!" he cried;
"My guardian gods have sent you to my side.
thou wondrous master minstrel, man inspired,
I thank the gods for thee," and sudden, fired
With transport as of lighting unaware
On some dear long-lost kinsman, held him there
Clasped in his greeting arms. And then they two
Exchanged the answering reverences due
By the fixed rites when stranger equals meet,
And named their names. And in the upper seat

Yu-Pe-Ya placed Tse-Ky, and called for wine

And drank the cup of honour to him. "Thine,

Tse-Ky, a boon to give me;" made he prayer,

"Stay with me these few hours while in the air

The night stars rule until to-morrow be.

Let us hold converse, thou and I, thus, free

From hankering ears that know not and the scan

Of judging ignorances, and man to man

Take thought aloud. For me too soon will break

The morrow that divides us."

       So they spake

Through the still night together. Twice ere day

The captain came: "The clouds have rolled away;

Shall we put off?" and "A light breeze blows fair;

Shall we start now?" Yu-Pe-Ya bade forbear,

And turned him to Tse-Ky. And still their speech

Waxed yet more earnest; and both seemed to teach

And both to learn the things they most had known,

As though 'twere not to know alone

And each had missed the other heretofore.

And all the while Yu-Pe-Ya wondered more.

At length he said, "What fate or whim, Tse-Ky,

Controls thee thus amiss? Thou who shouldst be.

In palaces and schools and city ways

Where'er renown is loudest and sweet praise

Of thankful eyes most numerous, named and known

Our newest glory perfect and alone,

Why art thou here, a peasant hewing wood?"

He said, "My hatchet singly earns the food

Of father and of mother old and spent:

They toiled, I toil in turn and am content."

"Right, noble friend," Yu-Pe-Ya said; yet sighed

"'Tis pity on a star that far and wide

Should flash its glories, lost away from sight

Of the large world that would have loved its light,

Uselessly shining in a pathless haze."

"Not so:" Tse-Ky spoke back, "the lost star's rays

Behind the mist make light in one poor spot,

One lowly home where else the light were not.

Trust me, Yu-Pe-Ya, while those dear ones live

My joys are with them here: I would not give

My daily cares for them in change to win

My place among the princes of great Tsin,

Not to be throned to-morrow in the halls

Of counsel and of judgment, where the walls

Glow with the gilded titles of the wise."

  Yu-Pe-Ya, seeing him with thoughtful eyes,

Grasping his ready hand, "Friend, friend will found,

I dare not blame thy choice. Oh nobly bound

To an ignoble fortune, thou hast won

My closest heart thy lover. If the sun,

Who presently with his unwelcome glow

Will scare the kindly night and see me go

To life that knows thee not, see thee remain

A drudge among these wilds, yet not in vain

Have we two met who never more shall be

As though the other were not. Far from thee

I shall remember, 'Would he praise or chide?'

Thou in the toilsome days, and lone beside

The old folks dozing, weary with their age,

In winter evenings, brooding o'er the page

Thou hast forgot to turn, wilt think, 'Ah well,

The world holds one who knows me.' We shall tell

Our counted years from now, as women do

From when their firstborn came."

                    At that there grew

The silence of full hearts till, pouring wine,

Yu-Pe-Ya spake, "The eastward moon gives sign

Of morning and farewells to be, but now

Drink to me, talk again. What springs hast thou

Who yet mayst go by springtime?"

                    "Since my birth

Have twenty-seven springs renewed the earth

And made my spring brown summer now."

                    "Why then,"

Yu-Pe-Ya said, "I pass your years by ten.

Elder and younger brother meet to-night.

Oh brother, let it be; let troth and rite

Seal our adoption perfect and avowed."

  Tse-Ky half smiled; "Some little night born cloud

Bedims Yu-Pe-Ya's vision: with the day

Will come the keen-eyed waking. Brothers, nay.

My lord, I am a woodman and no more,

thou art a prince and ruler; this night o'er

We go our unlike ways and are apart."

"And does Tse-Ky then in his inmost heart
So measure men by only rich and low?
And having known me does he scorn me so
As count me but the puppet of my state?
Yet judge me rather as a man whom Fate,
Dowering loose-handed with her common dross
He could have spared, has left for lifelong loss
Not to have ever known an equal friend.
And now, if she have brought him but to lend
These few brief hours then take, I would, Tse-ky
I had not seen thy face."

     So, with the plea
Of a great heart that cries towards its twin,
Yu-Pe-Ya urged him. And they plighted kin,
Burning the incense, promising the vow;
And took them witnesses.

     And "Brother, now"
The woodman said, they two alone once more,
"The place of honour that was mine before.
Being thy stranger, is no longer meet;
Let me, the younger, take the second seat,"
And meekly placed himself. And each of them

Wondered like one who finds a priceless gem

And, so made rich past count, thinks, "What had been

If I had glanced aside and had not seen?"

And scarce can feel his joy for its surprise.

Yu-Pe-Ya then: "Ah brother, in the skies

The stars are not alone, and join their song;

But in the crowded world a life-time long

The singer goes his solitary way

And has not found his fellow." And this lay

He sang for gladness, and the lute's sweet chords

Spoke softer than the voice of loving words.

"Seeds with wings, between earth and sky

  Fluttering, flying;

 Seeds of a lily with blood-red core

  Breathing of myrrh and giroflore:

Where winds drop them there must they lie,

  Living or dying.

Some to the garden, some to the wall,

  Fluttering, falling;

 Some to the river, some to the earth:

  Those that reach the right soil get birth;

None of the rest have lived at all.—

 Whose voice is calling:

'Here is soil for winged seeds that near,

 Fluttering, fearing,

Where they shall root and burgeon and spread.

Lacking the heart-room the song lies dead.

Half is the song that reaches the ear,

 Half is the hearing?'

Oh, the soil and the heart and the hearing found!

My song in thy heart, the seed in the ground!"

 And presently, "No father guards his girl,

No husband the young wife, the secret pearl

Hidden within our home, with such a zeal,

As I this lute whose strings may never feel

Another hand than mine; never till now;

But, brother who art worthy, take it thou,

And let me hear thy heart in its dear voice."

 "Ah, no," he said, "when I would most rejoice,

Most sorrow, or most hope, I not like thee

Can breathe aloud, as the wind-harp on the tree

Answers all gales with sweetness, to their kind,

Of air-born music; but my tongueless mind

Within the secret silences of thought

Accepts the urging voices ever brought

To him who listens in this world of ours

From all things—sky, and river, and small flowers,

And gossip birds, and these dusk hills that brood

Beneath the cloud-wracks, and the murmuring wood;

From stir of toil, from children's causeless glee,

From books, from mine own heart, from Heaven maybe;

Know them, and has no answer save to know."

    Fingering the lute, "Such tongueless mind, I trow,

Speaks itself more than to man's tongue belongs;

The heart that sings not has the sweeter songs;

And, whoso sang them, they are thrice thine own,"

Yu-Pe-Ya said: then, in the sudden tone

Of one who finds the thought he did not seek,

"Nay, and shall one like thee indeed not speak,

If he keep silence, yet in many a voice

Of minstrel men who in his strength rejoice

As the blossoms in the root's strength where it lies

Deep under earth, and they shine in the skies—

Of minstrel men beside him who declare

(He and themselves aware or unaware)

His thought by theirs, and most repeat him then

When most they are themselves? Brother, ah when

Shall they who need thee in our distant plains

Have found thee in thy mountains?"

                "There remains

The day that is to come," Tse-Ky replied.

"Yea!" said Yu-Pe-Ya, "by-and-by is wide

To the halt traveller who asks for now."

"And yet," the other said, "men scarce allow

Now's self so clearly theirs as by-and-by:

To-day is always gone, to-morrow nigh."

From the respondent lute a prelude rang,

Lingering, then firmer, and Yu-Pe-Ya sang:

        "Waiting, waiting.'Tis so far

          To the day that is to come:

        One by one the days that are

          All to tell their countless sum;

        Each to dawn and each to die —

What so far as by-and-by?

　　Waiting, waiting. 'Tis not ours,

　　　This to-day that flies to fast:

　　Let them go, the shadowy hours

　　Floating, floated, into Past.

　　Our day wears to morrow's sky—

　　What so near as by-and-by?"

"Is the strain mine or thine?" he said; and then
Struck the still quivering chords and sang again:

　　"A bird and flower upon the tree,

　　　Sweet peony① and oriole,

　　　Each of them a perfect soul,

　　　Song and sweetness manifest:

　　The bird and flower we love the best

　　Side by side on the tall tree.

'Flower who art sunlight and fire, flower who art perfume and joy,

　　Sweetest of sweet,

Ah for the gift withheld! Ah for the given gift's alloy!

---

① The Moutan or tree peony, of which the fragrance and beauty are lauded to the skies by Chinese writers.

Why must thy spirit exhale only in beauty and breath?

Ah for the voice thou hast not! I by thy side on the tree,

Telling the world of love, pain, and all raptures that be,

Raptures of laughter and life, raptures of tears and death,

Singing my heart to heaven, singing to earth at my feet;

  Silence in thee.'

'Bird who art dew-drops and flame, bird who art rapture and song,

  Sweetest of sweet,

Lo there's a voice part mine, songs that to me too belong,

Songs that grew of my growth, voice that has breathed my breath.

Bird that while I sit mute singest beside on the tree,

Hast thou ever a song taking no perfume of me?

Give forth my sweetness in song; bird, thou art singing for both,

Singing our hearts to heaven, singing to earth at our feet.

  My voice in thee.'

  On the tree-top side by side,

   Sweet oriole and peony;

   Music rings through earth and sky,

   Sweet and sweet in sweetness lost:

   The flower and bird we love the most,

  On the tree-top side by side."

And while he sang a tremulous flickering blush

Shook through the pallid east: and the wide flush

Of fiery dawn had set the clouds aflame

When he made end. From the red verge up came

The smouldering sun and brightened to round gold;

And on and on to where, grown white and cold,

Tired stars died singly round the moon's thin ghost,

The daylight leaped, and moon and stars were lost

Into their flooded sky, and everywhere

The morning world stood clear against the air.

On deck the wakened crew began to stir,

And calls, and tramplings, and the thud and whirr

Of loosening canvas, jarred and shook the beams:

Even so have exiles, roused from better dreams,

Wearily waking on the cabin bed,

Heard the rough din of starting overhead.

Tse-Ky arose, and would have given goodbye:

Yu-Pe-Ya took a cup and brimmed it high

With scented wine: "Ah, yet a moment long.

Pledge me this cup;" and gave, and, grasping strong

His brother's hand, he gazed with yearning eyes,

And felt the dizzy pang of that surprise

Which is in every parting, when at last

We know that come we in the moments past

Saw far remote by all the infinite

Of moments counted then. "Oh the despite

Of such a meeting!" sighed he, "since 'tis o'er.

And oh the wasted night! for so much more

I should have learned of thee, I should have told;

And now we part! Ah brother!"

                                                     In his hold

The golden cup was trembling, down his face

Did the rebellious tear-drops slowly chase,

One after one, and mingle in the draught,

But noting spake Tse-Ky, till, the cup quaffed,

He kissed Yu-Pe-Ya's hand: "Farewell, my lord;

Brother, farewell." and with no other word

Made reverence and turned him round to go.

   Yu-Pe-Ya said, "I will not lose thee so.

Share but my voyage then. So few days still

And the great town is reached; and at thy will

This ship shall bring thee back."

                                              "It may not be:"

The woodman answered, "they have need of me,

My father and my mother."

　　　　　　　"Yet to go

Some little day or two, no more than so,

Then by their side to serve them as before?

Oh friend, go to them, ask them. 'Twere no more

Than to have flown a moment from the nest,

As the nest's guardian flies that loves it best,

And bring new gladness with the swift return.

Will thou not ask, Tse-Ky?"

　　　　　　　He said, "I yearn

As a caged bird might yearn for room to fly

To now go forth with thee. But friend, put by

The idle tempting: old they are and lone,

Having but me; they must not feel me gone."

Then spake Yu-Pe-Ya, "Yes, it may not be:

thou hast said well. But I return to thee.

Not soon; but when 'tis summer and next year,

When this ripe month of leaves and gold is hear

Scattering red rose-bays on thy hill as now,

Watch down the river for the carven prow

Where my devices glitter. Trust me not

If half the month be wanted ere in this spot

I moor my bark and hail thee on thy strand

Waiting as I wait till our welcoming hand

Can grasp the other's, thou beside me thus

And the great river throbbing under us,

And all to-day be come to us again

Save but this parting." And the brothers then

Changed last farewell at length: yet even at last,

And while Tse-Ky in patient sorrow passed,

And gave no backward look, beyond the door,

Again Yu-Pe-Ya stayed him: "One word more.

Yield me my brother's due our bond has made,

Nor scorn me in my gift," and sudden laid

Two golden ingots in his hands. Perplexed,

Tse-Ky a moment pondered, but the next

He looked upon Yu-Pe-Ya: "Brother, yes."

Then gained the deck and donned his leafy dress,

And girt his axe, and in his hand he took

And poised the mountain staff; then, with one look

Answering Yu-Pe-Ya where he followed him,

Strode to the prow and from its outer rim

Leaped on the shore, and climbed a little height,

And sat to watch the ship pass out of sight.

奥古斯塔·韦伯斯特《俞伯牙摔琴谢知音》

And so Yu-Pe-Ya went his way alone.

And earth and skies were fair, but there was gone

A beauty from them and from the fresh air

A something of its fragrance; and the glare

Of noonday vexed him, and the dusk seemed chill.

And ever he mused, "If he were with me still

How would he praise this loveliness with me, "

And in the joy he had must yet more see

The joy he lacked that felt all incomplete.

So reached he the last port; and then, to meet

His king that waited for him, rode amain

Through the long highways of the corn-clad plain

To the great royal city. And the roar

Of thousand welcomes shook the streets and bore

His name into the skies, and any man

Who saw him pass felt taller by a span

And told his neighbours after as a thing

Scoring to his more merit; and the king

So greeted him as never heretofore

One not a king, and the wrought ring he wore

Put on his hand and gave him from his side

His jewelled sword whereof the sheath was dyed

In royal colours, and he made yet more

His riches and the honours which he bore.

   Then, dwelling in his city, in his home
Amid the wonted splendours, where would come
The thronging suppliants and the guests elate
And singers and grave sages, proud to wait
If he should lend a moment long his ear,
Where, did he speak, a hundred longed to hear,
And, did he listen, a hundred longed to speak,
He (as, when out-door airs have long been bleak,
In rooms the captured summer still embowers,
We sicken of the breath of house-born flowers
And yearn for some one blossom of the spring
Green from its hedgerow where the wild birds sing)
Yearned for the far-off voice, the heart not there,
And needed but Tse-Ky.

                           The trees grew bare;
And then grew rough with buds; and by and by
Had spread athwart the woods their canopy;
And now Yu-Pe-Ya, on a prosperous day
When the king's heart was glad, chose time to pray
Leave for his journey, and, at first denied,
(For the king loved him ever at this side)

Told of his bond-tie with the peasant man

Whose home was mid the steeps of Niao-Ngan

In the wild confines of Tsou's farthest shire,

And of his promise and his heart's desire.

So the king gave him leave. And "Tell Tse-Ky,"

He said, "there wait him for the love of thee,

And for his worth thou say'st, welcome and grace

The day that he shall look upon my face."

Because Yu-Pe-Ya said, "When to the last

His duty is fulfilled and they have passed

Into the sleep that needs no watcher by,

Who are too old to change their wonted sky

And are too old to lack him in their home

And, having lost him, live, then will he come."

And like a man who in some alien clime

Perforce has waited wearying for the time

When the might seek his home, and, hurrying there,

Sees every landmark never yet so fair

And longs but to have passed it, making haste

Yu-Pe-Ya now in joy the way retraced

He came last summer sorrowing. But the tide

Pushed at his vessel; from the counter side

The river breeze blew steady. Then at length,

A rugged giant sleeping in his strength

Among his lesser brethren, the black height

Of Niao-Ngan loomed in the pallid light

Before the day-break reddens; and the wood

And the brown headland where Tse-Ky had stood

Shone near before them in the evening sun;

And as night fell the little creek was won.

And all was still. "Tse-Ky," Yu-Pe-Ya cried,

"Tse-Ky, my brother, here!" But none replied,

And nothing stirred along the darkening shore.

And on he waited till the grey dusk wore

Into void blackness ere, with the long sigh

Of one constrained to let a hope go by,

He owned unto himself, "He hath not come:"

And went, and in the cabin's blazoned dome

Sat lonely in his chafed and wondering mood,

Unwont to not have had the thing he would.

But when the uprisen moon ere long had rent

The blackness round the stars and, straight, it went,

And there was lustre of a silver day,

He came upon the deck and, bidding lay

The pile of silken cushions at the prow

Where fell the shadow of a cypress bough,

Rested and watched the stillness; and him-seemed

As though he lived again that night, or dreamed,

Wherein he knew Tse-Ky. And he was here,

Lo! on the very night of all the year,

Told by the tale of circling moons and days

(So careful chance and willed it), but his gaze

Was vain along the shore, vain on the hill,

Asking Tse-Ky. "Why doth he linger still?

Or hath he then forgot?" he inly cried.

And then: "My brother hath not well espied

My flag and my devices; and there go

So many passing vessels to and fro

On this broad river-road, how should he note

Mine in the many? Let the sounds but float

Of my remembered lute through the still air

Into his woods; and maybe reach him there

While now he wanders looking down the stream

Time upon time to see my sails, agleam

In the white moon-ray, pressing here to-night;

And instant he will know the voice aright

And rush to me as, boisterous leaping out,

River to river after ended drought:"

Then called his pages, and with speed they brought

An ivory table with the casket wrought

Of scented woods and set with precious jade

Wherein the lute was locked, then by it laid

The golden censer breathing perfumed clouds.

But when, unfolded from its broidered shrouds,

The lute was wooed to speak, the strings denied

Their vibrant resonance and but replied

With muffled whispers, save when one long wail

Rang from the chord of Wen-Wang. Then he, pale

And chill with sick surprise, dropped in his lap

The voiceless lute, and thought. "Some woeful hap,"

He mused, "withholds my brother: the lute moans

And will not call him; and its tremulous tones

Are a great sorrow's; and that long shriek rang.

From the sixth chord, the grief chord of Wen-Wang.

Surely my brother mourns. Ah, in his home,

Taking an easy booty, Death has come;

Tse-Ky sits guardian by the sacred bed

Of father or of mother lying dead.

Oh, leal and loving, couldst thou choose but break

Thy faith to me for such thy duty's sake?

Now let the slow night hasten and pass by

And longed-for morning dawn into the sky,

Morning when I shall reach thee and be glad."

    And sorrowing because his friend was sad
Yet must he hush a little mingling thought
Too much like joy, springing to mind unsought
(As an unwelcome weed that yet is fair),
Because Tse-Ky was robbed of half the care
That held him in his wilds, and when we see
One yellow leaf of two drop from the tree
We look not for the other long to cling.

    And, fain for sleep to hide the stars and bring
By ignorance of night a speedier day,
He sought his couch. But all the hours he lay
Troubled and eager, counting how they went
Slower and slower and night was never spent.
Then when at last the first wan glimmer crept
Athwart dark skies where the sunk moon had slept
He started with the throb of one released
From some long bondage on a sudden ceased;
And rose and clad himself alone in haste
In simple garb. And in his belt he placed
A purse that held in gold ten acres' worth,
Thinking, "Where death comes ever comes there dearth.

Tse-Ky may need it for the present stress."

Then he went forth; and from the obsequious press

Of prompt attendants waiting sign or look

One little favourite page along he took

To follow him and bear the lute. And so

The two were landed on the beach below;

And up the track along the steep they went

And turned into the wood; and pungent scent

Of the warm pines, and sweet exuberant air

Of morning on the hills, and everywhere

Unclosing blossoms and birds' wakening joy

And insects' hum and twitter, filled the boy

With heady glee, and scarce he could restrain

His steps to measure nor his voice refrain

From little glad exclaimings; and well pleased

Yu-Pe-Ya marked, for his own heart was seized

With even such a lightness, and he smiled

And loosed the blithesome prattle of the child

With playful questions. So they followed on

Some while their winding pathway, and anon

Came on a small green plot of cultured land

Girdled with mountains; thence to either hand

Eastward and westward the cleft pathway went

By a low hill that jutted prominent,

Like a headland in a sea.

        "And now, which road?"
Yu-Pe-Ya cried, perplexed, and there abode
Pondering in vain to choose the likeliest;
For if the village stood to east or west
Was nought to show him. Where a great stone lay
In the shadow of a cliff upon the way
He sat to wait if any would pass by
And tell him whitherward his steps should hie
To reach the woodman's home. And from the right
Soon a white-bearded peasant came in sight,
Leaning upon his staff and moving slow
As one that drags a burden on, although
None bore he save the toy that lightly hung
Upon his arm, the little basket strung
Of shining reeds.

        And, when he had come close,
For homage to his years Yu-Pe-Ya rose
And bent his head before him ere he brake
His courteous silence; and the old man spake,
First making calm and seemly reverence,
And asked his need. And, when he heard, "From hence

These parted roads, " he answered "round the hill

In one like aim and, east or west, go still

By equal distance only to Tsy-Hien.

But half our few huts stand in the ravine,

Half on the ledge above: by this way go

To the high village, that best gains the low."

"Aye?" quoth Yu-Pe-Ya, musing: "How to tell

If in the high or in the low he dwell? "

And the old man, not loth to talk a while,

Noted his dubious mood with a quaint smile,

And "Nay," he said, "if chance or choice be guide

And guide amiss, small evil need betide;

A clamber down or up a rugged lane

And wrong comes right with little loss or pain.

But, stranger sir, if it shall please you, speak

His name you look for: trust me where to seek.

I have lived very long, sir; only three

Among our village folk count years with me,

And all the others I might almost say

I have dandled on my knees or taught to play;

Man, woman, child, no soul is living here

But knows me and I know. Aye, many's the year

I've been among them—time to know them all—

I am old enough to stand by and see fall

Good-timber to the axe that I had known

Saplings just to my breast ere I was grown;

And look, that moss-caked bridge o'er which you came,

I saw it making. Sir, what is his name?"

"A woodman named Tse-Ky," Yu-Pe-Ya said.

The old man looked on him: "My son is dead,"

He answered slowly; and then hid his face

And wept aloud. But, rooted in his place,

Yu-Pe-Ya stood and spoke not. And "My son!"

The old man sobbed, "Ah me! what had I done

To lose thee ere I died! Sir, this Tse-Ky

Was my one child, the light of life to me

And to my wife, our joy, our help, our stay;

But he is gone. A stranger came this way,

Passing along the river, a year since

In the summer time, a great and learned prince,

And lighted on Tse-Ky and so they knit

A solemn friendship, and in pledge of it

Yu-Pe-Ya gave my son a gift of gold.

And he bought books, and toiling as of old,

To earn our bread, all day, he through the night

Was lost in study, and the morning light

Would oftenest find him watching. So ere long

And ere we ignorant parents saw aught wrong,

Being unlettered folk, he sapped his strength,

So fell into a wasting and at length

He died."

  At that Yu-Pe-Ya gave a cry,

Piercing as though torn forth by agony

Of some great wrench by torture, and he sank,

Quivering and white, upon a ploughed-up bank,

With tightening fingers clutching in the moulds,

And gasped for tears that came not. As beholds

A child, who witless sets the sluice-gates wide

Of his father's garden weir, the sudden tide

Rush forth he knows not why and, breaking bounds,

Dash at the hedge and waste the flowery grounds,

The old man saw, and wondered "Who is this?

What grief have I awaked?" "Himself it is,

The lord of Yu-Pe-Ya's self," into his ear

Whispered the little page. Then he drew near

And would have soothed him while he held his head

Leaned on his bosom; but Yu-Pe-Ya said

"Comfort me not, but tell me more of him.

Alas my brother! when the twilight dim

Grew dimmer while I called thee, did my cries

But vex thy patient ghost? When my strained eyes

In the pale moonlight sought thee, wast thou there,

Helpless besides me, dumb and bodiless air?

Oh me disloyal to chafe at thy delay

And doubt and seek excuses for thy stay

As though blot of unfaith on thee *could* lie!

How knew I not thy death? But thou to die!

Old man, how long ago."

                    Then ere could come

The peasant's answer, "Stay," he said, "thy home

Is childless; let me for my brother's sake

Be called thine other son, and henceforth take

The name of father from me. He, meseems,

Will know, and gentlier dream the dead man's dreams,

Trusting ye both to me, whom his true arm

No more can labour for and fend from harm.

Now, father, tell me all."

                    "What shall I say,

Who knew not till the end?" spake Lao-Pay,

The white-haired peasant. "But the night he died

He spake to us mute watchers by his side—

Father and mother, scarcely even at last

Perceiving it must be—'Dears, it is past.

My life has not been long, and could I choose

I yet would live, part that you might not lose

The due and happy service I have done

And live your last days lone, without a son:

Part for some hopes I had. But now I lie,

The struggle and the bitterness gone by,

Patiently in Death's arms and am content.

Give me farewell, for I am well-nigh spent

And sleep is coming. Bury me where the hill

Curves and looks down the river; so I still

Shall keep the tryst, waiting Yu-Pe-Ya there.'

And, sir, we buried him as was his prayer;

'Tis near the pathway, underneath a pine—

A long way sooth for these old limbs of mine,

But since it pleased him. And he there has slept

A hundred days; and now the tryst is kept,

For he was lying there as you came by

Hard by the pathway. Aye, 'Twas young to die;

But who can tell the future? He is dead

Who should have closed my eyes, and I instead

Go my sad way to my son's grave to light

These gilded papers in the mourner's rite."

"And I will go with thee," Yu-Pe-Ya cried.
And they together, slowly, side by side,
Went riverward; and the old man still talked,
Telling his pitiful story as they walked,
Pleased to be heard and weeping o'er his dole.

And so they came to their fond errand's goal,
And saw a solitary earthed-up tomb,
Where now the little weeds began to bloom,
Beneath a sombre pine that singly stood
In a slant blossomy jungle of the wood;
And far beneath the silver furlongs shone
Of the great river winding on alone.

"Tse-Ky," Yu-Pe-Ya cried, "see, I am here,
Tse-Ky, my brother! Through the impatient year
Did never I know more worth in any day
Then for a stepping-stone upon my way
To this day, and was this day to be so?
Do we thus keep the tryst?" And his strong woe
Broke like a tempest o'er him. And where near
Poor folk were gathering faggots did they hear

The strangling sobs, and, curious and amazed,

Came and stood not far off and, whispering, gazed,

Shouldering each other in a bashful row,

And "Lo, a stranger of the towns!" and, "Lo,

His goodly dress! Some rich great man, may be.

What ails him to cry out on our Tse-Ky?"

Then Lao-Pay unrolled the golden leaves

Wherewith the living tells the dead he grieves[①],

And with him knelt Yu-Pe-Ya, and they prayed

And set the leaves aflame, and weeping paid

Their sad memorial homages. And now

Yu-Pe-Ya took the lute. "Speak for me, thou"

He said, and with shrill sweetness pierced the skies

And made the echoes song. In glad surprise

The faggot-gatherers heard, then praised the strain

And blithely took them to their task again,

Cracking loud jests; save one young child that wept

And asked its mother, as it closer crept

And clung upon her gown, "What have I done?

Why does the music scold me?"

---

① The sycee paper burnt by the Chinese at the tombs of their dead.

                    Then when none

Were left beside Yu-Pe-Ya save the lad,

His page, and Lao-Pay, "My heart was sad

As never yet," he said, "the while I played,

And all the sorrow that upon me weighed

Sounded more plain to me in my lament;

Meseemed that never yet my mind's intent

So thrilled my lute and spake articulate,

And it so wailed for me and his young fate

That wept I not for grief then must I weep

For hearing such a grief. And, lo, they leap

With boisterous antics as though I had rung

Some jig to tug their heels, and every tongue

Wags merry out of tune as loosed by wine!

What should it mean? Has then this skill of mine

Grown naught for anguish, and do my marred ears,

Hearing along the sound of inward tears,

Take merry notes for sighs and but betray

My senseless fingers, bidding them gainsay

My piteous will and mock me with ill mirth?"

   Said Lao-Pay "No coin has greater worth

Than what the land 'tis spent in has to sell;

No words, whate'er their wisdom, more can tell

Than what the hearer's wisdoms understand.

Here in our desert and unscholared land

We count all tunes are merry and for sport,

And work is over hard and time too short

For us to sit and learn to find a sense

In notes and chords and hear more difference

Than loud and soft and galloping and slow.

Myself, sir, in my young days, long ago,

I was a sort of judge and might have guessed,

But now my ears are dull, and like the rest

I could have thought 'Here's mirth on hand,' may be,

And helped it with a laugh, were't time for glee,

Though sooth the strain to me seemed sad, but then

I am sad myself, and 'tis the way with men

To reckon of without by what's within."

  But the page went and hushed their jocund din,

And they went deeper in the wood, and left

A silence after them. Forth from his cleft

A lizard stole and thought himself alone

Close at Yu-Pe-Ya's foot; on the flat stone

Where roughly painted shone the dead man's name,

In the still shade, a little wren, that came

Inquiring from her copse, perched confident,

Turning her neck and gazing, as intent,

On one and on the other of the twain

Who sat too still to fright her. Then again

Yu-Pe-Ya waked his lute, and, "Hear, Tse-Ky,"

He said, "Yu-Pe-Ya's dirge he makes for thee."

"Dead, my beloved! This small purple weed

    That grows upon thy grave shall have its time

To ripen and to wane, to bloom and seed;

But thou, strong doer, might'st not wait thy deed,

But thou, oh noblest, might'st not wait thy meed:

        Dead in thy prime!

Gone, my beloved! I that held thine hand

    Left sudden in a joyless waste alone!

I tossing on life's sea, and thou to stand

Hidden in the shadows of the silent strand.

Thou seeing me from where I may not land!

        Gone from me, gone!

Sleep well; but what for me who still must wake?

    Dream joys; but what for me who can but weep?

Oh, darkened days where never dawn shall break!

Oh, weary troth-plight I with sorrow make!

But thou, rest peaceful, care not for my sake.

  Dear, sleep thy sleep."

 Then, kissing the poor lute, he sighed "Farewell;
I need thee not; he is not who could tell
The thing thou wouldst have said, lie in his grave.
Farewell, I need thee not; I will not have
A friend except him dead, not even thee."
And, lifting it and calling on Tse-Ky,
Dashed it against the mound: the gold and jade
And carved and scented woods and gems inlaid
Lay in a thousand shreds; in one long shriek
The strings had rent apart.

     Afraid to speak
The old man saw, aghast, and fingered o'er
The tatters that should be a lute no more,
And sighed and shook his head and muttered low
"The pity of it! The pity of it, though!"
Yu-Pe-Ya said "Now will I go my way.
Old man, I dare not see thy home to-day,
My heart would break: but I will find thee there
Ere many weeks be gone. Thou art my care,
Thou and his mother. Spend this gold, and think

Tse-Ky hath given it thee. And buy a brink
About the grave of some few feet of ground,
That it be only ours, and fence it round
That no foot tread too near nor careless hand
Touch where he lies but we alone may stand,
We whom he loves beside him, many a day
Coming to tend his grave. And let them lay
Here at this feet, into the earth, this wreck
That was the lute we loved."

      Then on his neck
He fell, and kissed him as a son. "I go;"
He said to him, "and give thee farewell so
From son to father: for when I shall come
'T will be to carry to another home
My parents whom my brother gives to me,
And we shall hide in silence and be free,
And the loud world forget Yu-Pe-Ya's name.
For I am weary; and no more the same
Are joys or honours as in years gone by;
And hopes and nobler joys—lo, there they lie
To moulder with Tse-Ky. Now must the king
Release me from my greatness and I bring
A worn-out life back to my native earth:

Since in the fair dear land that gave me birth

Will I seek out some hushed, untrodden, nook

Where we may dwell and my tired eyes shall look

Upon the hills and plain my boyhood knew.

Farewell."

　　And almost he was lost to view

Adown the winding path amid the wood

Ere well the old man knew him gone, who stood,

While the quick page went leaping down the hill

To reach his master, dazed and fingering still

The fragments of the lute and, all in vain

Trying to piece them, murmured still again

"The pity of it! The pity of it though!"

Till in a while two specks passed far below,

Yu-Pe-Ya and the boy, towards the beach,

And dipped below the cliff. And in the reach,

That lay all wide and flashing in the sun,

Presently came a ship and glided on

Adown the river, motionless and swift,

Like a strong swan taking the current's drift.

思　考

1. 阅读奥古斯塔·韦伯斯特《俞伯牙摔琴谢知音》的英译文，谈谈你对此译文的看法。

2. 比较《俞伯牙摔琴谢知音》帕维法译文与英译文有何差异？

参考文献

- *YU-PE-YA'S LUTE, A Chinese Tale, in English Verse*, by Augusta Webster, London: Macmillan, 1874.

- *Selections from the Verse of Augusta Webster*, by Augusta Webster, London: Macmillan, 1893.

扩展阅读

- *Le Luth Brisé, nouvelle historique, Choix de Contes et Nouvelles*, Par Théodore Pavie, Paris: Librairie de Benjamin Duprat, 1839.

- "The Broken lute or Friendship's last offering by L. M. F.", *The Far East*, Vol. Ⅲ, No.3, 1877.

乔利《红楼梦》（第一回）

（1892—1893）

导　读

作为中国小说的巅峰之作，《红楼梦》自十九世纪三十年代已引起西方人的关注。如德庇时曾从《红楼梦》第三回"托内兄如海荐西宾　接外孙贾母惜孤女"中选译了描写贾宝玉的两首《西江月》，载于《皇家亚洲文会北华分会会刊》（Journal of the North-China Branch of the Royal Asiatic Society）1830 年第 2 卷。罗伯聃（Robert Thom，1807—1846）将《红楼梦》第六回"刘姥姥一进荣国府"的情节内容译成英文：Extract from the Hung-Low-Mung，收入其编撰的《正音撮要》（The Chinese Speaker）等等。但在乔利（H. Bencraft Joly, 1857—1898）《红楼梦》英译本问世之前，则多为《红楼梦》的零星译介。

乔利是英国在华外交官，曾任澳门领事馆副领事，他翻译的《红楼梦》英译本题为：Hung Long Meng: or The Dream of The Red Chamber。译文是《红楼梦》第一回至第五十六回的全译，分两册由别发洋行（Kelly & Walsh）于 1892 年和 1893 年出版，译本同时在香港、上海、横滨和新加坡发行，是《红楼梦》最早的译文单行本，也是《红楼梦》第一个较为系统的外文译本。

乔利在《红楼梦》英译本序言中曰：

"This translation was suggested not by any pretensions to range myself among the ranks of the body of sinologues, but by the perplexities and difficulties experienced by me as a student in Peking, when, at the completion of the Tzu Erh Chi, I had to plunge in the maze of the Hung Lou Meng.

Shortcomings are, I feel sure, to be discovered, both in the prose, as well as among the doggerel and uncouth rhymes, in which the text has been more adhered to than rhythm; but I shall feel satisfied with the result, if I succeed, even in the least degree, in affording a helping hand to present and future students of the Chinese language.[①]"

（"我翻译《红楼梦》，并不是要以汉学家自居，而是在北京学习《自迩集》时，亲身体会了学习汉语的困惑而艰难的过程。我必须再次置身于《红楼梦》的迷宫之中。

我自知，译文中无论是散体文的翻译或韵文的翻译都有很多缺点，而韵文的翻译我则更多地遵循文意而非韵律。但是，如果我的译文能对现在或将来学习汉语的人有些微的帮助，我亦可聊以自慰。"）

乔利将《红楼梦》比拟为"迷宫"，形象地描绘出翻译《红楼梦》的个中况味。而乔利为译本的定位或期许，则反映出乔利翻译《红楼梦》的动机主要是为外国人学习汉语提供帮助和借鉴。然而，作为《红楼梦》最早的、较为系统的外文译本，乔利译本在《红楼梦》西译史上无疑具有重要作用。此处译文选自乔利《红楼梦》英译本之第一回。

---

① *Hung Lou Meng: Or The Dream of The Red Chamber*, by H. Bencraft Joly, Shanghai: Kelly &Walsh, 1892, Book I, Preface.

译 文

THE DREAM OF THE RED CHAMBER

Chapter I

Chen Shih-yin, in a vision, apprehends perception and spirituality.

Chia Yü-ts'un, in the (windy and dusty) world, cherishes fond thoughts of a beautiful maiden.

This is the opening section; this the first chapter. Subsequent to the visions of a dream which he had, on some previous occasion, experienced, the writer personally relates, he designedly concealed the true circumstances, and borrowed the attributes of perception and spirituality to relate this story of the Record of the Stone. With this purpose, he made use of such designations as Chen Shih-yin (truth under the garb of fiction) and the like. What are, however, the events recorded in this work? Who are the dramatis personae?

Wearied with the drudgery experienced of late in the world, the author speaking for himself, goes on to explain, with the lack of success which attended every single concern, I suddenly bethought myself of the womankind of past ages. Passing one by one under a minute scrutiny, I felt that in action and in lore, one and all were far above me; that in spite of the majesty of my manliness, I could not, in point of fact, compare with these characters of the gentle sex. And my shame forsooth then knew no bounds; while regret, on the other hand, was of no avail, as there was not even a remote possibility of a day of remedy.

On this very day it was that I became desirous to compile, in a connected form, for publication throughout the world, with a view to (universal) information, how that I bear inexorable and manifold retribution; inasmuch as what time, by the sustenance of the benevolence of Heaven, and the virtue of my ancestors, my apparel was rich and fine, and as what days my fare was savory and sumptuous, I disregarded the bounty of education and nurture of father and mother, and paid no heed to the virtue of precept and injunction of teachers and friends, with the result that I incurred the punishment, of failure recently in the least trifle, and the reckless waste of half my lifetime. There have been meanwhile, generation after generation, those in the inner chambers, the whole mass of whom could not, on any account, be, through my influence, allowed to fall into extinction, in order that I, unfilial as I have been, may have the means to screen my own shortcomings.

Hence it is that the thatched shed, with bamboo mat windows, the bed of tow and the stove of brick, which are at present my share, are not sufficient to deter me from carrying out the fixed purpose of my mind. And could I, furthermore, confront the morning breeze, the evening moon, the willows by the steps and the flowers in the courtyard, methinks these would moisten to a greater degree my mortal pen with ink; but though I lack culture and erudition, what harm is there, however, in employing fiction and unrecondite language to give utterance to the merits of these characters? And were I also able to induce the inmates of the inner chamber to understand and diffuse them, could I besides break the weariness of even so much as a single moment, or could I open the eyes of my contemporaries, will it not forsooth prove a boon?

This consideration has led to the usage of such names as Chia Yü-ts'un and other similar appellations.

More than any in these pages have been employed such words as dreams and visions; but these dreams constitute the main argument of this work, and combine, furthermore, the design of giving a word of warning to my readers.

Reader, can you suggest whence the story begins?

The narration may border on the limits of incoherency and triviality, but it possesses considerable zest. But to begin.

The Empress Nü Wo, (the goddess of works,) in fashioning blocks of stones, for the repair of the heavens, prepared, at the Ta Huang Hills and Wu Ch'i cave, 36,501 blocks of rough stone, each twelve chang in height, and twenty-four chang square. Of these stones, the Empress Wo only used 36,500; so that one single block remained over and above, without being turned to any account. This was cast down the Ch'ing Keng peak. This stone, strange to say, after having undergone a process of refinement, attained a nature of efficiency, and could, by its innate powers, set itself into motion and was able to expand and to contract.

When it became aware that the whole number of blocks had been made use of to repair the heavens, that it alone had been destitute of the necessary properties and had been unfit to attain selection, it forthwith felt within itself vexation and shame, and day and night, it gave way to anguish and sorrow.

One day, while it lamented its lot, it suddenly caught sight, at a great distance, of a Buddhist bonze and of a Taoist priest coming towards that direction. Their appearance was uncommon, their easy manner remarkable. When they drew near this Ch'ing Keng peak, they sat on the ground to rest, and began to converse. But on noticing the block newly-polished and brilliantly clear, which had moreover contracted in dimensions, and become no larger than the pendant of a fan, they were greatly filled with admiration. The Buddhist priest picked it up, and laid it in the palm of his hand.

"Your appearance," he said laughingly, "may well declare you to be a supernatural object, but as you lack any inherent quality it is necessary to inscribe a few characters on you, so that every one who shall see you may at once recognise you to be a remarkable thing. And subsequently, when you will be taken into a country where honour and affluence will reign, into a family cultured in mind and of official status, in a land where flowers and trees shall flourish with luxuriance, in a town of refinement, renown and glory; when you once will have been there..."

The stone listened with intense delight.

"What characters may I ask," it consequently inquired, "will you inscribe? and what place will I be taken to? pray, pray explain to me in lucid terms." "You mustn't be inquisitive," the bonze replied, with a smile, "in days to come you'll certainly understand everything." Having concluded these words, he forthwith put the stone in his sleeve, and proceeded leisurely on his journey, in company with the Taoist priest. Whither, however, he took the stone, is not divulged. Nor can it be known how many centuries and ages elapsed, before a Taoist priest, K'ung K'ung by name, passed, during his researches after the eternal reason and his quest after immortality, by these Ta Huang Hills, Wu Ch'i cave and Ch'ing Keng Peak. Suddenly perceiving a large block of stone, on the surface of which the traces of characters giving, in a connected form, the various incidents of its fate, could be clearly deciphered, K'ung K'ung examined them from first to last. They, in fact, explained how that this block of worthless stone had originally been devoid of the properties essential for the repairs to the heavens, how it would be transmuted into human form and introduced by Mang Mang the High Lord, and Miao Miao, the Divine, into the world of mortals, and how it would be led over the other bank (across the San Sara). On the surface, the record of the spot where it would fall, the place of its birth, as well as various family trifles and trivial love affairs of young ladies, verses, odes, speeches and enigmas was still complete; but the name of the dynasty and the year of the reign were obliterated, and could not be ascertained.

On the obverse, were also the following enigmatical verses:

Lacking in virtues meet the azure skies to mend,
In vain the mortal world full many a year I wend,
Of a former and after life these facts that be,
Who will for a tradition strange record for me?

K'ung K'ung, the Taoist, having pondered over these lines for a while, became aware that this stone had a history of some kind.

"Brother stone," he forthwith said, addressing the stone, "the concerns of past days recorded on you possess, according to your own account, a considerable amount of interest, and have been for this reason inscribed, with the intent of soliciting generations to hand them down as remarkable occurrences. But in my own opinion, they lack, in the first place, any data by means of which to establish the name of the Emperor and the year of his reign; and, in the second place, these constitute no record of any excellent policy, adopted by any high worthies or high loyal statesmen, in the government of the state, or in the rule of public morals. The contents simply treat of a certain number of maidens, of exceptional character; either of their love affairs or infatuations, or of their small deserts or insignificant talents; and were I to transcribe the whole collection of them, they would, nevertheless, not be estimated as a book of any exceptional worth."

"Sir Priest," the stone replied with assurance, "why are you so excessively dull? The dynasties recorded in the rustic histories, which have been written from age to age, have, I am fain to think, invariably assumed, under false pretences, the mere nomenclature of the Han and T'ang dynasties. They differ from the events inscribed on my block, which do not borrow this customary practice, but, being based on my own experiences and natural feelings, present, on the contrary, a novel and unique character. Besides, in the pages of these rustic histories, either the aspersions upon sovereigns and statesmen, or the strictures upon individuals, their wives, and their daughters, or the deeds of licentiousness and violence are too numerous to be computed. Indeed, there is one more kind of loose literature, the wantonness and pollution in which work most easy havoc upon youth.

"As regards the works, in which the characters of scholars and beauties is delineated their allusions are again repeatedly of Wen Chün, their theme in every page of Tzu Chien; a thousand volumes present no diversity; and a thousand characters are but a counterpart of each other. What is more, these works, throughout all their pages, cannot help bordering on extreme licence. The authors, however, had no other object in view than to give utterance to a few sentimental odes and elegant ballads of their own, and for this reason they have fictitiously invented the names and surnames of both men and women, and necessarily introduced, in addition, some low characters, who should, like a buffoon in a play, create some excitement in the plot.

"Still more loathsome is a kind of pedantic and profligate literature, perfectly devoid of all natural sentiment, full of self-contradictions; and, in fact, the contrast to those maidens in my work, whom I have, during half my lifetime, seen with my own eyes and heard with my own ears. And though I will not presume to estimate them as superior to the heroes and heroines in the works of former ages, yet the perusal of the motives and issues of their experiences, may likewise afford matter sufficient to banish dulness, and to break the spell of melancholy.

"As regards the several stanzas of doggerel verse, they may too evoke such laughter as to compel the reader to blurt out the rice, and to spurt out the wine.

"In these pages, the scenes depicting the anguish of separation, the bliss of reunion, and the fortunes of prosperity and of adversity are all, in every detail, true to human nature, and I have not taken upon myself to make the slightest addition, or alteration, which might lead to the perversion of the truth.

"My only object has been that men may, after a drinking bout, or after they wake from sleep or when in need of relaxation from the pressure of business, take up this light literature, and not only expunge the traces of antiquated books, and obtain a new kind of distraction, but that they may also lay by a long life as well as energy and strength; for it bears no point of similarity to those works, whose designs are false, whose course is immoral. Now, Sir Priest, what are your views on the subject?"

K'ung K'ung having pondered for a while over the words, to which he had listened intently, re-perused, throughout, this record of the stone; and finding that the general purport consisted of nought else than a treatise on love, and likewise of an accurate transcription of facts, without the least taint of profligacy injurious to the times, he thereupon copied the contents, from beginning to end, to the intent of charging the world to hand them down as a strange story.

Hence it was that K'ung K'ung, the Taoist, in consequence of his perception, (in his state of) abstraction, of passion, the generation, from this passion, of voluptuousness, the transmission of this voluptuousness into passion, and the apprehension, by means of passion, of its unreality, forthwith altered his name for that of "Ch'ing Tseng"(the Voluptuous Bonze), and changed the title of "the Memoir of a Stone" (Shih-t'ou-chi), for that of "Ch'ing Tseng Lu", The Record of the Voluptuous Bonze; while K'ung Mei-chi of Tung Lu gave it the name of "Feng Yüeh Pao Chien", "The Precious Mirror of Voluptuousness". In later years, owing to the devotion by Tsao Hsüeh-ch'in in the Tao Hung study, of ten years to the perusal and revision of the work, the additions and modifications effected by him five times, the affix of an index and the division into periods and chapters, the book was again entitled "Chin Ling Shih Erh Ch'ai", "The Twelve Maidens of Chin Ling". A stanza was furthermore composed for the purpose. This then, and no other, is the origin of the Record of the Stone. The poet says appositely: —

> *Pages full of silly litter,*
> *Tears a handful sour and bitter;*
> *All a fool the author hold,*
> *But their zest who can unfold?*

You have now understood the causes which brought about the Record of the Stone, but as you are not, as yet, aware what characters are depicted, and what circumstances are related on the surface of the block, reader, please lend an ear to the narrative on the stone, which runs as follows: —

In old days, the land in the South East lay low. In this South-East part of the world, was situated a walled town, Ku Su by name. Within the walls a locality, called the Ch'ang Men, was more than all others throughout the mortal world, the centre, which held the second, if not the first place for fashion and life. Beyond this Ch'ang Men was a street called Shih-li-chieh (Ten Li street); in this street a lane, the Jen Ch'ing lane (Humanity and Purity); and in this lane stood an old temple, which on account of its diminutive dimensions, was called, by general consent, the Gourd temple. Next door to this temple lived the family of a district official, Chen by surname, Fei by name, and Shih-yin by style. His wife, née Feng, possessed a worthy and virtuous disposition, and had a clear perception of moral propriety and good conduct. This family, though not in actual possession of excessive affluence and honours, was, nevertheless, in their district, conceded to be a clan of well-to-do standing. As this Chen Shih-yin was of a contented and unambitious frame of mind, and entertained no hankering after any official distinction, but day after day of his life took delight in gazing at flowers, planting bamboos, sipping his wine and conning poetical works, he was in fact, in the indulgence of these pursuits, as happy as a supernatural being.

One thing alone marred his happiness. He had lived over half a century and had, as yet, no male offspring around his knees. He had one only child, a daughter, whose infant name was Ying Lien. She was just three years of age. On a long summer day, on which the heat had been intense, Shih-yin sat leisurely in his library. Feeling his hand tired, he dropped the book he held, leant his head on a teapoy, and fell asleep.

Of a sudden, while in this state of unconsciousness, it seemed as if he had betaken himself on foot to some spot or other whither he could not discriminate. Unexpectedly he espied, in the opposite direction, two priests coming towards him: the one a Buddhist, the other a Taoist. As they advanced they kept up the conversation in which they were engaged. "Whither do you purpose taking the object you have brought away?" He heard the Taoist inquire. To this question the Buddhist replied with a smile: "Set your mind at ease," he said; "there's now in maturity a plot of a general character involving mundane pleasures, which will presently come to a denouement. The whole number of the votaries of voluptuousness have, as yet, not been quickened or entered the world, and I mean to avail myself of this occasion to introduce this object among their number, so as to give it a chance to go through the span of human existence." "The votaries of voluptuousness of these days will naturally have again to endure the ills of life during their course through the mortal world," the Taoist remarked; "but when, I wonder, will they spring into existence? and in what place will they descend?"

"The account of these circumstances," the bonze ventured to reply, "is enough to make you laugh! They amount to this: there existed in the west, on the bank of the Ling (spiritual) river, by the side of the San Sheng (thrice-born) stone, a blade of the Chiang Chu (purple pearl) grass. At about the same time it was that the block of stone was, consequent upon its rejection by the goddess of works, also left to ramble and wander to its own gratification, and to roam about at pleasure to every and any place. One day it came within the precincts of the Ching Huan (Monitory Vision) Fairy; and this Fairy, cognizant of the fact that this stone had a history, detained it, therefore, to reside at the Ch'ih Hsia (purple clouds) palace, and apportioned to it the duties of attendant in Shen Ying, a fairy of the Ch'ih Hsia palace.

"This stone would, however, often stroll along the banks of the Ling river, and having at the sight of the blade of spiritual grass been filled with admiration, it, day by day, moistened its roots with sweet dew. This purple pearl grass, at the outset, tarried for months and years; but being at a later period imbued with the essence and luxuriance of heaven and earth, and having incessantly received the moisture and nurture of the sweet dew, divested itself, in course of time, of the form of a grass; assuming, in lieu, a human nature, which gradually became perfected into the person of a girl.

"Every day she was wont to wander beyond the confines of the Li Hen (divested animosities) heavens. When hungry she fed on the Pi Ch'ing (hidden love) fruit—when thirsty she drank the Kuan ch'ou (discharged sorrows) water. Having, however, up to this time, not shewn her gratitude for the virtue of nurture lavished upon her, the result was but natural that she should resolve in her heart upon a constant and incessant purpose to make suitable acknowledgment.

"I have been," she would often commune within herself, "the recipient of the gracious bounty of rain and dew, but I possess no such water as was lavished upon me to repay it! But should it ever descend into the world in the form of a human being, I will also betake myself thither, along with it; and if I can only have the means of making restitution to it, with the tears of a whole lifetime, I may be able to make adequate return."

"This resolution it is that will evolve the descent into the world of so many pleasure-bound spirits of retribution and the experience of fantastic destinies; and this crimson pearl blade will also be among the number. The stone still lies in its original place, and why should not you and I take it along before the tribunal of the Monitory Vision Fairy, and place on its behalf its name on record, so that it should descend into the world, in company with these spirits of passion, and bring this plot to an issue?"

"It is indeed ridiculous," interposed the Taoist. "Never before have I heard even the very mention of restitution by means of tears! Why should not you and I avail ourselves of this opportunity to likewise go down into the world? and if successful in effecting the salvation of a few of them, will it not be a work meritorious and virtuous?"

"This proposal," remarked the Buddhist, "is quite in harmony with my own views. Come along then with me to the palace of the Monitory Vision Fairy, and let us deliver up this good-for-nothing object, and have done with it! And when the company of pleasure-bound spirits of wrath descend into human existence, you and I can then enter the world. Half of them have already fallen into the dusty universe, but the whole number of them have not, as yet, come together."

"Such being the case," the Taoist acquiesced, "I am ready to follow you, whenever you please to go."

But to return to Chen Shih-yin. Having heard every one of these words distinctly, he could not refrain from forthwith stepping forward and paying homage. "My spiritual lords," he said, as he smiled, "accept my obeisance." The Buddhist and Taoist priests lost no time in responding to the compliment, and they exchanged the usual salutations. "My spiritual lords," Shih-yin continued; "I have just heard the conversation that passed between you, on causes and effects, a conversation the like of which few mortals have forsooth listened to; but your younger brother is sluggish of intellect, and cannot lucidly fathom the import! Yet could this dulness and simplicity be graciously dispelled, your younger brother may, by listening minutely, with undefiled ear and careful attention, to a certain degree be aroused to a sense of understanding; and what is more, possibly find the means of escaping the anguish of sinking down into Hades."

The two spirits smiled. "The conversation," they added, "refers to the primordial scheme and cannot be divulged before the proper season; but, when the time comes, mind do not forget us two, and you will readily be able to escape from the fiery furnace."

Shih-yin, after this reply, felt it difficult to make any further inquiries. "The primordial scheme," he however remarked smiling, "cannot, of course, be divulged; but what manner of thing, I wonder, is the good-for-nothing object you alluded to a short while back? May I not be allowed to judge for myself?"

"This object about which you ask," the Buddhist Bonze responded, "is intended, I may tell you, by fate to be just glanced at by you." With these words he produced it, and handed it over to Shih-yin.

Shih-yin received it. On scrutiny he found it, in fact, to be a beautiful gem, so lustrous and so clear that the traces of characters on the surface were distinctly visible. The characters inscribed consisted of the four "T'ung Ling Pao Yü," "Precious Gem of Spiritual Perception." On the obverse, were also several columns of minute words, which he was just in the act of looking at intently, when the Buddhist at once expostulated.

"We have already reached," he exclaimed, "the confines of vision." Snatching it violently out of his hands, he walked away with the Taoist, under a lofty stone portal, on the face of which appeared in large type the four characters: "T'ai Hsü Huan Ching", "The Visionary limits of the Great Void". On each side was a scroll with the lines:

When falsehood stands for truth, truth likewise becomes false,

Where naught be made to aught, aught changes into naught.

Shih-yin meant also to follow them on the other side, but, as he was about to make one step forward, he suddenly heard a crash, just as if the mountains had fallen into ruins, and the earth sunk into destruction. As Shih-yin uttered a loud shout, he looked with strained eye; but all he could see was the fiery sun shining, with glowing rays, while the banana leaves drooped their heads. By that time, half of the circumstances connected with the dream he had had, had already slipped from his memory.

He also noticed a nurse coming towards him with Ying Lien in her arms. To Shih-yin's eyes his daughter appeared even more beautiful, such a bright gem, so precious, and so lovable. Forthwith stretching out his arms, he took her over, and, as he held her in his embrace, he coaxed her to play with him for a while; after which he brought her up to the street to see the great stir occasioned by the procession that was going past.

He was about to come in, when he caught sight of two priests, one a Taoist, the other a Buddhist, coming hither from the opposite direction. The Buddhist had a head covered with mange, and went barefooted. The Taoist had a limping foot, and his hair was all dishevelled.

Like maniacs, they jostled along, chattering and laughing as they drew near.

As soon as they reached Shih-yin's door, and they perceived him with Ying Lien in his arms, the Bonze began to weep aloud.

Turning towards Shih-yin, he said to him: "My good Sir, why need you carry in your embrace this living but luckless thing, which will involve father and mother in trouble?"

These words did not escape Shih-yin's ear; but persuaded that they amounted to raving talk, he paid no heed whatever to the bonze.

"Part with her and give her to me," the Buddhist still went on to say.

Shih-yin could not restrain his annoyance; and hastily pressing his daughter closer to him, he was intent upon going in, when the bonze pointed his hand at him, and burst out in a loud fit of laughter.

He then gave utterance to the four lines that follow:

You indulge your tender daughter and are laughed at as inane;
Vain you face the snow, oh mirror! for it will evanescent wane,
When the festival of lanterns is gone by, guard 'gainst your doom,
'Tis what time the flames will kindle, and the fire will consume.

Shih-yin understood distinctly the full import of what he heard; but his heart was still full of conjectures. He was about to inquire who and what they were, when he heard the Taoist remark,—"You and I cannot speed together; let us now part company, and each of us will be then able to go after his own business. After the lapse of three ages, I shall be at the Pei Mang mount, waiting for you; and we can, after our reunion, betake ourselves to the Visionary Confines of the Great Void, there to cancel the name of the stone from the records."

"Excellent! first rate!" exclaimed the Bonze. And at the conclusion of these words, the two men parted, each going his own way, and no trace was again seen of them.

"These two men," Shih-yin then pondered within his heart, "must have had many experiences, and I ought really to have made more inquiries of them; but at this juncture to indulge in regret is anyhow too late."

While Shih-yin gave way to these foolish reflections, he suddenly noticed the arrival of a penniless scholar, Chia by surname, Hua by name, Shih-fei by style and Yü-ts'un by nickname, who had taken up his quarters in the Gourd temple next door. This Chia Yü-ts'un was originally a denizen of Hu-Chow, and was also of literary and official parentage, but as he was born of the youngest stock, and the possessions of his paternal and maternal ancestors were completely exhausted, and his parents and relatives were dead, he remained the sole and only survivor; and, as he found his residence in his native place of no avail, he therefore entered the capital in search of that reputation, which would enable him to put the family estate on a proper standing. He had arrived at this place since the year before last, and had, what is more, lived all along in very straitened circumstances. He had made the temple his temporary quarters, and earned a living by daily occupying himself in composing documents and writing letters for customers. Thus it was that Shih-yin had been in constant relations with him.

As soon as Yü-ts'un perceived Shih-yin, he lost no time in saluting him. "My worthy Sir," he observed with a forced smile; "how is it you are leaning against the door and looking out? Is there perchance any news astir in the streets, or in the public places?"

"None whatever," replied Shih-yin, as he returned the smile. "Just a while back, my young daughter was in sobs, and I coaxed her out here to amuse her. I am just now without anything whatever to attend to, so that, dear brother Chia, you come just in the nick of time. Please walk into my mean abode, and let us endeavour, in each other's company, to while away this long summer day."

After he had made this remark, he bade a servant take his daughter in, while he, hand-in-hand with Yü-ts'un, walked into the library, where a young page served tea. They had hardly exchanged a few sentences, when one of the household came in, in flying haste, to announce that Mr Yen had come to pay a visit.

Shih-yin at once stood up. "Pray excuse my rudeness," he remarked apologetically, "but do sit down; I shall shortly rejoin you, and enjoy the pleasure of your society." "My dear Sir," answered Yü-ts'un, as he got up, also in a conceding way, "suit your own convenience. I've often had the honour of being your guest, and what will it matter if I wait a little?" While these apologies were yet being spoken, Shih-yin had already walked out into the front parlour. During his absence, Yü-ts'un occupied himself in turning over the pages of some poetical work to dispel ennui, when suddenly he heard, outside the window, a woman's cough. Yü-ts'un hurriedly got up and looked out. He saw at a glance that it was a servant girl engaged in picking flowers. Her deportment was out of the common; her eyes so bright, her eyebrows so well defined. Though not a perfect beauty, she possessed nevertheless charms sufficient to arouse the feelings. Yü-ts'un unwittingly gazed at her with fixed eye. This waiting-maid, belonging to the Chen family, had done picking flowers, and was on the point of going in, when she of a sudden raised her eyes and became aware of the presence of some person inside the window, whose head-gear consisted of a turban in tatters, while his clothes were the worse for wear. But in spite of his poverty, he was naturally endowed with a round waist, a broad back, a fat face, a square mouth; added to this, his eyebrows were swordlike, his eyes resembled stars, his nose was straight, his cheeks square.

This servant girl turned away in a hurry and made her escape.

"This man so burly and strong," she communed within herself, "yet at the same time got up in such poor attire, must, I expect, be no one else than the man, whose name is Chia Yü-ts'un or such like, time after time referred to by my master, and to whom he has repeatedly wished to give a helping hand, but has failed to find a favourable opportunity. And as related to our family there is no connexion or friend in such straits, I feel certain it cannot be any other person than he. Strange to say, my master has further remarked that this man will, for a certainty, not always continue in such a state of destitution."

As she indulged in this train of thought, she could not restrain herself from turning her head round once or twice.

When Yü-ts'un perceived that she had looked back, he readily interpreted it as a sign that in her heart her thoughts had been of him, and he was frantic with irrepressible joy.

"This girl," he mused, "is, no doubt, keen-eyed and eminently shrewd, and one in this world who has seen through me."

The servant youth, after a short time, came into the room; and when Yü-ts'un made inquiries and found out from him that the guests in the front parlour had been detained to dinner, he could not very well wait any longer, and promptly walked away down a side passage and out of a back door.

When the guests had taken their leave, Shih-yin did not go back to rejoin Yü-ts'un, as he had come to know that he had already left.

In time the mid-autumn festivities drew near; and Shih-yin, after the family banquet was over, had a separate table laid in the library, and crossed over, in the moonlight, as far as the temple and invited Yü-ts'un to come round.

The fact is that Yü-ts'un, ever since the day on which he had seen the girl of the Chen family turn twice round to glance at him, flattered himself that she was friendly disposed towards him, and incessantly fostered fond thoughts of her in his heart. And on this day, which happened to be the mid-autumn feast, he could not, as he gazed at the moon, refrain from cherishing her remembrance. Hence it was that he gave vent to these pentameter verses:

> *Alas! not yet divined my lifelong wish,*
> *And anguish ceaseless comes upon anguish*
> *I came, and sad at heart, my brow I frowned;*
> *She went, and oft her head to look turned round.*
> *Facing the breeze, her shadow she doth watch,*
> *Who's meet this moonlight night with her to match?*
> *The lustrous rays if they my wish but read*
> *Would soon alight upon her beauteous head!*

Yü-ts'un having, after this recitation, recalled again to mind how that throughout his lifetime his literary attainments had had an adverse fate and not met with an opportunity (of reaping distinction), he went on to rub his brow, and as he raised his eyes to the skies, he heaved a deep sigh and once more intoned a couplet aloud:

> *The gem in the cask a high price it seeks,*
> *The pin in the case to take wing it waits.*

As luck would have it, Shih-yin was at the moment approaching, and upon hearing the lines, he said with a smile: "My dear Yü-ts'un, really your attainments are of no ordinary capacity."

Yü-ts'un lost no time in smiling and replying. "It would be presumption in my part to think so," he observed. "I was simply at random humming a few verses composed by former writers, and what reason is there to laud me to such an excessive degree? To what, my dear Sir, do I owe the pleasure of your visit?" he went on to inquire. "Tonight," replied Shih-yin, "is the mid-autumn feast, generally known as the full-moon festival; and as I could not help thinking that living, as you my worthy brother are, as a mere stranger in this Buddhist temple, you could not but experience the feeling of loneliness. I have, for the express purpose, prepared a small entertainment, and will be pleased if you will come to my mean abode to have a glass of wine. But I wonder whether you will entertain favourably my modest invitation?" Yü-ts'un, after listening to the proposal, put forward no refusal of any sort; but remarked complacently: "Being the recipient of such marked attention, how can I presume to repel your generous consideration?"

As he gave expression to these words, he walked off there and then, in company with Shih-yin, and came over once again into the court in front of the library. In a few minutes, tea was over.

The cups and dishes had been laid from an early hour, and needless to say the wines were luscious; the fare sumptuous.

The two friends took their seats. At first they leisurely replenished their glasses, and quietly sipped their wine; but as, little by little, they entered into conversation, their good cheer grew more genial, and unawares the glasses began to fly round, and the cups to be exchanged.

At this very hour, in every house of the neighbourhood, sounded the fife and lute, while the inmates indulged in music and singing. Above head, the orb of the radiant moon shone with an all-pervading splendour, and with a steady lustrous light, while the two friends, as their exuberance increased, drained their cups dry so soon as they reached their lips.

Yü-ts'un, at this stage of the collation, was considerably under the influence of wine, and the vehemence of his high spirits was irrepressible. As he gazed at the moon, he fostered thoughts, to which he gave vent by the recital of a double couplet.

'Tis what time three meets five, Selene is a globe!
Her pure rays fill the court, the jadelike rails enrobe!
Lo! in the heavens her disk to view doth now arise,
And in the earth below to gaze men lift their eyes.

"Excellent!" cried Shih-yin with a loud voice, after he had heard these lines; "I have repeatedly maintained that it was impossible for you to remain long inferior to any, and now the verses you have recited are a prognostic of your rapid advancement. Already it is evident that, before long, you will extend your footsteps far above the clouds! I must congratulate you! I must congratulate you! Let me, with my own hands, pour a glass of wine to pay you my compliments."

Yü-ts'un drained the cup. "What I am about to say," he explained as he suddenly heaved a sigh, "is not the maudlin talk of a man under the effects of wine. As far as the subjects at present set in the examinations go, I could, perchance, also have well been able to enter the list, and to send in my name as a candidate; but I have, just now, no means whatever to make provision for luggage and for travelling expenses. The distance too to Shen Ching is a long one, and I could not depend upon the sale of papers or the composition of essays to find the means of getting there."

Shih-yin gave him no time to conclude. "Why did you not speak about this sooner?" he interposed with haste. "I have long entertained this suspicion; but as, whenever I met you, this conversation was never broached, I did not presume to make myself officious. But if such be the state of affairs just now, I lack, I admit, literary qualification, but on the two subjects of friendly spirit and pecuniary means, I have, nevertheless, some experience. Moreover, I rejoice that next year is just the season for the triennial examinations, and you should start for the capital with all despatch; and in the tripos next spring, you will, by carrying the prize, be able to do justice to the proficiency you can boast of. As regards the travelling expenses and the other items, the provision of everything necessary for you by my own self will again not render nugatory your mean acquaintance with me."

Forthwith, he directed a servant lad to go and pack up at once fifty taels of pure silver and two suits of winter clothes.

"The nineteenth," he continued, "is a propitious day, and you should lose no time in hiring a boat and starting on your journey westwards. And when, by your eminent talents, you shall have soared high to a lofty position, and we meet again next winter, will not the occasion be extremely felicitous?"

Yü-ts'un accepted the money and clothes with but scanty expression of gratitude. In fact, he paid no thought whatever to the gifts, but went on, again drinking his wine, as he chattered and laughed.

It was only when the third watch of that day had already struck that the two friends parted company; and Shih-yin, after seeing Yü-ts'un off, retired to his room and slept, with one sleep all through, never waking until the sun was well up in the skies.

Remembering the occurrence of the previous night, he meant to write a couple of letters of recommendation for Yü-ts'un to take along with him to the capital, to enable him, after handing them over at the mansions of certain officials, to find some place as a temporary home. He accordingly despatched a servant to ask him to come round, but the man returned and reported that from what the bonze said, "Mr. Chia had started on his journey to the capital, at the fifth watch of that very morning, that he had also left a message with the bonze to deliver to you, Sir, to the effect that men of letters paid no heed to lucky or unlucky days, that the sole consideration with them was the nature of the matter in hand, and that he could find no time to come round in person and bid good-bye."

Shih-yin after hearing this message had no alternative but to banish the subject from his thoughts.

In comfortable circumstances, time indeed goes by with easy stride. Soon drew near also the happy festival of the 15th of the 1st moon, and Shih-yin told a servant Huo Ch'i to take Ying Lien to see the sacrificial fires and flowery lanterns.

About the middle of the night, Huo Ch'i was hard pressed, and he forthwith set Ying Lien down on the doorstep of a certain house. When he felt relieved, he came back to take her up, but failed to find anywhere any trace of Ying Lien. In a terrible plight, Huo Ch'i prosecuted his search throughout half the night; but even by the dawn of day, he had not discovered any clue of her whereabouts. Huo Ch'i, lacking, on the other hand, the courage to go back and face his master, promptly made his escape to his native village.

Shih-yin-in fact, the husband as well as the wife—seeing that their child had not come home during the whole night, readily concluded that some mishap must have befallen her. Hastily they despatched several servants to go in search of her, but one and all returned to report that there was neither vestige nor tidings of her.

This couple had only had this child, and this at the meridian of their life, so that her sudden disappearance plunged them in such great distress that day and night they mourned her loss to such a point as to well nigh pay no heed to their very lives.

A month in no time went by. Shih-yin was the first to fall ill, and his wife, Dame Feng, likewise, by dint of fretting for her daughter, was also prostrated with sickness. The doctor was, day after day, sent for, and the oracle consulted by means of divination.

Little did any one think that on this day, being the 15th of the 3rd moon, while the sacrificial oblations were being prepared in the Hu Lu temple, a pan with oil would have caught fire, through the want of care on the part of the bonze, and that in a short time the flames would have consumed the paper pasted on the windows.

Among the natives of this district bamboo fences and wooden partitions were in general use, and these too proved a source of calamity so ordained by fate (to consummate this decree).

With promptness (the fire) extended to two buildings, then enveloped three, then dragged four (into ruin), and then spread to five houses, until the whole street was in a blaze, resembling the flames of a volcano. Though both the military and the people at once ran to the rescue, the fire had already assumed a serious hold, so that it was impossible for them to afford any effective assistance for its suppression.

It blazed away straight through the night, before it was extinguished, and consumed, there is in fact no saying how many dwelling houses. Anyhow, pitiful to relate, the Chen house, situated as it was next door to the temple, was, at an early part of the evening, reduced to a heap of tiles and bricks; and nothing but the lives of that couple and several inmates of the family did not sustain any injuries.

Shih-yin was in despair, but all he could do was to stamp his feet and heave deep sighs. After consulting with his wife, they betook themselves to a farm of theirs, where they took up their quarters temporarily. But as it happened that water had of late years been scarce, and no crops been reaped, robbers and thieves had sprung up like bees, and though the Government troops were bent upon their capture, it was anyhow difficult to settle down quietly on the farm. He therefore had no other resource than to convert, at a loss, the whole of his property into money, and to take his wife and two servant girls and come over for shelter to the house of his father-in-law.

His father-in-law, Feng Su, by name, was a native of Ta Ju Chou. Although only a labourer, he was nevertheless in easy circumstances at home. When he on this occasion saw his son-in-law come to him in such distress, he forthwith felt at heart considerable displeasure. Fortunately Shih-yin had still in his possession the money derived from the unprofitable realization of his property, so that he produced and handed it to his father-in-law, commissioning him to purchase, whenever a suitable opportunity presented itself, a house and land as a provision for food and raiment against days to come. This Feng Su, however, only expended the half of the sum, and pocketed the other half, merely acquiring for him some fallow land and a dilapidated house.

Shih-yin being, on the other hand, a man of books and with no experience in matters connected with business and with sowing and reaping, subsisted, by hook and by crook, for about a year or two, when he became more impoverished.

In his presence, Feng Su would readily give vent to specious utterances, while, with others, and behind his back, he on the contrary expressed his indignation against his improvidence in his mode of living, and against his sole delight of eating and playing the lazy.

Shih-yin, aware of the want of harmony with his father-in-law, could not help giving way, in his own heart, to feelings of regret and pain. In addition to this, the fright and vexation which he had undergone the year before, the anguish and suffering (he had had to endure), had already worked havoc (on his constitution); and being a man advanced in years, and assailed by the joint attack of poverty and disease, he at length gradually began to display symptoms of decline.

Strange coincidence, as he, on this day, came leaning on his staff and with considerable strain, as far as the street for a little relaxation, he suddenly caught sight, approaching from the off side, of a Taoist priest with a crippled foot; his maniac appearance so repulsive, his shoes of straw, his dress all in tatters, muttering several sentiments to this effect:

> *All men spiritual life know to be good,*
> *But fame to disregard they ne'er succeed!*
> *From old till now the statesmen where are they?*
> *Waste lie their graves, a heap of grass, extinct.*
> *All men spiritual life know to be good,*
> *But to forget gold, silver, ill succeed!*
> *Through life they grudge their hoardings to be scant,*
> *And when plenty has come, their eyelids close.*
> *All men spiritual life hold to be good,*
> *Yet to forget wives, maids, they ne'er succeed!*
> *Who speak of grateful love while lives their lord,*
> *And dead their lord, another they pursue.*
> *All men spiritual life know to be good,*
> *But sons and grandsons to forget never succeed!*
> *From old till now of parents soft many,*
> *But filial sons and grandsons who have seen?*

Shih-yin upon hearing these words, hastily came up to the priest, "What were you so glibly holding forth?" he inquired. "All I could hear were a lot of hao liao (excellent, finality.")

"You may well have heard the two words 'hao liao', " answered the Taoist with a smile, "but can you be said to have fathomed their meaning? You should know that all things in this world are excellent, when they have attained finality; when they have attained finality, they are excellent; but when they have not attained finality, they are not excellent; if they would be excellent, they should attain finality. My song is entitled Excellent-finality (hao liao)."

Shih-yin was gifted with a natural perspicacity that enabled him, as soon as he heard these remarks, to grasp their spirit.

"Wait a while," he therefore said smilingly; "let me unravel this excellent-finality song of yours; do you mind?"

"Please by all means go on with the interpretation," urged the Taoist; whereupon Shih-yin proceeded in this strain:

Sordid rooms and vacant courts,

Replete in years gone by with beds where statesmen lay;

Parched grass and withered banian trees,

Where once were halls for song and dance!

Spiders' webs the carved pillars intertwine,

The green gauze now is also pasted on the straw windows!

What about the cosmetic fresh concocted or the powder just scented;

Why has the hair too on each temple become white like hoarfrost!

Yesterday the tumulus of yellow earth buried the bleached bones,

To-night under the red silk curtain reclines the couple!

Gold fills the coffers, silver fills the boxes,

But in a twinkle, the beggars will all abuse you!

While you deplore that the life of others is not long,

You forget that you yourself are approaching death!

You educate your sons with all propriety,

But they may some day, 'tis hard to say become thieves;

Though you choose (your fare and home) the fatted beam,

You may, who can say, fall into some place of easy virtue!

Through your dislike of the gauze hat as mean,

You have come to be locked in a cangue;

Yesterday, poor fellow, you felt cold in a tattered coat,

To-day, you despise the purple embroidered dress as long!

Confusion reigns far and wide! you have just sung your part, I come on the boards,

Instead of yours, you recognise another as your native land;

What utter perversion!

In one word, it comes to this we make wedding clothes for others!

(We sow for others to reap.)

The crazy limping Taoist clapped his hands. "Your interpretation is explicit," he remarked with a hearty laugh, "your interpretation is explicit!"

Shih-yin promptly said nothing more than,— "Walk on;" and seizing the stole from the Taoist's shoulder, he flung it over his own. He did not, however, return home, but leisurely walked away, in company with the eccentric priest.

The report of his disappearance was at once bruited abroad, and plunged the whole neighbourhood in commotion; and converted into a piece of news, it was circulated from mouth to mouth.

Dame Feng, Shih-yin's wife, upon hearing the tidings, had such a fit of weeping that she hung between life and death; but her only alternative was to consult with her father, and to despatch servants on all sides to institute inquiries. No news was however received of him, and she had nothing else to do but to practise resignation, and to remain dependent upon the support of her parents for her subsistence. She had fortunately still by her side, to wait upon her, two servant girls, who had been with her in days gone by; and the three of them, mistress as well as servants, occupied themselves day and night with needlework, to assist her father in his daily expenses.

This Feng Su had after all, in spite of his daily murmurings against his bad luck, no help but to submit to the inevitable.

On a certain day, the elder servant girl of the Chen family was at the door purchasing thread, and while there, she of a sudden heard in the street shouts of runners clearing the way, and every one explain that the new magistrate had come to take up his office.

The girl, as she peeped out from inside the door, perceived the lictors and policemen go by two by two; and when unexpectedly in a state chair, was carried past an official, in black hat and red coat, she was indeed quite taken aback.

"The face of this officer would seem familiar," she argued within herself; "just as if I had seen him somewhere or other ere this."

Shortly she entered the house, and banishing at once the occurrence from her mind, she did not give it a second thought. At night, however, while she was waiting to go to bed, she suddenly heard a sound like a rap at the door. A band of men boisterously cried out: "We are messengers, deputed by the worthy magistrate of this district, and come to summon one of you to an enquiry."

Feng Su, upon hearing these words, fell into such a terrible consternation that his eyes stared wide and his mouth gaped.

What calamity was impending is not as yet ascertained, but, reader, listen to the explanation contained in the next chapter.

思 考

1. 阅读乔利《红楼梦》译文,判断该译文译自《红楼梦》的哪个版本?并思考乔利采用了何种翻译策略?

2. 试论《红楼梦》在十九世纪欧洲的传播与接受。

参考文献

- *Hung Lou Meng: Or The Dream of The Red Chamber*, by H. Bencraft Joly, Shanghai: Kelly &Walsh, 1892.
- *A History of Chinese Literature*, by H. A. Giles, New York: D. Appleton and Company, 1901.

扩展阅读

- "Hung Lau Mung, Or Dream in the Red Chamber", *China Repository*, Vol.11, No.5, 1842.
- *The Chinese Speaker*, by Robert Thom, Ningpo: Presbyterian Mission Press, 1846.

道格斯《续玄怪录·薛伟》

（1893）

导　读

道格斯（Robert Kennaway Douglas，1838—1913）曾为英国在华领事官，1864年返回英国后，道格斯任职于大英博物馆东方藏书部，编有《大英博物馆馆藏中文刻本、写本、绘本目录》（*Catalogue of Chinese Printed Books, Manuscripts and Drawings in the Library of the British Museum*，1877）及《大英博物馆馆藏中文书目补编》（*Supplementary Catalogue of Chinese Books and Manuscripts in the British Museum*，1903）。1903至1908年，道格斯任伦敦大学国王学院汉文教授。道格斯对中国文学文化有较深的造诣，撰译的著作有《非基督教的宗教体系：儒教和道教》（*Non-Christian Religious system—Confucianism and Taoism*，1879）、《中国故事集》（*Chinese Stories*，1893）、《中国的社会》（*Society in China*，1894）、《李鸿章》（*Li Hungchang*，1895）、《中国》（*China, the Story of the Nations*，1899）等。《中国故事集》为道格斯编译的中国小说译文选集，共选译了《怀私怨狠仆告主》《夺锦楼》《女秀才移花接木》《夸妙术丹客提金》等十种中国故事，其中第七种根据《续玄怪录·薛伟》翻译而成，译作 *A Buddhist Story*，即《一则

佛教故事》。

《薛伟》载于唐代李复言所编《续玄怪录》,又见于《太平广记》卷四七一。明代冯梦龙将其改编为拟话本《薛录事鱼服证仙》,收入《醒世恒言》。与《薛伟》相比,《薛录事鱼服证仙》在内容上添加了薛伟之妻顾夫人为其请医、打醮,薛伟化鱼跳龙门,薛伟青城山遇老君,李八百点化薛伟夫妻成仙等诸多情节。这些情节均不见于道格斯翻译的《一则佛教故事》中。另外《薛录事鱼服证仙》通过李八百、太上老君等人物情节的增饰,赋予小说浓厚的道家色彩。而《薛伟》则具有较明显的佛教倾向。正如汪辟疆在《唐人小说·薛伟》按语中所指出的:"此事当受佛氏轮回之说影响,李复言衍为此篇,宣扬此法。"(汪辟疆校录《唐人小说》,上海:上海古籍出版社,1978年)道格斯将其译为《一则佛教故事》,与《薛伟》的主旨更为贴切。所以,道格斯《一则佛教故事》的中文底本似为《续玄怪录·薛伟》。

译 文

A BUDDHIST STORY

[The following story is of Buddhist origin, and has reference to the doctrine of transmigration of souls. According to this tenet of the faith every soul passes through a variety of existences, the conditions of the successive states of which depend on the amount of merit or demerit acquired in the previous life. Those who have done good pass into higher spheres of enjoyment and prosperity, while those who have done evil descend in the scale of creation by leaps and by bounds. Thus, a man who has kept most of the commandments of Buddha, but failed in others, may expect to be born a horse or one of the more respectable animals in his next state of existence; while one who has persistently broken the whole law, may think himself fortunate if he reappears as a fish or a dog. This doctrine, which represents all animated creation as being one and interchangeable, makes the killing of animals acts of murder and of possible impiety. For how can one be sure that in killing an ox or a horse one is not murdering a friend who, when a man, may have failed in some of his religious duties? or in crushing a beetle, that one is not cutting short the career of a near but perhaps dissolute relative? Eating animal flesh, of course, only adds to the crime of murder, and in the following pages we see how very easily Mr Le may have eaten his old friend Sin.]

Some years ago there lived in the village of "Everlasting Felicity", in the province of "The Four Streams", two officials, who from different causes had been relieved from the necessity of serving their country and their emperor. Mr Le, the elder of the two, was a somewhat heavy and morose man—one in whom it was difficult to say whether his appetite for his creature-comforts or his indifference to the feelings and opinions of his fellowmen predominated. In the last post which he had had the honour to fill he had been charged, his friends said unjustly, with having inflicted on innocent persons illegal torture, some refinements of which had emanated from his not otherwise inventive brain, and of having levied blackmail with so greedy a hand that the people had been driven to the verge of rebellion. When the storm was about to break Le wisely retired to the village of "Everlasting Felicity", carrying with him quite a little fortune which he had neither inherited nor had saved out of his official income.

Mr Sin, the younger of the two, was of an impulsive and a rather erratic nature. As an official his chief fault was the restlessness of his administration. He worried the people in his district; and when the infliction of constant worry is combined with an itching palm, even the sluggish Chinese nature will after a time turn on the worrier. And so it came about that he was recommended by his superiors to resign; and he also, having gathered together his ill-gotten goods, found his way to the same haven of rest to which Mr Le had turned his footsteps.

The similarity of their fates induced these two worthies to set up house together. Both being rich, they surrounded themselves with every comfort, and spent their leisure in entertaining those of their neighbours who could entertain them in return, and in discussing the ineffable wisdom of the moral maxims of Confucius. While pursuing the even tensor of this most inestimable way, it chanced that Mr Sin, having exposed his clean-shaven head unduly to the sun, fell sick of a fever. Mr Le, though annoyed at the circumstance—for he was expecting some rich friends to dinner that day—sent for a doctor and gave generally directions that Sin was to be looked after. In answer to the call the doctor arrived. He was an old man and lean, perhaps from much study, and he wore a pair of large horn-rimmed spectacles. His first glance at this patient showed him that the hot principle in Sin's nature was riding rough-shod over the cold principle, and had completely upset the equilibrium which should be maintained in all well-regulated constitutions. The symptoms of high fever were so plain that he thought it unnecessary even to feel the patient's pulse, but at once prescribed a decoction of powdered deer horns and dragon's blood, with pills made from hare's liver, to be taken at intervals. Before leaving the house he took Ting, Sin's valet, aside, and told him that on no account was he to leave his master alone. "At any moment," said he, "he may become delirious, and then Buddha alone can say what he may do."

Ting promised, with many asseverations, that nothing should induce him to leave his master's presence for an instant. But even Chinamen occasionally fail to act up to their professions, and when, after some restlessness, Sin fell off into a profound sleep, Ting, hearing sounds of merriment in the servants' quarters, persuaded himself that it would be quite safe to leave his master for a bit, and went noiselessly out to enjoy himself among his fellows. He had scarcely left the room, however, when Sin became restless again. He turned and twisted in bed and rolled his weary and aching head from side to side.

"Hot, hot, hot!" he moaned; "my head burns, the pillow scorches! I can't breathe! The room is suffocating me! Oh for a breath of the fresh air of heaven in the fields and woods! Why should I not go and enjoy it? I will!" he exclaimed, and in an instant he sprang out of bed, rushed out of the room, threw open the front door, and ran down the road into the neighbouring meadows.

"Ah," he shouted as he threw himself on a bank, "this is delicious!

Now I can live and breathe. The air of heaven cools my throbbing head, and I am myself again."

But presently the air again became oppressive. Shooting pains pierced his brain. His skin burned and his tongue became parched. "Oh!" he cried, "the fire-demon has followed me here! What can I do to cool my tortured head? If I might only plunge into a river of cold water I should be well." So saying, he rose from the bank and wandered on through woods and fields until, to his infinite delight, he saw before him a broad, cool, shining river.

"Now is my chance," he exclaimed, and without a moment's hesitation he plunged into the rolling tide. Being an expert swimmer he dived to the bottom, then skimmed along the top, his queue looking like an eel floating behind him on the surface, and presently stretched himself out flat on the water. "Ah," he said, "this is happiness. Who would live on land who can live in water?" As he ceased speaking, he heard close to him a kind of gurgling chuckle, something between the noise made by a person choking, and by water poured out of a bottle, and turning round he saw a large tench which was staring at him with round eyes, and with a contorted expression of mouth which Sin rightly interpreted to be the effect of laughter.

"What are you laughing at?" he asked.

"You!" replied the fish.

"And what do you see in me to laugh at?" he inquired, somewhat angrily.

"I heard what you said," answered the fish, "and the idea of a man knowing what the delight of living in water is, was so ludicrous that it sent me into a fit of laughter which has made me feel very uncomfortable, for I am not much accustomed to laugh."

"So I should imagine from the hideous noise you made," said Sin. "But tell me, how can you enjoy the water more than I do?"

"Why, you are a stranger and a foreigner to the element. For a few minutes you may enjoy swimming and diving, but your limbs would soon tire, those ugly limbs which make you look like a frog, though frogs have the advantage over you of moving horizontally, while you by some perversion in your nature are born to walk upright, for all the world like trees moving. And then, when you are hungry, you have to seek your food on land, while we, as we glide swiftly through the rushing waters without fatigue, and almost without movement, find the means of our nourishment in the midst of our enjoyment."

"If this is really so," said Sin, "I would give something to be like you."

"Do you mean that you would like to become a fish?"

"Yes; I would give up all the money I squeezed out of the people when I was a magistrate to enjoy the river as you enjoy it."

"Come with me, then," said the fish; and turning round, he swam upstream at such a pace that Sin was obliged to call to him to stop.

"Ah!" he said, in a tone of pitying contempt, "I forgot you were a man."

After going for a few minutes at a reduced speed, the fish led the way into a small bay in the bank, where, surrounded by attendant fishes, lay a huge carp whose size and gravity of deportment marked him out as a ruler of his kind.

As Sin's guide approached the monarch he indicated reverence and submission by wriggling towards him in the mud.

"May it please your majesty," he began, "I have found a poor man who wants very much to become a fish. Knowing your infinite benevolence I have ventured to bring him into your august presence." So saying, he motioned Sin to approach, who, being anxious to propitiate the king, began wriggling in the mud in imitation of his guide. But in so doing he made such a commotion in the water and stirred up so much dirt that the fishes all began to choke, and his own eyes were so completely blinded that he could not see where he was going.

"Stop! " shrieked the king. "What are you doing?" Sin was glad enough to obey, and when the water had cleared a little he lay prone before the carp awaiting instructions.

"Are you really desirous of becoming a fish?" inquired the king, in a husky voice, for his throat had not quite recovered from the effects of Sin's wriggling.

"I am, you Majesty," replied Sin. "This gentleman here has shown me that fishes alone can really appreciate life in streams, and as the slight taste of that existence which I am able to enjoy is so delightful, I am persuaded that the full enjoyment of it must be ravishing."

"You shall have your desire then," said the king, and turning to an attendant trout he told him to go and fetch a large fish's skin.

Presently the messenger returned with a carp's skin of a size which proved to be just the right length. At a word from the king the courtiers put Sin into it, and having tucked him in with the exception of his hands and feet, fastened him up. For a moment or two Sin felt very uncomfortable, but by degrees he became conscious of a physical change in his constitution. He limbs began to tingle and to lose their identities. His arms gradually contracted, while his hands flattened out and assumed the shape of fins. His leg became welded together, and his feet by degrees took the form of a tail. When this strange transformation was completed, Sin was desirous of trying his new powers, and so, with a bow and an expression of thanks to his Majesty, he turned to swim off.

"Don't be in such a hurry," said the king; "I have a word of advice to give you. Know, then, that men are always trying to catch us fishes, and that there are two methods which they especially employ—hook and net. Now, if ever you see a worm dangling in the water in the shape of hook, don't touch it, for if you do you will be a dead fish; and if ever you chance to see a net before you, turn round and swim as fast as you can in the opposite direction, lest you should be caught in its meshes."

"I thank your Majesty for your instructions," answered Sin, "and your words shall be engraven on my"—he was going to say heart, but he was not sure whether fishes had hearts, and so he said "memory". So saying, and with a reverent wriggle in the mud, he turned down-stream. At first he experienced some little difficulty, being unaware of the steadying force of his tail and fins. He wagged his tail as a man would kick out his legs, and the result was that instead of turning slightly, as was his intention, to avoid a stick, he made a complete circuit. And he more than once threw himself on his back by the too violent use of a fin. But by degrees he became master of the situation, and swam fairly along, the cool water gently lashing his sides as he glided swiftly with the current. Never in his life on earth had he felt so fresh and invigorated. The sensation of activity and power in an element which constantly refreshed without stint and without fail was exquisitely delightful. Every variety of movement added fresh enjoyment to the enraptured Sin, who was fairly entranced with the pleasures of his new existence. After a time, however, he began to feel the discomforts of hunger, and remembering that he had now to seek his own food, he devoted his energies to finding a worm. But whether through want of skill in the kind of search, or from scarcity of worms, certain it is that he was eminently unsuccessful. He prowled along the muddy banks, he dived down to the bottom, and he peered among the rubbish collected round the wrecks of punts and stumps of trees which strewed the bed of the river. But all in vain; and what made his failure the more distressing was that his appetite was becoming voracious.

In one of his predatory expeditions he saw a worm, and at first his joy was intense; but he was fain to recognise that it hung in the water in the shape of a hook, and remembering the king's words of warning, he passed by on the other side. After many fruitless swimmings to and fro, however, and when his strength began to fail and his energies to slacken for want of food, it chanced that he again found himself face to face with the dangling worm which he had before avoided. "Eat it," whispered the demon of hunger in his ear; "never mind what the old carp said. He is a fish of a past generation, and has not the knowledge and intelligence that we have. As to its shape, who ever saw a worm straight? And see, its tail is quite wagging with enjoyment." "Or pain," suggested prudence. "Not a bit of it," answered the demon. "But if you are afraid of gulping it down altogether, bite a bit off and then you can put it to the proof." Weakened by hunger, Sin yielded to the temptation and nibbled off a piece. The taste of food and the innocuousness of the first mouthful broke down the little hesitation he had felt, and with greedy maws he swallowed the whole worm.

Never was delight turned more instantly into pain. The hook, which had been concealed in the worm, pierced the roof of his mouth with an agonising prick. In his pain and terror he tried to swim away, but every movement, every writhe, added to his misery, and to complete his horror, he found that he was being pulled up towards the surface. When he became conscious of this he struggled violently, regardless of the torture it entailed, but all in vain. In spite of his efforts he was drawn out of the water, when, looking upwards, he saw, to his surprise and relief, that his captor was his own boatman, Chang.

"Let me go this instant, Chang," he said, "I am not a fish, but your master Sin. Take this horrid hook out of my mouth and put me back in the water at once."

"Well," thought Chang, "I never heard a fish make a noise like that before. But he is a wonderfully fine one, and I will just take him home to Mr Le." So thinking, he seized the fish, tore the hook out of his jaws and threw it down in the boat.

"Ah, your scoundrel!" shouted Sin. "How dare you treat your master in this way? You have broken my jaw, and injured my side. I dismiss you from my service. Put me back into the water."

"I have heard old women tell tales of birds that talked," said Chang, aloud, "but I will be bambooed if I don't think I have got hold of a fish that talks. But I daresay he will eat just as well as one that does not."

"What are you talking about, you fool?" said Sin. "I am not a fish, but you master. Once again I order you to let me go." These brave words ill consorted with the terror suggested by Chang's word "eat". The idea of being served up as a meal was almost more than he could endure.

At this moment the boat touched the shore, and without more ado Chang lifted the fish by its gills, and stepped on to the bank.

"Oh! oh! oh! you will kill me!" shouted Sin. "How dare you behave to me in this way? I will have you flayed alive for this. Oh, for an hour of manhood!"

By this time Chang had learned to disregard the strange noises made by the fish, and he trudged home with it, fully only of the thought of the "cumshaw"① which Mr Le would probably give him for bringing home

---

① *I.e.*, present

so fine a carp. Sin, also, who was beginning to feel weak from pain and the absence of water, determined to reserve his energies until he should come to his house, when he felt sure that the old porter would certainly know him.

On arriving at the gate, they were met by the porter, who, on seeing Chang and his prize, exclaimed, "Hai-yah! Chang, you are in luck to-day. What a splendid fish you have got! Mr Le has just sent out to know whether you have brought in anything."

"Porter," said Sin, "I am not a fish, but you master Sin, and this insolent fellow Change has tortured me inexpressibly, and refuses to put me back in the river. I depend on you to take me back at once."

"Now, by Confucius! Chang," said the doorkeeper, "you have got hold of a queer fish. I never heard a carp growl and snuffle like that before. You had better take it in at once to Mr Le."

Alas! thought Sin, it is useless trying to make these fools understand me. I must wait until I can explain myself to Le. His opportunity soon came, for Chang carried off his prize straight to Mr Le's apartment.

"Well, Chang, what have you got there?" asked Le.

"May it please your Excellency, I have brought one of the finest carp I ever saw."

"Le," said Sin in the loudest voice he could now command, "listen to me a moment. I am your friend Sin, and I put on this fish's skin merely to try what it is to be a fish. Alas! I know now only too well what that is. This villain Chang has tortured me beyond endurance. Tell him, as he will no longer obey me, to take me back to the river, as I should be glad now to resume my former shape. I have had enough of fins and scales." And hooks and worms, he might have added.

"Why, Chang, you have got hold of an extraordinary beast. He grunts like a pig. However, I daresay he will make a good dish." ("Oh!" groaned Sin.) "Take him to the cook."

"What! Eat your old friend Sin? Impossible, Le!"

"And tell him to split him open and grill him with some of that hot sauce I had yesterday."

"Le! Le! Le! Has it come to this—that you will eat your old friend?" screamed Sin. "Alas that my end should be to split open and grilled! My only chance now is that the cook may know me."

But even this last hope was destined to be disappointed. As Chang handed the fish to the cook, Sin said, as loudly and as distinctly as he could—"Cook, I am not a fish, I am Mr Sin. I have always been kind to you, cook, and I now beg you to take me back to the river."

"Your carp makes strange noises, Chang," said the cook, "but I will soon stop his grunting. Give me the chopper."

"Oh! spare me! spare me my life!" screamed Sin. But, regardless of his cries, the cook complacently placed him on the kitchen block, and lifting the chopper, gave him a violent blow on the head.

"Oh!" exclaimed Sin, sitting up in bed and thoroughly aroused, "What a knock I have given my head against the bedpost!" At first he could scarcely realise that he was safe in his own bed, his sensations had been so vivid. But at length he fell back with a sigh of relief, for, behold! It was a dream.

思 考

1. 仔细阅读道格斯《续玄怪录·薛伟》的译文，分析道格斯在译文中做出了哪些改写？
2. 试论道格斯对中西文化交流的贡献。

参考文献

- *Chinese Stories*, by Robert Kennaway Douglas, Edinburgh and London: William Blackwood and Sons, 1893.
- 汪辟疆校录《唐人小说》，上海：上海古籍出版社，1978 年。

扩展阅读

- *Catalogue of Chinese Printed Books, Manuscripts and Drawings in the Library of the British Museum*, by Robert Kennaway Douglas, London: Printed by order of the Trustees of the British Museum: sold by Longman, 1877.
- *Society in China*, by Robert Kennaway Douglas, London: A. D. Innes & co., 1894.

师多马《俗话倾谈·横纹柴》

（1895）

导　读

师多马（Thomas G. Selby，1846—1910）为十九世纪英藉在华传教士。作为卫斯理公会派的传教士，师多马于1868年抵达中国，在中国居住十二年左右，主要在岭南地区从事传教事业。他翻译和撰写的著作主要有《中国小说中的中国人》(*The Chinaman in His Own Stories*, 1895)、《耶稣的传教士》(*The Ministry of Lord Jesus*, 1896)、《现代小说神学》(*The Theology of Modern Fiction: Being the Twenty-sixth Fernley Lecture*, 1896)、《国内的中国人》(*Chinaman at Home*, 1900)等。其中，《中国小说中的中国人》是师多马选译中国小说结集而成，1895年在伦敦由查尔斯·肯尼（Charles H. Kenny）出版社发行。

师多马认为研读当地国小说是了解一个国家的思想生活、行为处事、家庭结构、社会习俗及宗教哲学最便捷且准确的方式，因此他从晚清岭南小说家邵彬儒编撰的粤方言小说集《俗话倾谈》中选译了《骨肉试真情》《好秀才》《瓜棚遇鬼》《泼妇》《横纹柴》《九魔托世》

---

① Thomas G. Selby 直译为托马斯·G. 塞尔比，习称其为师多马（Saint Thomas）。

与《生魂游地狱》七篇故事，作为英语读者了解中国人及其生活的媒介和参考。此处所选译文为师多马《中国小说中的中国人》中《横纹柴》之译文。

译 文

MADAM CROSS-GRAIN

In the reign of the emperor Kang Hi, there lived a Master of Arts whose name was On Wai Shing, of the Shung Hing prefecture, in the Sz Chün province, peaceable in disposition, and with a character free from grave fault. He had two sons, the elder of whom was called Tai Shing, or Great Completeness, and the younger, I Shing, or Secondary Completeness. Tai Shing's disposition was filial and friendly, but I Shing's was of a contumacious turn. In his fortieth year On Wai Shing was seized with sickness and died, leaving these two sons, who were insured at least against want by their small patrimony of fields and orchards. Tai Shing's mother, whose maiden name was Cham, was of a perverse disposition, and indifferent to what was equitable, accustomed to take her own course, and accounting might right. She was despised by all the neighbouring women, and nicknamed Madam Cross-grain. Her whole get-up may be imagined.

When Tai Shing had attained the age of twenty, Madam Cross-grain arranged his marriage. The maiden name of the bride was Cheung Shān

Ū(Coral). In appearance she was beautiful, and of very attractive manners. She waited upon her mother-in-law with gentle words and bated breath; never failing each morning to approach and ask about the welfare of her new relative, offering at the same time cakes and tea. Fastidiously neat in dress, she manifested her reverence by a grave deportment. But, lo! Madam Cross-grain, who had always been indolent and slatternly in her habits, felt ashamed at seeing Coral so neat and presentable, and began to revile her in a loud voice, saying: "It is quite a commonplace duty for the bride to wait on her mother-in-law; do you think it is some festive gaiety? Why need you be so pert and prim and spick and span, giving such heed to voice and carriage, and deporting yourself as elegantly, as though you had come to my place to put your figure on sale? When I was first a bride, I had ten times as good an appearance as you, and never thought that by to-day I should have grown ugly with age some thirty per cent or more."

This reprimand Coral heard silently with bowed head, not daring to speak in reply. On the following morning she again presented tea and cakes, attired now with severe simplicity, and wearing a well-washed blue tunic, but with neither grease on her hair nor paint on her cheeks. Madam Cross-grain grew angry at the first glance, and said: "Because I spoke a word to you yesterday, now you refuse to wear a single flower, to powder your face, or to put on new clothes. You simply want to exasperate me. You think I don't know! You think I don't know!"

Coral again bowed her head without speaking, inwardly reproaching herself for not understanding the etiquette of service. After this, when

Madam Cross-grain ran against a stool, Coral was sworn at. When the fowls would not eat their rice, Coral must again be sworn at. Returning home to visit her parents for three days, on her return she was sworn at for ten days. When Great Completeness saw that his mother was not pleased with his bride, he took Coral and beat her, to comply with his mother's wishes. Madam Cross-grain was pacified for the moment, but at length the disease broke out again. Her eccentricity passed all bounds, and she was without kindness or principle.

When the habit of swearing has been contracted, it is just like the vice of opium-smoking; you can scarcely live without indulging. Like intermittent fever, it is sure to come on once in two or three days. Evil spirits are the cause of swearing no less than of fevers.

A FIT OF TEMPER

One night, because of some trifling matter, this testy old woman stood in the doorway and swore a great volley of curses. Coral brought a bamboo chair, and invited her mother-in-law to be seated. Madam Cross-grain accepted the invitation, sat down, and with back bent, hand pointed to the sky, and feet pawing the earth, swore in a continuous stream without stopping to take breath. Coral boiled a dish of tea and presented it, asking her ladyship to assuage her thirst a little. After Madam Cross-grain had drunk the tea, her throat was mollified, her temper rose, and her voice waxed louder, and she swore away till the third watch of the night, when at length her voice gradually lowered, and her strength fell by degrees, and her breath gave out; for even a dog's voice will fail through excessive barking. Coral then knelt and entreated her, saying: "I have received what you have to teach me, and shall know how to do better in the future. Now please go to bed and rest, lest you should catch a chill from the breeze, and be calling out all night with stomach-ache."

Madam Cross-grain said, "I must swear! I must swear!" and, propping herself up the night through without sleeping, she swore till daylight. Coral was weeping by her side, and the neighbours came in to exhort the fury to desist. Having lit a lamp, Coral led her to her room to rest, spreading out the bed-quilts, arranging the mosquito net, putting the pillow straight, and then withdrew, wishing her mother-in-law a quiet sleep.

The first thing in the morning, Coral went to enquire after Madam Cross-grain, and saw at once that she could not speak. Her eyes were open, but without light or movement, her hair dishevelled and twisted about her head, and the whole appearance as of one already dead. Coral almost fainted away with fright, but at last ran to inform the old women of the neigh-hood, who came in a group to see how matters stood. The women chuckled loudly, and said to Coral: "You needn't fear; she only stretched her mouth too wide last night, and, having spent her breath, inflated herself with cold air, with the result that the circulation was checked. Her vital energy is exhausted, but with two or three days' quiet nursing she will soon be hale again."

When Coral understood the reason, she at once brought medicated ginger, and green cassia tea, and spirits of peppermint, to drive away the bed effects of the cold wind. She also purchased medicines to strengthen the constitution, and after several doses the patient could just begin to speak a little, and take her rice. But Madam Cross-grain insisted that some flesh should be brought to make soup which would lubricate her system, and Coral complied with her wishes, and offered it.

It chanced there was much cold and phlegm in the system, and its channels were not yet completely open, and after eating a few mouthfuls of pork, the fat pressed upon her throat, and made her so that she was unable to speak for ten days. At that juncture a doctor was summoned, and when he came he turned out to be a beginner, who did not understand his science. Thinking that inflammation was spreading internally, he gave a decoction of yellow nitre boiled very thick. After Madam Cross-grain had partaken thereof, and it had duly wrought, her eyes sank in her head, and she was so exhausted in all her limbs that she could not sit up, her face becoming yellow, and her bones poking out, so that she scarcely looked like a human being. Her vitality, moreover, became so depressed, and her stomach so weak, that food and drink lost their taste, and she dried away more and more each day. The doctor was skilful in healing chronic virulence, although a prentice hand in other branches of his profession.

Afterwards her son called in a physician who was fairly efficient, so that after a time she could begin to speak again, though with difficulty. And so things went on for some months, and there was to all appearance calm after storm. Coral was secretly delighted, thinking that as her mother-in-law was gaining flesh a little, she would now be able to sleep without anxiety. But, lo! as her voice became a little stronger, she began to curse and to swear, because Tai Shing had left home to study. And inasmuch as the old sickness was pressing on her, she swore at Coral, saying that she had bewitched her husband with fine dressing, and impaired his original disposition, threatening withal that she should pay for it with her life if Tai Shing should chance to die. She also swore at her son himself, because he was a worthless fellow, unable to distinguish between good and evil. Taking little heed of himself, he was demented by doting on his wife.

A HEARTLESS DIVORCE

Tai Shing knew that Coral was really virtuous and filial, but there was no help for it as she did not meet his mother's tastes; he wrote a deed of divorcement, and said to Coral: "I have heard that the reason for a man's taking a wife is that she should serve his mother. Why do I then still wish to keep you on as wife? I give you a bill of separation. You are now free to seek some new nest, and to marry another husband. There is no need for you to continue any longer an inmate of my house." Having so said, he turned round, walked out of the door and went away. When Coral heard this, her heart left her, and taking the document, she tore it into fragments and put them in the fireplace, and then went to her room and wept all night in the darkness. She knew that the past could not be undone, and all that was left for her was to pack up her bundle. So she chose out two or three articles of necessary clothing, but had no heart to think of the list of things she had brought with her as a bride. After rendering a farewell obeisance before the tablets and shrines, she came to her mother-in-law, desiring to speak, but could not frame her voice. With runlets of tears on her two cheeks, drooped head, and downcast spirit, she went slowly on step by step till she had got outside the door, where she paused a moment. Here she recalled how on the wedding day her father, brothers, and uncles, in ceremonial hats and long tunics, had followed her with lighted lanterns till she alighted from the bridal chair, earnestly exhorting her to be dutiful and affectionate towards her mother-in-law. But now, alas! she was driven forth for her unfilial conduct. Cast out on such grounds, how could she return home and face father, brothers, and uncles again! The best thing was to die. When she had thus thought, she drew a pair of scissors from her sleeve, placed them towards her throat, and began to cut with all her might. At that juncture happily a woman came up alongside, who, observing her fierce and excited demeanour, made a strong effort to seize her hand, and, thrusting it aside, said at the top of her voice, "Why are you so furious?" The scissor blades had already gripped her throat, and cut the skin, so that blood was flowing in a stream. The woman stanched it at once, and, taking the cloth Coral wore bound about her head, hastily bandaged the gash, crying out at the same time, "Save life! Save life!" All the neighbours then came running wildly, bringing pills and powders for wounds and abrasions, which, having been duly applied, arrested the flow of blood. Coral rested herself before the door, her face the colour of the earth. All who saw pitied her, some of them sighing aloud at the sight. Madam Cross-grain only cursed, saying: "You are making a pretence of killing yourself for the sake of involving me. If you want to die, go home to do it. Don't gather a crowd of people before my door to disturb me."

There was a widow in the same clan as Coral, whose maiden name was Wong, who had already heard of the excellent disposition of this disconsolate creature. She knew that Coral had been expelled by her mother-in-law, and, seeing that she was unable to walk because of weakness caused through loss of blood, she led her to her own house and bought medicines to heal her. In less than ten days the mark of her wound had disappeared. After a time Madam Cross-grain came again, and swore, saying, "You low, mean creature, discarded by your husband! Why don't you go back to your own parents rather than stay here to be a beam in my eye, and a burning fire in my heart?" The widow whose maiden name was Wong exclaimed: "Eheu! Eheu! what a perfectly ridiculous Madam Cross-grain you are! Your son has already given her a deed of divorce, and put her in the position of a common wayfarer. Is she still your daughter-in-law, that you presume to come and swear at her? Is not such conduct simply beneath contempt? Coral is a distant relative of mine, and if my relative comes to visit me, you, forsooth, must not allow her to stay!" And she in her turn swore at Madam Cross-grain till that venerable person was dumbfounded, and could only swallow her shame and go straight home in dudgeon.

Coral then said to her hostess: " I cannot make this my permanent resting-place. I must now be taking my departure." Packing up her bundle, she went away to live with a great-aunt on her mother's side who had married a man named Lok. She was cousin to Madam Cross-grain, and related therefore to Tai Shing. Advanced in years, and a widow herself, she had a daughter-in-law also a widow, and a little grandson. They lived some distance from Tai Shing, but had been to visit Coral, and had seen how filial and affectionate she always was. Coral accordingly entered their house, and told them some little of what had taken place.

"I know something, " said the old aunt, "of my relative's awkward disposition, and how inconsiderate she is. That was the reason why I was rather remiss in going to visit her. It is very cruel that you should have received all this oppression and ill-treatment from her."

"It is not after all on account of my mother-in-law. That I did not understand the art of being filial and conciliatory was my own fault, and I was therefore fated to provoke her at every turn. I know my sin, and ought to die for it."

"You must not speak thus, " said the old aunt. "I know you are concealing things."

A VISIT FROM CORAL'S MOTHER

After the lapse of some days Coral's mother came to visit her, and said: "I was away from home at the time, and did not know at once what had taken place, but have since heard our son-in-law has given you a bill of divorce. Why did you not come back home, rather than find your way here, to moil and disquiet your great-aunt? What reason could you have for taking this course?"

Coral replied: "Your daughter could not shame to face her father, brothers, and uncles again. I am resolved to stay here, and spin and embroider for a sip of coarse tea and a mouthful of rice, and here I will finish my days."

"Who could have foreseen the depths of your miscalculation, my daughter? With all your fine qualities and charms, you need not give way to despair. I shall find a new husband for you with plenty of money and an easy disposition, and with no mother to worry and oppress you, and I shall again give you in marriage."

"I have heard, " replied Coral, "that a faithful statesman does not serve two sovereigns, nor a faithful wife marry two husbands. Whilst I still have a mother-in-law I am unable to minister to, how could I have the effrontery to go into another family? If you insist that I must marry someone else, I shall leap into the river, hang myself, or take poison, and there will be an end of it. I have no wish to live a stolen life in the world of men.

When blow spring's wet breezes, and the bulb's growth is small,

And the pools are all pitted with the rain-drop's thick fall,

On the ooze of the pond-floor the lotos roots seize,

Unlike the limp willow blooms, adrift with the breeze."

Before she had finished the sentence, there came a choking sensation in her throat, and she fell on the ground sobbing, but unable to give articulate expression to her agitation.

Her hostess, seeing the tear-drops in her eyes, said: "Do not force her too much. Let her have her own way a little. If you press her unduly, she may cast away her own life in a spasm of perplexity, and how would you feel then?"

The mother, wiping her eyes, answered: "I cannot understand how it is that heaven has made you such an incarnate little demon. You may have happiness, and yet you push it aside. You may be a respectable and well-placed person, and you decline the prospect. Your heart is still set upon that miserable old mother-in-law, and you reproach yourself for not having served her with a devotion sufficiently perfect. You think she humbled and tortured you too little, forsooth! She did not restrain you with enough force, indeed! When I think of the demented old witch, I would like to bite out a couple of mouthfuls of her flesh; and yet you cannot bring yourself to part with her! Your tastes must surely be somewhat mean. Your mother will take the responsibility of finding you a new position, where you will have food and clothing at will; and you will not go, and have set your heart on living a life of starvation. Is not that a sign of unconquerable vulgarity? When you are dying of hunger or cold, do not blame your mother with your last breath. If you will not hear me, I will mutilate myself as the sign of an oath that I have cast you off, and no longer regard you as one of my own children. Then you need not be afraid I shall come to look after you again."

Coral cried incessantly, her mother cried and stormed, whilst the hostess chattered volubly, desiring to play the part of mediator. When her mother saw that it was impossible to change her purpose, she paced to and fro and shook her limbs, and prepared to depart, never even answering the invitation that was given to stay and eat rice. When she had reached the door, she turned her head about, and, pointing with her finger to Coral, said: "After this I shall not recognise you as my daughter, and you need no longer address me as your mother." Thus speaking, she went off in a rage.

When the mother had taken her departure, Coral remained with the aged relative, to quietly carry out her resolve.

NEW WIFE SOUGHT FOR TAI SHING

Soon after the flight of Coral, Madam Cross-grain called together the go-betweens, and said: "I have a good son, and should not be sorry to find a wife for him. Now, you matchmaking women, set your wits to work, and find up a taking girl as soon as possible, and send in her horoscope, and when the terms of marriage are settled, I shall fee you handsomely. Other people give two hundred copper cash, or thereabouts, to their go-betweens, but I am going to be spendthrift and pay in silver dollars."

As soon as the go-betweens had received their orders, they each went their way and enquired on all sides; but Madam Cross-grain's reputation was pretty well bruited abroad; and far and near parents who had seen the issue of the first betrothment were rather shy of dealings with the family. Who would be willing to let his daughter marry the son of such a harridan? And thus it came to pass that for two years not a solitary horoscope of maiden was brought back to see if its conditions would dovetail into that of Tai Shing. Madam Cross-grain then sighed, saying: "Most extraordinary! Can it be that my house is not a good building to live in, and that my rice is not a good grain to eat? How is it that I can hear of no family willing to intermarry with mine? Hard indeed is it to find any explanation of the fact."

MARRIAGE OF I SHING

Now because I Shing had already reached his majority, it was necessary that steps should be taken to consummate his marriage. The patronymic of the new daughter-in-law was Chau, and her name Tsong Ku, or Paragon Aunt. As soon as the bride reached her future home, Madam Cross-grain began to instruct her that she must be filial and docile, and that with bended head and bated breath she must minister to her mother-in-law. Above all, she must not imitate the evil disposition of the first daughter-in-law (a direction which she carried out to the letter). "Better than she was you must certainly be. In a word, if you are good, I shall be good. Why should not a mother-in-law be fond of her daughter-in-law? The only difficulty that can arise is when the daughter-in-law is not clear about her duty, and the mother-in-law gets a little provoked. If you are only willing to obey, my heart will get into my heels, and make me dance for joy."

But who would have thought it? The wife of Secondary Completeness, in spite of her high-sounding name, Paragon Aunt, was nicknamed "The Heaven-Usurping-Get-Up, " and also "The-Gutter-Poultry's-Imperial-Chancellor." If her mother-in-law gave expression in one sentence to a little displeasure, she would stick out her lips and reply with a dozen sentences or more. Every morning she slept till the sun was more than thirty feet above the horizon, and after she had risen, she would set her mother-in-law to wash the plates and bowls, and to cook vegetables and boil the rice; when her mother-in-law would not do it, she swore at her in ringing tones. "Several tens of years old, and cannot do a little simple, light housework. You won't boil a small meal of rice for us to eat a mouthful even! You think you can live with us young folk, and smooth your hair at your leisure, and powder away at your cheeks, and stick in your flowers, and you must moreover keep binding your feet round turn after turn till now." In boiling rice Madam Cross-grain would now put in too much and now too little water, and at one time the rice was too soft, and at another too hard. The Paragon Aunt would then mutter under her breath, and curse in a whisper, as though she were invoking the gods. And she now called her mother-in-law an old tortoise-wife, and now an old dog.

When Madam Cross-grain heard it, she would wax angry and say, "Have you come here to curse me, indeed?" and the Paragon Aunt would protrude her eyeballs and shout: "If I do curse, what shall you do next? I have no fear of your temper. If you like, you can fight it out with me before you sit down to rice." And with the word she would roll up the sleeves of her tunic, and tighten her headgear, and spread out her body, and make a display of strength very much like a fierce tiger stalking down the mountain side in anticipation of a good meal of human flesh.

Now Paragon Aunt was by birth tall, stout, large-boned, muscular, and fierce and savage in temper withal. When Madam Cross-grain saw the fury rushing into her face, as she had been afraid of her thirty per cent. to start with, now that this daughter-in-law was making a practical display of her majesty, Madam Cross-grain rushed out of the door, calling for help and crying for life as noisily as a whole market-place full of people, and jumping about like a live shrimp, and exclaiming, moreover: "I do not know why these dogs of broken-down families should have been brought together to hold me at bay. My whole life long I have been a good and honourable woman, as all my neighbours can testify; how is it that you young people should be so intolerable? Is there any such doctrine as this? Is it not hard indeed that a daughter-in-law should be more ferocious than her mother-in-law?" But Paragon Aunt took no heed to what was said, and the neighbours hid their mouths with their hands and laughed.

That night mother-in-law and daughter-in-law stood at the open door and had a pitched battle of words. Madam Cross-grain cursed till the third watch, and then left off work. But Paragon Aunt cursed on till the fourth watch without shutting up her mouth. Madam Cross-grain now knew that she was outmatched, and gulped down her indignation.

CONNUBIAL ASSIMILATION

One day the old harridan began swearing at her second son, I Shing, saying: "What an old bone of a beggar, what a head of a blind grub are you, to paly the part of a son in this fashion! You must surely see your wife is a presuming vixen, always cursing and swearing, and you are her husband, and do not shout a single syllable at her, or give her one passing taste of the stick. What does it all mean?"

I Shing replied: "She is rude to me as well as to you. What could come of beating her?"

"According to your view, I Shing, she need be subjected to no restraint whatever, and may be licensed to ill-treat her mother at will."

"You are a bit too snappish with me, and always were. Formerly you said of my brother's bride that she was no good. And now you say my bride will not do. Who upon earth will suit you? My wife says of herself that she is very good, and as for me, my verdict is that she will pass muster."

When Madam Cross-grain saw that I Shing was in this mood, she grew still more angry, till at last it brought on sickness. But in her affliction only Tai Shing would call in the doctor and prepare her medicine and tea. I Shing and his wife neither knew the general character nor the particular details of her illness, but simply ignored the matter.

Tai Shing then said to I Shing: "Brother, you know how it is our mother is prostrate on her bed with sickness. It comes from the irritation caused by the unseemly conduct of yourself and your wife. You seem not only to be incapable of changing the disposition of your wife by exhortation, but you yourself have degenerated into an unworthy son. Your wife comes of people with a different patronymic. It was through your mother you received your birth into the world. You never reflect how, when you were little, if you were sick your mother would sit all night with lighted lamp nursing you in her lap and ministering to your needs without ceasing, and how, with tears scarcely dry at dawn, unkempt hair, and unwashed face, she would put you on her back and go off to the doctors and get medicine to administer, and pray the spirits and entreat the Buddhas for your recovery, beating her forehead into a wounded pulp with her many prostrations. When you had sickness, your mother was stirred to her inmost soul. Now your mother is sick, and you pay no heed to it whatever. Hereafter you hope to have children and grandchildren. What blessing and honour is there pertaining to parenthood if the offspring is to act as you act? Now, brother, you must attend to what I say. Tomorrow just present yourself at your mother's bedside and enquire after her progress. Ask if you should call in another doctor, if she will eat rice or congee, or if there is any dainty she can fancy. Ask this with a soft voice and bated breath, so that you may comfort your mother's heart a little. That will be more like fulfilling the duty of a filial son. Now can you remember all I have said?"

I Shing, who had borne this just about as long as he could, answered: "Do you think I am stupid? You fear I cannot remember?" And having said thus, he went away.

The next morning, very early, he was in the act of getting up, and Paragon Aunt stormed at him, saying: "Are you mad? It is scarcely daylight, and you are getting up, and rolling the clothes aside and chilling my shoulders. Where are you going?"

"I am going to my mother's room to enquire after her health."

"Do not adduce this pretence of false piety to trifle with me. I know you pretty well, and am sure you are not one of that sort. Who directed you to do this?"

"My brother bade me, " replied I Shing.

"You ought to use your own judgment in giving ear to other people, and see if they are worth listening to. You will listen to your brother, and your brother is an idiot; for if he had had any wit about him, he would not have been wifeless now. Probably you intend to discard your wife and follow in the steps of your elder brother? You deserve a downfall if you take pattern by him. In the end you will certainly rue your mistake. Now listen to me, and you may have a happy career. I shall not permit you to go; and if you dare to go, I will bolt the door very early to-night, and not allow you to return to sleep."

"If you wish me not to go, I do not know that there is any very great difficulty in complying with your request. I will come back to bed and lie down again."

Paragon Aunt then laughed. "Now you are a good husband."

When a slow-hearted son and an evil-tongued wife recline on the same couch, they may be compared to a snake and a rat sleeping together.

Tai Shing had expected that his brother would certainly go and ask after his mother's health, but he had hoped in vain; so now he thinks within himself that, as his mother's sickness sprang from care and annoyance, he ought to arrange and have someone always with her to divert her attention and dissipate her vapours by constant conversation. After he had knit this brows and mused for a time, he suddenly brightened up and exclaimed: "I have hit upon the right plan. There is a female relative who is well advanced in years, and has plenty of time upon her hands. why should I not invite her to come and be a companion to my mother, for the gossip of an old crony may unlock her heart."

When he had come to this conclusion, there was, as it happened, someone going to Mrs. Lok's neighbourhood, and he availed himself of the opportunity to send a message, and the invitation was accepted. Form the arrival of the old dame, Madam Cross-grain's forlornness began to relax a little. In the still watches of the night, when tea was wanted, water was always ready, and the views and feelings of the old ladies jumped together, and not a little conversation went on to beguile the time.

The daughter-in-law of this companion always sent her cooked food from home every day. At one time it would be pork boiled with cutter-fish, at another fresh fish, soup, or oranges large or small, or sugar cane, or candied fruits. The old companion did not eat much, but Madam Cross-grain tasted and swallowed everything with the utmost recklessness, and satisfied all her fancies. At last, having broken out into a snatch of a song in her merriment, she said: "Well, old crony, fortune has been kind to you. Only think how blessed you are in having such a filial-tempered daughter-in-law. Why, when you have come to see a relative, she follows you with constant presents. Who can say what stacks of viands you must have to eat when you are at home?"

The old companion replied: "The woman who knows how to show herself a good mother-in-law naturally has a good daughter-in-law. We must take things as they come in this world, as you and I both know. For even a little to eat we must be thankful."

"I have no such good daughter-in-law, " sighed Madam Cross-grain. "Look at mine, got up as if she owned the firmament and all it contains. I would not even expect mine to buy presents of food for me, but should be satisfied if she were a little less passionate. My only desire is that she will not provoke me so much."

"But when Coral was with you, she was good-natured. If you swore at her, she only dropped her head; and if you beat her, she had not grievance to complain of. The fact of it is, you were rather awkward-tempered in your treatment of her, and, to put it gently, did not err on the side of indulgence."

Madam Cross-grain then groaned aloud and said: "I now see from contrast with the vices of my second daughter-in-law that my first daughter-in-law was really very good. I indeed repent, but it is hard to retrace one's steps. I do not know whether she may be married again, and where she may be gone by this. It is difficult for the north of the earth and the south of the heaven to cross each other's path again. When my ailment is better, I will go and have a peep at your daughter-in-law, and that will do."

MADAM CROSS-GRAIN VISITS HER FRIEND

After about twenty days, when the sickness was overpast and the old relative had gone back home, Madam Cross-grain came to pay the promised visit, and, as soon as she had entered and quietly seated herself, said: "Now this good daughter-in-law of yours, where is she?"

And the relative answered: "My daughter-in-law is not good. It is you who have the good daughter-in-law."

"I do not know where my daughter-in-law may now be—probably married again in some strange place to a new husband. Good or not good, I have no share in her affections and no right to her service."

"Your Coral is still here, weaving cloth at my house for a livelihood. The things sent as presents when I was with you were all bought out of her savings."

Now, when Madam Cross-grain heard this, her heart was stirred, and she gave a long cry: "Pity her, pity her! I cannot understand why she has been so good a daughter-in-law, for she was very badly treated. But if she is in your house, why is she not to be seen?"

Coral then came forth from her room and knelt before her mother-in-law, saying: "Your daughter-in-law has been unfilial, and was unversed in the art of ministering to her mother-in-law. I hope you will be lenient to my sin."

With two hands Madam Cross-grain then helped her up and answered in a fluster: "You are perfectly filial. From antiquity till now you have been unequalled. You top the list. The only thing amiss is that I am old, stupid, and useless, and cannot distinguish between light and heavy in my swearing and railing. Do not blame me. If, after eating rice, you will follow me back home, you will be the blessing of the household."

Coral replied: "If my mother-in-law will only receive back her daughter-in-law and give her a home again, the grace and favour will be like that of heaven itself. I hope you will point out the defects of your daughter-in-law and teach her."

"There will be on need to teach; none whatever, " Madam Cross-grain said. "Your old style of filial piety will more than suffice."

The old relative then killed and cut up a fowl and spread a repast, so that they could all feast together in joy. Coral chose out one piece of delicate fowl and offered her mother-in-law, and Madam Cross-grain chose out several tit-bits and pressed them upon Coral. She also begged Coral to drink wine, saying: "It is a good omen for young people to drink wine brought on with the fowl."

When Madam Cross-grain had sipped several tens of cups, her face began to get as red as the rising sun and her neck so relaxed that her head was bobbing to all points of the compass. After the repast was over, and her spirits had risen, and she had fanned herself cool again, she led back Coral home, swinging her arms with great vigour on the way. When she reached the entrance to her own alley, quite a number of people stood by the wayside, and Madam Cross-grain addressed them, saying: "My daughter-in-law had not married anyone else, and she said she must come back home to wait upon me. I could not very well bear to give her up, so I brought her back with me. Is it not a good plan?"

"Good beyond all forecast. Good beyond all forecast, " they cried with one consent. "She is a daughter-in-law it would be hard to match."

Upon their arrival, husband of course loved wife, and mother-in-law loved daughter-in-law, and the family was happy and harmonious with the breath of spring in their faces.

HIVING OFF

But what sort of pleasure was it that Coral's return gave to I Shing and his wife? I Shing grew angry, and said: "My brother declared at first he did not want his wife, and now receives her back with the utmost ostentation. How can he look men in the face if he goes upon this principle? My mother is still more demented. At first she said her first daughter-in-law was not good; now she turns round and makes her out a gem. What does it mean? This thing does not suit my taste. I must have the patrimony divided, and we will keep separate tables."

When Tai Shing heard this, he replied: "Brother, if you wish to divide, we will divide."

"I insist upon a division, " said I Shing.

So when they had assembled together paternal and maternal uncles and aunts of different degrees, and the old men of the family whose office was to assess, arbitrate and formally witness to the division of the estate, I Shing said, "I must have five or six extra acres of the low-lying field, and seven or eight acres extra of the land on the island, and ten extra fruit trees."

The great-uncles then said: "The proper rule for the division of property left behind by a father is for each brother to take on half. But if the eldest son or grandson who is the responsible representative for the family should desire a little more, there would be no unreasonableness in that; however, why should you want a larger portion than your elder brother?"

I Shing answered: "My brother was at school for more than ten years, and has been in to the examinations seven or eight times. When my brothers was married, two bands of musicians were engaged for his weeding; but when I was married, there was only one band of six flute-players. I therefore want a little more out of the estate to make things equal."

Tai Shing said: "Brother, I shall not strive with you. Take your first choice, and I will have what is left."

And thus I Shing got the best fields and the best land and the best of everything, and Tai Shing did not even think of making comparisons. The uncles said: "Such an elder brother is not a man to be made light of, but is one of a thousand. For the past seventy years we have been present at divisions of property times without number, and have seen men contend for a foot of land at the top of a field or the corner of an allotment, and the strife reached such a pitch that skulls were crushed and brows cleft open, and enmities sown that led to deadly law-suits. Sometimes they have striven because of some little inequality in the size of vessels and articles of furniture, and have made so much of their petty apportionments that they have grown red in the face and eyes, and have thereafter been accustomed to meet without speaking. But you seem to look very lightly on these things, and are indeed unexampled in your disposition, belonging to quite a superior grade to the rank and file of mortals."

Tai Shing replied: "The rule for division of parents' property is not inexorable. If he wants a little more, I will think of it as though our parents had left a little more behind them. Had they left two or three more children to share it, I could not have stubbornly insisted upon taking as much as I have now."

The uncles then clapped their hands with delight, and said: "The ten years' education your father gave you was not wasted. You can understand, and practise what you understand."

Now Tai Shing went out as a school-teacher, so as to be able to maintain his mother, and Coral occupied herself with embroidery and cloth-weaving, so that she might be able to minister to her mother within the house, all dwelling together in joy and peace. I Shing and his wife were secretly glad, thinking now that there would be no ties and no restraints, and that they would be able to have everything to their minds. They set up a table of foreign fashion japanned with gold lacquer, and two bamboo chairs in which they could stretch out their backs, and ivory chop-sticks, and plates and bowls of fine china, and teapots and flower-vases and the like, every article of which was fresh and bright. And thus they dwelt at their ease, the wife as gay as a millionaire, and insisting at every meal upon the best of wine.

One morning, when she had got half through her wine, she bade her husband go out quickly and get some toasted pork thoroughly salt in flavor. He had just wrapped it up in a lotos-leaf when he ran against his mother, who said, "What have you got there?"

I Shing answered: "It is not for you to ask. We have separate tables, and you do not superintend our cuisine now. Well, in fact, this is dragon's flesh. No concern of yours."

Madam Cross-grain was greatly provoked. "Blind grub-head, " retorted she, "how contemptuous and insolent you are, speaking without deference in your words and insulting your own mother! I won't allow you to eat it."

With the word she stretched out her hand and made a grab which had the effect of breaking open the parcel and scattering the strips of toasted pork upon the ground. At that very moment there were two great dogs by the roadside, who became perfectly frantic as they made a rush for the viands. I Shing, stooping to gather them up, found himself launched into a contention with the dogs, who in a trice loosed their grip of each other and bit him several times. Their teeth went through a finger and the drops of red blood trickled down, upon the few pieces of toasted pork he had recovered, and also stained the earth. At the side of the road there was a string of beggars, who clapped their hands and laughed away in audible guffaws. I Shing went home, cursing under his voice, in a high state of fury.

When Paragon Aunt had enquired the cause, she also was equally angry, though sorry at the misadventure. Both agreed in blaming their mother and censuring her for lack of kindness. At the four divisions of the year and the eight festivals, they never asked their mother to eat a meal or rice, or invited their brother to drink a cup of wine. When the wife's uncle came with presents and compliments, they bought fish and flesh, and did everything that was possible to fete him. And when Paragon's own mother came, they filled heaven and earth with their merry-making, killing ducks and fowls without number.

On the thirteenth of the eighth moon, they invited Paragon's mother to come to a birthday, and prepared a great fowl, four pounds five ounces in weight, and stewed it with lily seeds, chestnuts, red dates, bamboo shoots, vegetables, ginger, and all kinds of condiments. After it was stewed, the fragrance floated round into the next house. I Shing had two sons, and Paragon Aunt even would speak in high terms of their promise. Now the first-born was several years old, and as he saw the dish of stewed fowl awaiting his maternal grandmother, he asked his father, "Shall I go and invite the paternal grandmother also to come and eat rice?"

I Shing said: "First ask your mother, and then we may come to a decision."

Paragon Aunt replied: "You must not go. What would you invite her for? She is an old dog of a mother."

Ought not such language to be punishable with death? A dog indeed she would feed, but not this creature.

Afterwards Paragon Aunt told her little boy to go and buy a pot of oil, and gave him his orders, saying: "If your grandmother sees you buying oil, and asks, 'What have you for dinner to-day?' you must say that we are having raw bean curd. You must not let it out that we are indulging in fowl."

When Madam Cross-grain heard this, she was greatly incensed, and said to Coral: "The universe has in it folk of this sort, who have heart and have it to excess. When the outside mother comes, they kill fowls and exercise hospitality, but man and wife never ask their own mother to eat a mouthful. What use is it rearing sons and finding wives for them?"

Coral laughed and answered: "Well, do not suppose every one is after their cut. There are some who are good and there are some who are bad; but the world assuredly could not be carried on if all were to take pattern by them. Suppose you were invited there to a meal, how much could you eat? To-morrow I will go to the market and buy a plump fowl, and make duck sausages and other things, and you can eat your fill."

Madam Cross-grain said: "How do you make that sausage? I am getting past middle life, but have never eaten such dainties as yet."

The next day Coral was as good as her word. Madam Cross-grain ate to the full, with very great gusto, and stroked her paunch and straightened her backbone in a spirit of perfect contentment, and afterwards, when she met anybody, could do nothing but talk about the virtues of Coral. The physical wants of old people ought always to be divined in this fashion.

DOMESTIC TYRANNY AND ITS FRUITS

Paragon Aunt in the meantime was becoming more fierce and contumacious than ever, till at last her lack of self-control brought serious consequences. One day, because there was something that did not just suit her, she seized the slave-girl and beat her most unmercifully, and by one careless stroke fractured the skull, and the poor creature bled to death.

The father of the house-slave was greatly enraged, and said: "Because of poverty, I sold my daughter that you might employ her labour, not that you might beat her to death. Do you think, when you buy a slave-girl, it is according to some private code of your own? Possibly my daughter might hereafter have been wife to a rich man. Who can tell? Could you see into her future destiny? And then there would have been no more selling of daughters into servitude for generations. Now you have killed my daughter, and I have sworn an oath that I shall give you no rest, but shall petition the mandarin to put you on your trial."

He was as good as his word, and made a complaint to the chief magistrate, who forthwith sent out police to arrest Paragon Aunt. Placing chains round her neck, they led her away.

The mandarin, having opened the court for the trial, said: "You mean woman of bad disposition, you took human life, accounting it a thing to be sported with. Now what punishment do you think should be awarded you? Be quick and confess."

The Paragon Aunt, then kneeling, made her petition, saying: "Great officer, your discernment is lucid. I, the humble housewife, have hitherto been a lover of virtue and good works. On the first and fifteenth days of the moon, I have always burned incense and worshipped the gods. How can it have come about that I am charged with murder? It is only because this slave-girl was in the habit of stealing rice to eat, and I caught her in the act, and struck her several times with my fist, and unwittingly fractured her skull. She fell to the earth and died. What strength is there in a poor housewife's fist? It was because this slave-girl had some internal complaint, and her time to die had come. The accident has been used against me, but I cannot be fairly charged with her death."

"Your slave-girl stole rice because you did not give her enough to eat, and she could not bear hunger. You had no compassion on her, and went the length of using your fists upon her body. The poor thing had no strength, and no wonder she died under your evil hand. And according to the statute book, what is the penalty for murder?"

"It is murder to kill with knife or the sword. Is it the same thing to only strike with the hand? This humble housewife cannot subscribe to that doctrine."

"I direct that this low, turbulent woman, who tries to darken the question by talk and deception, shall receive a hundred blows on the mouth."

The police then plied their terrors till the gums of Paragon protruded, and blood trickled on all sides, and her two cheeks stood out as large as a pig's head. Paragon kept alternately sobbing and cursing, and pointing with her finger at the mandarin, asserted that he presumed upon the strength of his position to oppress her. This exasperated the mandarin, who called back the police and bade them give her a hundred more with the rattan canes. They beat till blood and flesh mingled with each other, and yet she would not confess. Calling the police, the mandarin said, "Take this wretched woman and put her in a cell, and at the next court day bring her before me to be charged again."

The father of the slave-girl again pressed his petition, and a second time Paragon Aunt was brought out for judgment, trusting as usual in the sharpness of her teeth and the volubility of her argument. The mandarin then bade the police bring out the press boards, and thus they tortured Paragon till tears and fire mixed themselves in her eyes, and her ten fingers were broken. The pain was so intolerable that she rolled upon the ground, and her breath more than once seemed quite gone, and she had to be revived by copious sprinklings of cold water. When she came to herself, she wept and cried aloud, "I confess I beat her to death."

The mandarin then said: "Now, as she has confessed, you can take her back and shut her up in the cell."

When I Shing saw the suffering through which his wife had gone, it was as though a knife had pierced through his heart, and he hurried home, and went round to men of means, attempting to borrow money with which to save his wife. But nobody would make him any advances, and he was compelled to sell his lands and fields, which realized some three hundred taels or a little more. Out of this he gave one hundred to the father of the slave-girl for "tear-stopping dollars". Another hundred he distributed at the mandarin's court for expenses incurred when the warrant was issued sentencing her to imprisonment for two months. At her release, her face was withered always, and her appearance most ghost-like. The skin had contracted, the flesh shrivelled up, and she was yellow and slender as a piece of firewood, quite unlike the bouncing woman of former days. Thus each received the recompense of earlier misdoings,—the husband in property losses because of his former selfishness, and the wife in terrible personal suffering, the providential penalty for ill-treatment of her husband's mother.

After Paragon Aunt had returned home, I Shing bathed her wounds with medicated wine, and administered sundry pills. Every morning he asked after his wife's health, and when she could begin to walk, humbly assisted her to hobble. The neighbours laughed at his stupidity; but I Shing said: "You need not laugh. She is my wife, and I am following heavenly doctrine. Ought I not to love her?" Alas! he could only love his wife, and could not fulfill the chief duty of loving his own mother.

A DREAM OF HIDDEN TREASURE

One night, when Tai Shing was sleeping heavily, his father appeared to him in a dream, and with a pleased expression of countenance said: "You are a truly good son, Tai Shing, and to find a wife the equal of yours would need a long search. Your mother was always of a more or less awkward disposition. Could I have lived with her as a husband for half a lifetime and not have found out that? Your wife, however, has been kind and patient with her, for she is an adept in meekness and reverent affection, and may be accounted truly filial and gracious. The filial merit of both yourself and your wife has been reported monthly in the Western Heavens by the God of the Furnace, and thence reported to great Yuk Tai. Yuk Tai is much pleased, and will hereafter enable your two sons to become literary graduates. For the present he gives you a boon of two jars filled with silver."

Tai Shing answered: "The attainment of literary honour by our two sons is a thing for coming years; but as for two jars filled with silver, where might they be?"

To which the father made reply: "The silver is in the back garden, under the root of the red thorn tree. I, the humble ghost, have come to announce that fact to you. To-morrow you may dig and take up the treasure."

When the father had thus spoken, with an expression of great benignity upon his face, he passed out of sight.

As soon as Tai Shing came to himself, he aroused his wife, and told her of the matter made known to him by his father.

Coral said: "Are we two then so extraordinarily filial? To speak plainly, if the sons born to us come up to your mark, and if, when we take them wives, the wives come up to my mark, for my own part, I shall be content."

"Well, we must take things as they fall out, " replied Tai Shing; "and our first work is to follow the directions heaven has given us."

"If we really find money when we dig, we must first buy a litter of pigs to fatten, and afterwards we must buy several oxen and give them in charge of someone to keep, and every year we shall get a little rice as the price of their hire. When your brother sold his lands and fields too, it was at a very low price; it would be a good thing to buy the property back again. With the remainder of the money we might open a pawn shop, or start a sugar factory, or buy rank and build a library and a large house. Now would not that be capital?"

Tai Shing laughed. "Do you want to be a rich woman all at once?"

And Coral replied: "Well, it is not an uncommon wish after all."

After they had heated water and washed their faces, Tai Shing said to his wife: "Just go into the back street to uncle A Mi's and borrow a wrought-iron spade, and then turn into the next alley to grandfather A

Tak's and ask the loan of a second spade."

Tai Shing then took off his gold-broidered cap, his shoes decorated with silk butterflies, his white stockings and long tunic, and, rolling up his trousers and turning up the sleeves of his inner garment, he seized hold of one of the spades, Coral herself taking the other. At first they were full of high spirits and physical strength, and quite taken up with the novelty of the work, and both delved with a will till they touched the roots of the tree. But Coral was accustomed to weaving and needlework only, and after thirty or forty turns began to complain that her arms were feeling weak. Tai Shing laughed and said: "Well, if you have no strength, you can rest a little. Sit down for a few minutes, and after getting your breath, you can dig again."

Tai Shing himself was a man more used to the fan and the pencil than manual toil, a genteel scholar, and how could he be expected to have much physical strength? Lo! after he had dug seventy or eighty spadesfuls, he found himself out of breath, and must stretch his back, forsooth! He also complained of pains in his arms, and said to Coral, "You get up and dig a little, for it is my turn to rest now."

Coral laughed and replied: "Well, you need not boast. You of course intend to exchange literary for military pursuits and learn archery." At which Tai Shing laughed loudly.

After they had been digging half the morning, he said to Coral: "Now go home and boil rice, and buy a little pork shank to make soup, and warm a few ounces of good samshoo, so as to animate our spirits and strengthen our arm-bones. And mince a few ounces of lean pork and fry it with an egg for our mother."

"I will keep in mind your instructions, " Coral answered.

As they sat down to rice, Madam Cross-grain said: "You two ought not to undertake all that work of digging at the tree roots. Would it not do if you were to hire someone to grub it up?"

Tai Shing answered: "It won't split up into very much firewood, and would scarcely repay the cost of the labour. We have nothing else in view but to take it up for firewood."

After lunch they again betook themselves to work, and digged till late in the afternoon. They had got under the root, and were making apparent headway. Again they applied themselves, till at last a ringing sound was heard, and the glimmer of something white seemed to burst forth. Pushing aside the earth, they made a careful inspection, and, lo! there lay rows of things, white in colour, round in shape, and large as the mouth of a teacup, and a whole jar packed full of them, and they knew that these were dollars. Husband and wife then capered for joy, chuckling to themselves silently all the while.

Just at that moment I Shing came to survey the situation, and in an excited manner, pointing at his brother, said: "Brother, you have no conscience. The stump of the red thorn tree was left us by our father, and I have a share in it. When you took it upon yourself to dig it up without taking counsel with me, you certainly wished to deceive me. Such proceedings will never do. Never. You must give me my half or I shall go to law with you."

Tai Shing replied: "Do not distress yourself; it shall be equitably divided."

"It is all as plain as the figure one, " said I Shing. "We surely need not call a family council to settle the matter. Whilst we keep watch here, you can send my sister-in-law into the ancestral hall to fetch the scales."

Coral went forthwith, and Paragon, having heard of the matter, came rushing in post-haste with several baskets full of chaff and emptied the contents on the floor; it would be impossible to say how much there was, the stuff seemed to fill the whole place. And having brought the baskets, she rushed away to put the stand of the scales level and to see that the scale pans were accurately suspended. I Shing handled the weights and kept a close eye on the indicator. Paragon then shuffled the silver into the scale and thence turned it out into the baskets, each basket being about a hundred-weight. The scaleful which fell to Tai Shing was light by a few ounces, and that of I Shing heavy, because the younger brother managed the scale. After all had been weighed out, each brother carried his portion into his own house.

I Shing clapped his hands and jumped in the air, saying: "After all, the great thing is for a man to have a conscience. Never have I injured anyone all my life long, therefore heaven does not hold back from me its good things. When because of that unpleasant business in the law courts I had to spend some hundreds of dollars, it was not with any great mental delight; but now I have got these several baskets full, it is many time more than I lost. Riches are a great help to courage. Hereafter I will buy several more slave-girls, and if they are beaten to death, what will it matter?"

"Such cases can always be managed with money," Paragon said.

To which I Shing replied: "At that time the wheel of fortune had not turned, and made me into a rich man. To-night we will drink a cup of wine and be merry."

I SHING GOES SHOPPING

I Shing, having brought out a couple of dollars from his store and walked as far as the market turned into a candied fruit and dried meat shop, He ordered samshoo and white rice and a roast goose and two pounds of roast meat, and brought out his dollars to be weighed in payment.

The cashier turned upon him and said: "Brother I Shing, these are counterfeit dollars. Why do you try and pass them off at a shop where you are so intimate?"

I Shing answered: "They were dug up from under a tree root. How can they be counterfeit? They were certainly deposited there a very long time ago, and in the course of centuries the colour of the silver has changed. If you are in doubt, why not take an awl and bore to the inside, and then you will find out that I am an honest man."

The cashier bored with the awl and said: "Every bit of it is white brass, and it is of no use whatever. It is not even silver-coated, for then the silver of the outside could be used."

I Shing, seeing there was no way out of this strange incident, asked him to put the things down to his account, but the cashier answered: "Well, that gives us unnecessary trouble. You had better not have the things."

He then took back the rice and emptied it out into the hopper again, and poured the samshoo back into the jar, and hung up the roast goose and pork where they were before. And I Shing, crestfallen, went home, not appreciating the flavor of the thing at all, and said to his wife: "As we enter upon this new turn of life, it is thrown in our faces that the dollars are counterfeit. Is it not mortifying? Boil a fowl, and let us have some samshoo and drink to our better luck."

After they had drunk, he said to his wife: "To-morrow you must be quick and starch a new tunic for me. I must go to the capital of the province to buy things."

Paragon asked, "Why?" and he replied: "At the small market-shops of our rural districts the men who profess to be cashiers have never spent a fortnight even in learning the art of their trade. They say good silver is brass. Is it not absurd? The silver we have dug to-day has changed its colour through age. The silversmiths of the city, however, will, I think, be sure to know it. I will bring home two hundred dollars worth of goods to open their eyes, so that when I go to them again to make purchases, they will not give themselves out to be so dreadfully clever."

All night long the worthy couple were talking of their plans for buying fields and lands, of building houses and purchasing rank, and of all the things suitable to rich people. They got scarcely any sleep; for when they had finished talking, they laughed, and when they had finished laughing, they talked again, till daylight came before they were aware.

The next morning Paragon went out into the street, and her speech was blustering and her voice high and sounding. You might speak to her three times without getting her to pay heed, for she was altogether absorbed in chattering about their own affairs and the security they now had against the fear of poverty. Some who were not altogether disinterested came rushing to their house to sit and talk, congratulating, flattering and praising them by turns, and saying, "How good-hearted and virtuous in disposition they must be, and heaven had used its eyes and at length given them rank and high estate!" Paragon was of course delighted.

It having been arranged that her husband should go to the city on the third day, a list was prepared of the things he was to purchase. It being the cold season of the year, of course they must have silk bed-quilts, crape mosquito nets, lacquered pillows, finely woven mats, long fur robes, and every kind of wearing apparel. Paragon said: "I must also have gold pins and jade bracelets, pearl clasps and silver buttons, a red petticoat and flowered tunic sleeves, every kind of clothing of the grandest description." And lots of ebony tables and chairs and old vases were to be bought in addition. It took two sheets of paper to write out the complete list.

After going on board the boat, whenever I Shing came across a fellow passenger, he would ask which was the best silk shop in the city, and which was the best establishment for furs and also for matting. He would ask those in the forward cabin, and then repeat his interrogatories to those in the aft cabin, and then he would go and ask those sitting on the roof of the boat. And the people said: "You will find out when you get to the city. Do not brag so much."

I Shing retorted: "Do you think it is inferior articles I am going to buy? The sage himself has said, 'Enquire about everything, ' and I am just carrying out the classical precept. Do you despise me for one who does not know propriety?"

Everybody in the boat laughed; but I Shing felt no sense of shame, and only made a display of himself, as if it were something very extraordinary in which he was occupying himself.

When he reached the city, he sought out the largest silk and braid shop with as much assurance as though he were a great wholesale merchant, and his mouth wagged and his finger pointed as he said, "I want this and this, " and he looked at them all, sample after sample, to see if it was just what he required. At last I Shing said: "Now, you must let me have these at what is a fair figure, and I shall have other transactions with you hereafter. I shall be a customer not for once in a way only." And the cashier gave a shake to his reckoning-beads, added up the bill, and asked the honoured guest to produce his dollars and put them in the scale to be weighed. I Shing fumbled about in a very large style, and at last brought a bag of dollars out from under his waist-band, about a hundred, or perhaps a few over that number. The cashier, having looked at them, said, as he changed colour: "These are all brass dollars. The man is certainly an impostor." And he called aloud to his fellow shopmen to come and search him. All at once the shop was in an uproar, and no chance of explaining himself was allowed to the poor fellow. They bound him with hempen cords right off, blacked his face with ink, and handed him over to the street watchman, who beat him most mercilessly the round of his ward.

The following day I Shing took boat to return home. Paragon, knowing that her husband had arranged to be back on a fixed day, in the evening of the appointed date engaged four or five porters to go to the landing and carry home the furniture and clothing. As soon as the boat had come to anchor, she saw her husband steadying himself by the boat roof and crawling up out of the cabin with down-bent head and dejected mien. "The men are here, " she said. "You can put the things you have purchased into their care to carry home for us."

I Shing nodded his head and waved his hand, saying: "Do not be so impatient. Wait till they have got all the cargo out. If they come again tomorrow morning at daylight, it will be ample time." And so the porters went off to their homes.

Paragon said: "Are the things at the bottom of the boat?"

I Shing replied: "Ay."

When they reached home, his wife said: "I think you are looking a little out of sorts. Possibly when you were in the city, holding high jinks in some of the wine-shops or flower-boats, you ate too much frizzle and roast, and your system has consequently become a little feverish. But of course I do not know positively."

I Shing then pulled up the after part of his tunic, and disclosed his wealed back to his wife's view, saying, "Just look at this."

She, of course, saw that his loins were black and blistered, and in her alarm said: "You have employed some man to scrape you as a counter-irritant. How comes he to have cut you so frightfully as this?"

I Shing exclaimed: "Cut, indeed! May the thread of your life be cut!" He then explained that he had been beaten with the rattan, and to mistake this for surgical scraping and cicatrising was nonsense.

Paragon said: "You are now a rich man; what need had you to go and play thief, and get caught and be beaten?"

"I have not been playing thief, " retorted I Shing; "but people said that I was an impostor, and had been using counterfeit dollars in payment for genuine goods. And thus I came in for a gratuitous castigation."

"Are all of the dollars bad, then? Your brother is a miscreant indeed. I hear the dollars he uses are all right, and, strange to say, ours are all counterfeit. It is clear he is taking advantage of your dullness. Go at once and insist on having them changed, and if he is unwilling, you need not be afraid to fight him. He is a schoolmaster, and, I will vouch, is no match for you in strength. And if he is still unsubmissive, I will go and tumble down on the floor of his house and sham dead, and do you fear he won't give in then? "

"Capital! Capital!" said I Shing. And again they talked over their plans in bed.

Paragon then hurried off to buy sundry herbs and powders, and, having made them up into doses, rubbed them on his back. I Shing thought: "She is first-rate. Her kindness of heart leaves on room for criticism. What an uncommonly good wife she is!"

Paragon observed: "Neither your brother nor your mother comes to ask a word about you. He forgets that he is the same flesh and blood, and she forgets that you are her offspring. If there were any such lack of mutual kindness in us, we should soon grow tired of each other."

I Shing replied: "Well, least said, soonest mended. Let us keep our own counsel. People who act in such ways are scarcely human."

HAVING CHANGED PORTIONS WITH HIS BROTHER, I SHING AGAIN SHOPS

Early next morning he got up and went off to his brother's schoolroom, saying: "Brother, you are bereft of all conscience, for you have given counterfeit dollars as my share of the treasure-trove, and kept the genuine for yourself; and I have been arrested, and had my face smudged, and made to pose like a black tortoise, and been cruelly scourged. It is intolerable. I do not want these, I want those; change the dollars, and that will do."

Tai Shing replied: " At the time we shared up the money, you held the scales, and your wife held the baskets and shovelled the silver in and emptied it out again. My wife and I never moved a finger in the transaction. How then could we show any partiality to our own interests?"

"Well, I cannot take any notice of all these trifling details; I want to change portions, and there is an end of it."

"Well, if you want to change, that is a very little matter, and it shall be as you wish."

The younger brother then brought his several baskets of dollars, substituting basket for basket, till all had been changed. That night I Shing was happy beyond expression, and said to his wife: "The look of these dollars is very different from the others. I need not be afraid of getting into disgrace now. The provincial capital is not a lucky locality for me. I will go this time to the great trading mart of Lung Tsai, to buy clothes and other things."

After two days, he again got out his paper to write down the lists of intended purchases, recalling them one by one, and asking Paragon from time to time if that were correct or no. Paragon said: " I too forget. Why do you not copy out again the list you took the other day?"

Her husband replied: "At the time they were tricing me up with hempen ropes, I lost my consciousness even, and do you think I had presence of mind to pick up my list and bring it home again?"

After they had thought and conferred together, however, they managed to make out a fairly full list, corresponding for the most part to the earlier one.

I Shing then said: "There is still one very important item I have not remembered to write. I must buy a jar of wine to strengthen my back, and all the joints of my body."

Paragon chimed in: "A little of it might do me good. When I was in goal, those execrable police, who have no thought of human life, beat madly, and thumbscrewed without any restraint; and although there are now no open wounds in my flesh, whenever there is cold wind or rain, my bones ache more or less."

"Why did you not tell me earlier? If that is so, we must put on our memorandum five pounds of the sinew of northern deer, twelve ounces of tiger-bone grease, and a branch of the tsam herb, and I must bring these things back to strengthen you."

Paragon was delighted, and said: "Be sure you remember. Buy those things first of all."

I Shing replied, "Do not fear lest my memory should fail."

And so he took passage by one of the regular ferries, and reached the great trading mart of Lung Tsai. Having sought out and entered a great silk-shop, he pointed with his finger to the shelves, and said, "Mr. Foreman, I want this, and I want that"; and when they were lifted down, he chose according to his fancy. Having agreed upon the price, I Shing clutched one parcel of dollars, of about fifty taels in value, and passed them over for the proprietor to examine. That person gave a sudden start and said: "Whoever knew the like of this? Yesterday a man took me in with thirty brass taels he tendered in payment, and now you want to try the trick with fifty." He then called the shop assistants to seize and search him. Upon his person they found a hundred and fifty taels, all counterfeit. And they blackened his face, and bound him with hempen ropes, and delivered him over to the street police.

A posse of street police then led him off to the City Hall, swearing at him in their loudest tones, and saying: "People of your order will only suffer themselves to eat rice; our kith and kin you will not suffer to live. We are the guardians of the streets, and why upon earth need you come to patronise us with your custom?"

I Shing whined and said: "From all this you may infer, honoured brethren, that originally I am nothing but a rustic farmer, perfectly straightforward and trustworthy. My brother is a schoolmaster, who will be surety for me, and settle up the whole business. This money was dug from beneath a tree in our back garden, and has not been surreptitiously cast of brass. Ten thousand times I speak the truth, and am not deceiving you." He then prostrated himself before the street guard, and knocked his forehead on the ground, and begged to be let go.

To his entreaties the police replied: "Your many words are of no avail. Strip off his clothes, and beat him."

As soon as they had taken off his clothes, they saw that his back was all black and blue, and scarred with the rattan beating he had previously received. The police then said: "If you are a law-abiding person, how is it you have been beaten after this fashion? You are certainly an imposer, and there is no room for two opinions on that point."

I Shing had no words with which to reply, but he besought them pitifully not to beat him, for the pain of the former beating had not yet gone. "Do you think I am a mere cowhide?"

The police then said: "If you do not wish to be beaten, we must rope you up."

I Shing had never seen anyone suspended with ropes, and thought this must surely be milder than beating. He said therefore, "Well, I will submit to be bound and hung up."

The police then took him and did him up after the fashion called "trussed pig in the roasting-dish". After they had kept him for half the night, crying out alternately for life and for death, and not able to get his wish gratified in either direction, his shrieks for help rending the skies, and his throat well nigh splitting open, the police unbound him. I Shing then knelt before each of the police, knocked his head on the ground, and confessed his sin.

On the following day he met in the street a man with whom he had some slight acquaintance, and borrowed money to pay his boat-fare home. Paragon knew on what date he would return, and, as on the previous occasion, engaged porters to meet the boat and carry back his purchases. As soon as the boat was moored, she saw this martyr of fate coming out of the cabin leaning on a bamboo staff, with bent waist, bowed head, sickly appearance, and walking very slowly and carefully. The clean new clothes he was wearing when he left home had disappeared, an old undershirt only being left to him, such as might be used for stuffing up holes and crevices. Her heart palpitated as soon as she saw him, and she thought within herself, "It is the same mould of bean curd over again." She waited till I Shing had come ashore, and then asked in a whisper how he had fared. "Not a word," said he, "not a word. Help me away home."

After dismissing the porters, Paragon led off her husband, who had to lean helplessly on her shoulder. As they crept slowly along, he talked to the effect that they were not destined to be rich, and that the fates were against them, and that he only got vexation and disappointment for his plans and toils. "This money I intend giving back to our brother."

Paragon said: "The sooner you return it the better. I am afraid that if our luck gets very much worse, we may all be dying together, and how then? Ill-fated we are, but must not repine."

That night husband and wife rediscussed the whole question, one moment proposing to give back the money, and the next finding it exceedingly hard to part with. The following morning they lighted candles and incense sticks, and worshipped the idol, and then asked for his guidance through an oracle. At first, when they divined with the flat and round tree roots, the intimations were uncertain; but when they divined with bamboo strips, all the indications were to the effect that it would be unlucky to keep the money. Should they keep it, certain calamity would follow in its train. So the younger brother made up his mind to return it, and bade his wife take it back forthwith.

Upon entering the house, she said to Tai Shing: "Brother, the money is unlucky; we wish to give it back to you."

When Tai Shing reflected a little, he thought it strange, and unconsciously smiled.

I Shing said: "Brother, you need not laugh at me. In the end you yourself may get beaten."

Strange to say, when Tai Shing spent the dollars, the coins were praised for the fineness of the silver, which far surpassed that of common dollars. Every coin weighed a full ounce and two-tenths, and the silver-miths would give an extra tenth of an ounce in exchange for it. Tai Shing, however, was not avaricious, and paid out his coins at the standard rate. Well says the couplet—

True heart makes true coin.

Heaven sheds grace on the filial son.

I Shing could not disguise his astonishment, and said: "What an extraordinary thing! Can it be that our father's grave is a place which is lucky for my brother and not lucky for me? When the feast of the graves comes round, I must take a hoe and scratch my father's last resting-place, and waken him up a bit, and tell him to turn round, and not send his luck-making magnetism out on one side only."

When the elder brother heard this, he thought it was very ludicrous. Seeing that his brother's hands were bound, he could scarcely avoid taking pity on him. He constantly gave him money, but the money had no sooner come into his brother's hand than it invariably changed into the hue of brass. It became necessary for Tai Shing to pay his brother's bills with his own hands, and then the money became good again. I Shing said, "Can it be that my brother's two hands are jewel-mines?" and Tai Shing himself could not explain how this came about.

The older repeatedly urged his younger brother to be more filial towards their mother; but, alas for it! I Shing would not regard it, and continued to treat his mother as though she were an adversary.

FILIAL PIETY PREACHED BY AN APPARITION

One night I Shing's father appeared to him in a dream, angrily cursing and saying: "What an odious and unfilial fellow you are! That mean, frisky wife of yours is far from good, and her husband has grown quite unworthy of his upbringing. How truly you illustrate the proverb that people of different characters do not get up out of the same bed! You and your wife have not behaved well to your mother. Do you think I am not cognisant of it? You treat your wife as if she were a pearl or a precious stone, and you treat your mother as if she were clay or mud. It was your mother who gave you being, and not your wife; your mother who, in the weakness of your infancy, attended to your wants, and not your wife; your mother who found a bride for you, and not your wife. How is it that you only understand the art of loving your wife, and do not understand the art of loving your mother also? Your unfilial sins have already been announced by the God of the Furnace in heaven, and the record of them has been handed on to Yuk Wong, and Yuk Wong is greatly incensed, and has sent forth an unlucky star, so that you may receive the recompense of your evil in scourgings and ropings-up. And—who could have anticipated it?—you are still without repentance; and if you continue as in the past, you and your descendants will soon be cut off, and in your own two persons you must go and be punished in the Fung To Purgatory, whence there is no transmigration." And when the father had thus spoken, he went away in anger.

I Shing awoke in a fright, perspiring at every pore. He called to his wife, who grew angry, and said, " I was sleeping so soundly—why did you wake me up?"

Her husband then repeated to her the angry and vengeful word which his father had uttered.

Paragon said: "It was a touch of indigestion from which you were suffering. Could a man's real father come running in and talking with his lips, especially when there was a daughter-in-law sleeping at her husband's side? He would certainly observe a little more propriety than that. The fathers-in-law of other women do not generally come into their rooms, and it is very improbable he would come right up to the edge of the pillow to carry on a conversation with you."

"There is, after all, reason in your criticism," replied I Shing. "To-night I drank a little wine and ate some pork and slat turnips. It perhaps does arise from the stomach."

"According to his account, you were not filial. Wherein have we lacked that virtue? Have you beaten your mother? or have I beaten my mother-in-law? At the worst we have simply shown a little temper. Let her speak on this subject. How often has she, who is the older, called me first? How often have I, who am the younger, commenced the quarrel? Am I so ill-bred as that?"

"Yes. Your statements are reasonable. I scarcely thought you had fulfilled your duties so well. You talk as acutely as one of the judges of a Superior Jurisdiction Court."

"When I was before the court some time ago, the mandarin was no match for me in speech. He overbore me with his ferocity and his bands of police. It was not as a fair conclusion to the argument that he had me so shockingly beaten. Your mother has a reputation. How is it that she is afraid of me?"

"I always give in to you, for you are a clever woman," said I Shing.

In the eleventh month of the year in which these events occurred there was an epidemic of smallpox amongst children, and the two sons of this couple, seven and five years of age respectively, died. I Shing and his wife were very sad, and wept night and day.

The murmuring of I Shing could not be checked, and he kept ever saying: "We two have never injured people at any time in our lives: I do not know why Heaven should be so very wroth against us. We have never impoverished anyone, and I do not know what reason Heaven can have for impoverishing us." And every day he repined against Heaven, and murmured against earth, and cursed ghosts, and cursed the good spirits as well.

An old woman belonging to the same clan, who was of a somewhat crabbed and outspoken disposition, and had no fear of provoking resentments, exhorted him, saying: "Your assert that you have never injured anyone, but you have done little else besides injure your mother. You say you have never defrauded anyone, but all along you have been defrauding the one who is nearest. I speak without the slightest fear of your wife. It is lucky that I am not the Ruler of Hell, for if I were, I would take the pair of you and drive you into the last abyss of punishment, and there should never be any rebirth for either of you again."

Having thus delivered her testimony, the old woman shook her sleeve and marched out.

When I Shing heard this speech, it made him very angry at the first, but he afterwards reflected that this speech was in perfect accord with what his father had said. "Are my wife and I really undutiful children, so that the universes cannot tolerate us? Those who are hated by men are first disliked by the sprits, and possibly the idols are punishing me."

As Paragon was reclining on the bed, she began to weep, and I Shing rushed into the room, saying: "You need not weep. When I reflect, we really are at fault. Our brother and sister are perfectly filial, and therefore they become rich and have children born to them. We have lost both of ours. When sin is great, it is difficult to secure a plentiful destiny of blessing. If we do not turn round, our woes will thicken, and we shall not be able to escape the sufferings of the abyss. We had better make a new beginning and go back to filial piety, and possibly through the favour of Heaven our past sins may be forgiven. What say you?"

Paragon answered: "As I was lying last night thinking, and comparing my disposition with my sister-in-law's, I felt that I was vastly beneath her level. My temper is turbulent, and you are not very clear-sighted and have been more or less carried away by your wife. If you know how to repent, I am ready to follow you."

Husband and wife that night relented, and set about making themselves filial. They shelled peanuts forthwith, and at the fourth watch got up to make congee, so that they might offer food to their mother the first thing in the morning. I Shing also bought a packet of meat patties to present, and the man and his wife were both delighted to render this trifling ministry to their mother, and were full of kindly dispositions. When she had taken one bowl of congee, they pressed another upon her, and when she had eaten one cake, they plied her with another, and when she could eat no more, they were quite overpowering in their entreaties that she would still continue to eat.

After they had departed, Madam Cross-grain laughed and said: " Extraordinary! For ten years they have scarcely interchanged a word with me. How is it that they are so zealous in service this morning, like A Pang's dog that changed its nature when it grew up?"

When Paragon got home, she at once boiled water, killed a fowl, and sent her husband to buy pork, and that morning they invited their mother to come and breakfast with them, and husband and wife offered the winecup, first one showing the mark of respect and then the other, and the old lady drank away to her heart's content. Then turn and turn about they pressed her to take slices of fowl, till the pile on the old lady's bowl of rice, when she took it up to eat, rose higher than her nose. "I cannot manage all this, " she said.

"Eat the fowl and leave the rice," said Paragon. "You do not often come to our place." And they urged their mother till she was both full and drunken, so drunken that it was difficult for her to walk, and they led her to a chamber where she could sleep her excess off a little.

In the meantime, Paragon went to her mother-in-law's room, intending to straighten up her bed and spread out her mat and quilt, and put things in order, and perhaps patch or darn, wash or starch a little; but, lo! everything, from mosquito curtain downwards, was so perfectly clean and in order, that she knew Coral's hand was always at work there. Paragon sighed and said, "My fault is great, and there is no wonder at my sister-in-law having such abundant prosperity."

Every day after that, I Shing and his wife were most attentive to their mother, and also deferential to their brother and his wife. But as Fate had determined, after the lapse of about a month, their mother, who was already old, took a chill, sickened, and died. Tai Shing and his wife carried out the funeral ceremonies in a style required by the principles of filial virtue; but I Shing and Paragon cried aloud, and fell on the ground, and rolled lengthways and rolled sideways, just as gourds might roll and their eyes were swollen to the size of hens' eggs. The Shing U Hau says—

When the tree yearns for stillness, loud roars the storm's blast;
When the child would be filial, both parents are passed.

Paragon in the course of time had more than twelve children; but none of them lived for very long: some dying at three or five years, some living one or two months, some two or three days, and some dying at birth. She wept till her eyes were dry.

One night she said to her husband: "I could never have imagined that my destiny would be so evil. I only see them born and do not see them live. I have no desire for children, and yet they come; and when they come, they will not stay with us. What can it all mean?"

I Shing said: "I see it all. They are evil spirits which have become incarnate. Other people are remorseful, and ascribe their trouble to the lack of self-culture in a previous life, but you and I have neglected the primary virtue in this life. When I think of our past undutifulness, I do not know how many more downfalls may be in store for us."

Paragon said, "We have already known our fault and become filial."

To which her husband replied: "But, alas! the time was so short, our beginning was too late. If it had only been earlier by three or five years, perhaps our children would not have died. Or if our mother had lived three years longer, we might have reduced the sum of our sin a little. But, alas! everything was against us, and when we wished to be filial, our mother died. Little heed is it that Heaven pays to human wishes as it makes ready inevitable downfalls."

The man and his wife lamented as they lay on their pillows till the third watch, when I Shing again dreamed, and saw his father approaching him with the message on his lips: "To punish your sin it was just that your children should be taken away. You and your wife deserved after death to taste the pains of hell, but because of your repentance and amended conduct towards your mother-in-law, and the sincere filial service you rendered for the space of two months before her end came, you are still preserved in life. Your destiny originally was to have had five sons and ten grandsons, but that has been changed because of your shortcomings in filial virtue. As for children beyond this number, they are only unhappy ghosts, who have stealthily glided into the life of the flesh, and have come of set purpose to afflict and anger your wife. The overbearing tyranny of your wife was hard to expiate, and had to be punished in this way."

I Shing then enquired, "Father, have the children I buried escaped hell?"

And he answered: "They have escaped. Lucky were you in being able to show so much zeal and energy before your mother died. If it had not been so, within the space of a month you would have been reaping your reward amongst the sword-bristling mountains and knife-studded trees of the underworld."

I Shing then said, "Am I to be left without incense and worship after my death?"

The father answered: "You may beg a child from your brother and adopt him as your successor, but you will leave no legacy of blessing as his heritage. His descendants will be few and unprosperous, unlike your brother's succeeding generations, rich and renowned age after age."

After thus speaking, his father vanished.

I Shing awoke in great fear and told the dream to his wife, who said: "We must take our vexations and disappointments quietly and without murmuring. But when the subject of purgatory was introduced, how was it you only asked about yourself and not about me? All your life long you have been forgetful of others."

Coral born three sons, two of whom became doctors in literature, and Tai Shing gave over one of his younger children to his brother for adoption as his successor. To the present day the descendants of Tai Shing flourish in a remarkable way, but for three generatioins I Shing's descendants were only few in number and comparatively poor.

思　考

1. 分析比较《俗话倾谈·横纹柴》与《聊斋志异·珊瑚》的异同，并判断该译文是译自《俗话倾谈》还是《聊斋志异》？

2. 思考《俗话倾谈》与《圣谕广训》的关系，及其在十九世纪欧洲有哪些译介？

参考文献

- *The Chinaman in his own Stories*, by Thomas G. Selby, London: Charles H. Kenny, 1895.
- ［清］邵彬儒《俗话倾谈》，沈阳：春风文艺出版社，1997年。

扩展阅读

- "Sacred Instructions of the Ta Tsing Emperors", *Chinese Repository*, 1841.
- "Chinese Fiction", by E. W. Thwing, *China Review*, Vol.22, No.6, 1897.

后 记

文化的交流与传播总是双向的。明清时期，与"西学东渐"相呼应，以介绍和传播中国传统文化为旨归的"中学西传"成为一种文化现象。其中，中国古典小说的西译构成了"中学西传"的重要组成部分。1735年至1911年的近两百年间，百余种中国古典小说被译介成西文，成为西方人了解中国和中国人最生动和有效的媒介，并给西方社会带去了回味隽永的中国风尚，又成为构建西方人眼中"中国形象"的重要镜像。"中学西传"与"西学东渐"是一种双向的、互动的文化交流，一起推动了人类文明的共同进步。

编者自2005年起以"中国古典小说的早期西译"为博士论文选题，至2009年博士论文初成，再至2017年书稿《"中学西传"与中国古典小说的早期翻译（1735—1911）》的正式付梓，走过了十二度春夏秋冬。这些年来，我深知中国古典小说西译文本第一手资料的重要性。因此着手编选了《中国古典小说西译文选读》一书，旨在提供中国古典小说早期西译的经典译文，便于读者进行文本细读，亦可与《"中学西传"与中国古典小说的早期翻译（1735—1911）》一书相互参阅。书中选取了十种具有代表性的小说译文：如殷弘绪翻译的《庄子休鼓盆成大道》是最早翻译成西文并正式出版的小说之一；帕西《好逑传》英译本在十八世纪的欧洲流传甚广，促使《好逑传》成为十八世纪欧洲声名最著的中国小说；乔治·亚历山大的《貂蝉》将《三国演义》中与貂蝉相关的情节编译成一部五幕的英国戏剧形式，成为跨文体跨文化的一次成功实验；乔利《红楼梦》英译本则是《红楼梦》第一个较为系统的西文译本；师多马的《中国小说中的中国人》不仅最早将《俗话倾谈》部分故事翻译成西文，亦是较早将中国方言小说纳入西人翻译和研究范畴的译本……

仅以此书向中国古典小说西译的先行者致敬，并供对中国古典早期西译及中西文学文化关系感兴趣的读者参阅。